UNFORGIVABLE

LUST&RELEASE

Book 3 of the *UNFORGIVABLE SERIES*

UNFORGIVABLE

LUST&RELEASE

Book 3 of the *UNFORGIVABLE SERIES*

SHAY LEE SOLEIL

S.L. Soleil Publishing
Belle River, Ontario,
Canada, N0R 1A0
www.shayleesoleil.com

Cover design: Damonza.com

Library and Archives Canada
Soleil, Shay Lee, author
Unforgivable Lust & Release / Shay Lee Soleil. —First Edition.
(Unforgivable Series; book 3)
Issued in print and electronic formats.
ISBN 978-0-9952342-4-6 (paperback)—ISBN 978-0-9952342-5-3 (eBook)
    I. Title. II. Title: Unforgivable Lust and Release.

Fiction, Erotic Romance

Distributed to the trade by The Ingram Book Company

DEDICATION

To my sister, Lily. (April 9, 2017) There isn't a day that goes by without me thinking about you. Every birthday, holiday and the day you passed is heart-wrenching for all of us. You send subtle hints letting us know you are still here with us. We hope you are happy flying with your new wings. The only thing that gets me through this is our great memories. We will see you again one day. Miss you so much it hurts. Love you, Lil!

To my mom. You have inspired me my whole life. You are the sweetest, most loving person I know. I am lucky to have you in my life. You are my number one supporter and fan reading my books first and loving them, waiting patiently for the next release. I tried to hurry, knowing we're not getting any younger. I wanted you to read this series while we still have our wits and minds. You've told me how proud you are of me and I want you to know, you are the best mom anyone could have. You guide me through life with your strength and love. You are a ray of sunshine we all love to be with. I did it Ma! Can you believe it? I finished the Unforgivable Series! Love you, mom!

To my husband and children, thanks for tolerating me during this six year obsession of the Unforgivable Series. Thanks for enduring the painful ramblings about my books and supporting me on this amazing journey, my dream.

ACKNOWLEDGEMENTS

To Lynne Melcombe, my editor. I have great appreciation and respect for you. We had a rough start but you instantly fixed the issue and surprised me with how fast you completed my manuscript. You are amazing! Your suggestions and expertise have transformed this book and it has improved tremendously because of your talent and skill. You are a genius! Thank you for your hard work. My appreciation is endless.

To the best readers around the world, thank you for following me on this incredible journey. I cannot thank you enough for your patience and encouragement.

To Damonza, my cover company. You have done it again! Thank you for designing a magnificent cover and for formatting my manuscript. You always go above and beyond to make authors happy. I described what I wanted and you created a masterpiece, better than what I imagined. And in record time! I'm ecstatic! It looks fantastic! I appreciate it more than words can say.

Unforgivable Series
by Shay Lee Soleil

Unforgivable Lust & Fire Book 1
Unforgivable Lust & Restraint Book 2
Unforgivable Lust & Release Book 3

1

I T'S BEEN THREE days since I last saw Bryce at the fire station. I've only seen him that mad when he was directing his anger at my stalker, Jake, or Colton. Never at me. His words and loud, furious voice still ring clear in my mind. *Keera, quit talking! I don't want to hear it! The pictures say it all. But there is one thing I want to know. Did you arrange this rendezvous with him when you were in Aruba?*

It didn't matter what I said at that point. He wasn't listening. He told me to *stop talking and leave.* He said he *couldn't look at me.* I left the fire station with tears in my eyes and a broken heart—devastated.

I'd hoped he'd show up today since he's not working, but nothing so far and it's already eleven o'clock. If he were coming to Huntsville, the latest he would've left Barrie would have been nine-thirty in the morning. He would've been here by ten-thirty. I've come to the conclusion he's not coming. He hasn't called. He hasn't texted. After the look he gave me, I have no idea what our future holds. It was pure hatred in his eyes and it replays over and over in my mind.

I've cried so much, I think I'm out of tears. I can't sleep. I'm hardly eating. When I do sleep, I dream of him. I see his face everywhere in this house and I envision all the times he made love to me—on the kitchen table, in the shower, on the living room floor, the couch, whatever surface was close when desire burned hot and wild.

Part of me is missing and I won't be whole again until Bryce returns.

Bryce has been my only love. The only man who could break through my defensive wall. I was damaged after almost being raped as a teenager by a friend I trusted. No one has ever affected me like Bryce. Our first encounter at the grocery store had me hoping I'd see him again. I did. He showed up at the bar when my friends and I were coming out of the washroom. Turns out, he was there watching over me. He was protecting me from a stalker he caught looking through my windows. That stalker has set fires and left notes professing his love for me. We've had several encounters with him and Bryce has protected me since the day we met. Gramps, Leena, and Katie have also been my rocks to lean on, helping me through the grief from when my parents died.

I was eighteen at the time. It was a head-on collision with a logging truck around a corner. Neither one saw the other coming. I always think, if I hadn't got out of the car that day, maybe I would've seen the truck and they'd still be alive today. I think of them constantly and talk to them when I'm alone. I've always remembered their passionate relationship and wanted that for myself. I thought I'd found it with Bryce.

Even though I wasn't good company, Leena stayed with me Wednesday night but has to work the rest of the week. Thursday, she texts to see if I'm okay. My only answer is that I'll eventually be okay.

I haven't gone out, I haven't called anyone, and I can't listen to music right now. I love music but every song reminds me of what Bryce and I shared.

My life is turned upside down because of a bad decision. I went to dinner with Colton after the photo shoot.

I told myself last night I would take a shower today and get some groceries, but I still haven't convinced myself to get out of this bed.

As I'm thinking, *I have to get up,* I hear a snowmobile circling my house.

Bryce!

Excited, I leap out of bed and run to the kitchen window hoping the sound I hear is Bryce taking his snowmobile for a ride. My heart drops when I see it's Jake. "Damn it!" I quickly duck my head and scurry low so he doesn't see me. Sitting on the edge of my bed, I hear his boots on the deck and the sound of crisp, crunching snow.

He bangs on the door. "Keera. Keera, are you home?" He hesitates before walking back across the deck.

I wait for the roar of his engine but there is no sound. Peeking out my bedroom curtains, I see he's not at his snowmobile.

What is he up to? I get low again, creep out to the kitchen, and steal a look out the window.

He's looking in my garage.

Damn it! He sees my Journey.

Yeah, but you could be with Bryce.

If only you hadn't screwed things up, you'd be with him right now.

He turns toward the house and I scurry low, back to my bedroom.

It strikes me then to use my security system. I'd forgotten about the cameras strategically positioned outside. I haven't used the system much since that lunatic stalker was put in jail. I fire up the computer and get a split screen showing four different angles of my yard. Jake is walking up the deck stairs for a second time and knocks on the door.

"Keera, are you here? I need to talk to you." He hesitates, looks around the yard, and knocks again. "Keera?"

Give it up, Jake, I'm in no mood to talk.

As if he hears me, he walks down the deck to his snowmobile, puts his helmet on, and takes off.

"I'm in no mood to talk to anyone."

Jesus, Keera. Snap out of it! How long will you torture yourself?

I drag myself to the bathroom, brush my teeth, and wash my face. *Okay, that wasn't so bad. Now get your ass in the shower.*

I look in the mirror and inspect myself. *Far cry from Tuesday when you looked fantastic in that red dress. Get your shit together and get in the shower.*

I turn the water on and wait for it to warm up, looking at my reflection in the mirror as my mind wanders to what my mom said years ago. *Don't go for the bad boys. They'll break your heart.*

I didn't. I fell in love with the responsible one.

Where did that get me Ma? He broke my heart anyway.

Shaking my head, I climb into the shower and stand under the spray until I notice the water cooling off a bit. *Damn it, Keera, wash your hair before you end up doing it in ice water!*

Towelling myself off, I realize, I feel a bit better. The flu-like aches and pains seem to have subsided, at least for now. Feeling faintly hungry, I remember I don't have much food in the house and convince myself to get some groceries.

On the way to the store, I see several black pickup trucks. More than usual. Or am I paying attention more? I don't know.

Once I arrive at the grocery store, I rush to collect the items I need, throwing them in the cart quickly. In the pasta aisle, I reach up to the top shelf for spaghetti sauce and look down the aisle remembering the first time I saw Bryce. The vision in my head seems real. I can almost see him standing at the end of the aisle with his powerful stance and the hunger in his eyes for me. We stared at each other for the longest time, neither one of us able to look away. I remember the sensations coursing through my body at that moment—a tingling warmth between my legs, an ache in my chest, weakness in my knees. No one has ever affected me like that before. I miss that feeling.

The tears start to flow again, and I curse at myself to stop. As the vision of Bryce disappears, I start racing down the aisles, collecting the rest of the items on my list.

The thought of Bryce runs through my head again while I'm cashing out. I turn away to keep the cashier from seeing the tears welling up in my eyes.

By the time I get home, the aches and pains are back and I'm crying like a fool. Placing the perishables in the fridge and leaving the rest in bags on the floor, I climb into bed, my mind overflowing with memories of all the amazing moments I've spent with Bryce.

After about ten minutes, my security system alerts me that a UPS truck is in the driveway.

"Why can't people leave me alone today?"

I hesitate, thinking, not wanting to interact with anyone, but decide I'd better before he leaves. Otherwise, I'll have to pick it up at the parcel depot later.

In my rush to get out of bed, my foot snags on the sheet. I stumble but quickly recover and sprint across the living room, opening the front door to a man in a UPS uniform. "This package is big, not heavy, but awkward. I'll place it on the floor." He gently sets it down. "And I'll have you sign right here," he says.

"Thank you," I say as he turns to head down the stairs.

To close the big wood door, I have to move the box out of the way so I bend down and lift it up, trying not to scratch my hardwood floor.

When I turn to shut the door, who is standing outside the screen door?

2

*B*RYCE.

My face must show shock and surprise.

"Hey," Bryce says as he looks me over.

"Hi." I do the same and I can't hide the delicious shiver running through me.

Bryce notices and smiles. "Can I come in?"

My brain finally functions and moves into motion. "Oh, yeah. Sure. Come in." I open the screen door and Bryce slips in. Time suspends in the air as we stand face to face, staring, trying to read each other's minds. I can almost feel a tangible force field of energy crackling between us.

How I've missed this feeling.

"Here. Let's close this door. Keep the heat in." Bryce gently closes the door and locks it.

Once again, we're staring at each other and I'm waiting for him to say something.

He obviously came all this way for a reason.

Either to tell me face to face that we're done, or, he believes me.

He doesn't touch me but I have a feeling he wants to.

It seems like an eternity of awkward silence stretched between us. "I couldn't stay away but I needed to know you were telling the truth." Bryce says, easing our discomfort.

"We don't lie in this relationship." I stare right in his eyes. *Oh my God, those eyes. Get a grip, Keera.* "We have to have trust." I wait for his response, feeling calm and anxious at the same time.

Eventually he takes a breath and says, "I know. I know we need trust. But let's turn this around. If you saw pictures of me and Lindsay like that, wouldn't you find it hard to believe it was completely innocent?" I don't have time to respond before he says, "I don't think so. I think it would rip your heart out, like it did mine."

When I allow that unpleasant thought to enter my mind, a stabbing pain hits my heart. "You're right. I'm so sorry. I should never have gone to dinner with him."

"Then why did you?"

"Because I was starving and we were in a snow storm." His head tilts a bit to one side as he cocks an eyebrow. His unspoken words have me backpedalling, fast. "I know that's no excuse. And I did try to keep my distance from him. But you know what Colton is like, how persuasive he is."

"Persuasive? Really? So now you're saying he persuaded you to do-what?"

"No, that's not what I mean. That's the wrong word. I mean … manipulative. It doesn't matter what anyone says to him. He finds a way to do whatever he wants. I'd say no, but a minute later he was beside me. And of course, every time he did touch me a paparazzi was right there taking pictures. I'd never cheat on you, Babe. I'm not like that."

"Okay, but you have to understand that's why all that crazy shit went through my mind when I saw those pictures, and I couldn't stop thinking about it until I read your letter and got your side of the story. I believe that bastard set up the photo shoot to see you and I'd put money on it that he's trying to break us up." In the silence that follows, Bryce takes my hand. "Come with me."

His fingers skim my sensitive skin and I wonder if he's feeling the same spark as I am. Then he smiles and I know he is.

He tugs me further into the living room and we sit on the couch. Looking over at me, he asks, "Still something on your mind?"

Crap! Do I tell him this or do I not say a word? Just tell him! "Umm … I don't know how to say this."

"Just say it, Angel."

"Colton says he's coming back in three weeks. I don't know if he means it or not."

"Like fuck!" He shouts, jumping up from the couch. "He's not getting anywhere near you." Bryce shakes his head in disgust. "That fucker has balls. Does he know where you live?"

"He knows I live in Huntsville but he doesn't know where. And it only came up because we were talking about how much snow we get up here." A thought pops into my mind. "Unless he gets my address from Chaz. I think they're good friends." I point to the box at the door. "That's what's in the box. Pictures of the photo shoot and the clothes."

Without sitting down, Bryce asks, "Did you talk to Jake the snake?"

"What?"

I look at him, feeling my eyes squint and my head cock to one side in confusion. "How'd you know Jake was here? That was two hours ago."

"I was watching, down the road. You didn't answer me."

"No. I didn't feel like talking to anyone. Why were you watching down the road? Why didn't you come to the door?"

"I needed to know you were telling the truth. I didn't want to come here and catch you with Colton. It would have killed me. I could only make sure by watching your house for a while."

I take his hand in mine and look deep into his eyes. "Babe, I love you. No one can do what you do. The way I feel when you're around me, the way my heart skips a beat and the energy that surrounds us. I know you feel it too. We were meant to be together. I don't want Jake and I don't want Colton. I love you and I'll love you until the day I die. And I'll keep loving you after that."

Bryce takes my face in his hands. I can almost see the tiny lines around his eyes smooth over as he relaxes and allows the thick defensive wall he surrounds himself with to crumble. "I love you. Fuck, Angel, I've missed you."

Our lips meet in a heated rush and we don't stop. He lowers himself back onto the couch, pulling me on top. His big strong arms hold me in a tight embrace. I can feel all the anxiety and torment he's been going through this last week fading away as he rubs his hands gently up and down my back and lightly kisses my face, neck and shoulders. His hands slide down my back to my butt, and he pulls me into his hard cock. His tongue is deep inside my mouth when he suddenly pulls away. "Angel, forgive me for telling you to leave. I was angry. Christ, I'll never forget the look on your face. I'm sorry."

"I deserved it. I should never have gone out for dinner with…"

Before I can speak Colton's name, Bryce's lips cover mine again in a frantic kiss. I feel passion in his tongue and desperate need in his trembling hands and I realize my hands are trembling, too. When our lips separate we're panting.

Bryce runs his finger over the two-heart necklace he bought me.

"You never took it off."

"No. This necklace helped me through our break-up."

"We never broke up." Bryce stares directly into my eyes. I see how important this is to him. "Do you know what got me through this?"

"What?"

"All the memories of us making love flashed in my mind, but also I kept remembering that first day I met you in the grocery store. I'll never forget the way I was feeling. Then after, when Austin pulled me away, I found you again. I was watching you. I couldn't take my eyes off you. I saw you smiling and I wondered if you were thinking about me, too. Then I saw your nipples through your tank top and I was hoping—hoping that was for me."

"It was. I was thinking about you. Nobody has ever affected me like that before. I couldn't think straight after seeing you and when I went home, I couldn't get you off my mind."

Bryce holds my face in his hands. "Let me make love to you." *Thank God I took a shower!* "Yes." The word falls from my lips.

"I need you, Angel. I need to know we're okay."

"Babe, I need you. I need to know you still love me."

"Angel, even though I was mad, I never stopped loving you. I couldn't stay away. I was going through hell without you. And Dante and Jax weren't helping. They were pissing me off. I couldn't handle it when they were all over you Wednesday at the station."

The thought of Bryce hanging out the door yelling at Dante and Jax, saying the Chief wanted them inside, runs through my mind. Bryce was trying any tactic to coax them away from me.

"I haven't been good myself. Pretty shitty, actually. I stayed in bed, crying. Today is the first day I made myself take a shower and get some groceries."

"I can tell you haven't been eating." His voice is deep but loving. "It looks like you've lost five pounds. Come with me. Let's get you something to eat." Bryce slides me off him and rises from the couch in one smooth move and holds his hand out for me to take.

I hesitate. "But I thought you wanted to make love to me?"

"You have the cutest pout. And yes, I do want to make love to you. But that can wait. You need to eat first."

I sigh. "But I'm not hungry ... for food."

Bryce smiles down at me, obviously amused, as he leads me into the kitchen.

We agree on sandwiches so it's fast and easy. We have other things on our mind.

"So tell me what happened," Bryce says after swallowing a mouthful of ham and cheese. "I want to hear it from you."

I finish chewing and swallow. "Well, I got to the Alaina building and everything was fine. They ushered me into Chaz's office and gave me some paperwork to fill out. While I was writing, Chaz got on the phone and was talking to someone. Now that I think about it, he was probably talking to Colton. The conversation was very cryptic. I remember him saying something about a gold mine and being alone, no one else. Then he mentioned something about pictures being ready and asked if he was in the air. He said he'd see him later. I had no clue at the time except Chaz was looking at me strangely and I felt a bit uncomfortable. Later, I found out Colton was there to pick up his pictures from a photo shoot that had taken place at Alaina last month."

"Bullshit! Those two fuckers orchestrated the photo shoot to get you there, so Colton could see you again."

"I don't know. Colton can be very persistent. He most likely wouldn't have stopped until Chaz gave into his demands. Chaz probably only went along because he wanted to get Colton off his back."

"Colton had one thing on his mind and that was getting you alone to break us up."

"I think you're right." I see Bryce is tense and shuffle my chair close to him to touch his thigh.

He relaxes, slightly.

"So anyway, the photo shoot went well. But once the snow started piling up outside, that's when I noticed everyone rushing to finish so they could make it home safely. I sent you a text but you didn't answer. I was thinking I could drive back to Barrie if I drove slowly."

"No. That wouldn't have been possible. They shut the highways down because everyone was getting stuck."

"So then I thought I would get a room for the night. I wasn't sure but I thought there was a hotel near the Alaina building."

"What happened to that idea?"

"Colton showed up before the shoot was done and stuck around, waiting to talk to me. My stomach was growling from hardly eating all day, so he convinced me to go to dinner with him. I'm sorry."

"Continue, please."

"The limo was having a hard time plowing through the snow and cars were stuck everywhere so Colton thought of different transportation, except I had no idea his favourite restaurant was in Niagara Falls. When I found out where we were, I lost it!" I rub his thigh. "I'm sorry, I see how this is bothering you."

"Angel, continue please."

"He took me to the Hilton hotel. We ate dinner and then he asked me if I want to see the Falls. I said yes because I vaguely remember being there with my Mom and Dad when I was five or six. I thought seeing them again might bring the memory back more clearly, and it did. That was when the paparazzi started taking pictures. I didn't kiss him. I was giving him shit for kissing me. That's probably the picture you saw. Anyway, I got cold, so we went back to the hotel to wait for his pilot to fly us back to the Alaina building. Umm, I don't know how to tell you this."

"What? Just say it, Angel."

I take a deep breath. "Umm, he convinced me to go see the final copy of the video while his pilot was getting busy with a blonde."

"And where was that?"

"Umm, next door to the pilots room."

Bryce gets up and starts pacing, running his hands through his hair. "Un-fucking-believable!" Bryce raises his voice. "And you went with him to his room?"

"Don't yell at me! You know how convincing he is."

"He set this up. How naïve can you be?"

"You know what?" I jump from my chair and start to walk to my bedroom. "You asked me to tell you, and you've told me twice to continue, and now you're yelling at me? Don't talk to me if you're going to be like this!"

Bryce stands in front of me, holding my arms. "I'm sorry. I didn't mean to yell. You know what I'm like when he's around you. I lose my fucking mind." He wraps me in a hug but I'm stiff, not hugging him back. He holds my face in his hands and kisses my lips gently. "I'm sorry. I won't yell. Please, come over here and eat. I won't say a word."

He pulls me by my hand and I sit at the table.

After taking a few moments to calm down, I bite into my sandwich and he waits for me to continue.

"So what happened when you got in the room?"

"He showed me the video. Then he saw a news article that said Colton Von Jobin was missing, and the band members were worried. I told him he needed to call Reese to let him know he was okay. He needed some convincing, but he finally listened to me. Then we waited for his pilot to finish and I was getting a little irritable because I was tired from getting up early and I fell asleep. I asked Colton why he didn't wake me when the pilot was done and he said his pilot was still going at it. So this time I went with him because I thought he was stalling. Colton woke the pilot and we headed down for breakfast and waited for him again. Then we headed back to the helipad and flew to the Alaina building. And then I got in my car and drove home."

"I saw a picture of Colton talking to you between two glass doors. What did he say?"

"That was when he told me he was coming back in three weeks."

Bryce grumbles something and I can tell he's trying hard not to explode again. "Anything else happen?"

"No, that's about it. I'm sorry. It'll never happen again."

"Yeah, I know because he's never getting near you again."

When I take my last bite, Bryce holds his hand out, pulling me up from my chair and leads me to the bedroom. As we're walking he asks, "Did he try anything?"

"He tried to kiss me a few times but I gave him shit when he did. Nothing happened. I love you, Babe. Colton knows I love you. I was constantly telling him." I take his face in my hands and kiss his lips. "I'm sorry. I never wanted to hurt you."

"Come here." Bryce tugs me over to the bed and cradles me in his lap. "We'll get through this." He holds me tight, breathing me in. I do the same, snuggling into his neck, smelling him and the scent of his cologne. "You belong in my arms, Angel. I can't stand to be separated from you."

Bryce notices a small scar on the underside of my forearm by feeling it. "What happened here, Angel?"

"That's from the bleachers at school. A sharp piece of metal was sticking out and I happened to find it by running my arm across it."

"You marked your beautiful skin. High school?"

"Yeah." I touch his left triceps muscle, running my finger over the scar. "What about this one, here?"

"Ontario fire college. Can't remember how I did it. Just covered it up right away. Didn't want anyone to see I was hurt." The corners of his mouth turn up and he raises his right eyebrow. "You know, you have to prove you're tough enough for the job."

"I can see you doing that. You're stubborn, like your father."

Bryce's eyes scan over the mountain of Kleenex piled high on my nightstand and then his eyes follow the trail to the wastebasket I was trying to throw them in. "Angel…"

Embarrassed, I hurl myself onto the floor grabbing the wastebasket and start cleaning up. "Crap, I forgot about these."

"This place is a pigsty!" Bryce teases.

That's one thing you don't say to a clean freak. I turn to look at Bryce as I'm down on all fours. He's looking at my ass with a big smile on his face, and then he bends slightly to get a better look. "Aren't you funny?" I say twisting my body to see his reaction, and then turning back to finish picking up.

The heat of his body cocoons mine as he gets down on one

knee, hovering over me. He rubs my butt cheek and whispers in my ear. "How I've missed this sweet ass of yours." Then he switches to the other one and I'm frozen, enjoying every sensation.

"Your punishment will have to wait, but I'm itching to redden those cheeks."

Punishment?

My eyes widen, knowing he can't see the expression on my face.

Where did that come from? Oh Bryce, some of your dark thoughts scare me.

He pulls down my yoga pants to reveal my butt cheeks. *Oh crap, I think he's changed his mind.* I wait for a smack but instead, I feel his lips grazing across each cheek and then he gently kisses each one several times, sending a delicious shiver through my entire body. His finger slides inside me and a whimper slips from my lips as he tortures me with a slow rhythm. My hips circle and I moan with my head resting against the mattress.

Bryce can do whatever he wants at this moment. I surrender! "Babe I've missed this. I've missed you." I moan softly.

He pulls his finger out and my eyes open quickly to see why.

He's sucking on his finger like a lollypop. "I've missed my sweet, sweet pussy. I need to taste you, now!" He picks me up and spins me around fast, surprising me with his speed and dominance. Now I'm facing him.

He pulls my yoga pants down to the floor in an instant. "Commando. I love that!" Then he's pulling my t-shirt over my head. Bra, gone, flying across the room.

Damn, he's fast.

Bryce pulls his t-shirt off, his muscles contracting as he flings it … somewhere. He drops to his knees in front of me. Taking hold of my butt cheeks, he pulls me to his waiting tongue.

In a panic, I hold his face to stop him. "Babe, I haven't shaved."

He takes hold of my wrists, pinning them to my side. "You think that will stop me from eating my sweet pussy." he asks in a deep husky voice. "You worry too much." His tongue hardens, spearing me, sliding between my pussy lips, lapping the moisture he finds there.

I moan from the sensation and lift my leg onto the mattress.

"That's it Angel, open those legs." He returns to feasting for a few minutes and then his black silky hair falls back off his brow as he looks up at me, his lips glistening. "Damn, woman, you taste so sweet, I've missed tasting you."

The sight of him at this moment is something I'll remember and treasure forever. I run my thumb along his bottom lip. "Babe, I love you so much."

And just when I thought I couldn't cry anymore, a single tear drops down and hits his shoulder.

He rises to stand before me. "Angel, please don't cry." He holds my face in his hands. "It kills me to see you cry."

"I thought I lost you. I thought you hated me."

3

"NEVER! YOU'RE MY life, the air I breathe. Staying away from you was my own stubborn pride and I'll never do it again. And as for hating you … I could never hate you. I might get mad but I'll always love you." Bryce holds me in a tight embrace and then our lips meet in a slow, sensual kiss.

When we separate I look deep into his eyes. "Love me. Please."

"My pleasure." He strips out of his pants and kicks them away.

Our lips meet again as he lowers me to the bed with him on top, skin on skin. I feel the heat of his body, every hard muscle, and all his weight, a welcome feeling I've missed. Our bodies tangled like a puzzle, the passion in his kiss as his tongue probes my mouth.

Everywhere he touches, leaves trails of fire, making me want more. And how I've missed his scent and the smell of his cologne. I nuzzle, taking deep breaths as I kiss my way around his body. "Babe you smell so good. I've missed you."

His grip tightens as he inhales sharply into my hair and then down my neck. "Angel you have no idea how I've missed you. I'm never letting you out of my sight again." Bryce spreads my legs with his and settles between them. His tongue slips inside my mouth, our tongues intertwine in a delicious dance. His hand slides down my right side until it reaches my butt. Then he tugs me into his steely erection as he grinds on that perfect spot.

"I love your body," he says as his other hand fondles my left breast, first feeling the weight of it and then tugging my nipple between two fingers. "They're perfect." He runs his large hand beneath both breasts, touching gently. His lips flutter across my cheek and then to the soft spot behind my ear. "This body was made for me. I'll never get enough. You're so beautiful. The way your body responds to me, to my touch."

"Only you can do this to me, Babe."

"Open," he whispers in my ear. "Let me taste you." I open my legs wider as Bryce kisses his way south to his destination.

"Relax and enjoy," he says, his tongue diving for the moist flesh between my legs. His finger slides deep inside and out again, slowly.

My body has been wound tightly from the moment he stepped foot in my house. When he took his coat off, he was wearing a tight white Henley with the jeans I love and my eyes instantly devoured his muscular body. And now, I have him. He's all mine.

This is what I want.

I moan and circle my hips. My fingers lace through his silky jet black hair as I hold his head in place.

He picks up the pace, his tongue and finger moving at lightning speed. He doesn't stop.

My breathing quickens, from panting to sharp tiny inhalations. Small beads of sweat mist my skin. I clamp down on his finger, tightening my hold on him. My body is wound like a spring, begging for release, climbing higher and higher as every muscle contracts.

"Babe! Right there! Just like that! Don't stop! Don't— ooohhh!" An orgasm of unbelievable intensity rips through me. My hands let go of his hair to grasp the sheets and my head thrashes from side to side.

Bryce doesn't stop. He circles my clit, lapping my juices and pumping his finger inside me.

As the last waves of my orgasm recede, I try to push him away but he ignores me. "Babe?"

"No, Angel. One more."

"It's too sensitive."

"Give me one more and then I'll fuck you." His sinful mouth returns to my clit and his finger curves slightly inside, pumping the hell out of me. The sensitivity subsides as I quicken again. He teases me with that amazing finger by gently outlining my trembling entrance and then he plunges deep inside, again and again, his finger thrusting fast and hard. Seeing how close I am, he keeps up the same relentless pace and pressure as the hurricane builds in my body once more. I run my fingers through his hair and tighten my grip to keep his beautiful mouth securely in place.

I'm gasping for air thinking of how good it feels. Every muscle in my body tightening has me aware that it's happening again, and so quickly. Clenching down on his finger, I feel every muscle straining as a second orgasm sends me reeling. "Babe, you're doing it to me again! Oh my God! It's so good!"

Bryce only stops when he sees me go limp. Lost in euphoria, it barely registers that he's now standing at the foot of the bed. His large strong hands take hold of my ankles, pulling me down to my original spot in the center of the bed. Letting his weight fall on me, he laces our fingers together at the side of my head, capturing me so I can't move. His eyes bore into mine.

"Angel, you're mine. I'm the only one who sees you like this."

"Yes, Babe, and you are mine."

He moves slightly but his eyes stay locked on mine as he repeats in a stern voice. "I'm the only one who will see you like this!"

"Yes, Babe. You're the only one who will ever see me this way."

I know he's satisfied with what I've said because he continues making love to me.

"Open." He says in that deep commanding voice.

I open my legs wide to accommodate him.

He continues teasing me, the head of his cock entering slightly and then backing out, over and over again, saturating the tip with my arousal. I wrap my legs around him and lift my hips, inviting him in, whimpering every time he withdraws, until suddenly, with one fierce thrust, he slams balls deep into me.

"Babe ... your cock ... it feels so good inside me."

He pulls all the way out and slams into me again. "This will be the only cock that enters this pussy."

Bryce needs the reassurance that I didn't fuck Colton. He rams once more, pulls out and hesitates, waiting for me to speak.

"This is the only cock that will ever enter my pussy. I want you. Only you and your beautiful cock."

He seems satisfied with my response, tightening his hold, returning to fucking me hard. Nailing me to the mattress.

His cock is hard as stone and every thrust goes deeper than the last, hitting that perfect spot way up inside. He's drilling me with the knowledge that no one will ever be able to satisfy me like him. His to do with whatever he pleases.

But I already know.

I am possessed, thinking of him every moment of every day.

I am his.

"Feel that? Feel how hard my cock is for you?"

"Yes."

"Christ, Angel. You drive me crazy." He pulls me up so I'm sitting on the edge of the bed, my legs still wrapped around him. "Play with your clit."

I reach down between us and do as he says.

I know Bryce struggles with his feelings for me, they overwhelm him at times.

I try to put myself in his position.

How would I have reacted if I found out Bryce had taken Lyndsay out for dinner and then she'd fallen asleep on his lap?

I know how I would react. I'd most likely break up with him and wouldn't listen to his explanation until I cooled down, weeks later.

I see the torment and emotions that have been building inside him for the last few days and realize his strange mood is because of me. Bryce needs the reassurance that he is the only one I will ever love.

I scrape my nails down his back, easing his discomfort.

Losing myself again, I feel my orgasm building like a raging storm. I clamp my muscles tightly around his cock and watch as his control slips away.

"Fuck!" Bryce groans. "Come for me, Angel."

"Babe, you fuck me so good." I pull him into me by his ass cheeks, holding on for dear life as my orgasm peaks and sends another tidal wave of sensations through me.

The second I let go, Bryce gives up his own fight for control. I watch his beautiful features change. His eyes close and then open, his muscles tense and release as he slams into me three more times, emptying himself into the deepest part of me. The full weight of his body falls on top of me. It's a feeling I've missed.

We lie tangled together, kissing, caressing, soothing, reassuring, reconnecting. We remain there in silence, both lost in our own thoughts. Bryce pulls the covers over our bodies. We snuggle like spoons, my back curling into his strong chest. His muscular arms hold me tight.

Breaking the silence, I say, "I'm sorry this happened. I never wanted to hurt you."

"We'll get through this." He gives me a reassuring squeeze. "It will make our love that much stronger."

"You're so good for me. I love you so much."

"I love you, too," he says. "But I need you to promise me something."

"What? Anything."

"Promise me we'll stay together. We'll spend as much time with each other as possible. Life is much simpler when we're not separated. Come with me to Barrie when I have to work and when I get time off we'll come back here to your place or the cabin."

"Yes, I promise." Turning over to face him, I reach up and run my thumb across his cheek. "I love being with you."

"We can make it through anything if we have love."

"I believe that." My stomach growls loudly and I giggle. "That workout you gave me must have brought back my appetite."

Bryce smiles and kisses my cheek. "You're so beautiful. And this body." His hands roam the curve of my butt. "I think I could go again, but I can't let my Angel get weak from lack of food." Tossing back the blankets and standing in one seamless move, he extends his hand and says, "Come with me. Let's get something to eat."

As we're moving around the kitchen preparing dinner, he in his jeans, me in his shirt, I feel an immense need to touch him and rub against him. I can't help myself. He's like a drug for me. The pull and ache I feel are almost unbearable. Even though I had three explosive orgasms, I want more. I can't get enough of him. Peeking up at him, I give him my seductive smile.

His glimmering eyes stare down at me and he grins.

Oh, what that gorgeous dimple does to my heart!

"You keep that up and you'll be spread out on that kitchen table again before we finish dinner."

"I just need to touch you."

He wraps his big, strong arms around me. "I'm an idiot."

I look into his eyes. "What do you mean?"

"When I was pissed at you, I couldn't see straight. I don't know how I thought I could live without you, even for a second. Dante and Jax opened my eyes. Dante, the fucker, kept getting his digs in, but the final straw was when he said he was glad it was over between us because having me out of the picture would give him a chance."

"What happened?"

"I threw the first punch and then all hell broke loose. Jax and a couple of the guys had to tear us apart. The little bastard always knows how to get to me." He looks back into my eyes. "I'll have to thank him."

"See, I almost lost you."

"Never! I love you too much. It's my damn temper. When anyone says something about you I don't want to hear, I'm like a bull seeing red. I have to learn to control it."

I stand on my tiptoes and kiss him softly. "I'll have to thank Dante and Jax for bringing us back together."

"And so you know, I never broke up with you. I just needed time to think."

"Good I'm glad. I didn't have a clue what was going on because I didn't hear anything from you. But I hoped and prayed you would come back to me." The water on the stove starts to boil over and, as we return to cooking our pasta dinner, our intimate moment slips away.

I play some music and we sit at the kitchen table, eating in silence with Bryce resting his hand on my thigh and rubbing his foot against mine.

After dinner, we bundle up and head outside to blow the driveway and shovel the decks.

Bryce steps through the snow drift at the side door of my garage and hits the remote for the big door. Pushing the snow blower to the edge of the huge drift that's accumulated at my garage entrance, he looks back and forth from my Journey to the drift and asks, "How did you make it into the garage through all that snow?"

"No problem, I just gunned it and quickly let off to brake before I went through the back wall."

He shakes his head. "Angel, you scare me sometimes."

"You worry too much. I have angels looking out for me."

"They've got their work cut out for them."

"Are you saying I'm reckless?"

"You've got no regard for your own safety. So yes, at times you're reckless."

I smile at him and we get back to work removing the remnants of Tuesday's snowstorm from the driveway and sidewalks.

When we finish, Bryce stores the snow blower in the back corner of my garage and tugs me into his side. "Let's get warmed up."

In the house after we strip off our winter clothing, Bryce loads the fireplace with wood and I open the box from Alaina. I pull out a beautiful flower arrangement in a crystal vase.

"What is that?" Bryce asks, looking over his shoulder from a crouched position in front of the fireplace.

"They sent me flowers." I frown, my brow furrows in confusion.

"Read the card," Bryce says, standing up and closing the gap between us. "Out loud."

"Shit!" I cringe, my face wrinkling. "Do you really want to know?"

Bryce snatches it from my hand and reads, *"Thank you for the best two days of my life. Missing you! Badly! Love Colton."*

Red, climbs up Bryce's neck to his face and he looks like he'll explode from anger. "For fuck's sake!" He grabs the floral arrangement out of my hand, opens the doors and tosses it off the front porch into the snow.

Shock and surprise must show on my face when he slams the doors.

"What?" Bryce demands.

"Nothing." I hold up my hands in surrender. "Didn't say a word."

"That mother—" Bryce grumbles but I ignore it, returning to pulling items out of the box.

My gaze focuses on a huge brown envelope taped to the side of the box. "The pictures!" I say excitedly as I go sit on the couch, spreading them out on the coffee table.

I can't fit them all so I set aside the last few in a pile to look at later.

Bryce sits beside me. "Wow! Look at you, Angel. You're beautiful. You look totally different with the fancy clothes."

"Is that a good thing or a bad thing?"

"Good and bad."

I frown, not knowing what he means.

"Let me explain. Good, because you look like a supermodel. But bad for me because you're a hot commodity now. Every modelling agency and magazine will want you, which means less time together for us."

"Babe I'm not going anywhere. I like my simple life. That was okay to do once. I don't know if I'd do it again."

A thought enters my mind. "I want to show you something." I run back to the box and pull out the red dress, holding it against myself. "What do you think? It's beautiful, eh?"

"You're beautiful. The dress is nice, too."

I return to Bryce, still holding the dress against myself. "Thanks, Babe, but you've got to check out these pictures." I drape the dress over the chair and search through the remaining pictures, finding four of me wearing the red dress.

"Jesus, Angel, I'm getting hard just looking at these pictures. You are hot!"

I pick the dress back up and hold it against myself again, fluffing the bottom. "I don't know where I'd wear it? But I have it to keep in case we go to some ritzy event."

Bryce flips through the rest of the pictures and comes across the ones of me in the bathing suits, a groan vibrating in his throat. "You pranced around the studio like that?"

"Yes, Babe. It's part of the job."

Skipping forward, he reaches the last picture: the group photo I'd forgotten about. Colton is standing beside me with his hand on my hip.

Crap! Dropping the dress back down on the chair, I try a

diversion, pointing out everyone in the picture. "This is Josie and Anna. They did my makeup and hair—"

"That jackass had to be touching you, eh?" Clearly, the diversion didn't work.

"Babe, every time he did touch me I was thinking of ways to back up so he wasn't so close."

"Look at that smug grin on his face," Bryce shouts. "This is a big fuck you, Bryce, I've lured your girlfriend here and now I've got her in my arms."

"Babe, Chaz yelled out 'group photo' and we all gathered around and Colton ended up beside me."

"I don't believe that for a second. That fucker devised a scheme to get you there and his plan from the beginning was to break us up. I can see it in his face."

I look at the picture closely but only see Colton smiling like the rest of us. "So anyway, this is Chaz and this is Brent the photographer. Brent was easy to work with. He told me what to do and I did it."

"Did they have their hands all over you, too?"

Oh crap, he's in a pissy mood now. "Babe." I hold his face in my hands and look into his eyes. "I've never seen you like this before. This mad and ... jealous."

"I'm still having a hard time with this."

"I know. I'm sorry." Can this relationship get any harder? And it's all because of me. "I really did think you gave up on me because of everything we've been through."

Both of us turn toward the sound of footsteps on my front porch and then look at one another again and ask, "Who is that?"

4

FIRST THE DOORBELL rings, then we hear the screen door open and a knock on the door. "Keera? I know you're in there."

"It's Jake," I whisper.

"Un-fucking-believable!" Bryce says loudly, shaking his head. "All I need now is for Colton to show up to make this day outstanding!"

"We don't have to answer the door."

"No, let's answer it and see what's so fucking important that he has to come to see you twice in one day."

The moment Bryce opens the door, I tense. I still don't feel comfortable around Jake.

Jake holds the flower arrangement in his hands. "Bryce!" he says, acting surprised, though he must have been able to hear Bryce's voice. Then Jake turns to look at me. "Keera, here. I found this in the snow on your front lawn." Bryce grumbles something too quietly to understand.

"Thanks." I place it on the bench Gramps made for me and Bryce, and then turn to see Bryce's big body covering the doorway.

Jake peers around Bryce and asks me, "Where the heck have you been?" Then he steps back, looks at Bryce and frowns. "Can I come in and talk to Keera?"

Bryce moves slightly and Jake enters, standing just inside the door.

"I haven't seen you for three weeks now," Jake says. "You disappeared."

Bryce is holding the wooden door looking like he wants to close it on Jake.

"Yeah, we've been busy."

"Umm, can I talk to you? Alone?"

"Whatever you've got to say, you can say it in front of me." Bryce's voice is clipped. He sounds annoyed.

"Fine. Can I come in at least?"

"Sure. Would you like something to drink?" I ask politely even though I want him to leave.

"A beer, if you've got it."

Bryce strides to the fridge with that powerful walk. Jake and I pull out chairs at the kitchen table. Bryce plops a beer down in front of Jake with a thud and then gently places mine. "So what's so fucking urgent that you have to bother my girlfriend twice in one day?" Bryce demands, leaning back against the counter with his arms and legs crossed.

Jake looks directly into my eyes. "I was worried because I haven't seen you around and what's with all the caution tape at Leena's? Jesus, I thought someone was murdered. I pumped the cops for information and all I got out of them was that it was an ongoing investigation, though they did at least tell me no one was murdered."

I look at Bryce. His face is expressionless.

"Problem is taken care of," I say vaguely. "Everything's good now."

"Oh come on Keera. Haven't we been good friends all these years? I'm concerned about your safety."

Bryce almost chokes and I look at him, eyebrows arched. He

rolls his eyes slightly, so I know he's gotten the message: quit being so rude.

"Jake I don't like to talk about it. Okay? Maybe someday I'll—" I'm a little emotional still, so I stop talking.

Bryce comes over and rubs my shoulder. "Are you finished asking questions?"

Jake reaches into his coat and pulls out a poster of me running on the beach in my white bikini. "Is this you?" he asks. "One of my employees had this taped inside the door of his locker. When I asked where he got it, he showed me the video of Von Jobin's "Let Me Be the One" and then all the other crap that's on the web about you."

"Yes, Jake that's me. And don't believe everything you see on the internet."

"What the hell's been going on?"

"It's too long of a story to tell, Jake."

"So obviously you're not with Colton Von Jobin."

"No, Jake. Bryce is my boyfriend."

"Oh. I thought—"

"Yeah, I know what you thought. If she was with Colton they'd probably break up and you could slither right in there. Right? Not happening. She's mine. Now, are you finished? I don't mean to be rude but we've got to meet someone."

I flash a look at Bryce again. "We've got to meet Leena and Austin," I say, backing up his story. "We don't have much time to talk. Maybe next time I see you."

I stand up, and Jake takes the hint. At the front door, he says, "Maybe next time you can fill in all the holes. I just want to know you better, Keera."

"Yeah, maybe next time. Bye, Jake."

"Bye, Keera." Jake touches my arm and I stiffen. He doesn't look at Bryce as he turns and leaves.

As I'm closing the door, Bryce stomps to my bedroom, returning with my laptop in his hand.

My heart drops. *Aw, crap, here we go.*

Setting it on the kitchen table, he sits down and fires it up.

Settling in on his lap, I apologize again. "I'm sorry this crap is happening all at once. When you got here, I was so happy and I was hoping we could have a nice peaceful day enjoying each other's company."

"Angel, it's not your fault these dickheads keep sniffing around, thinking they can get into your pants instead of moving on to find their own girlfriends."

"Jeez, where were you after my parents died? I was lonely and needed a shoulder to cry on."

"You don't know how bad I wish I knew you back then. I would've helped you through the bad times. Both of us together. Hell, we'd be married by now and you'd be popping out a couple of my babies and all these dogs sniffing around would know your mine."

The video starts to play and I tense with worry.

As Bryce watches, he starts to gradually tense himself. His whole demeanour changes when Colton mentions the kiss, and his grip on my hip tightens. "Did he kiss you in Aruba?"

"Ummm." I stammer.

"Tell me the truth, Angel," he says softly.

"Yes. He tried."

Bryce plays the video again. "What does Colton mean when he says you've shared something he'll never forget?"

I shake my head and shrug my shoulder. "I didn't share anything with him. I don't know what he means."

That's not really a lie. Colton never did say what that meant. I assumed it was when Bryce and I had sex in the tropical forest and Colton was watching.

"He should have asked your permission to use the footage of you running on the beach. And you coming out of the water."

"Yeah, it's a little embarrassing."

Bryce hits play again.

"Babe! Stop! You're torturing yourself. We can't change anything and in time this will all blow over and we'll forget about it."

"See, the rat bastard is saying right in the song that he'll steal your heart away from me. He's been trying to break us up from the beginning. I'm done with this shit!" Bryce closes my laptop harder than what he normally would. "He's never getting close to you again. Come with me. Let's go to bed. I want to get lost in you and forget about the last couple of hours."

We do. It starts with us cuddling, then touching, then kissing that progresses quickly to gentle pecks to tongues entwining and then a desperate need to show each other that our relationship will be fine.

I hope that no matter what obstacles we have to face in our lives, we'll still love each other in the end. Our love will conquer anything.

The morning light startles me awake with the thought of Bryce no longer in my life. But with Bryce's arm wrapped around me and his legs tangled with mine, I soon realize it's a bad dream. I stretch a bit, remembering why my legs and arms are so stiff: from the amazing, wild, untamed, animalistic, erotic sex we experienced hours ago. I'm toasty warm next to Bryce but my nose tells me it's cold outside the covers which leads me to believe the fire must've gone out during the night. I try to get up but Bryce's arms tighten around me. "Where do you think you're going?" His deep voice curls my toes.

"To throw a couple logs on the fire and warm things up in here."

"No. Let me do that. You stay here under the covers. I'll be right back."

I watch his gloriously naked body scramble to find clothes. As I watch him strutting over to my chair, and then rummaging through one of his drawers in my dresser, the sight of his muscular back and tight ass leaves me shaking my head and smiling. He turns and my eyes instantly lower to his beautiful cock. As he slips one leg into his warm jogging pants, I watch his ab muscles contract. Bryce shivers. "Christ, it's cold in here." He quickly throws on a sweatshirt.

Laughing, I watch as he leaves the bedroom, but then I grab a warm throw to wrap around me while I head to the kitchen to put the kettle on for myself and make coffee for Bryce.

When we both meet back in my bedroom with chattering teeth, I hand him his coffee before dropping my blanket and climbing back into bed with him.

"Brrr." Bryce groans.

"Coffee warming you up?"

"Ummm, hot coffee and my angel's warm, naked body next to mine. This is the life. You know I'll never want to get out of this bed."

"Good. Let's stay here all day."

Bryce sets his coffee on the night stand and turns toward me, propping his head on his hand while his other hand caresses my stomach. "Angel, I'm sorry, but we need to discuss something."

I turn toward him. "What's wrong?"

"When I talked to Grant he said the investigation showed forcible entry at the back door of the Ericson's house. Leena didn't forget to lock it."

"We'll have to let Leena know. She still feels bad."

"There's one more thing."

"What?"

"I don't know if you want to hear this."

"Yes. Please, tell me."

"I hate seeing what it does to you."

"Babe, I need to know."

Bryce hesitates, letting out a deep sigh. "Grant also said they found sex toys and several articles of lingerie in that room."

"I had a feeling they'd find something."

"They're using them for evidence in the case. Grant also mentioned it would be more effective if you wrote a victim impact statement and if you were at the trial."

I tense. "No. I can't! I don't ever want to see him again."

"I told him, I don't think it'll happen. It's okay, Angel." Bryce rubs my side to calm me. "He suggested it, but that doesn't mean you have to do it."

"Good. Because I can't!"

"I know, Angel. Grant said he'd keep me updated."

"Okay, so let's forget about this and move on to our amazing weekend together."

"You're right. I had to tell you to get it out in the open."

"I know, Babe. Thank you."

In our few moments of silence, my mind flips to that lunatic stalker and how he's been collecting my lingerie whenever he's entered my house. *If Bryce hadn't come into my life at the right time, where would I be today?* I cuddle next to Bryce, shivering, trying to dismiss my terrible thoughts.

"Are you okay, Angel?"

"Yeah, I'm good." I push myself up, leaning on my elbow so I can look in his gorgeous hazel eyes. "Do you know how much I love you?"

"Yes. I see it in your eyes." He grabs my butt cheeks, pulling me into him. "With all the chaos and bullshit going on in this relationship, I want you to know we will get through the tough times together. We'll be stronger because of it. And if we end up like this, in bed with love in our eyes, we're doing something right. I love you, Angel."

He squeezes me hard and I melt, hugging him back.

After a few minutes, the room falls silent as we lose ourselves in our own thoughts again, sipping our coffee and tea.

My thoughts turn to when Bryce came down the hall with my laptop in his hand and I almost had heart failure hoping Colton hadn't sent the e-mails, like he said he would.

Who knows what Colton would send? I need to tell Bryce—and soon—to get it out in the open so I can stop feeling guilty. I want to be truthful in this relationship.

But today is not the day. I want one full day with Bryce, spending quality time together.

For a moment, I imagine a future with no stalker, no Jake, no Colton, no Lindsay. Why can't they find new loves and move on?

Draining my tea cup, I scramble out of bed to get another one. When I return, Bryce lifts the covers for me and I quickly drop my blanket, set the cups down on my night stand, and cuddle in beside him. "Jesus, Angel, your freezing!" He wraps me in a warm hug.

"Yeah it's cold out there but you're nice and warm." I shiver and rub my pussy against his leg.

"Ready for round three?" he asks.

"You can't go again!"

"Yes, I can. Angel, I'd fuck you all day if you'd let me."

I prop my pillows up and hand Bryce his coffee. "Here," I say, "drink this before it gets cold."

"Are you trying to change the subject?"

"Let's just say I want to walk later," I say, smirking.

When the house finally warms up, we get dressed and make some breakfast. While Bryce cooks the bacon, my attention turns to the red dress lying across the chair and the box full of clothes in the living room. "Be right back, I need to hang up the clothes."

"No problem," he says, holding up the silicone tongs. "Got it all under control."

I pick up the red dress, place it across the awkward box and carry everything to my walk-in closet.

When I finish hanging the clothes, I notice an envelope at the bottom of the box with my name on it. I open it and take a quick glance. It's handwritten and it's long. I scroll to the bottom and see it's from Colton. I don't have time to read it so I place it back in the envelope, stuff it between some clothes, and then go help Bryce finish cooking.

During breakfast, Bryce tugs my chair close so he can rub my foot with his and rest his hand on my thigh. I rub his foot back, a gesture I love and hope we'll share forever.

His mood is different than yesterday. He's seems content.

"What do think about staying at the cabin for the rest of the weekend?" he asks. "I'd like to check on it after the snow storm."

I run my hand through the hair at the back of his neck, grabbing a handful and tugging gently. "I don't care what we're doing as long as I'm with you."

Bryce squeezes my thigh. "I don't want anything to interrupt this day. And by anything, I mean Jake."

"Yeah, okay. Let me do the dishes, we'll take a shower and then we'll pack up and head out."

Routinely, when we leave my house for any amount of time, we shut the water off and turn the heat up to fifty so the pipes won't freeze. Then we lock up and grab the mail.

As we're driving to the cabin, I text Leena and Austin to let them know everything's good and back to normal.

Leena texts back:

The reason I'm not blowing up your phone is because I heard through the grape vine that Bryce was visiting Huntsville. I predicted everything would be fine. And besides, we're having a sex marathon.

I text back:

Is that all you two do all day? LOL! Sorry, didn't mean to interrupt. Continue and have fun.

By the time we arrive at the cabin, a new snowfall is starting. We don't want it to pile any higher so while Bryce lights the wood stove to warm up the cabin, I fire up the snow blower to clear away the remnants of Tuesday's storm.

After we've stored the snow blower away, Bryce fires up the engine of his snowmobile. It starts right away. He hits the throttle a few times to make sure it's running smoothly and then quickly shuts it down. "Want to go for a ride?"

I close the gap and rub against him. "Always. You know that."

"Great. Lets go in for a bit to get warmed up and then I'll take you for a ride." He smirks down at me and the hidden promise revs up my hormones.

I nudge him in the ribs. "Owww!" he says, holding his side like he's wounded. "What was that for?"

"Nothing. I just like to touch you."

"How's this for touching you?" He scoops me up in his arms and cradles me like a baby all the way to the cabin.

I giggle as he puts me down.

"I love that sound, Angel."

"I love you."

He squeezes me extra hard.

"But. I. Can't. Breathe."

"That's how much I love you," he says, releasing me. "Do you ever feel pain in your heart from it?"

"All the time, Baby. All the time."

5

*T*HE SNOW WAS falling lightly when we first arrived at the cabin and now, three hours later, the snow is coming down steadily. The flakes are huge, the temperature is below freezing, and there's no wind, so it's accumulating quickly. It's one of those snowfalls that lure you outside to spend countless hours enjoying the peaceful tranquillity and beauty of it.

Bryce pulls the snowmobiles outside the garage and then fusses to make sure my helmet is done up properly. Climbing aboard, I study him as he flips his hair back, placing the helmet on his head and straddling the seat. It doesn't matter what he's doing, it's the way he moves that is awe inspiring to watch.

Bryce drives Austin's snowmobile and I follow him down the trail on Bryce's machine. Once he sees I can drive a snowmobile (even though I told him we used to own one and I drove it often) then he finally relaxes. Letting his guard down, he goofs around kicking up snow and acting his age for once instead of being Mr. Responsible. I enjoy seeing this side of him.

As we race through the trails, I can see he's impressed at my ability to keep up with him, even when we pop out of the tree line onto a deserted logging road that snakes and curves dramatically. We race down the smooth roads for a few miles and he slows every now and then to look behind, making sure I'm close and safe. After about an hour of climbing and descending through the mountain trails, we end up at one of the waterfalls. Once we take our helmets and gloves off and stretch our legs, Bryce points out the heavy wet snow blanketing the pine trees, its weight causing the branches to collapse.

"It's so beautiful out here. Look, Babe, a cardinal," I say, pointing.

"You're beautiful."

I smile, liking his comment. "That was fun and exciting. Bet you didn't think I'd keep up, eh?"

Bryce struts toward me, using that panther-on-the-prowl walk that gets me going every time. How I love to watch him. "What are you doing driving that fast?" His fake scolding expression and the slight grin tells me he likes it when I'm aggressive.

"Keeping up with you." I smile proudly.

"We'll be slowing down now. I don't want you hurt."

Crap! He's changed back to Mr. Overprotective.

"But—" I start to protest and Bryce shuts me up with a scorching kiss that travels all the way to my toes.

When we separate, I continue. "But that got my adrenaline pumping. And so did that kiss. Wow!"

"It did, eh?" Bryce takes his leather coat off smoothly, throwing it on Austin's snowmobile seat.

"What are you doing?"

He stands before me, the corners of his mouth turned up mischievously and one eyebrow raised. "I'm taking my clothes off. And so are you." He unzips my coat and pushes it off my shoulders. A moment later, it flies past me to land on Austin's snowmobile seat next to his.

He has that hungry look in his eyes, the one that tells me, I'm taking what I want.

His lips meet mine, kissing me like he can't get enough-like he's dying from thirst and I'm the water that will replenish him.

But then he breaks away abruptly. "I've been thinking about this since you said you wanted to go for a ride."

"You're serious? Out here?"

He unzips my snow pants and pulls them down. "Dead serious. Nobody for miles, Angel." He quickly spins me, pulling my yoga pants down and pushing my upper body over with his big hand on my back. "Hold the seat, Angel. Don't let go. This will be a quick and hard fuck."

Out of the corner of my eye, I see Bryce pull down his snow pants and jeans. His cock springs out at full attention and then his warm body encases mine as he slides his finger inside me, testing to see if I'm ready. "Christ, Angel you're soaked," he says appreciatively.

I twist my body to glance back at him. "That's from the vibrating seat."

"You like that, don't you? It makes you hot and wet."

Turning back to rest my head on my arm, I circle my hips to drive him wild. "Mmm, yes."

He pulls out quickly and smacks my ass. "You love driving me nuts, don't you? This tight little pussy's been dying for my cock."

I widen my stance and circle my butt suggestively, wanting him deep inside me. Filling me. Stretching me. "Yes. I need you."

"You need my cock." Bryce slaps his cock across my pussy, saturating the tip.

I moan. "I need you. All of you. Every inch of your gorgeous body."

"You want this?" He pushes the head in a fraction.

"Yes."

"Are you sure? Right here, right now?" He's such a tease.

I was reluctant before but now I don't care who sees us fucking. I want him that bad.

"Fuck me!" I push back onto his cock. "Fuck me hard!"

His grip tightens on my hips and his groan echo's over the

sound of rushing water nearby as he sinks balls deep. "Fuck, Angel, this pussy of yours. You're so warm and tight on my cock."

He slams hard into me, time and time again. Pleasure builds and spikes.

Holding onto my hip with one hand, he slides his other hand up my sweatshirt and pulls down my bra to fondle my hardened nipple. He tugs and circles it with his fingers, sending tingling sensations directly to my pussy. He falls down on my back holding me tight, gathering control. "All I want is to bury my cock deep inside you, live in this sweet pussy, forever."

He lifts and drives his cock deeper than the thrust before.

I turn to see him slamming into me. "You do. And it's where I want you to be. Buried deep."

He reaches around and as soon as his finger touches my clit, I clamp down on him. "I want you to come. Give it to me, Angel."

Nothing could be more beautiful than it is right now.

The huge snowflakes falling, the beauty of the waterfall, the sound of rushing water and the smell of clean mountain air.

Bryce holds my hips tighter yanking me down onto his cock, his balls slapping my pussy.

Fire courses through my veins. My temperature rises. My pulse and breathing quicken as my orgasm brews like a storm.

The sensations are too much to suppress, sending me over the edge and my orgasm tears through me.

"Babe! Don't stop. Please, don't stop." I keep up the same rhythm, pushing back on his hard cock, gripping the seat tighter as I quiver and shake.

"Aw, fuck!" Bryce groans as he slams into me a few more times and then rears up, almost lifting me off my feet. His upper body weight collapses on top of me, holding me there, holding me tight.

His cock twitches, erupting long and hard inside me. "Christ, Angel, I can't control myself around you."

"Good. I don't want you to. I want you to be as crazed and turned on for me as I am for you."

"You never have to worry about that. I'll never get enough of you. You're my drug. I'm addicted."

A clean rag magically appears from the compartment at the back of the snowmobile. I smile, realizing Bryce planned this. When he pulls his cock out, his large hand cups the rag between my legs and he meticulously cleans me up before focusing on himself, a selfless act I love and admire about him.

I shiver.

"You're cold." Bryce rushes to dress me before focusing on himself, then steps over to Austin's snowmobile to retrieve our coats.

"I don't think I'm shivering from the cold." I give a seductive smile.

He stands before me, helping to pull my coat on. "That's good. Hold that thought until we get back to the cabin." Then he pulls his coat back on and shivers.

"You're cold," I say.

"I think all the blood went to my cock and it's still there," he says with a boyish grin.

I run my hand across his cheek. "I love you. You're irresistible."

Bryce hugs me. "I love you, Angel." He squeezes me harder. "Now let's go find a restaurant and get warmed up."

"Sounds like a great idea. I'm starving."

"You should tell me when you're hungry."

"I just did."

He shakes his head, smiling, and strolls over to start Austin's snowmobile, every step exuding power and strength. Few people get to see the vulnerable, boyish side of him. But I get to see that. Just me.

The snow is falling more heavily now and it's hard to see. I wipe my face shield often to get a better view of Bryce and the trail in front of me. Fifteen minutes later, Bryce has found a small restaurant off the highway.

He asks for a booth across from the fireplace and we melt into the seat thawing, waiting for the waitress to take our order.

Bryce takes my hand in his. "Thank you for fulfilling another one of my fantasies."

"That was fun. We'll have to do that again sometime. It was so beautiful, the way the snow was falling. I think that's my favourite waterfall."

Bryce rubs my arm. "It's my favourite too, now."

The waitress appears and takes out her notepad. "Kay, what would we like here?" she asks me before turning to Bryce. Her eyes widen. "Oh," she says, turning red, a typical response to my boyfriend's good looks. I almost roll my eyes.

Bryce squeezes my hand. "You go first, Angel."

"I'll have the clubhouse sandwich with salad and ranch dressing, please."

The waitress turns to Bryce. "And you?"

"Same, but for an appetizer, can we get deep fried dill pickles?"

She kicks into gear and starts writing. "All right then. And to drink?"

"Bud light lime and a Molson Canadian, please," Bryce says politely.

"Shouldn't take long," she says, and disappears.

Bryce takes my hand again. "This has been a great day."

"Yes. I've really enjoyed it."

Bryce runs his finger around the base of my ring finger. "When we're together, by ourselves, nothing else matters and we always have a good time."

"Yes, I've noticed that. All worries disappear. It's just you and me enjoying each other's company."

"The way I feel about you, Angel, I could do this for the rest of my life."

"I could too. I love you that much."

He laces his fingers with mine. "The love I feel for you is too hard to describe, so I'll have to show you every damn day."

"I like the sound of that."

The waitress comes back with our drinks and pickles and we

automatically separate our hands but Bryce keeps contact with my leg beneath the table. "Shouldn't be too much longer," she says and disappears again.

We dip the pickles into the ranch dressing and take a bite. "Mmm, these are good. And hot!" I say, trying to cool my mouth.

Bryce chuckles. "Yes, they're hot, Angel. Be careful. Is this the first time you've had them?"

"Yup. I think they're my new favourite."

We eat in silence and my thoughts wander. I'm amazed at how far I've come with the idea of marrying Bryce. After almost losing him and knowing how it ripped my heart out, I realize I never want to feel that again. There's no place on earth I'd rather be than with him.

The waitress brings our food and we dig in.

"The ride here was smooth. I've been on trails that were like a plowed field," I say.

"Tuesday's storm and the four inches from today helped with that. They are smooth, but on the way back we need to take it easy. It'll be dark when we leave here. I want you staying right behind me."

Bryce is back to Mr. Overprotective.

I salute him with two fingers to my forehead like Leena does. "Yes, sir!"

Bryce leans in and lowers his voice. "I think you need a spanking."

I smile and change the subject. "So did you ever apologize to Dante?"

"I will. When I go back to work."

"Think he's still mad over your fight?"

"No. He set me up. He knows how to push my buttons, to get me thinking straight. He used to pull the same crap with me over Lindsay, except, he wanted us to break up. He saw how that relationship was affecting me."

"Good friends do that. Subtle hints that make you think."

"Dante's a good friend."

When we're finished eating, the waitress brings our cheque and then stands with a couple other waitresses in the doorway of the kitchen, giggling and looking our way, waiting to catch a glimpse of Bryce.

We slide from the booth and I close the gap between us, taking hold of his sweatshirt, spinning him around so they can see his beautiful face.

"I love having you all to myself. This has been a great day. One I'll remember forever."

Bryce smiles down at me. "This day will be in my memory forever." He chuckles wickedly and tosses money on the table. He wraps his arm around my waist and tugs me close. "Let's get you back to the cabin."

I glance back at the doorway. The ladies are smiling.

I drive closely behind Bryce as we make our way back to the cabin through the trails in the darkness. The headlights are bouncing, reflecting off the trees. The huge snowflakes are still falling. They're blinding but beautiful as we climb and descend through the mountain trails. The smell of pine trees wafts up into my helmet. The scent must be more prominent than usual from the moisture of the snowfall.

Bryce has slowed down considerably now because the darkness changes everything in our path, including the one trail we were supposed to turn down. The snowfall has covered our tracks and we're both disoriented. Bryce stops, giving me a hand signal to turn around. I follow.

After driving on this trail for a few miles, Bryce slows and stops again. He comes back to talk to me and I shut down my snowmobile engine. In his headlight, a moose and her calf are standing in the middle of the trail. "We have to wait until they leave. Don't want to piss Mama off."

I fumble to get my gloves off and my phone out of my pocket in a hurry, hoping to take a few pictures, but there's not enough brightness from his headlight and they're too far away. It's not long before mom and calf make their way back into the trees.

"That was so cool! I've seen them on the side of the road before but never that close."

"Incredible animals. Taste good, too."

"Yes, the moose burgers were delicious. I don't know if I could shoot one, though."

"I bet you could." Bryce gives me a squeeze. "You've got the shooting part down pat."

"I'd love to go hunting with you."

"You'd be the sexiest hunter alive."

"No. I don't think so."

"You don't think so? What hunter could be sexier than you?"

"You."

The snow is falling more heavily as we get going again. White-out conditions are making it hard to see so Bryce slows further. I wonder if his adrenaline is pumping as fast as mine from driving in the darkness with obstructed vision. It's very exhilarating and I'm enjoying it immensely, but it is a little scary, too. But then, along the way, Bryce points out all the deer he sees darting through the trees in the bouncing headlights. It's awe-inspiring.

After driving for about an hour we make it back to the cabin and store the snowmobiles in the garage. Chilled to the bone, we rush inside the cabin and Bryce throws wood on what remains of the fire.

Laying out a plush blanket on the couch, he pulls me down into his arms and we cuddle while we wait for the cabin to warm up.

The kisses start out slow and sweet and progress to hot and steamy. Bryce pulls away, maneuvering his big, hard body up so he's standing beside the couch looking down at me. His eyes are filled with lust and desire as his chest heaves. "Jesus, Angel, you get me so worked up." He shakes his head.

"You do the same to me," I say, panting.

"Okay, we need to tone it down for a few seconds, because I've got something in mind."

"Oh, yeah? A surprise?"

Bryce grabs the remote and flips on the TV. "You sit here, and I'll be right back."

"Okay."

I hear him in the kitchen and wonder what he's up to now. I'm flipping through the channels, killing time, waiting for him, when I stumble onto the music awards and stop to watch as they interview some of the musicians on the red carpet.

Suddenly, the crowd starts to cheer and the camera scans over to a limo as its occupants disembark.

It's Von Jobin, and they're all wearing tuxedos, looking hotter than hell.

6

J LOOK OVER MY shoulder toward the kitchen.

Bryce is busy in the fridge, not paying attention. *Should I change this, or … hell, no. I'm watching this.*

The beautiful blonde in the sexy pink dress gathers the band members together to interview them. "That's quite a loud reception, don't you think?"

Reese and Drake pump their fists in the air, working the crowd into a roaring frenzy.

The beautiful blonde practically yells into her microphone. "So your new album will be released in two weeks?"

Colton responds. "Yes. The fans will love it! Quite a few love ballads on it."

"No date tonight, Colton? Thought we heard you had a new love in your life." She holds the microphone to Colton's mouth waiting for his response.

The crowd settles down and Colton lowers his voice to answer. "No date, she had to go back home, but you'll be seeing her next time."

"Does this mean you're off the market for now?"

"Yeah. She's the one."

"Ooh, listen to the crowd. Broken hearts all over the world. Thank you, I hope you win an award tonight." She moves on to the next band, taking the camera with her.

I change the channel. *Good! Hockey.*

Bryce returns from the kitchen with tea and coffee cake. "Red Wings and Toronto. Could be a good game."

"Thanks, Babe." I take them from him. "Aren't you sweet."

Bryce grins. "You'll know in about ten minutes." His eyes and his deep sexy voice drip with the promise of long, hard, explosive sex. "You drink up and I'll be right back."

"Okay."

"You keep looking at me like that and I'll take you right now."

"Oh? Am I looking at you in some strange way?" I tease, remembering how he said that exact phrase to me the first day we met when he was seducing me right out of my thong.

"If you didn't have that tea in your hand, I'd be tickling you to death."

"Well, it looks like you'll have to wait."

"You wait. You're going to get it. Hard!"

"Promises, promises." I give him my full white-teeth smile. As he shakes his head and walks into the bedroom, my eyes widen and I sigh in relief. *That was close!* Bryce didn't see or hear the TV.

Why would Colton say that? Especially on TV. *"She had to go back home, but you'll be seeing her next time." "She's the one."*

He can't be talking about me. There has to be someone else in his life.

I replay our last conversation in my head.

"Everything that's in my heart I write on paper and then I create a song. And don't think it's about someone else because I know what you're like. You keep denying my love for you. You're the one I want. I will only write about how I feel for you."

Aw crap, maybe he was talking about me.

Will this new album cause more heartache for me and Bryce when it comes out?

Shaking my head, I dismiss Colton from my thoughts.

I hear Bryce moving furniture in the bedroom and my heart quickens. He makes me smile.

Finishing my tea and dessert, I wait patiently for him to return. Finally, he comes to stand before me in his black thong, showing quite the impressive package.

My eyes scan his body. "You look yummy."

"I do, eh?" As he smiles down at me, I notice he has one hand behind his back. "Will you wear something for me?"

I'm almost hopping off my seat with excitement. "Sure. I'd love to."

"You go into the bathroom while I make the final preparations for our room. I'll come to get you."

Our room? I love how that sounds.

Bryce takes my hand, pulling me from the couch, and hands me the bundle of white lace he's been hiding behind his back.

I stop to eye him up and down again and then run my hands down his tight abs. "So hot!"

Bryce stops my hand abruptly as his stare bores right through me. "No touching!" He spins me fast. "Get!" He smacks my ass so hard it sends me forward out of the living room.

"Ouch." I rub my butt cheek all the way to the bathroom.

Upon closer inspection, I see what I'm holding in my hand is the lace bra, pearl thong, garter belt, and lace top stockings I bought from the naughty shop.

Bryce must have grabbed them from my house before we came here. I love that he likes my taste in lingerie and that he thought about this well in advance, preparing for this. *Can he be a more perfect boyfriend than he is right now?*

I hear him banging things around while I dress. As I'm clasping the last garter to the stocking, I hear a tap at the door. "Are you ready?" Opening the door, his eyes travel over my body. "You blow me away every time I see you like this."

"So I take it you like?"

"More than like. I love this on you." Unexpectedly, he tugs my hand, flattening me against his hard body. His finger slides inside the cup of my bra teasing my nipple until it hardens and peaks. His hands caress my back until they reach my butt cheeks, and then he pulls me in hard against his steely erection.

"Oh my, feel that." A hint of a smile crosses my face.

"You'll feel it, all right. That's what you do to me." As he lifts me up, I wrap my legs around his waist. He rubs his hard-as-stone cock deliciously on the right spot.

I giggle as he carries me into the bedroom and lowers me into the leather swing. "Hold onto the ropes, Angel." After he positions my butt where it's supposed to be, he walks behind and hoists me higher, securing the ropes when I'm at the perfect height. He swings me, my hair dangling and swaying. Then he picks up his phone from the dresser and takes a picture. "So beautiful. You're perfect. I'm keeping this. Spank bank material." His dimpled smile has the strangest effect on me.

"Babe, you're irresistible."

"I am, eh?" He takes a few more pictures at different angles. "I bet that photographer was fantasizing about doing this."

What? Where did that come from? Oh Babe, the way your mind works. "Babe, Brent was very professional."

"Yeah, right. He's a typical guy and that's what he would be thinking. Every guy thinks like that. Do you want me to ask Austin, Dante, or Jax?"

"Can we not fight over this? Can we get back to where we were?"

"We're not fighting." His voice is deep and husky. "We're talking, and I'm saying all guys think this way." He places the phone back on the dresser. He stops me from swinging and positions himself right at my pussy. He holds onto my butt so I can't swing away.

"Damn you're sexy! Look at this? The pearls are pulled tight in your pretty pink flesh." And just like that, his thoughts have changed.

"I can't see it, but I feel it."

"That's hot!" He says appreciatively. "Can you feel this?" He runs his tongue up the pearls.

"Mmm, yes. I like that."

"So do I." His voice resonates. "Tastes so sweet." He licks again, up one side, then the other, with long, unhurried strokes of his talented tongue. "I didn't get to taste you when we were fucking on the snowmobile and I miss that. I'll remove these." Bryce undoes the pearls at the top of my thong. "So I can feast on my sweet, sweet, pussy." I feel him searching for a toy of choice in the compartment below. "I plan on driving you wild. You'll be begging me to let you come." His deep voice is laced with pure, erotic, unhurried sex.

Oh, crap! Prepare to be tortured.

Bryce does just that, coaxing my body to the brink of orgasm over and over again. Whenever he sees I'm close, he stops and chooses another toy from his goody bag. He keeps going until I'm begging for him to let me come. When he finally does, it's one of the most explosive orgasms I've ever had and I'm totally exhausted afterwards.

Delirious from my orgasm, I feel Bryce lower the swing. He moves around at lightning speed between my thighs and swings me onto his awaiting hard shaft. "You are so sexy in this swing. Fuck, Angel, you get me so hot."

I gasp as his cock fills me hard and fast, right to the end, not able to go any further. My back arches from the intense feeling. He thrusts in and out, pulling on the handles at the side of the swing and I glide effortlessly onto his hard cock.

His movements are skilled and methodical, as he pleasures me, tenderly touching every inch of my stomach. He reaches for my breast, rolling my nipple between his thumb and finger. "I've never seen such a perfect pair of tits. And they're mine."

He pulls out to the tip, slamming balls deep, again and again. The more turned on he gets, the rougher he grows, as lust and desire consume his self-control. Suddenly he pulls out, using the head of his cock to prod my clit, rimming my entrance as he tries to gain control. With our hearts racing, he tunnels deeper than the time before, deeper than I thought was possible. I gasp.

Our orgasms build like a storm, chests heaving for our next breath, sweat forming at my temples as I clench around him. "Reach down and play with your beautiful clit. I won't last much longer."

"Babe, your cock. I love it. You're doing it to me again."

Before I know it, I'm coming apart at the seams. My legs shake and I grip the sides of the swing so tightly it's almost painful. "Babe! Ohhh! It's so good!" I scream in ecstasy.

"Take it, Angel! Take all of me! Every … last … inch!" Bryce follows, gripping the handles tighter, pulling me deeper as his head falls back and his pelvis thrusts forward into me. "Christ, that's deep!" He comes with an animalistic growl, tightening every muscle in his body, struggling to give me every last drop.

Once he gathers his senses, he reaches for some Kleenex and holds it at my entrance when he pulls out.

Then he lowers the swing and lifts me out of it, cradling me in his arms. He carries me to the bed and holds me tight on his lap as he kisses every inch of my face. "You're so beautiful."

"Wow! I've never come so hard in all my life, except when I was in the swing with the music piped into my ears. That was amazing, but please don't do that to me again."

How ineffective my plea is when I can't erase the ridiculous grin on my face.

"You loved it and you know it."

"You love to torture me, don't you?"

"I'm taking you and your body to places you've never been before. I'll test your limits and beyond to see how far I can push you." His eyes are dark and mysterious as his lips meet mine in a slow sensual kiss. "You'll be surprised how much you can take. And you'll love all of it and beg for more."

Something in his eyes has me a little scared of what's going on in his head but I have to trust him. I know he'd never hurt me and I have enjoyed everything he's ever done to me. How does he know my body better than I know it myself? Experience with other women?

Don't go there. Get that out of your head right now.

"Ready for more?" Bryce picks me up and places me in the middle of the bed. He unclasps my bra, sliding the straps down my arms, slowly, skimming across my sensitive skin. Then he tosses it, hooking it on the bedpost. A rope magically appears, hidden from my view and he ties it securely around my wrist. He walks around the bed gloriously naked, tying my ankles and my other wrist to the bedpost as my eyes glance over his washboard abs and the sexy V at his hips. I can't take my eyes off him. I want to run my hands all over his body. Damn, he's hot!

"Not too tight?" He asks, his voice is deep and husky.

"No," I say, mimicking the same sexy stare he's giving me.

"Can you get loose?"

I pull on my restraints, testing them. "Nope."

"Good. Now you're mine to do with as I please."

Dominating Bryce is back.

A shiver of excitement runs through me. "Can I tie you up after this?" I ask.

He turns and I get a glimpse of his gorgeous dimple as his sexy ass saunters over to the kinky cabinet. When he comes back, he sits on the side of the bed next to me with a white silk blindfold. Leaning, he runs his hand over my cheek. "This is for your pleasure, Angel." He cocks his head to the side and smirks. "And mine. But mostly yours."

He covers my eyes with the blindfold. "Can you see?"

"No."

He thinks I've forgotten he's avoiding the question.

"You're beautiful. You look like an angel dressed in white, tied to my bed. Fuck you're hot!" I hear him taking more pictures as he makes his way around the bed.

"Bet that photographer had dirty thoughts of you like this, too. But too bad, you're mine! And I'm the only one who will ever have pictures of you like this."

He still can't get over it. It's still bothering him?

"Babe, like I told you before, everyone was very professional, including Brent."

Is it because he saw a picture of Brent and noticed he's good-looking? Or is it because Brent took pictures of me? Bryce, what is going on in that head of yours?

He's silent after that. I hear him rustling things around in the kinky cabinet. I hear his feet padding on the floor as he comes back around the bed. He places something on the nightstand and then the door opens. I hear his feet on the hardwood, fading as he approaches the kitchen. He opens the fridge and closes it again.

What is he up to now? A thrill of excitement darts up my spine as I await his return.

He strolls back in the room and places something else on the nightstand. Then I feel the bed dip as he positions himself and his skin grazes my calf. Now I feel no movement at all. I wait for a sound or movement. Nothing.

Is he staring at me?

After what seems like at least a minute he finally speaks. "You make my cock so hard. Fuck!" He drops down and straddles my hips. "You do know, I'll never let you go."

"Good, I don't want you to."

Bryce falls on me, his warm body covering mine, and he hugs me. His lips separate mine and his tongue explores my mouth.

My tongue darts out to meet his. It's a slow, sensual kiss that gets me hot all over again.

He lifts himself, straddling my hips, cupping my breasts, feeling the weight of them. "So beautiful. Your skin is flawless and so soft." He pauses for a moment. "They're perfect. I'll never get enough of this body."

The bed shifts and I wonder what he's up to now.

He straddles my thigh and then leans over, as if reaching for something on the nightstand. I wait for some kind of touch or feeling, but nothing. He knows how to wind me up tighter than a rubber band.

I squirm.

"Stay still."

"Babe?"

"What? Missing my touch already?"

"Yes."

After one long minute, I feel ice cold water dripping on my breasts. I gasp and my back arches.

"Stay still." He warns me.

"It's hard."

"I know, Angel."

Drops of ice cold water trail down my lower belly until I feel it there, hitting the target. I swear my clit grows to twice its size.

"I love how your body responds to the things I do to you."

"Mmm yes, I like that."

What takes me by surprise is the feeling of warm droplets and then ice-cold right after, dropped on the same spot on my leg. I'm guessing its wax and ice.

What a sensation.

"I experimented on myself. How's that feel, Angel?"

Isn't he sweet? Always looking out for my safety.

"I like that, too."

He repeats the process. Warm then cold droplets across my breasts and belly—and I enjoy every bit of it.

All at once, I feel pressure on each nipple. Nipple clamps? Then he lets go of whatever this device is and I feel a cold chain across my chest. The weight of each one tugging. "Does that hurt?"

"No."

"I tested them on my nipples." He then moves on to running something down my body, which causes a tingling sensation that leaves a trail of fire in its wake. The bed shifts again and again.

Damn, he's busy! And this is all for my pleasure. He really does enjoy this.

He's between my legs now and I feel something cold running across the flesh of my pussy. "You like this?"

"Mmm, yes." My hips start to move, wanting more. I feel something different now, more rigid, but still cold.

"How's this?"

"Yes, I like that too." Various fruit? I'm guessing.

I feel something cold poking at my entrance and then it enters and I feel the weight of it.

One of the pretty glass dildos?

Ice-cold droplets of water hit my clit one after another. My body is all sensation. I move more impatiently now, tugging on my restraints. "Babe?"

"I know, Angel, I'm getting there."

"I can't wait." God, he drives me insane.

Bryce goes to work untying my legs, but he leaves my wrists tied.

He pulls off the nipple clamps, yanks out whatever was inside me and replaces it with his warm cock. His lips and tongue spend the same amount of time on each nipple easing the slight sting from pulling the nipple clamps off.

I moan and arch my back. "Your cock is so warm inside me. I love your cock."

"Fuck, Angel, you're killing me with your sensual movements." Bryce pulls the blindfold off. "I want you to see me fucking the hell out of you." Bryce reaches to the bedpost and unties both my hands. "I want to possess your mind, body, and soul." He pulls out to the tip and slides back in. He hands me a thin vibrator. "Start that baby and place it on your clit."

I do as he says and Bryce does as he promises, fucking me hard and fast.

It's only a matter of seconds before I quicken.

We're both panting and sweating and as soon as I clamp my muscles around his cock he lets out a regretful groan.

"Come for me!" he demands.

"Babe! Don't stop!" My eyes close and then open. I moan, my head thrashing from side to side as I fall apart beneath him.

When the aftershocks fade, I see Bryce is still struggling with his control. "Babe, let go. Come for me," I urge him.

He grips my butt cheeks, rocking me into his next hard thrust. He buries himself deep inside, making me gasp. "I want to feel your warm cum inside me."

A groan escapes from deep in his throat as every one of his muscles tighten and release. He slams into me twice before explod-ing, flooding me with his warm cum. His weight falls heavily on top of me and he nuzzles in my neck.

We lie in silence for a while, feeling each other's hearts beat, waiting for our breathing to return to normal.

"Too many things on my mind," Bryce says breaking the silence.

"I'm confused. Is that an apology for giving me one of the best fucks of my life? Babe, I loved every second of it."

"I like to come with you."

"You did. Sometimes these things can't be perfectly executed or rushed."

"Yeah." Bryce is deep in thought and it has me a little worried that he saw something I haven't seen in the media with all the pictures circulating.

I have to get on my computer, but when?

"So what's on your mind?" I ask in a soft voice.

"I'll get over it in time."

A vague answer. Is it still bothering him that Brent took pic-tures of me? Maybe he'll eventually tell me.

"Babe, it kills me to see you hurting like this." I take his beau-tiful face in my hands and look directly into his eyes. "But know this: I'm not going anywhere. We'll be together forever. Think you can handle me, pain in the ass that I am, for the rest of your life?"

Bryce's semi-erect cock starts to grow inside me and his hips move rhythmically. Leisurely. "First, you can't help that you're beautiful and men are attracted to you. Second, think you can handle my temper and jealous streak for the rest of your life?" Bryce lifts his upper body weight and does that expert roll of his hips, slowly.

"Yeah. I can handle it. Yours is mild compared to mine. Remember what I was like when you gave Lindsay that look?" The thought makes me seem foolish now that I know he loves me, but at the time it was tragic.

Bryce rocks into me, in and out, working me up until I'm hot and needy again. He chuckles. "Huh, yeah, how could I forget? You tried to break up with me. But I wouldn't let you."

"At least you were rational. I wasn't."

"But we worked through it like we'll do with every situation that arises." He thrusts harder now.

"Yes." My attention to the conversation slips as I become preoccupied with how good it feels.

"Do you want me to stop?" Bryce teases in that deep, sexy tone.

"No."

"That's what I thought."

After we both have another mind-blowing orgasm, we're so exhausted we fall asleep wrapped in each other's arms.

In the morning, I wake to the light shining through the outer edge of Bryce's camo drapes, feeling hot from Bryce tangled around me like a vine.

"Angel." Bryce says, as he moves slightly. I rise to look at him and see he's breathing heavily. He's in a deep sleep. His arm instinctively wraps around me, squeezing tighter.

I lie there thinking, *He really does love me!*

7

J COULD'VE LOST HIM. *I could've lost this.* I snuggle closer, wanting to feel every inch of his body.

My mind replays our beautiful weekend together, the numerous times we had sex and the mind-blowing orgasms I've had.

Thinking this way sends tingles to all the right places, making me hot and wanting more. It also has me thinking about the way he diverted the question about me tying him up and it has me searching to see if the ropes are still tied to the bed.

They are.

I gently nudge his arms and legs off me and silently rise. He grumbles something incomprehensible and then falls back to sleep. I quickly go to work, tiptoeing over to the kinky cabinet, gently pulling the doors open, and pick out the black leather dominatrix ensemble.

I slide the thong on and look in the mirror as I fasten the collar around my neck. I then clasp the bra behind my back, if it can be called a bra. It's really just three leather straps that barely cover my nipples. One long leather strap down my stomach connects the collar, bra, and thong together. It is very sexy, showing mostly skin.

One by one, I pull on the lace top silk stockings, running my hand down the back of my legs to make sure the seams are perfectly straight. Then I grab a few weapons of choice and lay them at the foot of the bed within easy reach for teasing and taunting.

Next, I gently lift one of Bryce's wrists and tie a knot around it. He moves slightly and I duck down at the side of the bed, frozen in place as I wait for him to fall back into a deep sleep.

As his breathing changes, I peek up from the side of the bed. Seeing his eyes closed, I move on to tying his ankle. It's very time consuming.

I then creep around to the other side of the bed and repeat the process.

I'm proud of myself when I finish tying him to the bed, without him waking. I whisper "Yes!" Raising my head and arms in the air, cheering like I'm at a game.

Pulling the comforter down to the footboard, I leave only the sheet on his hips.

Climbing on the bed with the leather whip in hand—the one with two-foot cattails—I gently tickle Bryce's eight-pack abs.

I feel like I'm going to explode from pure excitement.

I'm like a little girl with a new toy—a hunky new toy, I've captured.

I wait for him to wake. He stirs slightly. Pulling the sheet down, I use the cattails to tickle his thigh.

He stirs again. I run the cattails across his nipples, muscular pecs, and down his abs. He opens his eyes. "What are you doing, Angel? Nice view by the way." His deep, resonate voice sets me off.

"Yes, I know." My eyes scan the length of his body and I lick my lips.

As Bryce moves slightly, he notices he's tied. He pulls on the ropes and I hope I've secured them tightly enough that he can't get free. "Angel…"

I cut him off. "Can't get loose?" I ask in a teasing voice.

He pulls hard on the ropes.

I flop down, straddling his hips, holding his arms to calm him. "Stop! I don't want you hurting yourself, or the bed."

"I told you, it was for your pleasure." He doesn't sound pleased, but he hasn't demanded I remove his restraints either.

"Can't I have a little fun?"

He tries to hide the smirk on his face, but I see it. "Have your fun." He rolls his eyes like he's pacifying me.

I guess, in his eyes, big, burly, tough guys are not supposed to be tied to the bed. But it sounds like he'll give me my way, just this once.

Time is of the essence. I don't know how long he'll let me have my fun, so I have to work fast. I run my hands down his arms, feeling every bulging muscle along the way. "So damn sexy in this pose." I decide to keep going because he feels so good beneath my hands. I grab his muscular pecs and give a quick, little lick to both nipples, he squirms. "Stay still."

"You woke me out of a dead sleep and you're licking my nipples," he says. "How do you want me to respond?"

"Good point. I'll let this one slide." Continuing, I use my finger to outline every muscle across his stomach. His muscles tighten further with my touch. I glance at his fully erect cock but I don't touch it. I want to drive him wild like he does to me. I run my finger down his happy trail, tickling him. He squirms again.

"Stay still," I warn him.

He chuckles but doesn't say a word.

"I think you've seen enough." He's heard that line before. Out of his own mouth. I reach back and pick up the dark purple blindfold.

"Playing that card, eh?" he says in a deep, tough guy voice.

I place it over his eyes. "Can you see?"

"No."

"Good. Now I can do whatever I please with you and if you're not quiet, I'll gag you with the strawberry ball."

"My little dominatrix."

"Quiet!" Cattails in hand, I slap his hip and leg.

He tries to hide his smile, but he doesn't fool me: he's enjoying this. His cock is hard as stone.

I shimmy off the bed, open the door, pad across the kitchen floor and open the fridge.

The deviant me is smiling, knowing my absence will make him a little bit anxious, wondering what I'm up to. From the fridge, I take my time gathering whipped cream and various fruits.

Back in the bedroom, I see he's still trying to wiggle out of his restraints. I place everything on the nightstand next to his head and then touch his wrist. "Stop!" I whisper next to his ear. "You should know, I'm a fireman's girlfriend and with my experience, I know how to tie good knots. You won't get loose until I decide to untie you."

"Aren't you adorable?"

I pick up the cattails and swat him. "Quiet! What did I tell you?"

He tries to hide his smile. He doesn't speak this time.

Laying the various weapons I've chosen around him, I skim his skin ever so slightly, knowing it will drive him mad. I climb on the end of bed, standing between his spread legs, and take a picture.

I can see why he likes this so much. I'm having the time of my life!

Moving around the bed, I take pictures at different angles and then move back to my original position: standing over him, not moving a muscle, staring silently at the gorgeous male specimen I've captured. A minute later, I flop down, straddling his thigh. I lean over him, my breasts close to his face, and drop my phone on the nightstand. Picking up the whipped cream, I squirt it in various, strategic places.

He reacts to the cold cream.

"Don't move," I warn him.

After placing pieces of fruit on his nipples and stomach where

I've applied the whipped cream, I take another picture. Moving fast before the whipped cream starts to drip, I put my phone back on the nightstand and get to work. Hovering over him, I lick the whipped cream around each nipple, leaving the cold fruit.

He squirms again and a moan escapes from deep within his throat.

Ha! You're not immune. This is driving you wild and I'm loving every moment.

Picking up the fruit, I run it across his nipple then place it close to his lips. "Open." I stick it in his mouth. "Bite."

"Mmm."

"Quiet!" I swat his hip.

My mouth closes over his nipple and I lick and clean the remaining whipped cream.

His nipples harden into tight peaks.

I repeat the same process on the other side, but this time he doesn't make a sound. I pick the three remaining pieces of fruit off his stomach and feed them to him, then lick the rest of the whipped cream off him from top to bottom. The light dusting of hair tickles my nose as I lick once more making sure the sticky residue is gone. Then, picking up another whip—this one has feathers on the end—I lightly touch all the spots my tongue has neglected.

Quickly shifting on the bed, nestling between his legs, I start the vibrator and run it gently down his balls.

His body jerks.

"Your body tells me you're enjoying this." My voice is slow and seductive.

He doesn't respond.

"Is this what it felt like the first time you tied me up? When you took me from the bar and brought me to the cabin, did you stand over me staring, holding your cock in your hand, fantasizing about shooting your warm cum all over my tits and belly?"

His cock grows harder with my words and seductive tone. He groans.

"Were you dying to know what my pussy and tits looked like? Or did you look?"

Another groan, this one escaping from deep within his throat.

I had no idea talking dirty could get both him and I so turned on. I run my hands down each thigh, making sure to graze his balls.

He squirms a bit.

"Were you fantasizing about sticking your cock in my mouth? Were you wondering how tight my pussy would be and if it would squeeze you like a fist?"

His jaw tightens, but he's silent.

Whipped cream in hand, I squirt it from the tip of his cock in a straight line to his balls. I lick all the way up and I'm rewarded with a body jerk and a drop of pre-cum. His balls need attention too, so I cover them with the whipped cream and take my time licking my way around with feather-like licks. I don't think I've ever seen them this tight.

He groans and I know he can't take much more.

"Were you wondering how sweet my pussy tastes?" His tongue darts out of his mouth and he runs it along his lower lip as if he tastes me. I squirm.

Bugger! I'm supposed to be teasing you.

I slap his hip with the cattails. "Quit! You know what licking your lip does to me."

"Fuck!" Bryce says when I cup his balls and take his cock in my mouth. "Angel, untie me so I can fuck you!"

I ignore him and keep up the same torturous rhythm.

"Angel, I don't want to come in your mouth. Stop!"

His cock pops out of my mouth, still standing straight as a soldier.

"I was waiting for you to beg." I pull the blindfold off. "Welcome back Mr. Tall, Dark, and Gorgeous."

"Untie me." His eyes, half lidded, are filled with desire. I make my way around the bed, doing as he wishes. As soon as I get the last rope off, he yanks my arm, surprising me as he tackles me to the bed beneath him.

I giggle. "I can see why you like doing this. Babe, I'm on fire. I really enjoyed that."

"You did, eh?"

"You liked it and you know it. Say it!"

He straddles my hips, capturing my hands, with our fingers entwined at the side of my head.

"You're a bad girl. What should I do to you?"

"Love me."

His eyes are alight with amusement, his mouth twisted in a mischievous grin. Suddenly, he leans over and seals his mouth over mine. Our tongues tangle and I savour the mingled tastes of fruit and whipped cream. He kisses me like he's been starved for years. "You get me so fucking horny. You're a gift from heaven. I never thought I'd find someone like you. To have what we share? You're a miracle. My Angel!"

"So you liked?"

"Yes, I liked. I'm the luckiest man alive."

He hugs and kisses me with such passion I'm overwhelmed by my feelings for him.

We continue making love as if the hours on the clock don't exist for us, taking our time, touching, exploring, and enjoying each other's bodies. When we finally separate, exhausted, a moment later, we jump up, remembering time does exist and we scramble to collect our things to make the trip back to Barrie.

Passing the Gravenhurst exit, the memory of the accident and Ken's death is still clear in my mind. It's had such an impact, I doubt I'll ever forget it.

I reach over and run my fingers down Bryce's forearm, remembering how he helped extricate Susan from the crushed car. I'm proud he's mine.

He squeezes my knee, giving me a knowing smile.

Just then, the picture I took of Gramps pops up on my phone. My heart drops in my chest and my eyes widen.

I show Bryce and he looks concerned. "He never calls me," I say. "I always call him." Placing the phone at my ear, I say, "Hi, Gramps. Is everything okay?"

"Yes, we're good here. But a man named Chaz from Alaina modelling agency called and was looking for you. I told him I would relay the message to you."

That's right, I remember. *I gave him my home phone number when I filled out the paperwork. And the first time we talked, I had called from Gramps' house. It must be important.* "Thanks Gramps. I'll call him back. So what did you think of that snow storm? Did you get much?"

"A foot. Not as much as Toronto. I saw the news. They were buried." I hope he didn't see anything about me and Colton on the news. "How about you?"

"We didn't get as much as Toronto," I say, "and that's weird because we usually get the brunt of it."

"When are you and Bryce coming to visit again?"

"I'm not sure. Most likely around Christmas when he has time off." I put my phone on speaker so Bryce can hear too.

"Great. I look forward to seeing both of you."

"I'll talk to you next week. Love you, Gramps."

"Love you too, Giggles."

Oh good, he didn't say he saw anything on the TV so maybe I'm in the clear. Or maybe he did see something and he's asking about Bryce to see if we're still together?

Keera! Don't get yourself all worked up for nothing.

"See Babe, he likes you. He wants to know when you're coming back to North Bay with me."

"He's a good man under that hard-ass shell. He had me on my toes, but I think I broke through it."

"Got to love my Gramps."

I didn't want to bother Chaz on Sunday, which is most likely his only day off, so I make a mental note to call Monday morning.

Bryce's alarm startles me, waking me from a dead sleep with the sound of sirens blaring. My arms shoot out, slapping Bryce across his abs. He gasps for air and then rolls over to shut it off.

"Sorry, Babe. It scared me."

Bryce rubs his stomach. "Good left hook. Knocked the wind out of me." Bryce rubs the spot where my hand made contact.

I roll on top of him, straddling his hips, splaying our fingers together on the pillow beside his head. "That didn't hurt. You like teasing me." I roll my hips, grinding against his semi-erect cock.

"Who's teasing who here?" He shakes his head. "I love waking up like this." He grips my hips pulling me into him. "You're beautiful. Look what you're doing to me already."

"Mmm, yes. Would be a shame to waste this." I move down the bed so I'm straddling his calf and take him deep in my mouth.

His throaty groan curls my toes. I pop him out of my mouth. "This is for you. You can owe me." My mouth surrounds his cock again as I set out to give him one of my best blowjobs ever.

"Only too happy to repay you, Angel." His voice is slow and deep and the tingle travels down my body, zapping me right there. I clench my muscles instinctively.

He gathers my hair into a ponytail and wraps it around his forearm, grabbing the base, helping my head bob up and down until he starts to lose control. Then his grip tightens at the back of my head and he aggressively pulls me up and down his shaft at his own pace, fucking my mouth.

I'm so hot and turned on by his aggressive thrusts pumping deep in my mouth that my pussy clenches greedily. When he shoots his cum to the back of my throat, I almost come from rubbing against his leg.

I swallow quickly, wiping the excess off with the back of my hand. I crawl up his body, kissing my way up until I reach his lips, and then I kiss him slowly, sensually. "You taste good."

"Jesus, Angel." He shakes his head and smiles. "You're killing me. I'll be thinking about this all day and I'll be a walking hard-on until I get inside you again."

"I'll be waiting." I hop out of bed, walk to the doorway, and turn my head to give him a seductive grin. "And I'll be dripping."

"Aw, Christ."

I turn to walk down the hall totally naked and I hear Bryce yell after me, "You can't do this to me, Angel."

I smile and whisper, "I just did."

But then I realize I'll be the one climbing the walls waiting for him to come home.

I'm surprised he let me finish. Most likely because he's pressed for time and has to get to work.

I hear the water running for the shower while I make his coffee, which I bring to him in his favourite fireman's mug as he's exiting the shower.

His smile lights up the bathroom. "My Angel." He hangs up the towel and sips his coffee. "Damn, that's good." His eyes travel the length of my body. A smile forms at the corner of his mouth showing me his dimple. "This morning couldn't be more perfect." He steps close to me, gloriously naked.

I scan the length of his body, taking in the beautiful sight before me. "Well, I hope you have a good day and I hope you think of me," I purr.

He tugs me against his hard body, rubbing my butt cheeks. "My mind is consumed by you, all day, every day."

"Good. Because I'll be thinking of you too."

"That's what I like to hear." He runs his thumb over my bottom lip and grins at me mischievously, knowing how he's affecting me. "So, what are you doing today?" he asks as he walks toward the bedroom.

"Maybe I'll play with myself all day." I grin at him.

"You like to drive me insane, don't you?"

I smack his butt cheek. "Get dressed, I'll make you breakfast."

He calls out to me as I'm walking down the hall. "Yes, you do like to drive me insane."

He makes me smile, he's so irresistible.

After Bryce finishes his breakfast, he hesitates at the front door, peppering me with kisses. "I don't want to leave. This was the best weekend and this morning was great! Life feels so good having you here with me." He kisses me again.

"Yes, we had an amazing weekend. You and I together, feels so right."

He hesitates for a few more seconds, searching my eyes and then hugs and kisses me for the fourth time before heading out the door.

I feel lonely the moment I close the door behind him. I haven't taken two steps away from the door when he pops back in, wraps his arms around me and bends me backwards, kissing me long and hard in a tongue-on-tongue passionate kiss that leaves me reeling with hot, greedy need. "I love you, Angel."

I can hardly speak through my face-splitting grin. "God, do I love you."

"Bye, Angel."

"Bye, Babe."

This time I know he's gone because I hear his truck start and pull out of the driveway.

I sit down with my second tea in front of my laptop and call Chaz.

He answers right away. "Chaz here."

"Hi Chaz, this is Keera. How are you?"

"I'm good. Where have you been? I've been calling your house and then I checked through my phone and saw you had called me from another number."

"That's my grandfathers house."

"Keera, modelling agencies and cosmetic companies have seen

your pictures and they want you to endorse their products. You are one hot commodity. Don't you answer your e-mails?"

"I just sat down in front of my laptop now. Sorry, I've been busy."

"I sent you a list of the companies that want you, and the money they're willing to pay for a contract with you. Pick through it and decide who you want to work for. Send them an e-mail and tell them your demands. They'll bend if they want you bad enough. If you have any questions, send me an e-mail. Keera, you can make a lot of money. Oh, one more thing, I sent you an invitation for Alaina's formal gala in two weeks. It's the most popular event of the year. It is something to see. You have to be there! Top executives will be scouting our leading models this year. It'll be great for your career. And you have to wear the red dress! I'll send a limo for you and your guest. Got to run. Talk to you later."

And just like that, he's gone. I stare at the phone. "Busy man," I say, talking to myself. But as the news sinks in, I start to smile. I get to wear the red dress to a formal gala. Never been to one. "What do you do at a formal gala?"

Opening my e-mail, I see fifty-four in my inbox. What? I've never received so many e-mails at one time in my life. I start at the top and glance down the list. I see there are a few from Colton. Shit!

I check out Chaz's e-mail in case he calls back.

He's listed offers from fifteen companies, from the lowest—two-thousand dollars—to the highest—a one-hundred thousand dollar job. I look at it again.

That has to be wrong. How can a company afford to pay a model that much money?

There are many more offers from other companies below Chaz's e-mail.

Just because they like my pictures? I scroll through the other e-mails and delete the ones in Europe off the list because I'm not spending ten or fifteen hours flying to my destination. I put a star next to the ones in Canada and the US.

I don't have to decide right this second. Maybe Bryce can help me later.

That's when my eyes focus on the first e-mail Colton sent last Wednesday after I dropped him off at the airport.

8

From: Colton Von Jobin
Subject: Missing you already
Date: Wednesday, November 19, 2014

I can't stop thinking about you. I replay every look you gave me, every touch, and every kiss. These two days have been outstanding, the best of my life. You've made me the happiest man alive.

Thank you, beautiful. Like I said, missing you already and I haven't landed yet.
Love, Colton

Oh, Colton. I read his next e-mail

From: Colton Von Jobin
Subject: Hope everything went well
Date: Thursday, November 20, 2014

I fired Craig the minute we landed yesterday and had a new replacement in two hours. He should have known not to mess with me.

So how did it go with Bryce? I've been worrying. I wish I could pick up the phone and call you. Can you call or e-mail me back, please? Thinking of you constantly.
Love, Colton

I knew you'd fire him, you were pissed.

From: Colton Von Jobin
Subject: Really worried about you
Date: Friday, November 21, 2014

Just left Detroit after Wednesday and Thursday's concerts. On the bus heading to Ohio for a concert tonight, so I have a lot of time on my hands to answer your call or e-mail in case you want to talk or send me one. I hope you're okay. Worried! And thinking of you.
Love, Colton

From: Colton Von Jobin
Subject: I'm dying, not knowing if you're okay
Date: Saturday, November 22, 2014

Just flew into Vegas for the music awards. Wish you were here with me. I'd show you off for the whole world to see and then you could meet my parents and sister. As soon as you get this, please let me know if you're okay.
Thinking about you constantly.
Love, Colton

I throw my hands in the air, raising my voice. *"Colton, why can't you give this up?"*

From: Colton Von Jobin
Subject: You're scaring me!
Date: Sunday, November 23, 2014

I'm going to send a search party for you. Or maybe I'll cancel the concert in Chicago on Monday and go look for you myself? Please answer me. The silence is driving me crazy!

Love, Colton

Jesus, what do I say to him? Just tell him the truth. Don't sugar coat it. Just tell him straight out.

From: Keera Johnson
Subject: Just got your e-mails
Date: Monday, November 24, 2014

This is the first chance I've had to look at my computer because I was with Bryce all weekend at the cabin. No internet. I'm doing fine. Everything is good. I hope you won an award.

Keera

He sends one back immediately.

From: Colton Von Jobin
Subject: Finally!!
Date: Monday, November 24, 2014

You are one hard person to find. You're on my mind constantly. I've been going crazy, worrying about you. I miss you so much. We won two awards in Vegas and when we played "Let Me Be the One," we got a standing ovation. They loved it! I wish you could have come with me to see the show. Did you find my letter in the box from Alaina? Can you call me? Please.

Love, Colton

Colton, please give this up.

Tell him Keera. You have to break his heart, but he'll move on and find someone else.

From: Keera Johnson
Subject: Last e-mail I'm sending
Date: Monday, November 24, 2014

*Colton, you have to stop this. I love Bryce. I will not
e-mail you again. This causes problems in my relationship with him. I wouldn't want Bryce e-mailing another
woman. This has to stop! You need to find someone you
can love. She's out there and I know you'll find her and
be happy for the rest of your lives.*
Goodbye, Colton.

I hit send and close my laptop, hoping he takes my advice and respects my wishes.

I need to show Bryce these e-mails so we can get this out in the open. I don't want Bryce to think I'm hiding something from him. It would make things worse.

But when?

While I lay awake last night, an unsettling thought crossed my mind, and it wasn't the first time: I thought of Lindsay and Bryce fucking in his bed. I made a mental note to do something about it first thing in the morning.

Since I'll be spending a fair amount of time in Bryce's bed, I decide to change the mattress and bedding to something of my choice.

I get out the phone book and call around to a few stores.

After setting up delivery of a mattress, sheets, and comforter, I prepare a lasagna for tonight's dinner, clean Bryce's house, and workout to keep myself busy. Bryce calls me around noon, and talks dirty to me, revving up my hormones.

Before I know it, the delivery truck shows up with the new mattress.

I make the bed and jump on top to try it out. It's much higher than the old mattress and it's like floating on a cloud. I love it.

Five o'clock rolls around and I have dinner in the oven. I'm sitting on the stairs naked with a beer in my hand. Bryce's dark purple tie is wrapped around my neck.

"How was your day, babycakes?"

Bryce stands at the doorway with his hair falling over one eye looking hotter than hell in his navy blue uniform.

He clears his throat and smiles, making his eyes crinkle in the corners as he closes the door. "It's great now." He inhales deeply. "Mmm, smells good."

"Yes, that's our lasagna in the oven." I stand so he can get a better view.

He strolls toward me but halts a few feet away, eyeing me up and down. "It's you who smells delicious."

The magnetic pull and the electricity charging between us are unbearable. He's so close, I feel my body straining toward his. He waits—getting ready to pounce, I hope.

I can barely stop myself from launching into his arms.

I've been wound tightly all day since our early morning escapade. With Bryce talking dirty to me this afternoon, I'm shaking with need and desperate for his touch.

He yanks on the tie, forcing me into his awaiting arms. I'm surprised at how quick he is. He holds me tight, breathing me in, not letting me go.

I frown. *Jeez, what's this all about? What's wrong?*

"This is where I want to be, Angel. Right here with you."

"Babe, are you okay? What happened?"

"Nothing in particular. It was a rough day."

Mr. Vague. Obviously, he doesn't want to talk about it. I hand him his beer. "Maybe this will help."

He stands close to the bottom step as he takes a sip of his beer. I'm on the second step but he's still taller than me. He focuses on the purple tie hanging between my breasts, his fingers gently grazing the outer edge and making my nipples tighten and peak to half an inch. His eyes ogle them as he runs his cold beer bottle across each one. I shiver. "I knew I could make them grow," he says appreciatively.

"Babe, all you have to do is breathe on them."

"Come. I want to lose myself in you." He sidesteps, squeezing between the banister and myself, tugging me gently by his tie up the stairs. I follow, willingly.

Once in the bedroom, I start to undress him while he drinks his beer. He watches me intently. I throw his shirt on the chair and go to work on his pants. After unzipping them, I hook my fingers in the waistband and pull down both pants and boxers. He kicks them away. "Now that we've got that out of the way," he says, tugging me by his tie toward the bed and places his beer on the nightstand. He glances at the comforter. "New bedding?"

"New mattress, too."

"You didn't like the other one?"

"Not especially. It was bothering me that you and Lindsay fucked on that mattress." I shrug my shoulders. "What can I say? I'm weird like that."

"I'm sorry, Angel, I never even thought of it." He wraps me in his big, strong arms. "I'm such a jackass."

"That's okay. I was thinking we'd change the mattress at my house too." An unwelcome thought enters my mind: that lunatic stalker doing, whatever, in my bed.

"Yes, the moment we get back. Now let's focus on this." He loosens the tie and slips it off over my head, quickly tying my hands in front of me.

Damn, he's fast.

Picking me up, he throws me on the bed and then climbs on—a black panther, ready to pounce on his prey.

He straddles my hips, lifting my tied hands above my head, leaning over and tying me to the bed. "At my mercy now, Angel." He leans back, admiring his handiwork.

"Oh yeah, what are you going to do to me?"

"Let's start with this."

Over the next ninety minutes, he pulls every trick from his book and every card from his sleeve, not stopping until I'm delirious from so many orgasms, I lose count. He showers every inch of my body with kisses, licks, nips, and bites and when he finally unties me, I return the favour. He fucks me senseless, and I have no choice but to have another mind-blowing orgasm. Only when he decides I've had enough does he allow himself to come, tunnelling deep into me, pumping every last drop inside me, and then letting his full weight fall on me as I run my hands down his back, soothing him as his aftershocks fade.

Emerging from my state of euphoria, I finally speak. "Wow, Babe, my legs are shaking."

"I don't think I can get up," Bryce says. "You wear me out."

"That's good. So you're satisfied?"

"More than satisfied. There will never be another like you. No one can make me feel what I feel with you."

"Aww, you're so sweet. I feel the same way you do."

Tangled together, we touch and caress for a while, alone with our own thoughts.

After about ten minutes, I decide it's time to talk to Bryce. "Babe, I called Chaz and he told me to check my e-mails because he had sent me a list of companies that want me to endorse their product and that's when I saw some e-mails from Colton."

Bryce tenses.

"I need you to see them so you know I'm not hiding anything. We have to be honest in this relationship. I've been trying to spare you unnecessary pain, but that hasn't been working out. So, if you want to see them, I'll show you. If you don't, I'll delete them."

Bryce turns his face away from me for a split second. When he looks back, something indefinable in his expression makes me wonder if he's hiding something.

"No! I need to see what Colton's up to." He kisses me and

climbs out of bed. "I need you to show me anything that has to do with him. Don't leave anything out to spare me the pain. I'm a big boy."

I dismiss the odd feeling that he's not telling me something and roll onto my stomach, kicking my feet as my eyes float down to his semi-erect cock, which is only two feet away from my face. "Yes. You are a big boy."

Bryce finishes his sentence, ignoring my comment. "I can handle it. Love the new mattress, by the way, and I'll put that money right back into your account."

"You don't know what my account number is." I roll out of bed, smacking his ass as we walk to the bathroom to clean up.

He stares back at me through the mirror. "You'd be surprised what I know about you."

"That's kind of stalkerish, don't you think? Wait—is that even a word?" I test it on my tongue. "Stalkerish."

His eyes crinkle when he smiles. "Not when it comes to you. We'll know each other inside and out."

"Oh. All-righty, then."

"Before I forget, our game Wednesday night has been changed to six o'clock. Dante and Jax want to go to The Bull for some drinks afterwards. Okay?"

"Am I invited?"

"Of course, Angel. You're always invited everywhere I go. I'm making sure you want to go. Lindsay never did. Sorry." He closes his eyes and makes a face. "I don't like mentioning her name to you."

"That's okay. Sure, I'd love to go." Why wouldn't she have wanted to go? Oh, yeah, she's anti-social. Or she's pissed off too many people.

Bryce's stomach grumbles.

"You ready to eat?"

"Yeah, I'm starving."

I pull him by his cock, walking backwards to the kitchen. "Jeez, you look like you could go again, big boy."

"You keep doing that to me and you'll see what happens."

"You like this, don't you?"

Suddenly, he pulls me hard against his body, stopping me in my tracks as he nuzzles my neck. "See what you do to me? I'm ready to bury myself inside you again." He lets me go and I continue to pull him by his cock to the kitchen. "But let's eat first. It'll give me time to regenerate some sperm for you."

I smile and run my hand over his cheek. "You are too adorable." Placing the mitts on my hands, I open the oven, bending to pull the lasagna out.

"Damn!" he bursts out. "That is hot!"

I turn to look at him sitting at the breakfast bar. His eyes are glued to my butt. "The lasagna?"

"You! I should take a picture."

I place the lasagna on the stove top and turn my body toward him. "Ya, snooze, ya lose."

"Come here. Bad girl!" Bryce comes around, meeting me halfway, wrapping me in his strong arms and nuzzling my neck again.

"Me? A bad girl? Nooooo."

"God! You drive me crazy. I love you so much."

"I love you, too." I look at him, wondering what's gotten into him, but he doesn't notice. "Jeez, you sure are frisky tonight."

"Haven't you noticed we can't be in the same room together without fucking?"

"Yes, I hope that never fades."

"Never, I'll love you forever."

"Good." I dish out the lasagna and we sit naked at the breakfast bar, eating.

"Mmm, this is delicious—like you." Bryce habitually plays footsie with me and grazes my pussy with his hand as he rubs my thigh.

After we're finished eating, I clear away the plates and he

opens my laptop. *Oh crap, here we go.* Bryce starts to read the first
e-mail Colton sent. Red, starts to travel up his neck toward his
brow. I sit on his lap, hoping to calm him. "I'm sorry, I hate this.
I hate what it does to you."

His grip tightens on my hip as he reads. "That motherfucker
got to spend two days with you and I didn't."

"Seventeen hours and I was sleeping for seven, so technically
it was only ten."

Bryce doesn't answer me. He's mad.

Way to go Keera, you're making things worse.

He continues reading.

"He wants you to call him? He gave you his phone number?"

"He gave me a piece of paper before the valet showed up with
my car and I stuffed it in my pocket. It must still be in the coat I
wore to the Alaina shoot."

"What letter?"

"When I was unpacking the clothes, I found it at the bottom
of the box. I glanced at it quickly, saw it was from Colton, slipped
it back in the envelope and stashed it between some clothes in
my closet. I didn't have time to read it because you were cooking
breakfast and I wanted to help you."

Bryce doesn't comment, he keeps reading the e-mail
Colton sent after I closed the computer.

From: Colton Von Jobin
Subject: I love you!
Date: Monday, November 24, 2014

*Please don't do this, beautiful. You're my lifeline. The
only one who gets me through the day. I love you!
You're all I think about. We'll e-mail each other for now.
We'll keep this as our secret. Bryce doesn't need to
know. Please answer me.
Love, Colton*

"He thinks he loves you? He doesn't know you." Bryce frowns. His deep voice is filled with anger. He deletes all the e-mails and closes the laptop. "I want to see anything and everything he sends you." He rises from the chair and so do I. He takes my hand. "Come, let's go watch the TV so I can forget about this shit."

Bryce's concentration isn't on the TV and neither is mine. It's like we're in two separate worlds, both lost in our own thoughts and I want desperately to know what is going on in his.

"Babe, what are you thinking about?"

"Nothing in particular. My mind is all over the map right now."

Mr. Vague again. Christ, help me out here. "Okay. Name one thing that's bothering you."

"Colton!"

"Anything else, like at work?"

He lets out a sigh. "They hired four new recruits and they're making my life a living hell."

"Why, what's going on?"

"For the past three years, we've had the same group of guys and we're all in sync. We all know what the other is doing. Now, this screws up the perfect system we had."

"But once they get trained properly everything will be back to normal. Right?"

Bryce grumbles. "Maybe." He leans forward like he wants to get up. "Come with me. Let's go to bed."

I rise from the couch and he stands right behind me. His fingers trace my ribs and I squirm. "That tickles."

Pivoting on my heel, my hair whips his chest as I take off down the hall, full tilt run, giggling all the way. Coming up behind me, Bryce tackles me to the bed, pinning me beneath him as he straddles my hips. "I love chasing you."

"I can see that. I love it too." I grab his hard cock with both my hands and he moans. "Did you play football in high school?"

"No time for that. Just hockey." His lips seal with mine as we moan into each other's mouths, tasting, licking, savouring.

Tuesday morning when I drop Bryce off at work, he kisses me like he can't get enough, even though, we made love twice last night. I also woke to him hovering over top of me rubbing his hard cock down my leg and licking my belly. Instantly aroused, I asked him if we had time and he said, "Always have time for you." It was one hard fuck that left me wondering again what was bothering him. I asked him and got yet another vague answer.

On the drive back to Bryce's, I conclude that the e-mails from Colton are the reason for Bryce's strange mood. I'm learning that every time there's an obstacle in this relationship, Bryce's mood changes and he's not himself. He tries so hard to live up to his tough-guy image, hiding his feelings, but I see right through him.

After parking the truck in the garage, I stroll back to the house to prepare dinner for tonight. The laptop on the counter seems to call out to me to take care of business so I send an e-mail to a Canadian company based out of Toronto. I set my terms, letting them know I only want to work the day shift, eight to four each day. If they don't go for it, I'll move on to another company.

I work out and take a shower. Within two hours, I'm back out the door to go shopping.

Roaming from store to store, I pick up some great gifts for everyone on my Christmas list. I also find some cute high-heeled leather boots and a new shirt for Bryce to wear on our Wednesday night trip to the bar. I spend countless hours enjoying myself with no strange feelings of anyone watching me.

Back at Bryce's, I put away my parcels, throw dinner in the oven, and go to the station to pick him up.

The normal ritual when I pick Bryce up at the fire station is that Dante and Jax follow him out to the truck to talk to me. But today only Bryce comes out.

I scoot over on the seat so he can drive. "How was your day, Baby?"

"Better now." He squeezes my thigh, kisses me, and tugs me closer.

"No Dante and Jax? I thought I would've seen them? I want to thank them."

"They're busy," Bryce grumbles. His voice and expression tell me he's annoyed. "You'll see them Wednesday."

Uh-oh! Are they not getting along? What's going on? Bryce drives in front of the bay doors and I see someone pressed against the glass, looking out the window at us. I can't make out who it is. Damn it! If Bryce weren't so stubborn and would talk to me, I might be able to help him with his problem.

"Angel, Grant called me today. He said the trial started."

And just like that, he changes the subject. He doesn't want me to know what's bothering him.

"Oh. Where is it?"

"Bracebridge."

"I'm curious about the time he's spent in jail so far. Does that count toward the time he'll receive?"

"I'll ask Austin. He knows the judicial system better than I do. Are you okay?"

"Yeah, I'm fine."

He pulls me closer, hugging me, kissing my temple.

"Mom texted me today. She wants to know if we can make it for dinner Thursday. I told her I'd talk to you."

"Yeah, sure. Ask her if she wants me to make something."

Bryce's eyes gleam. "You're my angel. I always think you'll give me some bullshit excuse about why we can't go, but you always surprise me."

"This is what relationships are like. We compromise. I go with you, you come with me. Together, always."

"You know, before you came along, the best part of my day was work. I dreaded going home. But now, you're the best part of my day. The day drags and I can't wait to see you again."

"See, you're a romantic. That is so sweet. I look forward to seeing you and having you in my arms again too, Babe. Nowhere would I rather be."

"Yeah. But don't say that romantic bullshit too loud."

"Before I forget, when I talked to Chaz he said he sent an invitation for Alaina's formal gala." I feel Bryce's arm twitch and then tighten around me, but I continue speaking, not skipping a beat. "He said I have to go because there will be some major designers and cosmetic companies at the event and it would be good for my career. He said he'd send a limo for me and my guest. Will you be my guest for the evening?"

"When is it?"

"He said in two weeks."

"Where is it?"

"I'm not sure. He's such a busy man he didn't have time to tell me, but the invitation is in the mail."

"Sure, I'd love to go with you." He gives me a squeeze.

After he backs into the garage, we make our way into the house and upstairs to the kitchen. "I'm taking a quick shower." He empties his pockets, takes his pager and phone off to charge them, and saunters down the hall, undressing along the way.

"Nice view. I'll check on dinner, should be done by the time you get out."

"Good, I'm starving." He disappears around the corner and I hear the water running.

As I'm putting the finishing touches on our salad, his phone dings with a text notification. I automatically look to see if it's Lindsay. The text shows a number I don't know. No name means it's not someone in his contact list.

Hey, Bryce. Got your number from Dante. He wants to know if you're going to The Bull Wednesday after the game.

9

HO THE HECK is this?

I scroll down and see the text Bryce's mom sent and a few from Austin, Dante, and Jax. And then some from none other than, Lindsay. She's still hounding him, but he doesn't answer. That's good.

Hearing the water shut off, I put his phone back on the counter and go back to what I was doing.

Five minutes later, Bryce walks out of the bathroom and down the hall toward me, gloriously naked, smelling of cologne and body wash, with his hair wet and tousled. He takes my breath away. I'm frozen, except for my eyes, which rake up and down his perfect physique greedily. He's still tanned from Aruba and his muscles flex, and relax as he walks. Those huge thighs and the package swaying back and forth catch my eye. *Damn!* The smirk on his face is proof that he knows what he's doing to me.

As he approaches me, he grabs both my arms roughly, turns me so my back is against his chest, and pulls my body hard against his. Moving my hair to the side, he kisses the back of my neck. I'm immobile. I moan as he licks down my neck and peppers me with kisses. Without warning, he stops, spins me around, and attacks my clothing. I'm stripped in a matter of seconds.

There is an urgency in his touch, a shaking need. It's almost like his world revolves around making love to me. Not that I'm complaining. I love all the attention he's giving me, but it worries me that he might have something other than Colton on his mind.

Bryce moves the salad and everything else over to the other counter and focuses his undivided attention on me. Tugging me close, his thumb traces the outline of my lower lip. His intense gaze makes me shiver: in this moment, I am adored and treasured by the man I love. His hands roam my back and my butt as he stares into my eyes.

Jeez, that look. Does he realize what that look does to me?

My hands do the same, roaming over his hard muscles. We caress and pet, lost in the moment, not taking our eyes off each other. I feel his cock, trapped between the two of us, as it hardens to stone. My nipples graze his skin, tightening to hard peaks. Our breathing accelerates to deep breaths. Our skin is warm as our temperatures rise.

He's silent, but so am I. We're too busy cherishing one another to speak.

His hands caress my sensitive skin all the way up my back, across my shoulders, and up my neck. He holds my face in his hands. "Words cannot convey how much you mean to me. But let me tell you, I'll never stop loving you like this. You're my everything!"

Wow! If that isn't a declaration of love, I don't know what is.

His lips lower to mine in a lingering kiss and then his tongue slides inside my mouth, slowly licking, savouring. It's one of those kisses that curls your toes and tightens every muscle from the waist down. By the time he pulls away, we're breathless, gasping for air.

He lifts me up to sit on the edge of the raised island counter and positions my feet on each side of the granite countertop. I'm spread wide open, totally exposed.

I lean with my elbows on the other countertop, which is resting at my back and I try to settle into a comfortable position.

Bryce stands back, admiring me. "My pretty little pussy is glistening for me."

"That's what your body does to me."

"I want to taste you."

I watch his wet, unruly hair lower to me and his talented tongue goes to work doing amazing things. His finger slides inside me probing around and then he teases me by pulling it out and rimming my entrance with the tip. I lift a fraction hoping he'll give me more. He notices my discomfort on the cold granite so he does his magic, working me into a frenzy in a matter of seconds with his sinful mouth and finger.

I lift my butt off the counter a fraction and hold the back of his head tight to my pussy with one hand, keeping the same pressure. Sweat starts to form at my temple and with a sudden muscle contraction, I'm clenching eagerly around his pumping finger. My head falls back and my chest heaves. "Babe, oh, oh, right there! Don't stop!" Every muscle in my body tightens and shakes.

When the aftershocks fade and my legs go limp, Bryce picks me up off the counter and carries me down the hall. He whispers in my ear. "I love making you come." He hugs me tight. "The sounds you make. You're so beautiful."

In the bedroom, Bryce gently lowers me to the bed. He climbs on the mattress and prowls up my body with an intense stare. "Promise me you'll never let anyone or anything get between us in this relationship."

He is struggling with something but if I ask again, I'll get another vague answer. "I promise, Babe. The only way I would give up on us is if you cheated on me. Everything else can be worked out."

"And you know that would never happen because I love you too much."

"I love you."

Our lips meet in a rapturous slow kiss that progresses to steamy hot. Our lips start to swell and we're gasping for air.

"I need to be inside you."

"I need you."

Bryce swipes his cock over my wet pussy, saturating the tip, then aims it at my entrance and sinks into me slowly.

I inhale sharply, scraping my nails down his back. When I reach his butt cheeks, I tug him further into me.

Lowering himself onto me, he kisses my neck. His hips move slowly, around and around, in and out. Then he lifts his upper body and picks up the pace, giving it to me hard.

Suddenly, he stops, rolls, and pulls me up onto his lap. "Come here. I want to feel you like this." We're face to face now, staring lovingly into each other's eyes, making sure his cock stays securely inside me.

I lift and lower myself back down onto his cock, using his shoulders for support while we find the perfect rhythm. His hands caress my back. My hands touch every well-defined muscle along the way. I can't take my eyes off him.

I hold his face in both my hands and lower my lips to his, kissing him sensually. "I love this position."

"So do I, Angel. I love watching you ride me. You're so beautiful."

My fingers snake through his hair and I tug, pulling back his head, opening his mouth to me. My lips lower to his and my tongue darts into his awaiting mouth. He grips me tighter and deepens the kiss, moaning in my mouth.

Our lips separate, my head falls back, and I ride him hard. The moment I clamp down on him, he rolls me over, pinning me to the mattress again, keeping his cock securely in place. He doesn't stop fucking me until I erupt, falling to pieces, a shaking, quivering mess.

As Bryce follows, I watch his facial features change. His muscles contract and release. His groans are heard throughout the room with each exhale. His cock twitches and I feel warmth spread inside me. Then he collapses on top of me and buries his face in my neck.

We kiss and caress each other lightly, waiting for our hearts to stop pounding and our breathing to return to normal.

"Babe, you're amazing."

"So are you, Angel. And you're good for my ego."

"No seriously, you give one-hundred-and-ten percent every time you make love to me."

"So do you, Angel."

"I'm just learning," I say softly.

"And you're a pro at it now."

"Think so?"

"You give me everything I need. You amaze me every time we make love." Bryce rolls off me and his cock slips out. "Stay right there, Angel." He walks to the bathroom, returning with a warm cloth to clean me up. I grab the cloth from his hand and wipe the cum off the end of his cock, cleaning him with the same care he shows me. I look up to see his reaction.

The love in his eyes does the strangest things to me. I feel it down there but also in my heart.

"I'm starving." He says.

"Yes, you worked up an appetite."

I stand on the bed and motion. "Turn." I climb on his back, wrapping my legs and arms around him, and he carries me to the kitchen.

I dish out dinner and we eat in silence. And then I remember the text. "Babe, while you were in the shower someone texted you."

"Oh, okay." He finishes his dinner, loads his plate in the dishwasher, and turns to look at his phone. He makes a face. Bryce texts back.

Who the hell is this?

Instantly he gets a reply. His face turns to anger, so I have to ask.

"Who is it, Babe?"

"Blake. One of the new recruits. Fucking Dante. I'll be clueing him in. I don't appreciate having my phone number handed out." Bryce returns the text and then places his phone back on the counter.

Bryce, sometimes you confuse me. You're hard to read. I don't understand your reaction. Why are you pissed off at Dante for giving your number to a rookie?

I want him to share his feelings with me when something's bothering him, but I think I'm asking for a miracle. Depending on the situation, I sometimes have to pull the smallest amounts of information from him. He keeps everything bottled up inside, protecting me so I don't worry.

I don't want to be the kind of girlfriend who nags and freaks out constantly. He dealt with enough of that in his relationship with Lindsay. I want to be the woman he loves to come home to. I want to be his best friend, lover, and the one he shares his deepest secrets with.

I'll let this one slide and maybe something will give me a clue and help me figure him out.

Wednesday morning, we wake up to four inches of snow. By the time he clears enough of the snowfall from the driveway to get his truck out of the garage, he has to rush to get to work on time. When he comes in to kiss me goodbye after putting the snow blower away, he grumbles, "I can tell this day will be crazy. Angel, can you check the weather to see when it will stop snowing?"

"Sure."

The weather report says snow until two p.m. and a total accumulation of six inches. I hand him two ham, egg, and cheese English muffins to go, so he can eat them on the way to the fire station. "My, Angel. Thanks. Bye, I love you."

"I love you. Get!" I smack his ass. "You'll be late."

He kisses me and rushes out the door.

I sit down with my laptop and tea to check my e-mails. The Canadian cosmetics company Avionté e-mailed to say they want me as their model. They've given me their phone number. The president of the company, Christina, answers the phone on the first ring.

She wants to know where I'm located so they can rent studio space nearby for the two weeks we'll be working together. I tell her I'm in Barrie but don't give her an address in case Colton is involved in this photo shoot in some way. I'm trying to be more cautious, looking for any signs.

We work out the details and she says she'll be in touch as soon as all the arrangements are made.

After hanging up with Christina, I scroll down to yet another e-mail from Colton.

From: Colton Von Jobin
Subject: I'm not giving up!
Date: Tuesday, November 25, 2014

This is the reason I'm not giving up.
He's inserted a picture into the e-mail of himself, holding me in his arms in Niagara Falls. I'm smiling and pointing my finger at him. He writes:

Look at the love we've shared, the love in our eyes for each other. A picture doesn't lie. Please talk to me. Don't do this. I need you!

Love, Colton

I wonder if I should delete this. It'll break Bryce's heart seeing this picture again. I don't know what to do.

I text Leena. Maybe she can help me with this one. After that, I text Katie to see how she's doing.

I can't keep up with the incoming texts from both of them so I create a group text.

Katie's a little lost in the conversation but we tell her we'll bring her up to speed when she comes home for Christmas.

When I ask Katie and Leena what they would do about Colton's e-mail, they say they wouldn't hide anything from Bryce. I decide to keep it.

Before ending the text thread, Leena and I tell Katie we'll see her soon and Leena tells me she has to work, but she'll meet me at the arena for the game since the time has changed.

When Bryce pulls into the driveway half an hour late, I have his hockey equipment packed, a change of clothes for after the game, and a sub sandwich for him to eat on the way to the arena.

Bryce rushes into the dressing room with only seven minutes to spare and I sit in my usual spot in the grandstand directly behind the firefighter's bench, beneath one of the radiant heaters.

People-watching is one of my favourite pastimes when I'm by myself and nothing is distracting me.

A mother and her six-or-seven-year-old son climb the steps and settle in three rows down from me to the left with their concession food. Across from me to the right, a father is trying to rein in his four kids, who are running up and down the stairs. After a few minutes of them not listening, he gives up and lets them do what they want.

But what really catches my eye is the two beautiful women walking across the grandstand toward me. One nudges the other and they give me a once-over, eyeing me up and down.

What is that all about?

When they go to sit on the other side of the firefighters and have their backs to me, I check them out. The one with long, brown hair is wearing a great pair of boots and I love her black leather jacket.

Movement in my peripheral vision diverts my attention to the ice. Both teams are filing out the doors.

Bryce is the last one to come out onto the ice. As soon as I see him, that familiar tingle travels to places that haven't been touched since last night. I squirm in my seat.

Leena slides in across the seat, surprising me as she plasters herself to my side. "Getting all hot and horny watching Bryce play hockey?"

"Hey. How do you know what I'm thinking?"

"You've got that I-want-to-be-fucked look on your face."

"I do not! Do I?"

"Yeah, you do. Hey, where's Austin?"

I point and Leena's eyes follow.

"I want to have the same fuck-me look as you. Have to get started."

I chuckle. "Are you and Austin coming to The Bull for a few drinks with everyone after the game?"

"Austin didn't mention it."

"Well, I am. And I want you guys to come."

"All right, then. We'll be there."

"Good. Look, Bryce and Austin are facing off again."

"Austin told me the cops won the game last Wednesday, eh?"

"Get out!"

"I wouldn't bullshit about that. But I guess only because Bryce was off his game."

"I totally forgot about the game with all the drama going on between me and Bryce." The unwelcome thought of Bryce holding up his hand, telling me to stop talking and leave enters my mind. "I talked to him at the fire station, shortly after five Wednesday night." I frown. "He actually went to the game after that?"

"Yeah, but I heard he was a mess. He was bitchier than all hell. Everyone was asking. 'What's wrong with Bryce?' And by the end of the night, everyone knew. Thanks to Dante."

"Dante was the one who showed Bryce the pictures of me and Colton."

"I remember that. And his excuse. 'There was no hiding it, it was all over the TV and internet.' Do you ever think Dante's trying to split you two up?"

"No. He was the one convincing Bryce to come see me. He told Bryce he was glad we were done because it would give him a chance with me. But he only said it so Bryce would stop being bullheaded and come to Huntsville."

"Did you just hear yourself?"

"Yeah. Now you've got me thinking. I'll have to pay attention to the way they're acting around each other because they did have a huge blowout. They tackled each other to the floor, beating the crap out of each other. The rest of the guys at the station had to pull them apart."

"Get out! Really?"

Bryce scores so we stop talking and pay attention to the game.

The intensity of game pushes Leena and me to the edges of our seats. There are two fights, which send a few players to the penalty box for two minutes. When one player shoves another from behind, the ref loses it and gives the player ten minutes. Every time Bryce gets a goal, he looks up in the stands at me. Austin gets two and stares at Bryce with a smug look. They both behave themselves trying hard to score the whole game. The arena is erupting with loud boos and cheers. The hat trick Bryce slips in helps win the game with two minutes left on the clock. The cops fight to catch up, but there isn't enough time. Final score: Firefighters 5 Cops 4.

Bryce is back with a vengeance.

The two beautiful women are obviously here for the firefighters because they've stood and cheered every time they've got a goal.

After the game, everyone in the stands file out to the lobby, where it's warm.

I glance at the sign for the ladies washroom and grab Leena's elbow. "I'll be right back, got to go."

"I'll look for Ma, Pa, and Ciara."

"Okay."

As I settle into a stall, I smile at Leena's ease and comfort with the Hamilton family. It's so like her to fit in instantly like that—and it's one of the reasons I love her.

Just as I'm sliding my jeans up, I hear two women come in, talking as they close the doors of the stalls on either side of me.

One of them says Bryce's name loud and clear. I freeze and listen to their conversation.

"What did you say to Bryce when you went over to talk to him at the bar last Wednesday night?"

"You saw me talking to him?"

"Yeah. He looked pissed. What'd you say?"

The woman with the great pair of boots is in the stall on my right. I can see them beneath the partition. "I told him, let me give you what you need, it'll feel so good. I'll make you forget all about her."

"No! You didn't!"

"Yup, I did. I get a little bold when I have a few drinks in me and I was well on my way by that time. Did you see the look on his face?"

Are they talking about my Bryce? Don't be an idiot, Keera. How many guys named Bryce are there around here?

"Yeah, he looked disgusted with your comment," the other one says.

"Obviously. He left right after that."

"He seems like he has an attitude with you. What's up with that?"

"He caught me watching him take a shower."

"You watched Bryce in the shower?"

"Yes I was really enjoying myself until that asshole Dante, ruined it for me."

"Get out! Bet you got an eyeful."

I've heard enough. I exit the stall and wash my hands.

"What a body! Jesus, Trish, I stood and stared. I couldn't pull myself away," says the one with the boots.

"Yeah, I can see he has a rockin' body in his uniform. And last week in his jeans and t-shirt. The man is hot!"

"Yeah, but with no clothes on ... Damn, I've never seen a body that perfect. I'm not done with Bryce yet. I've got plans for him."

That bitch! How does she know Bryce? I exit the washroom and look for Leena.

My face is beet red and I'm fuming.

"I can't find Ma, Pa, and Ciara," she says before turning to me. "Jeez, what are you pissed about?"

"You can tell?"

"Uh, yeah. What's up?"

I tell her what I heard in the washroom.

"If they mentioned Dante's name, too, they must be talking about your Bryce. That can't be a coincidence. But how do they know him?"

"I was asking myself the same question."

"You should've confronted them when they came out of the stalls. I would've."

Just then, the guys come bursting through the doors, freshly showered and carrying their equipment over their shoulders.

I can't take my eyes off Bryce as he struts toward me with that powerful sexy walk. His black hair is falling over one eye. His t-shirt is tight, showing every delectable muscle underneath. His jeans fit perfectly, outlining the bulge and his large muscular thighs. What a sight to see. I shiver as the smell of his cologne and body wash manipulate my senses.

Bryce and Austin drop their bags and sticks next to Leena and me. They each lean in for a kiss.

"Good game. We were on the edge of our seats the whole time," I say, looking into Bryce's eyes.

He wraps his arm around my waist and tugs me against him.

Austin leans over and mumbles next to Leena's ear, "Hat trick. Frickin' asshole."

Bryce smiles at Austin.

"You'll get them next time," Leena says.

Dante squeezes between people to stand next to me and grabs my elbow. "Hi, Keera."

"Hi, Dante. Good game."

Bryce spins and picks up his sticks and bag, hoisting it over his shoulder, hinting that he wants to leave. His hand rests gently on my hip. "Let's go to the bar."

"Oh. Okay. We'll see you there, Dante," I say, trying to smooth over Bryce's eagerness to leave. "Leena and Austin are coming, too." Bryce nods and we make our way through the crowded lobby and exit the arena.

At The Bull, Bryce navigates between people and over to the bar, slowing to greet the regulars he knows with a handshake or a slap on the back.

I'm holding his hand and trailing along behind him, ending up at the far corner of the bar.

Leena and Austin follow, settling onto the high-backed bar stools. In the truck on the way over, I didn't mention anything to Bryce about what I overheard in the washroom. Maybe later.

Bryce calls the waitress over and orders us a round of drinks, then pulls my stool close to his so he can snuggle into me. He talks next to my ear, above the music. "You look hot tonight."

"Thanks, Babe, so do you. I like your new shirt."

He smirks. "Thank you for that, by the way." He squeezes my thigh and then clears his throat a bit. "Angel, I want you to stay right beside me tonight."

I look at him, wondering again what he isn't telling me. "Okay," I say. "We can dance later, right?"

"Yeah, we can dance."

It's only nine o'clock on a Wednesday night, but the bar is already crowded. There's a mechanical bull fenced in on the opposite side of the bar and a line up to ride it. The décor has a country theme like The Lodge, our favourite bar back in Huntsville, where Leena, Katie and I love to dance.

The music is loud and the dance floor is huge with quite a few people dancing already. The atmosphere has me hopping in my seat, wanting and waiting to dance myself.

I lean over and Leena strains toward me to listen. "I think we should dance after."

"Yeah, I like this place."

"Me, too."

On the other side of the bar, I see Dante and Jax coming in, greeting everyone they know with a slap on the back. They hold their position, talking with a giant man at the bar. Later, they grab their drinks and make their way over to where we're sitting.

Dante shoves a beer in front of Bryce. "To the man with the hat trick."

"Thanks, dickhead."

"You're welcome." He turns to me. "And how's Keera?"

"I'm good." I lean over to talk above the music. "Thanks for helping Bryce find his way back to me."

"Had to. He was a miserable prick without you." Dante grins at Bryce, slapping his back.

Jax smiles at me. "I want to thank you, too," I say loud enough for Jax to hear.

Jax comes to stand next to me, pushing Dante out of the way.

I turn to look at Bryce and he's smiling.

He seems to be okay with Dante. This is good.

As the firefighters file into the bar with their girlfriends or wives, Bryce introduces me to them and then they sit at the tables next to us.

I look Dante's way and realize that bitch with the boots and her friend from the washroom are settling in next to Dante and Jax.

Bryce puts his arm around my shoulder, squeezing me a bit closer. It's a possessive gesture he uses whenever he thinks there's an obstacle in the path of our relationship. I look sideways at him to see the expression on his face. He does not look impressed.

What is she doing here? And who is she, anyway? How did she see Bryce in the shower? Every time I've been at the fire station, I've only seen men working there. Is she a secretary in the office?

She talks with Dante for a bit and then she and her friend make their way around the other tables where the firefighters sit with their girlfriends and wives. Dante and Jax follow.

When Bryce isn't looking, I look at Leena with wide-open eyes and then side-eye the two women.

Leena swivels in her bar stool, following my eyes and then gives me a look I can't read. I give her a different look and hope she knows the meaning of it.

We've always been in tune with certain looks we exchange. It's our silent way of communicating without bringing attention to ourselves.

I do a visual in my head of how Bryce would've reacted when he caught her watching him. He must have been pissed off because I've noticed he's not showering at the station anymore. He comes home to take a shower. Then it hits me. *That's why he's been acting strange all week. It not because of Colton. It's because of her! She's been hitting on him!*

"Let me give you what you need," she said, "It'll feel so good. I'll make you forget all about her." That bitch!

Calm down, Keera. You don't want anyone to see how pissed off you are right now. I glance at Leena and take a sip of my beer to defuse the tension in my body. I don't want Bryce to notice my anger.

Leena gives me the eyes.

I give her a half smile letting her know I'll calm down in a few minutes.

Just then, the bitch in heat and her friend come to stand next to Bryce. She touches his shoulder and I feel him tense. "Hey, Bryce. Are you going to introduce me to your girlfriend?"

I replay in my head the nudge she gave her friend when they first saw me at the arena. She knew who I was. But how?

"Keera, this is Blake and Trish. Two of the new recruits."

10

*J*CAN TELL BY Bryce's tone he's annoyed, but she doesn't notice.

"Nice to meet you." I glance at Blake and Trish, nodding.

Blake? This explains it all. She's the one who texted Bryce and wanted to know if he was coming to the bar. She used Dante as an excuse.

What a fool I am! All this time, I thought Blake was a guy.

How am I going to deal with this when they're working together?

"Nice to meet you," they say simultaneously.

"I've heard so much about you," Blake adds.

"Oh yeah? I hope it's all good."

"Of course."

Her sarcasm leaves me wondering whether she's seen the crap on the internet about me.

Bryce leans into me further, motioning with his chin, and then talks next to my ear. "The other two new recruits have Barrie fire t-shirts on. Mike on the left, Cruz on the right."

I thought Blake would get the hint that Bryce was ignoring her, but she doesn't. She stays right beside him.

Bryce tenses again and I know she's touched him or rubbed against him because he acted the same way when Fiona touched him. It was like someone poured acid on his skin. "Would you like to dance, Angel?"

"I'd love to."

Bryce moves off his bar stool and comes around to take my hand, leading me to the dance floor.

As he spins me, I see Blake looking over at us.

Austin and Leena join us.

When a slow song comes on, we hold each other close, rubbing against one another, and staring lovingly into each other's eyes. At the end of the song, in a moment of quiet before the next song comes on, I can't hold back anymore—I have to ask. "Okay, spill it. What's going on?"

Bryce looks into my eyes and I can tell he knows I mean business. "I'll tell you as soon as we get in the truck. It's too hard to talk over the music. Okay?"

"Sure. But promise me you'll tell me everything."

"Promise."

Dante taps Bryce on the shoulder and Bryce turns to see who it is. "Can I have this dance?"

"Fuck you! She's mine."

"I know she's yours. I want to dance with you, asshole. All the guys are talking over there. You're never living this one down. Fred!"

"Dickhead, get the fuck out of here." Bryce pushes Dante away with a smile on his face as he holds me tight.

I think my face is splitting from smiling so hard.

Dante holds his hands in the air like he's surrendering. "I'm just saying none of us knew you could dance like that."

"Can you leave us alone?"

"Sure." Dante goes back to the table.

We dance for a couple more songs and then go back to our seats. Blake and Trish have moved on to another table and Dante and Jax have followed.

I relax. Somewhat.

Bryce orders us another round and we talk above the music about the game, doing a recap with lots of laughter.

After our second beer, I nudge Leena. "Time to hit the john, girl."

"I'm with you." Leena hops down from her bar stool and I do the same. When I turn, Bryce is standing behind me, wrapping his arm around my waist.

We all turn to look at Austin. "Yeah, I'm coming." Then we head through a sea of people towards the washrooms on the other side of the bar.

Bryce protectively holds my waist in front of him. "See the way they're looking at you?"

I look over my shoulder at Bryce. "No."

"I'll wait right here for you to come out." Bryce points to the wall outside the men's washroom.

"Okay. I won't be long."

The washroom is loud and crowded with a bunch of women converging at the mirror to talk and touch up their makeup. Leena and I find stalls and slip right in. When we come out, the women are still hovering and a few of them move out of the way so we can wash our hands.

When Leena and I exit the washroom, Bryce and Austin are leaning on the wall, looking hotter than hell. Bryce rests his hand on my waist and leads me through the crowd. Out of nowhere, a short, stalky guy steps in front of me, blocking my way. "Can I ask your friend something?" he asks, directing his question at Bryce.

I glance over my shoulder at Bryce. His forehead is furrowed and his mouth tight-lipped. He's clearly annoyed. "Girlfriend! What?" His voice is clipped and angry.

"Is this you?" He shows me a picture on his phone. It's me in my white bikini.

"Someone who looks like me," I say, bending the truth.

"Oh, okay, sorry to bother you."

He moves out of the way and we continue through the crowd to our table.

Once I settle onto the bar stool, I lean into Bryce and talk next to his ear. "Sorry about that."

"You've got to stop apologizing. It's not your fault men think you're beautiful. I guess I should take it as a compliment and quit being jealous about it."

I smile at him.

Bryce orders another round and when the waitress leaves, I look over and see Blake talking to the short, stalky guy as they repeatedly glance at us. After a few minutes, she moves to the end of the bar and strikes up a conversation with an older gentleman who is taking pictures with an expensive camera. She speaks with him for a couple of minutes and then goes back to stand with Dante.

"Keera?"

I turn to see the short, stalky guy and a couple of his friends standing beside me.

"Keera Johnson?"

Did Blake give him my name? Or did she confirm it for him? What kind of game is she playing?

"Keera, why wouldn't you own up to this picture? You're beautiful." He flashes the white bikini picture on his phone again. "And this one." He shows the picture of me in the red dress.

How did he get that? "I don't like to draw attention."

"You're every guy's fantasy. I've been following you online ever since I found this picture."

"I don't know what to say."

He holds my arm and turns to his friends. "I told you it was her!" He turns back to me. "I have a poster of you and I wish I had it with me now. I'd have you sign it for me."

I look around the table at everyone as my face blushes, not knowing what to say.

"I won't bother you anymore. Have a good night."

As they're walking away, I hear, "I told you it was her!" They playfully shove each other and go back to the bar.

Bryce slides off his bar stool and holds his hand out for me to take. "Come with me. Dante's riding the bull."

"Oh, okay."

We make our way through the crowd and stand along the fence as Dante climbs on the bull. Simultaneously, we take our phones out and capture some good shots. Bryce tenderly holds my lower back and we snuggle into one another as we watch Dante start out slow, riding the bull with ease and then getting cocky, lifting both arms in the air. The bull operator cranks the joystick up and down. Dante holds on, trying not to get thrown. He lasts about five seconds before the jostling bull tosses him face first into the padded mat below. "Oooooh," we all shout in unison.

Jax enters the bullpen and high-fives Dante. Climbing aboard, he closes his hand around the saddle horn, punching it down with his other hand, squeezing it tighter. He digs his heels into the side of the bull and raises one arm like they do at the rodeo. He looks very professional. I think he must have done this before. Jax gives the operator a nod to let him know he's ready and the bull starts out slow but quickly progresses. Jax stays on, riding it like a pro throughout the entire eight-second rough ride. When he conquers it, he pumps his fist in the air and jumps down smoothly.

We all cheer.

Dante waits for Jax at the exit from the bullpen where they push and shove each other, hurling insults like a couple of high school kids. I can't help but laugh at their playful antics.

"Would you like to dance, Angel?"

"I'd love to, Babe."

We head to the dance floor with Leena and Austin for a slow song.

Bryce pulls me hard against him, holding me close, rubbing his cock on that perfect spot. He smiles down at me, knowing I love it when he's a little aggressive. We nonchalantly rub against each other for two songs until Bryce grows to where it's unbearable from his jeans constricting him. "Come on, we're leaving."

I look at Leena and Austin. "We're leaving."

"All right, we're with you."

We head back to our table to grab our coats and wave goodbye to everyone.

Jax and Dante are nowhere in sight, so we head for the door. Out of nowhere, the short, stalky guy is standing in my way again. "Can I ask you one more question?" he says, grabbing my arm.

"What?" I say politely, trying to have patience.

"You're not with Colton Von Jobin anymore?"

"Never was. Bryce is my boyfriend."

He lets my arm go and I continue through the crowd of people. I hear the short, stalky guy yell out, "If you and Bryce break up, I'll be here. Right here. In this bar. Waiting."

I look back at Bryce, "Sorry."

Suddenly, Dante sideswipes Bryce with a hip check, but it only moves Bryce back a few steps.

Jax, Blake, and Trish stand close by, watching.

Bryce hands me his coat and shoves Dante into a bent-over headlock.

Dante turns his head to look up at me. "You guys can't leave."

"Yeah, we can. And we are," Bryce says in his deep commanding voice.

"Come on, I want you to ride the bull."

"Not this time buddy. I've got other things on my mind."

"Just one more beer?"

"Nope. Got a date with an angel. See you in the morning."

Bryce lets Dante go and we follow Leena and Austin out to the parking lot.

When we get to the vehicles, I hug Leena. "Thanks for coming."

"Had a great time," Leena says. "I'll come to Bryce's in the morning. See you then."

"Bye guys. Love you."

"Look at her. She's got a glow on from two beers," Austin points out as he hugs me. "Cheap date."

"She's always so lovable," Leena says. "You're too cute, Keera."

Bryce tugs me close to his side. "Yes, and she's all mine." He swings me around so we're face to face and I look into his eyes. As he kisses me, I faintly hear Austin in the background.

"Don't even bother talking now. They won't hear you."

"Bye, Keera." Leena's voice is like a faint whisper in the distant background.

By the time Bryce breaks the kiss, my knees are weak. "Let's get you home."

"Okay." I look around to see that Austin and Leena have disappeared. When we get into the truck, Bryce derails me from asking questions about Blake by fondling me.

As soon as we step in the door at his place, he shoves me hard against the wall, kissing me fiercely, stripping off my clothes. We make love with such intensity and passion, I'll never forget.

Two hours later when we're snuggling, I press the Blake issue now that the booze is wearing off. "Okay, what's going on? And you better tell me everything."

Bryce exhales and hesitates before speaking. "Blake started last Monday and she's clung to me like glue. At first, I thought she was thirsty for knowledge, being a new recruit. But she's made it clear, real quick what her intentions are. I told her I have a girlfriend who I love very much but it's not registering. She doesn't stop. She rubs against me, she tries to talk to me ... and you'd think she'd get the hint when I only give her one-word answers. I finally got pissed and told her to stop or it could be her job. But she's not listening. She's still hounding me. I caught her watching me take a shower. I don't know how long she was watching for but Dante saved my ass."

"Are you flirting with her or sending her mixed signals?"

"No. From day one, as soon as I noticed she had a thing for me, I've been a complete dick to her."

"So she started last Monday? That's when you started acting weird."

Bryce props himself up on his elbow to look at me. "The only reason I was acting weird was because you were leaving for Toronto. I had a bad feeling and every time I do, something happens." He lies back down and relaxes.

"So when did she see you in the shower?"

"This Monday. Why are you asking that?"

"Trying to figure something out."

Bryce is silent as he thinks for a minute.

"Last Wednesday, when you left after I yelled at you, I felt like such an asshole. I went to the game to get my mind off it but all I could think about was the look on your face and how devastated you were. We lost the game because I couldn't think straight. If I could change how I handled that situation, I would, because I never want to cause you pain like that again. After the game, I went to the bar to get drunk so I could forget."

Our fight affected him as much as it did me.

"As I'm over in the corner of the bar trying to drink away the look you gave me, Blake comes over. I can't remember exactly what she said. It was something like, 'Let me give you what you need. I'll help you forget about her.' She pissed me off. I shoved back my chair and left."

"Anything else happen?"

"No. I've told you everything." He looks into my eyes again. "You can tell I have an attitude with her, can't you?"

"Yes."

"You sure are calm about this."

"I wanted to see if you'd tell me everything. I pretty much

heard it all in the washroom at the arena when Blake and Trish came in. They didn't see me. I was in the stall between them and when I heard your name I started listening. I'm calm now but at the time, I was pissed. Especially when I didn't know who she was and how she would have seen you in the shower."

"I'm sorry you heard that and have to deal with this crap, Angel."

"I don't like her already. There is something about her that rubs me the wrong way."

"Angel, she does nothing for me. I love you."

"I want you to tell me every time she hits on you."

"I don't want to cause you any pain."

"I'm a big girl. I can handle it. Just like you said when you asked me to show you anything Colton sends. Oh, that reminds me, he sent another e-mail." I cringe, making a face.

"You know what? We'll deal with that, and everything else, together. Just another obstacle to hurdle over in this relationship. And if we always end up in this bed, making love, we're doing something right." Bryce rolls slightly, reassuring me with a kiss. "I've come to the conclusion there will always be someone trying to break us up, but we won't let that happen. We'll work at this relationship every day and be together forever."

This feels like a major milestone—like we're growing, getting stronger.

"I love you, Babe. You always know what to say to make me feel better."

"I love you. Now sleep. Close those beautiful eyes." Bryce kisses me and we fall asleep tangled together.

In the morning I wake an hour earlier than Bryce's alarm because of a bad dream. I can only remember bits and pieces but what I do remember is Blake weaselling her way into Bryce's heart over time and there isn't anything I can do about it because they work together. I'm helpless.

Lifting myself up, I glance over at Bryce. He's still asleep. I can see the outline of his face in the darkness from the reflection of light on his alarm clock and I wonder why I have bad dreams when women get obsessed and fall for him.

Look at him. He's gorgeous. That's why. You don't want to lose him.

Lying back down, I look up at the ceiling and my mind roams, pointing out how Bryce reacted from his first encounter with Blake last Monday and a timeline including all the incidents afterwards.

When he came home from work last Monday, he was a bit moody but I thought it was because I was leaving for the modelling job at Alaina in Toronto and he didn't want me going alone because of his bad feeling. Maybe it was a little of both. She was hitting on him from day one.

Tuesday morning, he kissed me passionately in the driveway, holding me, not wanting to let me go.

Wednesday, I returned from Toronto after the snow storm finished and when he wasn't home by five, I went to the fire station to confront him. That didn't turn out well. I was so upset, I went home to Huntsville with tears in my eyes and a broken heart. Meanwhile, Bryce was drowning his sorrows over a few beers with Blake in his ear, telling him how she can make him feel good and how she can help him forget about me.

I grumble and scowl.

Thursday and Friday, she wouldn't have been able to talk to him because he was a miserable prick, like Dante said.

Monday he was happy again after our great weekend of making up, but that was when Blake saw him in the shower.

I get pissed about that every time I think about it. When he came home, I was sitting on the stairs waiting for him, naked, with his tie around my neck and a beer in my hand. We made love twice that night. That was also the night he turned away from me as if he was hiding something when I had just finished saying he should see the e-mails Colton sent so he would know I was honest in this relationship.

He said he was trying to spare me the pain.

With his vague answers?

Then it hits me like a sledgehammer. *He was friskier than usual. Did he get turned on from Blake watching him in the shower?*

Why didn't he tell me two women recruits were hired and one of them is obsessed with him?

He wanted to spare me the pain like I've done numerous times with Colton's encounters.

Tuesday, I picked Bryce up from work but when I asked him about Dante and Jax, he grumbled that they were busy. They were busy. Sniffing around the new female recruits. My mind does a replay of the person looking out the window at us when we were leaving the fire station in Bryce's truck. It was a woman. I bet it was Blake.

He came home to take a shower that night and afterwards we had a few intimate moments, like when he said, "I'll never stop loving you like this. You're my everything." We stared lovingly into one another's eyes, petting and caressing. He wanted me to promise him that I'd never let anyone or anything get between us. I told him the only way I'd give up on us would be if he cheated on me.

I hope he heard me.

Then, while he was in the shower, he got a text. At the time, I didn't know who Blake was, but it's clear now why Bryce was pissed off at Dante for giving his number to her.

Dante must have seen how she's been flirting with Bryce. Why would Dante give her Bryce's number? Is she so persuasive that he caves in? Or will Dante give her anything to get into her pants?

After analyzing the timeline in my head of Bryce's strange moods, the sirens on his alarm blare and I reach to shut it off.

"Mmm, I like waking up to you on top of me."

I look down and smile. "You do, eh? How about this?" I straddle his hips and place his cock between my pussy lips. I lean forward, entwining my fingers with his, capturing his hands on either side of his head. My hair blankets our faces and I grind along his fully erect morning hard on. "I like this too. Wish you had more time."

"We can finish this after we get home from dinner at Mom and Dad's."

"It's a date!"

Bryce tackles me, pinning me to the bed. "A date, I intend to keep."

"You'll have to show me your Ninja skills tonight."

"Count on it." He kisses me and then gets out of bed in one seamless move to take a shower. He glances over his shoulder at me just before that very fine, sexy ass disappears around the corner.

I shake my head and smile. "That is the sexiest ass I've ever seen."

I throw on my silk pyjamas and head to the kitchen to make us a quick breakfast.

When Bryce saunters down the hall, he is dressed in his uniform. My eyes scan his body.

He takes a few sips of his coffee, his eyes glued to my nipples. They're cold and erect, and clearly visible through the clingy silk. He runs his hands over both. "Look how hard they are. They're beautiful!"

Devouring his breakfast, he asks, "Angel, will you do me a favour and hit the button for the garage door and start my truck? I've got to grab my other coat."

Finding the leather jacket he wore last night draped across the chair, I reach in the pocket for his keys and find a piece of paper neatly folded. The keys are in his other pocket so I fish them out and hit the button.

As I'm reading the paper, Bryce comes down the hall, slipping on his coat.

"What's that Angel?"

"Seems to be a love letter from Blake."

11

"WHAT? LET ME see that." Bryce reads the letter. *I've seen everything on the internet about Keera and Colton. She doesn't deserve you. It's time for you to move on with your life. She's making you miserable. I've seen you happy and that's the way you should be. Give me a chance. I'll give you everything you need. Just think about it. Blake.*

"Un-fucking-believable! She's the one making me miserable. She must have stuck that in my pocket last night." Bryce holds my face in his hands. "I'm sorry you had to see that." He hugs me.

"I can handle it, Babe. I want you to tell me everything. Even if it's the smallest thing, I want to know."

"I'm taking care of this shit right now." Bryce folds the letter and shoves it in the pocket of his coat. "I don't need you worrying over this."

"Don't get her fired."

"I won't. But I'll be letting the Chief know what's been going on so he can talk to her because, obviously, she's not listening to me. Christ, I'm a complete dick to her. I don't understand it."

"I do. You are one of those men who instantly catch women's eyes. And now that she sees how you are with me, she wants what I have."

"Never happen. I love you."

"I love you." I pull him down for a searing kiss. "You'd better get going. You'll be late."

"I'll come home and take a shower and then we'll head to Ma and Dad's."

"See you then. Go." I slap him on the ass.

He spins like he's leaving and then grabs me, bending me backwards and planting another hot, luscious kiss on my lips. When he pulls me up, I'm breathless.

"Wow, Babe!"

"Think of that all day."

"You can't leave me like this. I'm weak in the knees."

"Good. Just how I want you. Bye. I love you, Angel." He opens the door and hesitates, waiting for my response.

"Bye, Babe. God, do I love you."

He gives me that gorgeous smile and disappears out the door.

I sit down with my second tea and fire up my computer. Another e-mail from Colton and one from Christina at Avionté Cosmetics are waiting in my inbox.

Christina says she found a four-thousand-square-foot second-floor studio. They're remodelling it and setting up the props—should be done by Monday. She gives me the address and wants me there for eight, Monday morning.

I e-mail her back to let her know I'll be there.

As I'm clicking on the e-mail for Colton, Leena bursts through the door. "Hey, girlfriend! How are you feeling this morning?"

"Good. Want a tea?"

"Sure."

"I've got a new job. I start on Monday."

"Doing what?"

"Modelling for a Canadian cosmetics company called Avionté."

"Get out!"

"Yeah. Do you believe it? They rented a studio nearby so I don't have to travel to Toronto. I'll be working from eight to four every day and they'll pay me seventy-five thousand dollars for two weeks of work."

"Jesus, I'm in the wrong business."

"Yeah, but you're the best baker they have. Who would make the delicious desserts if not for you?"

"I'll get fat if I stay there."

"See if you can get a leave of absence for the two weeks I'm in the studio and I'll pay your salary to be my assistant."

"Get out! You'd do that?"

"Yeah."

"That would be frickin' awesome. I'd get to spend time with you and Austin."

"Do it. Call them."

"Have to wait until Manny gets in there at nine. But I'm so excited." Leena claps her hands together.

"So guess what I found in Bryce's pocket this morning?"

"What?"

"A love letter from Blake."

"Who the hell is Blake?"

"Oh yeah. I guess you would've missed it with all the loud music." I couldn't tell her in the washroom because with the girls screaming, it was too loud. "Blake was the one I gave you the eyes to. She's the new recruit I overheard in the washroom when she was talking about Bryce."

"What? Oh, crap! She's pretty."

"Thanks. You're making me feel better."

"Sorry. You know I have no filter."

"That's okay. I can see it for myself. So anyway, Bryce was acting weird before I left for Toronto, but I thought it was because I was leaving him. I think it was a little of both. Blake was hitting on him from the first day she met him. How am I going to deal with this when they work together?"

"You'll have to trust him."

"Yeah." I'm lost in my own thoughts for a second. "Anyway, Wednesday, when she tried to hit on him at the bar, he got pissed off and left."

"That was the night you went back home."

"Yeah. Dante said he was a miserable prick the rest of the week, so she probably couldn't get anywhere near him. Monday he was happy again after our great weekend together and that's when she saw him in the shower. I want to ring her neck every time I think about it. I get so pissed off."

"Calm down there. We don't want you getting all crazy on us now."

"How would you feel if a beautiful woman cop purposely strolled into the men's washroom to watch Austin take a shower?"

"Okay. I get your point. I'd be flipping."

"Yeah, you would. More than I am." I lean on the counter and sip my tea. "So Tuesday, I could swear I saw her looking out the window at us when I picked Bryce up at the station. Wednesday at the bar, she was all touchy-feely and I'd put money on it that she gave my name to that short, stalky guy because I saw them talking as they were looking over at us. I don't know what kind of game she's playing but I don't like her. And then this morning, I find the love letter in Bryce's pocket. Bryce was pissed. He said he'll talk to the Chief. I told him not to get her fired."

"What did it say?"

"That she saw everything on the internet with me and Colton and I don't deserve Bryce. She said it's time for him to move on with his life. She's seen him happy and I'm making him miserable. She wants him to give her a chance and she'll give him everything he needs."

"That bitch! And you don't want to get her fired? What's wrong with you?"

"It would be nice if she went away. Or maybe, since Dante's been sniffing around her, she should go out with him and forget about Bryce."

"Yeah, like that will happen."

"Bryce is being a complete dick to her—and she still wants him."

"I noticed when they came to our table that Bryce gave them the cold shoulder. And then when she touched him, it was like his skin was crawling. Yup, he's acting like a complete dick."

"Oh, I forgot to tell you, she texted Bryce Tuesday night. She said Dante wanted to know if Bryce was going to The Bull, but Dante already knew we were going. He was the one who organized it."

"She used Dante as an excuse to talk to Bryce?"

"Yeah." I pour the hot water into the cup. "Bryce was pissed that Dante gave out his number to her. At the time I couldn't understand why, but then it became clear at the bar when he introduced her to me. All this time, I thought Blake was a guy."

"So since last Monday you've been wondering why Bryce has been a moody fucker."

"Yeah, he's been very vague with his answers. He said he was trying to spare me the pain but I made him tell me everything. And I'll be bugging him tonight to find out what happened today."

"You go, girl. So anything else happen?"

"No. I think I covered it all."

"What do you want to do today?"

"I was thinking you could make a dessert and I'll make my mom's famous spaghetti sauce with penne noodles for dinner at Ma and Dad's tonight."

"Yum." Leena awakens my laptop. "I want to check out a new recipe." Leena clicks away and reads. "Uh, Keera, did you see this e-mail from Colton?"

"No, I was about to look at it when you came in. Why?"

I come around the counter to look at the laptop. "Oh Jesus! Bryce will lose his mind."

"Was that picture taken in the hotel room?"

"Yeah, must have been when I fell asleep on his lap."

"Look at the smirk on his face. So Colton sent this one first?" She points to the picture of Colton holding me in Niagara Falls with him sucking on my finger. "And now this one?"

"Yeah."

"Has Bryce seen them?"

"No, not yet."

"What if he took other pictures of you while you were sleeping?"

"I never thought of that."

"Seems to me like he's playing dirty to break you guys up. He knows Bryce will see them."

"I think he's sending them to irritate me so I'll e-mail him back."

"No. By the looks of this one, he's trying any tactic. He wrote you a new song?"

"He did?"

"That's what it says here." Leena points to the message below the picture.

I'm missing you. Wish I could hold you again like this. I think about you constantly, replaying every moment. You have to hear my new song. I wrote it for you.

Love, Colton.

"Did you see the pictures of you and Bryce that someone posted from the bar last night?" Leena clicks to the internet. "And what it says?"

"No. What does it say?"

"'*Colton Von Jobin's model girlfriend moves on with someone new.*' There's a nice picture of you and Bryce dancing, looking like you're in love."

"Let me see that." I walk to the laptop to check it out. "That is a good picture of us. You know what? I saw a photographer speaking with Blake last night. I wonder if he took the picture. Holy crap!"

"What?"

"I bet Blake told the photographer my name and clued him in to the stuff on the internet about me."

"No doubt. She's up to something. But what?"

"I don't know."

"Jeez, look how many pictures he took of you guys. This is a good one of you kissing."

"Yeah, that's a good one."

"Clearly, anyone can see you're in love."

"I'll have to get an eight-by-ten of that one."

Leena searches for Colton's new song on YouTube and, as she scrolls down, she finds the lyrics of "You Belong in My Arms." Those were the exact words Bryce used when he held me in his arms after our fight.

Leena and I listen to the words and I tense.

In the song, Colton mentions holding me all night and how it was like running a knife through his heart, sending me back into the arms of another. He says he's fighting to get me back where I belong—back in his arms.

Leena listens to the rest of the song while I make another tea. "Keera he swears he'll get you back. Jesus, he won't give up. How does it feel having two hot men fighting over you?"

"You know I love Bryce. I have no contact with Colton. He'll eventually give up and find someone new."

"Is that what you're predicting?"

"That's what I'm hoping."

"You know, I think you should have a few fuck buddies to compare Bryce with before you tie the knot. Ma always told me, 'you have to try on the shoes before you buy them.' And when you think about it, Colton is the Louis Vuitton of all shoes. Don't you think?"

I giggle. "Yeah, I know. But I love Bryce."

On our way to the Hamilton's, I ask Bryce how it went with the Chief. "After I calmed down, I thought I would take care of it myself."

"Oh," I say softly, waiting for him to continue. He tries to reassure me with a squeeze to my knee. I ask another question. "Did she hit on you?"

"We were busy today."

"Oh." I look out the window.

I can feel Bryce looking at me, but I ignore it and stare out the window in silence.

"Angel. Look at me."

I turn slowly and wait for him to say something.

"I don't want you worrying. I'm taking care of this."

So, she did hit on him! That bitch!

His vague answers are starting to piss me off. I turn away in silence again and he knows I'm mad. "Christ! Do you know how hard this is to tell you? I hate seeing the hurt in your eyes."

"It hurts me more not knowing what happened, but also, when you hide something from me."

"Okay. I'm sorry. She asked me if I got the letter. I told her it has to stop. I told her I don't want anything to do with her. She came close to me and touched my arm. I backed away. She said, 'Bryce, please, listen to me.' I turned and said, 'Fine, I'll take care of this myself.' I walked away and she hasn't spoken to me since."

"See? Now was that hard?"

"Yes, it was. I hate hurting you."

"It only hurts when you don't tell me the truth."

Bryce tugs me close and kisses my hair as we pull into the driveway of his mom and dad's house. "I want you to know, I love you and I'm taking care of this."

"Okay."

Bryce kisses his mom when we enter the kitchen. "Keera made her mom's famous spaghetti sauce and noodles. It's delicious. I had a bite before we came here."

I place the crock pot on the counter and plug it in. "You had a bowl." I turn and smile at him.

"Correction. A bowl."

Deana laughs.

"Where's Dad?" Bryce asks.

"In the garage. He said he wouldn't be out there too long."

Bryce gently touches my lower back. "Be back in a few minutes. I have to talk to him."

"I'll help Ma."

Bryce smiles over his shoulder as he disappears out the back door.

"Leena made her famous turtle cheesecake. It's to die for," I say, helping Deana prepare the chicken and salad. "And in case you don't like cheesecake, she also made an apple pie."

"You girls have been busy."

"We hung out today. Got a few things done. I have a new modelling job. It's for a Canadian cosmetics company. I start Monday."

"Oh. How does Bryce feel about that?"

Crap! Deana must know everything that happened at my last modelling job in Toronto.

"He wasn't too happy about it until I told him it's right here in Barrie and I hired Leena as my assistant. I'll be working from eight to four. I'll be home with Bryce, and Leena will be home with Austin."

"That's good. It's probably a load off Bryce's mind knowing you don't have to travel to Toronto in the snow."

"Umm ... Did you see everything that's been on the internet about me?"

"Ciara showed me."

"Don't believe it, please! Colton showed up at the photo shoot during the snow storm..."

Deana hugs me. "Don't worry dear. Bryce explained everything."

"I need you to know I love Bryce and I would never cheat on him."

"I know. I see how much you love Bryce."

"I do. Very much."

"You can't help that you're beautiful and men will fall for you, be infatuated with you. Bryce will have to learn to deal with it and trust you."

I give Deana a hug. "Thanks. I was worried about what you thought."

"Do not worry. Life is a long road with lots of ups and downs, but you and Bryce have what it takes to stay together. I can see it."

"Thank you."

When Leena and Austin stroll in, they greet us with a hug. Bryce and Garrett emerge from the garage.

Ciara hears the laughter and joins us.

I take the cheesecake from Leena and stick it in the fridge. Austin and Leena grab a drink and settle in around the kitchen table.

Austin tells us briefly about a case he's working on and then drills Bryce about an accident his officers are investigating, hoping he can get more details. Bryce tells him what he saw and then Austin fills in some of the details Bryce didn't know. Garrett listens intently and adds a couple attributing factors. These conversations show how strong their family bond is. I love to watch how excited they get when they express their thoughts.

After dinner, when Bryce makes a trip to the washroom, Ciara scoots over on the couch to whisper in my ear. "You lucky little bitch. You've got Colton Von Jobin falling for you."

I don't know what to say but I can feel myself blushing.

Ciara grabs my arm. "I want you to fill me in on all the details when I can steal you away from Bryce."

I glance up, feeling Bryce before I see him. He's giving Ciara that look: *Let it go.*

She does and I'm saved from trying to explain.

Dinner at the Hamilton's is something we all look forward to and enjoy. Playful insults fly freely around the room and laughter fills the air.

The boys do a recap of the game for Mom and Dad, since they missed it, and Austin only comments on our fight three times making me blush every time. How he loves to embarrass me.

Bryce stays beside me throughout the evening, touching and caressing, and Ciara doesn't get her wish to steal me away from Bryce. He makes sure of it.

Back at Bryce's house, he places the crock pot on the counter, comes over to me, and holds my face in his hands. "I need you to know how much I love you."

"I know. I can see it in your eyes and feel it in your touch."

"Good. Now let me show you."

He tugs me to the bedroom, where he shows me how much he loves me by the tenderness in his touch and the way he worships every inch of my body. I do the same, showing him how much he means to me.

Afterwards, we lie together with my back to Bryce's chest, his strong arms holding me tight, and we fall asleep.

Bryce has two days off, so we head to my house in Huntsville.

The first thing I do when we get back is check the mailbox for the Alaina gala invitation.

"It's here!" I hold it up and shake it, squealing, I'm so excited. Bryce smiles at me.

I hold it to my chest waiting to open it once we're settled in the house.

Bryce places our bags in the kitchen and then walks to the fireplace. "I'll get the fire started."

"Thanks, Babe." I place the invitation on the table and then turn the water on and the heat up.

I glance over at the invitation but then I look at the bags in the kitchen. *Put them away first, Keera.* I carry them into the bedroom and then rush back.

I feel like a small child with a gift in front of me. I want to rip it open but I also want to be careful not to damage it. I want to keep it in the hope chest Gramps made for me. My hope chest is like a time capsule, full of mementoes that remind me of everything that's happened in my life. I cherish everything in it.

I walk to the living room, where Bryce is placing the last log on the fire. He turns to see me reading it.

"The gala is Saturday, December 6th. Dinner is at six, dancing to follow at the Royal ballroom, overlooking Lake Ontario. I have to RSVP and set up a time for the limo to pick us up."

Bryce closes the gap and holds his hand out. "Let me see that."

I hand him the invitation.

He looks it over and frowns. "I don't like this."

"What do you mean?" I ask, but I'm thinking, *Don't tell me you're going to give me grief over this?*

"Relax, I'm saying I don't like the idea of Colton getting my address from the limo company. He probably has the address of your house already from Chaz, his buddy, so in case he's behind this—"

I cut him off. "Babe, there's no way Colton could arrange a gala of this scale. From what I hear, it's supposed to be out of this world. It would be too costly for him." *Although, he does have a lot of money.*

"We'll take my truck to the limo company and go from there."

"Fine."

Bryce drops the invitation on the table and scoops me up in his arms. "Don't be mad at me." He bends his knees and searches my eyes. "I'm trying to protect us. I don't want the shark showing up at our door one day."

Our door. Isn't he sweet? He's looking out for us.

"I'm not mad at you. I see you're trying to protect our relationship and I love you for it."

We kiss and hug, and when we separate, Bryce takes my hand. "Okay, one thing solved. Now, show me the letter Colton sent."

12

*O*H CRAP, HERE *we go!*

This is why Bryce was intent on coming to my house. He needs to take care of unresolved business.

I have no idea what's in the letter.

Bryce pulls me by the hand to my walk-in closet, clearly on a mission. He must have been thinking about this from the moment he saw the e-mail.

I rummage through my clothes, trying to remember where I put it. When I find it, I hand it to him.

I'm thinking he'll rip it in two and throw it away. Instead, he tugs me over to the bed and opens it. As soon as he starts to read, he tenses and so do I.

Keera, my beautiful angel eyes. From the moment I saw you, my heart melted. But then I realized you were taken. I fought, trying to dismiss my feelings for you. The feelings grew as I got to know you. I tried to resist, knowing it was a dead end, but you're like a magnet, pulling me toward you. Every look, every smile, every touch made those feelings grow stronger. I couldn't concentrate on the reason I went to Aruba in the first place, and that's not like me. I'm focused, down to business, in control of everything in my life. But I can't get you out of my head. I envision every moment I had with you. I remember what you were wearing at the time. I remember those beautiful angel eyes, the way they squint when you giggle. I remember the sound you make when you laugh, how it would melt me in an instant to the point where I would start aching with an urgent need to hold you. I picture your hair blowing in the breeze. That body! I smile every time I see the video of you running on the beach. I lie awake for hours thinking of you. When I finally fall asleep, I dream of you. When I wake, I want to go back to sleep to finish my dream of us making love. But then my heart feels like it will explode from the pain of not seeing you in person. Like I told you before, I need to touch you. I need to hold you. You belong in my arms. I replay our kiss and it's like I can taste you all over again. Can you see how bad I've got it? I'm dying a slow death without you. Keera, you know a love like this will never go away. I realize it now. I'll love you forever. Please, tell me that if you and Bryce break up, you'll give me a chance. I'm hanging on to the thought that maybe someday I'll be holding you in my arms, having you by my side to experience this beautiful life together. I know you've heard it before but please listen to me. I could give you everything you want and need. Give me a chance, beautiful!

I love you!

Colton.

As he puts the letter down, Bryce turns to me. "When did he tell you he needs to touch and hold you?"

I hesitate for a second and then realize by the intense look on his face, I'd better answer fast. "In Aruba and in Niagara Falls. Babe, I'm sorry. I hate seeing you like this. What he says doesn't mean a thing. Only what you say to me matters."

"Angel, you have to stop apologizing. It's not your fault."

"I want you to know the letter means nothing and when he did say those things to me, it felt awkward and it went in one ear and out the other."

"When did he tell you he could give you anything you want and need?"

"In Aruba."

"When, in Aruba?"

"I'm not sure. Maybe when we were dancing. I hardly remember. It means nothing. It's already erased from my memory."

"Good." Bryce holds the letter out. "Do you want this?"

I look down at it. "No."

Bryce rips it in two. "Now, come with me." He takes my hand, picks up my laptop from the dresser, and tugs me into the living room. He tosses the letter in the fireplace before we continue to the kitchen.

Now that it's warm in the house, we take our coats off and I hang them at the back door.

Bryce sits at the table with the computer in front of him and I sit on his lap.

"What are you researching?" I ask.

"The e-mails from Colton. I haven't had time to check them."

"Oh," I say softly and cringe.

"What?"

"Are you sure you want to see them? Leena saw them and she thinks he's using any tactic to break us up. Please, keep that in mind."

Bryce looks at the first e-mail: the picture of Colton holding me in Niagara Falls, which he's seen before. He doesn't linger too long before moving to the next. "Un-fucking-believable! That mother fucker took that picture for one reason. Look at the smug look on that prick's face." Bryce nods his chin toward the screen of the laptop. "That right there." Bryce points to the expression on Colton's face. "That's a big, 'Fuck you! I've got her. I've got her in my arms.'"

I look at the picture, studying it and then turn to Bryce. "I'm beginning to think you're right."

"Fucking right, I'm right!"

"Babe we can't get worked up about this. Maybe we should ignore him."

"No! I want to see anything else that prick sends."

"Why? Why would you put yourself through that?"

"This way I can determine what his next move is."

"Oh, okay," I say, but I'm unconvinced.

"Don't delete them, Angel!" Bryce closes the laptop and looks directly in my eyes, waiting for an answer.

"I won't." *Sheesh!*

To change his deteriorating mood, I shuffle around on his lap, straddling his legs, taking him by surprise. My left hand weaves through his hair at the back of his neck while the right hand caresses his cheek. "Babe, don't get mad. He's trying to push your buttons. Ignore it because, you know what? You've got me and he doesn't."

"You are one-hundred-percent right." Bryce stands up and carries me to the counter, where he places my butt on it and settles between my legs. "Our time together is precious and no one's ruining it." He kisses me slowly, igniting every cell in my body before pulling away. "Let's get some groceries."

What? Oh sure, turn me on and then shut me down. I let out a sigh.

"And then we're finding a new mattress for that bed. And don't think you're paying for it. I am!"

Okay, Mr. Control Freak. "Fine!"

"You're learning."

"I'm not arguing because of the mood you're in." *And because I need to spring something on you.*

"Good. I'm on a mission to get this crap done so we can spend the rest of the weekend in each other's arms."

"All right, then. Let's go." I hop down from the counter. "Since we're going to be out, we should get you measured for a tux."

"Do we have to do that right now?"

"Will you have time this week?"

"Probably not. This week is hectic."

"Okay, then." We walk to the back door, pulling on our coats and boots.

Bryce opens his hand to me. "Phone number."

His comment throws me for a bit and then I realize what he's asking for. "Colton's phone number?"

"Yes."

"Oh." I turn and reach for the coat I was wearing at the time. "I think it's in this pocket." I fish it out and hand it to Bryce.

He looks at it, rips in two, and throws it in the garbage.

"Look at us taking care of business." I smile at him.

He must have been thinking about this since he saw the first set of e-mails from Colton.

I take his hand and lead him out the door, hopefully turning him to jelly. "Since you don't have time this week, we have to get your measurements done right now."

Bryce grumbles but he doesn't say no.

Biting my lip, I hold in a smile.

At the furniture store, I'm undecided between three mattresses, so I lie on one, then another, then switch to the third.

Bryce stands back watching me with an amused smirk on his face.

I rub it with my hand. "Babe, I think this is the one. Come here and try it."

Bryce looks down the aisle one way and then the next. A mischievous smile crosses his face and then—he jumps on me, grinding his cock into me like he's fucking me.

I giggle. "Someone will see us."

"Think I care? I don't care who sees how much I love you." He frowns. "I thought you like doing it in different places?"

"I do but everyone can see us here."

"I want to hear that giggle again." Bryce tickles me and I squirm, trying to grab his hands. "I love that sound." He stops, rolls off me onto his back, and rubs the mattress with his hand. "This one is good."

"Yeah, I think it's perfect." I look down the aisle both ways. Seeing no one is coming, I roll half onto Bryce and kiss him. All noise fades except for Bryce's pleasurable moan in my mouth. We kiss for—well, I don't know how long—until we hear someone clear their throat at the end of the bed.

I pull away and lift my knee over Bryce's hard on to conceal it.

We turn to see a salesman and a boy standing there.

"I told you there was someone making out on the bed."

"Do you like this mattress?" The salesman ignores the boy's comment as he stares back at us.

"We'll take it," Bryce says.

The boy looks back at the salesman. "My mom and dad told me to get off. Aren't you going to kick them off?"

"No. They're buying it. Shouldn't you be looking for your parents?"

The boy takes off down the aisle.

"I'll meet you up front and we can take care of the paper-work," the salesman says.

"Great. We'll meet you up there," Bryce says, trying to get rid of him.

It works. The salesman disappears.

Bryce rolls over to give me a long, toe-curling kiss.

When he pulls away, I smile up at him. "That was a little embarrassing," I say with a smile on my face.

"Why? We're in love and people should leave us alone."

"You're right. Absolutely right."

"Now, where were we?"

I pull back to look in his eyes. "Oh no! You've got that look on your face."

"You're getting to know me well," Bryce says in a deep resonate voice.

"We'd better get off this mattress before they call the cops."

"Yes. Camera right above us."

We both get up at the same time and meet at the end of the bed. Bryce steps in close, wrapping his arm around my waist. He leans down to talk against my ear. "Another one of my fantasies."

I give him a grin, tipping my head to one side, showing my right dimple, trying for a seductive look. "We'll have to work on that, but somewhere else. This place is too busy."

When we enter the formal wear store, a sharply dressed man rushes over. "Good afternoon, or is it still morning? It doesn't matter. I'm François. And you are?" he asks in a high-pitched French accent as he takes Bryce's hand and shakes it fast.

"Bryce," he says deeply.

"Would you look at the physique on this fine specimen?" François says as he circles Bryce, touching his shoulders as if he's measuring and then standing back, two fingers over his lips, eyeing him up and down.

Bryce frowns and I smile. François turns to look at me.

"I'm so sorry, I was too busy ogling your boyfriend. And you are?"

"I'm Keera." I shake his hand and I can't wipe the smile off my face.

"Pleased to meet you." He turns his attention back to Bryce. "And what can I do for you today?"

"A tux." Bryce's voice deepens even further.

My cheeks hurt. I can't stop smiling.

"Come with me and I'll have you try on…" François runs his fingers over the selection of men's formal wear.

"This one!" He pulls it off the rack and hands it to Bryce. "Right in here." He gestures for Bryce to enter the dressing room.

Bryce slips inside to change and François hooks his arm in mine, guiding me over to the plush, Victorian-style couch. "Come with me, beautiful, and this way you can watch." He gestures for me to sit.

When Bryce emerges from the dressing room, François, his over-enthusiastic tailor, pulls him over to the platform in front of a triple mirror. François is a treat to watch. He is talkative, tiny, and very feminine, clapping his hands together and performing hilarious hand gestures. I watch him as he falls all over Bryce, gushing at how good-looking he is, touching his muscles, and making sly remarks.

Bryce glares at me as if to say, *this is all your fault!* And I smile back affectionately, loving how uncomfortable he feels.

I pull out my phone and take a picture.

Bryce, unimpressed, frowns at me.

"This way, Bryce." François turns both of them my way and then he cuddles next to Bryce so I can take a picture. "Oh, this will be a good one! You'll have to send me a pic darling!" His hand gesture flutters my way.

Bryce looks down at him and frowns again.

Once the picture is taken, François gets back to work, down on his knees, taking a few measurements for the length of Bryce's pants. He circles him, again and again, taking measurements and writing them down.

Suddenly, he drops to his knees, tosses his notebook, and pulls at the material covering Bryce's overly large package.

Bryce steps back, holding his hand in front, guarding his jewels. "Are we finished here?" Bryce says annoyed.

"But I have to make sure you have enough room. You are very well endowed." His French accent is more prominent now. Bryce glares at me through the reflection in the mirror and I'm almost rolling on the couch with laughter.

"We're done!" Bryce says as he steps down from the platform.

I rush over to talk to François, distracting him. "François do you have a store in Barrie?" Bryce stalks to the dressing room.

"Oh yes, Huntsville, Gravenhurst, Barrie, and of course, quite a few locations in Toronto."

"Can you send Bryce's measurements to your Barrie store?"

"Oh yes, absolutely."

"Great. I'll pick the tux up on my way home from work Thursday."

As soon as we exit the store, Bryce tugs me into his side. "You were enjoying that way too much."

"I like François. He's quite the character."

"You like torturing me."

"I have to admit, that made my day."

Bryce smiles down at me. "Just wait. Paybacks are a bitch."

"Oh, come on Babe, he was funny."

Bryce grumbles.

"Let me take you out for lunch since I tortured you."

"We can go for lunch, but I'm paying," he says.

"Stubborn."

The restaurant we pick is tiny and cozy but very busy and it takes ten minutes before we are seated. We get comfortable sitting across from each other at a window table in the corner. Looking around, I notice the craftsmanship of the woodwork before I pay attention to the pictures of Elvis, James Dean, and Marilyn Monroe on the walls. It is always a habit to compare Gramps' craftsmanship with others. In my eyes, Gramps wins the competition every time because he always adds some intricate signature detail.

When the food finally comes, it's delicious—well worth the wait. Hand-breaded chicken parmesan, fresh spaghetti, and Italian meat sauce with warm cheese sticks, dipped in an amazing herb, garlic, and parmesan dressing. We talk and laugh about the boy at the end of the bed and François. Then we drive back to my house and cuddle on the couch, watching a movie. "This was a perfect day," I say. "Just you and me. No one bothering us."

"Yes, I enjoyed it. I appreciate every moment with you, Angel."

"You say the sweetest things to me."

Bryce moves like he wants to get up and I move with him, rising from the couch. He tugs me into his hard body. "Come, let me show you how sweet I can be."

In the morning, when we're making breakfast, there's an insistent bang on the door. As we go answer it, Bryce holds me protectively behind him.

Bryce opens the door and grumbles under his breath.

"Bryce," Jake says, ignoring the look on Bryce's face and searching around him for me. "Keera. There you are. Can I speak to you? Alone?"

"Whatever you've got to say, you can say it in front of me," Bryce says.

"Can I come in at least?"

Bryce opens the door wider, giving Jake the opportunity to move into the living room.

I lead the way into the kitchen. "It's early. Would you like a coffee?" I pull out a chair for him but he doesn't sit down. Anxiety and impatience drip off him in waves.

"Yeah, real early," Bryce says. "What's so fucking important today, Jake?"

"Cream and sugar?" I ask.

"Yes, please."

I pour the coffee and turn to hand it to Jake.

He takes a sip and then places it on the table before turning to me and taking hold of my arms. "Keera, I'm sorry for what I did when we were teenagers in Algonquin. I was young and stupid and my hormones got the best of me. I know that's no excuse, but believe me when I say, that day is the one thing I've always regretted in life."

Bryce slides his arm between the two of us. "Back it up there, buddy. You're too close."

"I need to apologize. Can I do that? Please."

"Yeah, you can do that. Without touching her."

Jake backs up slightly. "Please forgive me, Keera. I never wanted to hurt you. We were best friends for Christ's sake."

I can see the pain in his eyes and how he regrets doing that to me, but he has to know how it affected me. "Jake, I'm relaxing a bit more every time I see you. But what you did screwed me up for a long time."

"I know." He pulls me in for a hug. "I'm so sorry. If I could change what happened that day, I would." Bryce clears his throat as if to tell Jake to back up again, but Jake doesn't get the hint. "I want us to be friends again. I want you to feel comfortable around me."

"Okay, back it up! Can't you see you're making her feel uncomfortable now?"

Jake steps back, running his hands down my arms until he reaches my fingertips. Then he goes to sit. "Sorry, this has been bothering me for a long time and I needed to apologize." Jake takes another sip of his coffee and then turns to look at me. "I never wanted to hurt you. I'm sorry."

"It'll take time, Jake."

"I know." Barely missing a beat, he asks, "So what's on the agenda for you two today?"

"Breakfast first." Bryce turns to look at the pans on the

stove. "Then we're meeting Austin and Leena. We're taking the girls hunting."

This is news to me. Is this an excuse so Jake will leave?

"Oh. Well. My place is finished. I thought maybe one of these weekends you could stop by to check it out?"

"Next weekend is kind of busy but maybe another ti—"

"No," Bryce says, shaking his head. "Uh un."

"Great," Jake says, ignoring Bryce. "I'll stop by in a couple of weeks and then maybe you can come over. It looks good. My renovators did a great job. Quality work."

Bryce takes the eggs out of the fridge and gives Jake a raised eyebrow, hinting it's time to leave.

"I'll let you get back to your breakfast." Jake takes hold of my hands, bending his knees to look me in the eye. "I'm sorry again."

Bryce leads the way to the door. I follow.

Jake hesitates as he looks at me again. "I'm hoping someday we can be like we were."

"Bye, Jake."

"Bye, Keera." Jake squeezes my hand and then nods Bryce's way. "Bryce."

Bryce closes the door as soon as Jake is out of the door frame. Then Bryce turns and caresses down my back, hooking his thumb in my yoga pants, grumbling something I can't make out.

I look up at him. "What was that?" I ask, trying to figure out what he's saying.

"Jake the snake thinks he can slither right back into your life."

"Yeah, I don't know what he's thinking. It'll never be the same." I run my hand down Bryce's back as we walk into the kitchen. "He does seem sorry though."

"Don't trust him, Angel. He's got one thing on his mind. And that's to get you beneath him again."

13

"I DON'T KNOW, BABE, we were good friends. We grew up together."

"You're not paying attention to the way he's looking at you. I am. He's not looking for a friendship."

I'm quiet, letting Bryce's words sink in.

"I don't want you alone with him, ever. And if you go to see his house, I'm going with you."

"Fine."

After making our breakfast of scrambled eggs and toast, I place the plates on the table and we sit down to eat.

"I mean it, Angel. Don't trust him."

"All right." I turn to look at Bryce. "When were you going to let me in on the secret that we're going hunting? Or were you trying to get rid of Jake?"

"Austin mentioned it. I'll text him to see if we're still going."

Austin has to wrap up a big case he's working on at the police department but says he and Leena will be on the road heading to Huntsville in an hour. He says he'll meet us at my house and then we'll drive to the cabin together.

With Christmas well on the way and two hours to spare before we leave, I think this is the perfect time to dig out the decorations. My mom and dad always decorated inside and outside the house, making Christmas a memorable holiday. I keep the tradition alive every year.

"Angel, let me get that." Bryce picks up the huge Christmas tree box stored in the spare room closet like it weighs nothing.

"Look at those muscles." I appreciatively squeeze the bulge on his arm and he grins down at me.

He carries it into the living room and I follow with two large plastic totes piled on top of each other.

Bryce starts to pull the Christmas tree out from the box while I rummage through the lights. "Do you set it up in front of the window?"

"How did you know?"

"Had a feeling."

Bryce is learning I have a certain way of doing things. He tries to move heaven and earth to make me happy. He doesn't need to, but it makes me smile every time he does. I wonder if he got that trait from his dad.

I'm learning what pleases him too.

We work together well without any arguing. Bryce meticulously sets up the tree piece by piece, fixing the branches to perfection.

Once he's done, he turns to see me screwing new bulbs into the ancient string of lights strewn on the floor. "No." He shakes his head. "I'm not wasting time with those. I'm going to Canadian Tire to buy new LED lights. They're brighter and easier to hang."

"Oh. Okay. So I shouldn't hang these on the tree?"

"No. They're a fire hazard." He gives me a kiss and heads for the back door.

"I guess I'll wait until you get back then," I holler.

While he's gone, I organize all the ornaments on the couch. I get choked up reminiscing about our life together as I have every year since my parents died. I hold the ornaments in my hand—the multi-coloured humming birds and the blue and purple hand blown glass balls with a white feather inside—and I run my fingers over them. There's one each for Gram and Gramps, Mom and Dad, and me. Going to the spare room to collect more decorations, I find the ornament I bought for Bryce—a firefighter helmet with his name and number painted on the crest—when Leena and I were shopping. I place it with the others, then string the garland around the fireplace mantel and the banister at the front door, carefully, placing red ribbon and mistletoe for accents. My three-foot animated Mr. and Mrs. Claus go into their usual spot in the corner. From the front of the house to the back, I place the decorations my parents have collected over the years in their traditional places. There are lots of decorations and it takes a while to finish.

The final touch is a huge snow globe with our family picture in it. I sit on the couch, turning it upside down and back upright again, over and over, watching the snowflakes surround our picture. Gram and Gramps are sitting on chairs with me at their feet, and Mom and Dad are standing behind the chair. It was taken when I was fourteen. I remember exactly how old I was at the time. It makes me smile but then a tear falls.

Just then, Bryce comes through the back door. "Couldn't decide so I bought twenty boxes to make sure we have enough." Bryce sees me wiping away my tears. "Angel, come here." Bryce places the bags of lights down and hugs me tight.

"I'll be okay. I do this every year." I say, sniffling.

Bryce looks around, examining the decorations I've arranged. "You've been busy. Looks great!"

I give him a squeeze, letting him know without words how much I appreciate him distracting me from my grief.

"What colour did you get?" I dive into the bags and boxes. "Blue, purple and green. These will look great!"

Bryce takes them out of the boxes, plugging them in to make

sure they work. He stands back with a set in his hand ready to place them on the tree.

He shakes his head. "It doesn't smell like pine. What if we cut down a real tree today?"

My eyes light up. "Really! I haven't had a real one since my parents passed." I step closer and hug him.

"Why didn't you tell me you wanted a real one?"

"It's easier this way."

"I didn't have the balls to tell you your tree is scrawny," Bryce says, smiling.

I laugh.

"Angel, it doesn't matter what it is. If you have your heart set on something, I will get it for you."

"Thanks, Babe, you are too sweet." After giving him a kiss, I return to extricating the lights from their packages and watch as Bryce takes the artificial tree down.

Bryce dresses warmly and heads outside. When I hear him up on the roof, I rush to get dressed, hoping I can help. "Babe, you don't have to hang them on the roof. I usually place them on the railing."

"I plan to hang them there too."

Once Bryce is finished, we stand at the road admiring the lights and then hurry back into the house for the warmth of the fire. The aromas of the wood burning in the fireplace and the scent of the pine candle combine, bringing back memories of Christmas with my parents.

Bryce inhales deeply. "Mmm, smells good in here."

"That's the smell of Christmas. I remember it well. And at this moment I can feel my parents here with us. I know it sounds weird, but I feel them."

"It's not weird at all. You miss them."

"I do."

I find having Bryce in my life this Christmas makes it easier handling the grief than previous years.

Bryce walks to the mantle and picks up the snow globe inspecting the picture inside. "How old were you here?"

"Fourteen."

Bryce smiles. "You were gorgeous then too. I wish I'd known you then. That reminds me: where are your family pictures?"

"Seriously? You don't want to see those."

"Yeah, I do. Come on. Let's go find them." Bryce tugs me toward my room.

I open my hope chest and pull out the metal box containing everything I cherish. We take them to the living room where we can sit on the couch, and I scatter them on the coffee table in front of us.

Bryce holds a picture of me in his hand. "Look at you, Angel. How old were you?"

I flip the picture in his hand. "Three. My mom always wrote how old I was on the back."

"Our kids will be so damn cute."

My cheeks hurt from smiling. "Yes, they will." I hold his face in my hands. "Because they'll have your gorgeous smile." I give him a kiss and then he pulls away.

"Because they'll look like you."

"And you."

We search through the pictures and Bryce collects five in his hand. "Don't you ever take a bad picture?"

"Yes. Look at me." I cup his hand and point with my finger. "I look terrible. I was almost late for school that day and of course it was picture day."

"You're adorable."

Just then, Leena and Austin come through the back door. "Wow! Your house looks great!"

"Thanks."

"Dug out the old pictures again, eh?"

"Yeah, Bryce wanted to see them."

Austin picks up a picture and looks at it. "You were a scrawny little thing. But I have to admit, you were kind of cute."

"Thanks, Austin."

He winks at me. "We're ready to go. Or are we sitting around gawking at pictures all day?"

In the garage at the cabin, the guys give Leena and me their old camo gear from when they were teenagers. Austin brought them from home in Barrie. I wonder if he wants us to blend in with the trees to avoid being seen by the deer.

Bryce hooks up the sleigh to the back of his snowmobile and straps down a collection of tools.

Austin notices. "What's all that for?"

"I'm cutting down a real tree."

"For what?"

"Keera's house."

Austin grumbles. "Pussy-whipped. That will slow us down."

"Hun, I want a real tree too," Leena says.

"See what you started!"

Leena's eyes make contact with mine and we can't hide the smiles on our faces.

When we're near the hunting camp, Austin pulls the snowmobiles off the trail in a clearing and Bryce follows. Once they shut the engines down, it's peaceful and quiet. We can only hear the sound of the crisp snow beneath our boots.

"It's beautiful out here," Leena says.

"Quiet! No talking. We don't want to scare the deer."

"Oh, yeah, like the sound of the engines ripping through the trails didn't scare them off!" Leena says sarcastically.

The moment I take my helmet off, Bryce covers my blonde hair with a camo hat and tucks the remaining hair into my jacket.

His eyes gleam as he looks in mine. Then they follow to my lips and he gives me a scorching kiss.

"Jesus, we're in the damn bush," Austin grumbles.

"What's up your ass?" Bryce chuckles.

"We're parking them here and walking the rest of the way in. I want you quiet!" Austin says sternly.

Leena turns to look at me with big eyes and a funny face. Then we smile at each other. We don't need words to know we're both thinking how anal Austin is about his hunting.

Grabbing the supplies from the sleigh, we make the long trek down the trail. There is pine trees on both sides of the trail and the snow blankets the branches, heavily weighing them down. I pull out my phone and take a picture behind us. It's an award winning photo, it's so beautiful. Bryce stops and looks back at me and I rush to catch up. When we hit a clearing of less pine trees, the trail has changed to snow covered large trees and I know it's not much further to Austin's tree blind. Once we reach the hunting camp, looking up, you can see the wood Austin used to build this has weathered from the last time I was here and it now blends in with the trees. We venture up the wood steps Austin bolted to the tree trunk to the landing above. Austin clears the walls of cobwebs with a broken handled broom from the corner while Leena and I paint each other's faces to match the guys' and then take pictures.

Austin glares at us, trying to be serious. "Are you two finished? You have to be quiet. And no movement."

Leena cuddles into his side. "Come on, hun, this is our first hunting trip. You want us to have fun, don't you?"

Austin and Bryce don't fool us. The slight smirk on their faces tells us they're amused.

Leena asks me questions about the job we're starting Monday and the guys tell her to be quiet.

She thinks of something else and they tell her to zip it.

Leena opens her mouth to speak again and Austin covers it with his hand.

Finally, Austin gets fed up and sends me and Bryce to the other tree stand, to keep Leena from talking.

When we climb the metal pegs, Bryce stays close making sure I don't fall.

Once up top, he covers me with a blanket to keep me warm. "I'm fine, Babe. This suit is pretty warm."

"Humour me."

"Okay."

"Christ, Austin is a miserable prick today."

"I can hear you!" Austin grumbles from the other tree.

Bryce rolls his eyes and makes a face. Then he sits on the bench, tucks me into his side, and sets his rifle up, looking around and waiting patiently for the deer to come out of hiding.

Half an hour later, after seeing nothing, we venture back up the other tree to be with Leena and Austin again.

Austin is looking through his scope, watching the horizon, not paying attention to us, but Leena's excited to see us.

Ten minutes later, Austin points and motions for us to be quiet.

Our attention instantly shifts to where he's pointing. We find ourselves following Austin's lead by looking down our scopes to see what is in his sight.

Two men wearing camo gear and carrying rifles walk toward us in the distance.

Austin sits back on his heels and mouths to Bryce, *Trent*.

I look from Austin to Bryce and see they're both grinning mischievously. "Quiet. Don't move," Bryce whispers.

As they draw closer, we hear their conversation. "Look at this thing. Austin outdid himself."

"You could have a party up there."

Austin grins proudly but stays silent, waiting for them to climb up the tree.

When they make it to the landing, Bryce and Austin charge out the door, shouting, "RAAA!"

"Jesus! You guys scared the hell out of us!"

Austin and Bryce laugh. "I thought you were going to fall down." Austin pats Trent on the back and shakes his hand.

"Probably would've if you hadn't grabbed my coat."

They're all laughing when they see Leena and me standing in the doorway.

"You brought the girls?" Trent asks, sounding like it's taboo to bring females hunting.

"Hi, Trent," Leena and I say at the same time.

Austin sees Leena shiver. "We were heading back down but thought we'd stick around to scare the crap out of you guys."

"And I thank you for that," Trent says. "You got my heart pumping."

After saying our goodbyes, we drive down the trail for a few miles on the snowmobiles. When we come to a field of evergreens, Bryce slows and makes his own trail between the trees. Once he sees the perfect Douglas-Fir, he stops and takes his helmet off. He treks through the deep snow and shakes the tree to get the snow off the branches. "What do you think of this one?"

I take my helmet off and stand back, trying to picture it in my living room. "Think it's too big?"

Bryce reaches up, measuring with his arm. "No. It will fit perfectly."

"All right then. This is the one." Looking around, I see Austin shaking a tree for Leena. Then he moves to the next, shaking it. She decides on the fourth tree. Bryce is already lying beneath the branches of our tree, cutting the trunk until it falls over. After he hands the saw to Austin, we tie up our tree with string and haul it to the sleigh before helping Austin and Leena. We secure both trees with bungee cords and then rush to get back on the trail.

The restaurant is only five miles away but by the time we make it there on the snowmobiles with the wind whipping up, we are chilled to the bone. Once inside, we take our helmets off, placing them on a large shelf with the other snowmobiler's helmets.

Leena pulls me over to the massive stone fireplace and arranges our gloves on the hearth to warm them. Then she sits down and takes her boots off, pulling out the insulation. "Sit! Give me your foot."

"I can take my own boots off."

"Keera, give me your damn foot."

I sit quickly. "Yes, mother."

She yanks at my boots until they come off.

The guys drop their gloves next to ours and take off their coats, hanging them on a coat rack. While they settle in at a table across from us, Leena and I stand in front of the fireplace, flipping from front to back, thawing. "This feels good," I say.

"I swear with that wind, it's forty below."

"I know, eh? My buns are frozen. It's cold out there," I say. "I think the temperature is dropping."

"Speaking of buns, I have to tell you what happened. Ma wanted to hang out, have a girl's day. She wanted to go shopping and out for lunch. I said great, but I have to stop at Martina's to get my eyebrows done. She had no problem with it. So, there I am in Martina's private room, naked from the waist down, up on all fours on the table. We were laughing about something. Next thing I know, my mother, who was sitting in the waiting room, opens the door and asks 'what's so funny?' I spun around and I could see some guy looking at me through the crack in the door where it was open. So, Ma says, 'those are funny-looking eyebrows.'"

I laugh out loud. "Oh my God, that is too funny! What did you say to Ma?"

"I yelled, 'Mother get out!' I could've died, I was so embarrassed."

"You, embarrassed? Never!"

"Okay, only for a second. Then Martina said, 'Did you see your mother's face?' She mimicked my ma with her eyes wide open and her jaw on the floor and we both broke out laughing. My mother!"

"Wish I could've been there. Just love Ma."

"All day, we couldn't stop laughing. Ma kept saying it over and over. 'Those are funny looking eyebrows.'"

Once we've warmed up, we scurry across the floor in our socks, sliding in next to Austin and Bryce.

"I could go for a hot bowl of soup right now," Leena says.

"That's what I'm getting," I say as I look over the menu. "And a sandwich."

"Make that two," Leena says.

Having taken our orders without so much as looking at us, the waitress smiles girlishly at Bryce and Austin while taking theirs. Leena and I roll our eyes at each other, but the waitress is so busy smiling at the guys that she doesn't even notice. As soon as she disappears, our attention is diverted to the snow falling and the large group of snowmobilers pulling up outside the window. People are coming in at a steady pace, happy to be out of the cold. A couple of women shove their way through to get to the fireplace and warm themselves.

Austin and Bryce are in deep discussion, talking about the big case Austin's been working on. They don't notice the two women at the fireplace, but Leena and I do. And when the girls spin around to warm their backsides, they definitely notice the guys. One nudges the other and they both home in, staring.

I read the brunette's lips. "Wow, would you look at that!"

They laugh and then her friend takes her by the arm and pulls her away. The brunette stops dead. "Can't I stay here and stare?"

"No! You're embarrassing me."

They laugh again and then saunter over to the large table where their group is settling in.

Leena grabs my hand to get my attention. "You'll never believe this. The other night when I got home from work, I could hear Ma giggling in her bedroom. Never thought anything of it because Donovan's car wasn't in the driveway. Thought she was watching TV. Later, I come out of my room and guess who is standing in the kitchen with his boxers on?"

"Who?"

"Constable Grant."

"What? No! Get out of here!"

"I know, eh? He's been fucking my mother. How frickin' awkward is that?"

"What did you do?"

"I almost died. I didn't say a word, turned right back around and went to my room."

"What did you say to Ma?"

"I asked her what happened to Donovan? She said he was nice but she never felt like she does with Grant. She said Donovan just wasn't that good in bed. But she knew the moment she met Grant. Sparks flew, I guess." Leena rolls her eyes.

The waitress brings our meals and we devour them. "Man, being cold makes me hungry," Leena says.

We talk and eat and enjoy each other's company. It's a great day filled with laughter. With our bellies full now, we put our gear back on and head back out to the snowmobiles in the freezing cold. The snowfall is almost blinding and when the wind whips up, I can feel it through the opening beneath my helmet. I climb aboard behind Bryce and tuck my collar up, sealing the gap. When I wrap my arms around him and cuddle into his back, he knows I'm ready and squeezes my hand before heading out of the parking lot. Austin and Bryce rip through the trails, climbing and descending through the mountainous terrain. I find myself leaning to the right and left with Bryce to help us make it around the corners safely. A few times, I look back to make sure the sleigh is still behind us. Bryce and Austin are on a mission to make it back to the cabin in record time and get out of the cold. When we're close, I notice the tall rock face and the huge fallen tree in Austin's headlight behind us and know it's only five more minutes to the cabin. Bryce hits the button on his key fob, opening the large garage door, and we drive right in. The old wood stove in the corner of the garage still radiates heat. I hurry over to add more wood to the fire. Leena follows and we warm ourselves as the guys lift the snowmobiles and clean the tracks.

The evening is a relaxing one, watching movies and sipping hot chocolate with marshmallows.

Early in the morning, we drop Leena and Austin off to set up their Christmas tree at the Ericson's.

Bryce and I lug our big tree through the front door, placing it in the tree stand. He cuts the string and we separate the braches. We're pressed for time, so we work together decorating it. Bryce plugs in the lights and we stand back admiring it.

"Thanks, Babe. This is the best Christmas since my parents passed."

"Looks better than that scrawny one. It covers the window now." Bryce chuckles. "And it smells great."

Our two days in Huntsville have flown by. After we lock up my house, we pick Leena and Austin up. They drive my Journey behind us so I'll have it to travel back and forth to my new job at Avionté cosmetics. We head for Highway 11, for the hour-long trip back to Barrie.

Every now and then, Bryce and I get quiet. I don't ask what he's thinking about, but my thoughts are running wild, thinking about him going back to work with Blake. *What tactic will she use to get his attention this week?* I try to dismiss her from my mind.

14

MONDAY MORNING, I wake early from a bad dream about Bryce and Blake. I've been having the same recurring dream where she eventually charms her way into his life.

Bryce senses something is wrong. "Are you okay?"

"Yeah, I'm fine. Maybe I'm a little nervous about my new job."

"That's a normal reaction for everyone starting a new job. Tonight you'll wonder why you were stressing. Promise, you'll do fine." He pulls me in for a hug and he kisses my forehead. I melt into his hard body.

The dress I brought from home in Huntsville is perfect for my first day at work. I know it's a good choice when I come out of the bedroom and see the expression on Bryce's face. "You're wearing that?"

I smooth it down at the hips feeling self-conscious, even though it's already tight. "Why? Is something wrong with it?"

"No. You look amazing. I want you to wear that around me."

I move closer to Bryce. "I thought you liked me naked."

"I do." Bryce takes my face in his hands, caressing it with his thumbs and gazing in my eyes. "We're going out for dinner this week. I want to see this dress hit the floor when we come home."

"All right."

My day is already improving and gets even better when Bryce bends me backwards at the front door, giving me a smoking hot kiss.

He lifts me up and holds me tight. "Call me right away if Colton shows up there."

"Babe, I don't—"

He places his finger over my mouth. "Phone." He holds out his hand, gesturing. "Hand it over. I want to put the phone number and address of the studio in my phone."

"Fine, but I think your worrying for nothing." I hand it to Bryce and he adds it to his contact list.

"I don't put anything past the shark." He kisses me again and smacks my butt. "Have a good day at work."

I turn back around, grasp his butt cheeks with both hands and tug him into me. "I'll be thinking of you all day." I squeeze. "And this very, fine, sexy ass."

He bends me backwards and gives me another scorching, tongue entangling kiss. When he pulls me up, I'm light headed and dizzy. He holds me steady. "Are you okay, Angel?"

"Yeah. It's that kiss of yours. Makes me light-headed."

"Come with me. I'll walk you to the Journey."

"I'm okay. Really."

Bryce opens the garage and we walk around to the driver's door. I sink down into the seat and Bryce bends to give me another kiss. "Be careful! I'll see you tonight."

"You be careful, too. Love you, Babe."

"I love you, Angel."

Leena is ready and waiting when I pull up to Austin's house to pick her up.

"Hey, girlfriend. How's it going this morning?"

"Good." Leena claps her hands together as she slides in the passenger seat. "I'm so excited to be a part of this."

"Yeah, I'm excited too. Probably why I didn't sleep that good. Woke up early from that same recurring dream I told you about."

"I don't know what you're getting worked up about. Bryce loves you. You're all he sees." She rolls her eyes. "It's actually a little bit nauseating."

"That's the thing about bad dreams. They screw with your mind. It seems real. Five minutes after I wake up, I finally relax and tell myself it's a bad dream."

"I've had dreams like that."

"What would you do if Austin had a woman cop he worked with who was trying anything to get his attention? What would you do if she watched him in the shower?"

"I'd kick her ass. That's what I would do."

Chuckling, I pull onto St. Vincent until I reach Wellington street, then I follow that to Bayfield. My navigation sends us half-way down the road and we pull up to an old red-brick building with black awnings above the windows and doors. The railings around the balconies are black wrought iron and the combination looks fantastic.

"This is the place?" Leena asks, looking out the front window.

I look up too. "This is the address they gave me."

"Wow! Nice. Looks like it's been newly renovated. Look at the windows."

Leena and I walk up two flights of stairs and down a hallway to room two-twenty-two. We knock and we're ushered in right away by a happy brunette.

"Keera, so nice to meet you. My name is Shyanne. I'll be the one who oversees everything and one of your photographers for the next two weeks."

"Nice to meet you." We shake hands.

"This must be Leena. Christina told me your assistant would be coming. Let me show you around."

The studio is one large room, fifty feet long, sectioned off by the props they're using for the photo shoot. An outdoor café setting catches my eye, along with the thirtyish sheer, white panels of material strung from the ceiling to the floor. At the other end of the room are three sets of large French doors with black-accented half-moon windows above them. They are spectacular.

"What do you think?"

"This looks great!"

"Good. Let's get started."

The day is filled with wardrobe changes, makeup, and the hair stylist trying different techniques for some of the shots. Leena assists by sitting in with me for the café video and she's thrilled by the way they apply her makeup. She loves and wants to buy the form-fitting navy-blue lace dress they have her wear. Later, we stop for a catered lunch of soups, salads, and sandwiches and then get back to work shortly after. The day flies by and before we know it, Shyanne yells out, "Good job, people. See everyone tomorrow."

On the drive to Austin's, Leena can't contain her excitement. "Keera, that was amazing! Way better than the bakery. I don't think I stopped smiling all day."

"I was going to ask but then I figured it out. You were too quiet. What's up with that?"

"I'll show them the real Leena in a couple of days," she says, snickering.

"I enjoyed myself too. I told Bryce the first modelling job was a one-time thing but I'm liking this, and we get paid."

"Which is awesome!" Leena cuts in. "Bryce will have to adjust. He has a career and now you do, too. See you tomorrow," she says as she gets out of my Journey at Austin's house.

Bryce enters the front door of his house shortly after five. "Angel?"

I walk to the stairs overlooking the foyer. "How was your day?"

"The usual. How was yours?"

"Great."

"Anyone show up at the studio?"

Meaning Colton? "No."

Bryce minimizes the space between us and kisses me. A toe-curling kiss. "I'll take a shower and help you with dinner." He guides me to the kitchen with that simple touch to my lower back and then routinely takes his pager and phone from his belt.

"Thanks." I watch as he strolls to the bathroom and then I start dinner.

The sight of Bryce coming down the hall after his shower with his wet hair and towel hanging low on his hips takes my breath away, as usual. I wonder if I'll ever get used to his stunning good looks and perfect hard body. Probably not. The tingle is back, I'm instantly aroused thinking of his hands all over me and wild, animalistic, mind-numbing sex.

"Keep looking at me like that, see what happens."

I chuckle and bump his hip. "You can't go outside and bar-beque like that. Although the neighbours would get a treat."

"We're barbequing tonight?" He puts his arms around me. "Tomorrow we're going out for dinner and you're wearing that dress you had on this morning." He kisses my forehead, turns, and drops his towel, shaking that sexy ass as he struts down the hall.

"Tease," I call after him.

He turns his head slightly and I see him smirking.

After a few minutes, he's back beside me, holding my hip, resting his chin on my shoulder. "What else are you making?"

"Salad, baked potatoes, veggies."

"After dinner, we're going to the station to workout."

"We are?" I say.

"Yes, wives and girlfriends use the equipment with us."

"Oh."

After cleaning the dishes, we head over to the fire station. Bryce wears his low-hanging shorts and a tight t-shirt. I wear shorts and a tank top. As I emerge from the women's washroom, I see Bryce leaning against the wall, waiting for me. His eyes rake up and down my body inspecting me. A grin forms.

I think he approves.

As he guides me down the hall, I can feel several pairs of eyes on us. Some of the firefighters have stopped working to watch us as we make our way to the workout room.

Bryce looks back at them looking out the door. "I've never drawn attention like this before."

"Must be that sexy little ass of yours," I say, smacking his butt as we're rounding the doorway.

He smiles at me and shakes his head, amused by my comment, before striding over to use the weights while I step onto the treadmill.

Five minutes into our workout, when I haven't even broken a sweat, the sound of the fire alarm blaring resonates throughout the station.

Bryce stops and places the barbell on the rack, listening intently.

"Barrie dispatcher to Barrie Fire Station 1. We have a report of an MVA. Several cars and a transport truck involved, occupants trapped. Highway 11 and Highway 400 interchange. Time of dispatch 19:20 hours."

Bryce sits up and counts the firefighters running down the hall, racing to reach their gear.

"Are you going with them?"

"No. They can handle it." He stands and motions. "Come here."

I walk into his arms and he hugs me, grabbing both butt cheeks and squeezing. "I love your workout attire."

"You do, eh?"

"Come." Bryce takes my hand and leads me out of the workout room. We stroll down the hall, making our way to the lone firetruck left in the bay. The doors are closed and it's eerily quiet.

At the side door of the firetruck, he pulls out a blanket and captures me against the truck, kissing me slowly. He deepens the kiss, revving up my hormones. When we pull apart, we're panting softly. He tugs me along and climbs on the platform at the back of the firetruck holding out his hand for me. "Come here, beautiful."

I smile and place my hand in his and he pulls me up.

"Up you go." He follows and we climb the ladder to the top where the hoses are stored, then lays the thick blanket out and motions for me. "Kneel in the middle."

I clamber over and Bryce kneels behind me. He pulls my hair to the side, kissing my neck, sending chills down my spine. His hand slips under my shirt, grasping my breast.

I turn slightly to look at him. "Do you think everyone left?"

"I know they left. No one here, Angel." He continues kissing my neck. "Only me and you." Moving my hair, Bryce runs his lips across my shoulder and kisses the other side of my neck, raising goosebumps everywhere he touches. I shiver.

"I've wanted to fulfill this fantasy from the moment I met you." His husky voice against my ear travels to all the right places.

Instantly aroused, I relax and enjoy every sensation running wild. I unleash my inner goddess and let go, helping him achieve his fantasy, hoping it's better than he imagined.

He wraps his arm around me, splaying his fingers across my belly, pulling me against him.

"Mmm, I like that." I reach back and hold his hips, circling my butt against his hard cock.

"We've got too many clothes on. Let's take this off." Bryce lifts my tank top and extricates me from my bra. His large hands cup my breasts and his lips feather down my neck, sending chills down my spine.

I reach back, grasping his cock through his shorts. "I want this."

Bryce nips my ear. "For you? Anything."

I turn to face him and pull down his shorts. Taking his cock in my hands, I stroke it up and down. His body jerks from my touch.

With our lips sealed in a slow kiss, he lowers me gently onto the blanket. He strips from his clothes and then focuses on my shorts. His gaze floats over my body, inspecting me. He lowers himself on top and nuzzles in my neck. "So beautiful and you're all mine."

"Mr. Tall, Dark, and Gorgeous, and you are all mine."

He kisses his way across my collarbone, smiling, and then flutters his lips down to my breasts. His teeth capture my nipple and he gently bites. He flicks it rapidly with his magical tongue and then moves to the other breast, giving it his undivided attention. His tongue darts out and he licks a perfect line down my abs. He takes his time nipping and kissing each hipbone, pushing me close to insanity. "Babe."

Gazing up at me, he smiles, apparently pleased with himself, but doesn't say a word as he continues torturing me.

My pelvis lifts slightly but he ignores my plea. "Babe, please."

"I was waiting for that." His luscious mouth lowers to my pussy and his finger slides in and out. His talented tongue and hands, confident and skilled, drive me closer to orgasm.

Weaving my fingers through his hair, I tug on it, holding him in place. My breathing slows to small intakes of breath and my skin is misted with sweat.

I grasp tighter and clamp down on his finger, rocking my hips up to meet his every thrust. "Babe. It's so good. Don't stop!"

Bryce doesn't stop. His merciless tongue flicks my clit relentlessly as one orgasm rolls into another and then I'm pushing him away from the sensitivity. Mindless from the intensity of my orgasms, I'm vaguely aware of Bryce yanking me down to where he wants me, spearing me with his cock, sinking balls deep with one fierce drive.

I gasp. My hands grab onto his pec muscles and squeeze. "Your cock feels so good inside me."

"This is where I've wanted to be all day. Buried deep inside you." His movements are slow and precise as he expertly rolls his hips, angling his cock for maximum penetration.

"Angel, nowhere I'd rather be than with you."

"Mmm, yes, I feel the same way you do."

He picks up speed then, giving me everything he has, working me into a frenzy. His cock batters into me, growing beyond hard as steel. His balls slap deliciously against me while his chest heaves frantically for air. Then without warning, he freezes, collapsing on top of me, whispering next to my ear, "Don't move."

I run my nails down his back and grasp his ass cheeks.

Suddenly, he pulls out and kneels up, grasping my legs, flipping me over at lightning speed. "Hands and knees. I want you from behind."

I get into position and as I'm looking back he sinks into me. His leg muscles bulge to support his weight as he lunges in and they're spread wide as he holds onto the steel rafters on the ceiling. Turned on by his pose, I can't look away. "That's hot, Babe. Don't stop! Give it to me, hard!"

"Christ Angel, you turn me on. You're so sexy." Drenched with sweat, he tunnels deeper than the thrust before. He gives me what I ask for. Hard. And it's Heaven. "You like this? Fuck, is that deep." His fingers grip tighter on my hips. "That sweet, sweet pussy is going to make me come already. I want you with me."

I can hear in his voice he's close. With my left arm outstretched, I hold myself up and reach to touch my swollen clit with my right hand. As my muscles clamp down around his cock, it feels like I'm unravelling. "Babe! Oh, oh, it's so good. I want to scream!"

Bryce rears up, almost lifting me with his cock, and the feeling intensifies as my orgasm rips through me. When the last tremor fades, I look back again to see him ramming into me a few more times. "Angel!" A muffled curse leaves him as he spurts his cum inside, filling me with his warmth. The full weight of his body falls on me, draping over mine, and he holds me tight. We topple over, spooning with Bryce's cock jerking inside me. His arm lays across me, holding my breast in his hand, as he peppers my neck with kisses. Breathless, he whispers against my ear. "This was better than I fantasized."

"I was hoping. Glad I could help."

"You rock my world, Angel."

"You've rocked mine from the moment I met you."

"That's good. I don't ever want you wondering if someone else can make love to you better."

"Never, Babe. No one can do what you do."

My eyes widen at the sound of the door lifting.

Three beeping firetrucks are backing into the bays beside us. "Shit!" I giggle and duck down.

Bryce chuckles, placing his finger over my lips, motioning for me to be quiet. Looking up, I see my bra and tank top above my head. I quickly reach and pull them on. Fast. My shorts are by my feet. I don't want to lift my upper body or someone will see us so I grab them with my toes. Once Bryce and I are dressed, we lie basking in the afterglow of one of the best fantasies we've ever experienced.

We kiss slowly, sensually, running our lips down each other's throats, listening and waiting for the firefighters to clean and restock the trucks. We stare lovingly into one another's eyes, caressing and petting until we hear it's quiet again and climb down. After Bryce replaces the blanket, we make our way back to the workout room, undetected.

Tuesday morning, Bryce asks a few questions about the building Avionté cosmetics rents, which leaves me wondering why he's being over-protective again. Before I leave for work, he grabs me and holds me tightly, kissing me with such hunger, it has me shivering. *Is something bothering him again? Something he doesn't want to share with me?*

What could it be?

The only thing that enters my mind, is Blake.

What has she done now? I let it go for the time being because I'm running a bit late, but tonight I'll ask him what's wrong.

"Think about that kiss," Bryce says, smacking my butt as I walk out the door.

"I will. And I'll want more."

"I want to give you more."

I smack his butt and give him a kiss goodbye before we get into our own vehicles.

When I pull into Austin's driveway, Leena is waiting for me. "Hey, girlfriend," Leena says lowering into the passenger seat of my Journey.

"How was your night with Austin?"

"Erotic! The man can fuck!" She shivers. "I'm getting aroused thinking about him. How was your night with Bryce?"

I laugh. "Great! We went to work out at the fire station and when everyone left for a transport truck accident, I helped Bryce fulfill a fantasy of fucking wildly on the firetruck."

"Listen to you, opening up without me prying. It's about time," Leena says. "That's more exciting than being tied up and whipped." We both laugh. "How is Bryce?"

I look at Leena, wondering why she's asking how Bryce is. "Why?"

"Oh, umm." She hesitates for a moment and I know she's searching for something to say. "I was wondering if he was getting weird again about Colton."

I glance over at her a few times while I'm driving.

Knowing Leena well, I can see she's lying. *What is she up to?* "He asked if anyone showed up at the studio yesterday but when I told him no, he relaxed."

"Oh."

"He was acting strange this morning and I thought of Blake because he seems like he's hiding something from me." *Like you.*

"That could be."

We get down to work as soon as we enter the studio. The team applies my makeup and have me change into a tight, bubblegum-pink mini-dress with high heels to match. They paint my nails the same colour. Then they take some shots of me strolling through the sheer white panels of material hanging from the ceiling.

Shyanne shows me the pictures and video of how the pink dress stands out as I float through the sheers. Later, she wants me to change into a fabulous white chiffon dress with several layers and walk through the panels again, but this time, with a fan blowing lightly. I wonder how that will work out.

It is now after eleven. I've noticed sirens approaching for a few minutes, but now they're blaring right outside our window and everyone is rushing to look over the balcony and see what the commotion is.

There's a firetruck below and the firefighters are scrambling about, yelling orders, extending the ladder—up to our balcony!

I tap a few of the employee's shoulders, forcing them to look at me. "Come on, we've got to get out of this building! It's old. We don't have much time before it goes up in flames!" I walk back through the French doors, making my way to the exit sign at the other end of this large room. But before I make it there, Leena is grabbing my arm.

"Hold on a second. It might be a false alarm."

"We've got to tell everyone in this building there's a fire. We need to evacuate!"

"Calm down, relax." Leena grabs my hand off the doorknob.

I grab her shoulders and shake her a bit. "Leena, listen to me! We have to get everyone out. Why isn't everyone moving? Come on, let's go." I turn toward the door again in a panic, reaching for the doorknob.

"Keera, look." She spins me roughly to look back at the balcony doors. "Bryce will explain."

15

C LIMBING OVER THE balcony from the bucket of the ladder truck, Bryce hops down and struts toward me through the French doors with his powerful, confident walk. He looks amazing in his full firefighting gear. Taking his gloves off, he drops them along the way. Next, he takes off his helmet and by the strap, he gently places it on the floor, not slowing his pace at all. He is a man on a mission. I'm mesmerized, can't take my eyes off him. He walks toward me, and I step closer to meet him in the middle of the room.

Fishing into his pocket, he pulls something out. As he nears me he gets down on one knee. "Keera, Angel, will you marry me?"

My mind is spinning. Overwhelmed.

In the blink of an eye, a whole conversation runs through my head.

How can I tell him it's too soon?

You can't. He planned this.

Do you love him?

Yes. Madly. I couldn't live without him.

So what's the problem? This is every woman's dream proposal.

But marriage is a big step.
Do you want to spend the rest of your life with him?
Yes, without a doubt.
So extend the engagement until you're ready.
Great idea!

I come back to the moment as he opens the box. Inside is the same ring I tried on in Aruba.

My eyes float from the box to Bryce's beautiful, hazel eyes. There's so much love in them that my chest hurts. Tears well up and seep down my cheeks. I touch Bryce's face tenderly. "Yes."

He stands and hugs me, hard. Then he holds my face in his hands. "Say it again."

"Yes. Yes. I'll marry you."

Bryce takes my hand and slips the ring on my finger, making the moment last as he gently runs his fingers along mine. "To have and to hold from this day forward," Bryce says slowly in his deep, bedroom tone.

I look up from the ring to his glimmering eyes. "How?"

"I had it made." Bryce lowers his lips to mine. The kiss is so passionate it takes my breath away.

All sound disappears.

After a few moments, loud clapping in the distance brings me back to the here and now. I'm the first to pull away. "There's no fire?"

"No, Angel. No, fire." He grins at me.

I turn to look at Leena and she's grinning. "You knew!"

"We all did." She squeezes an arm around Austin, who looks like he's on duty with his partner because they're in uniforms. Then she scans around the room and so do I. The cameras are rolling and all eyes are on us. Dante and Jax and a few firefighters are standing back, smiling, and so is everyone who works here at Avionté.

Leena comes to hug me. "I almost gave it away this morning."

I point my finger at her. "I knew you were up to something," I say, laughing.

Leena grabs Bryce's arm to get his attention. "Bryce, you should have seen her. She was on a mission to get everyone out of the building. I had to stop her. She was leaving."

Bryce stares at me once again with love in his eyes. "Firefighter's fiancé." He plays with the ring on my finger, which he's holding to his chest. "You wanted to save everyone."

"I did."

There are hugs all around as people take turns congratulating us.

Later, when everything calms down, Bryce tugs me in for a goodbye kiss. When he releases me, his eyes wander down to the way my cleavage looks in this dress. "I'll pick you up at four-thirty for dinner. Ask them if you can borrow this dress. You look beautiful."

Just then, several pagers blare, filling the room with the dispatcher's voice. Bryce, Jax, and Dante have a car accident with people trapped and they need police assistance. Austin gives Leena a kiss and Bryce does the same to me.

Leena and I yell out, "Be careful" as they head for the door to take the stairs.

We get back to work.

During the day, I steal a few seconds for myself here and there staring down at my finger, playing with the diamond. It's blindingly beautiful.

Bryce had this stunning ring made for me, a replicate using the picture he took of it in Aruba. And he planned this amazing proposal. For me.

Here I was thinking he was worried about Colton showing up at the studio when really, he took my phone for the address to execute the perfect marriage proposal. Cunning.

How did he get the Chief to agree to this—taking the truck out of service for an hour? My heart swells with so much love for him, I ache. He did all of this for me. Everything he has ever done is for us. To keep our love and this relationship strong. He loves me. I can't believe I'm engaged. I'm getting married. *Holy crap, this is moving fast.*

Bryce arrives at the studio fifteen minutes early to pick me up and we're still working. Several eyes are on him as he strides his muscular, uniformed body halfway across the room over to Shyanne. His amazing build and powerful walk make me achingly aware that I want him right now. My muscles clench instinctively. I'm the luckiest woman alive. This Greek God loves me.

"Keera, I need you to look over here." A voice is speaking loudly, bringing me back from my lust-filled trip.

It's Parker, my photographer, and I give him my attention for as long as I can. But after a few moments, my gaze floats back to Bryce. "Someone needs to get him out of this room. He's distracting her," Parker grumbles.

My gaze locks on Bryce as Shyanne hands him a memory stick. *What is he up to now?*

"Keera, I need you to look this way. Damn it! Okay, we'll get a side view," Parker says, annoyed.

"Let's call it a day," Shyanne yells out, saving me. "We'll see everyone back here tomorrow."

I stand and walk toward Bryce. He does the same, strutting closer with his powerful walk. His eyes glimmer as his gaze floats up and down my body, inspecting me. With one hand on my hip, his other hand holds my lower back and he tugs me into him. "You're beautiful."

"Thank you. I love your uniform and the man in it. Too hot, Baby. I can't wait to get this off you."

Bryce grabs my hand and pulls me to the door. "The faster we get dinner over with, the faster I watch this dress fall to the floor."

The restaurant Bryce chooses looks like a stone castle from the outside. He has reservations and they usher us in right away. As the Maître'D guides us through the restaurant, I note how large and elegant the main dining room is. The interior décor, only adds to the castle theme. The carved wood chairs at the end of each table are huge, like king's chairs. Iron lanterns hang along the walls and down the hall, illuminating the way. Vintage hurricane candleholders grace the middle of each table and strings of tiny white lights, meticulously strung from the ceiling, set the atmosphere to "intimate." We follow the Maître'D down a hallway and through a maze of smaller rooms on each side, then up the stone steps to the second floor, straight to the third secluded room on the right.

When the waiter leaves with our drink order, Bryce slides the candle to the left of the table and takes my hand in his. He moves my ring back and forth on my finger. "I knew from the first week we were together I wanted to make you my wife. And now, it's happening. You'll be mine."

"Babe, I've always been yours."

"But it'll be official. I need that. I want what you want, Angel. A relationship like our parents."

"Yes, I've been watching your parents and they've got a remarkable relationship. They're perfect for each other and they're still in love after all these years. I can tell by the looks in their eyes. And you're right. I do want that." I caress his hand. "Your proposal will be with me forever. I'll never forget what you did for me." Tears start to well up in my eyes from the immense emotions I feel for him but I bat my eyes, holding them in. "I've been on cloud nine all day. And this ring is perfect. It blows me away that you had this made for me exactly like the one I tried on. Thank you." I squeeze his hand and change the subject so I won't cry. "How did you convince the Chief to let you take the firetruck out of service for an hour?"

"Didn't take much. When I asked him, he told me he used the truck for his proposal. Turns out he's quite the romantic."

"So are you," I say, rubbing my leg against his.

The waiter appears with our drinks and takes our orders.

As the waiter leaves, Bryce takes my hand moving my ring with his thumb. "I asked your Gramps."

"Oh, yeah. What did he say?" I remember when I overheard Bryce asking and how nervous he was, especially when Gramps tortured him with the silent treatment.

"He's a tough old bugger, let me sweat it out for a few minutes, but then he finally gave me his blessing."

"That's my Gramps. But I can tell he really likes you."

Bryce holds my hand in both his large hands. "Do you want to get married on a beach or in a church?"

"What do you want?" I ask, turning the decision back to him.

"We could get married in Hawaii, Greece, wherever you want. Or a church. But even if we do a destination wedding, we'll have to have a reception once we get home for family members. Big family. They'll be pissed if we don't have a party."

"Sounds good. I remember you saying you have a big family, but how big?"

"Ten kids on my dad's side, eight on my mom's side."

"Really? That's huge."

"Not to mention a lot of firefighters I work with, nurses and doctors who work with my mom, inspectors, captains, and chiefs working with my dad … could be a considerable size reception."

"How many people do you think?"

"I'm thinking around three-hundred-and-fifty."

"Wow!"

"Next question is, when."

Holy crap, he's been thinking about this for a while. The waiter appears with an appetizer, which gives me time to think.

But then he disappears and Bryce looks in my eyes, waiting for an answer.

"It could take up to a year to prepare for this," I say. "We'll have to decide on the church, book a reception hall…"

Bryce cuts me off. "We'll get it done in six months."

Six months. Holy. "You're rushing this don't you think?"

"Angel, what are you afraid of?"

"Marriage is a big step."

"You love me," he says.

"Yes, with all my heart."

"You're overthinking this. I'll guide you through it. I'll reserve everything if you want me to, or Leena can help. After we're married, you'll wonder why you were nervous."

"You're right. I am overthinking this." I take his hand in mine, reassuring him. "Why is it you always know what to say to make me relax? Leena would love to help with some of the arrangements. She lives for this kind of stuff."

The waiter comes in with our Caesar salads and soft, warm bread with whipped butter. "Another round of drinks?"

"Please," Bryce says.

The waiter disappears.

During our dinner, Bryce constantly touches my leg with his and when my hand is free he plays with my engagement ring. "Next question. How many children do you want?"

My eyes widen. "Umm, two, three. How many do you want?"

"Four or five."

"Oh." He has been thinking about this for a while.

As time goes by, I'm learning how Bryce wants and needs control of everything in his life and mine. I've been on my own for years, but now that Bryce is in my life, I find myself giving in and letting him take the reins. I know if I have a problem with any decision he makes, he'll compromise to make me happy.

The waiter enters our secluded room with our drinks and clears our salad plates.

"What did Shyanne hand you in the studio?"

"You saw that, eh?"

"Yeah." I lift my eyebrow waiting for his answer as he deliberately sidesteps my question.

"I had them film the proposal. I want to add it to the wedding video."

"Look at you. Taking care of everything. You always amaze me."

Bryce takes a sip of his drink and watches my lips intently as they touch the rim of mine. I take a sip and intentionally lick my lips afterward to get a reaction from him. His eyes squint and I see a slight smirk as his lips curl to one side of his beautiful mouth. He rubs my leg with his and then takes another sip, mimicking me, slowly sweeping his tongue along the seam of his lower lip. He can see the effect it has on me.

A thought enters my mind. I take my shoe off, lifting my foot, feeling for and finding his semi-erect cock. He hardens beneath the pad of my foot and his look seems to say, *You're asking for it and I'm the one to give it to you.*

The waiter enters and places our aged filet mignon with creamy wine sauce for dipping, loaded baked potato, and warm bread with whipped butter on the table.

Bryce's eyes never leave mine.

"Thank you," I say, glancing at the waiter. "Looks delicious." I curl my toes around his cock and his eyes squint. His lips bunch up as he tries to hold in a smile.

The waiter leaves.

"This feels delicious, too," I say, moving my foot a bit.

"You'll feel it." He shakes his head and smiles at me.

The waiter comes back in after we've finished our main course and asks, "Would you like some dessert?"

"No thanks. Just the cheque. Please." Bryce stares in my eyes.

The waiter pulls out the cheque, places it on the table, and disappears.

Bryce fishes in his pocket and pulls out some bills, throwing them on the table. "Let's get you home."

He drives faster than usual and takes a couple shortcuts to his house.

As I'm taking my shoes off at the front door, Bryce moves in close. He pulls my hair to the side and kisses my neck, making his way around to the other side, slowly.

I reach back holding his hips and circle my butt. I feel him smile against my jawline.

"Come with me." He says, pulling me up the stairs.

I stop abruptly, pulling him back. "Since you spoiled me today, let me spoil you tonight."

"No. Some other time. Today and tonight are all about you."

Wednesday morning after getting ready, I stand at the breakfast bar admiring my engagement ring, sipping my tea, remembering how Bryce took his time making love to me. His display of love for me showed through with every touch and every kiss. He caressed every part of my body, worshipping me.

I returned the favour, showing how much I love him and appreciate everything he's done for me. The proposal and the whole day were amazing, thanks to him—a memory that will burn bright in my mind forever.

Bryce strides down the hall toward me. My eyes travel up and down his muscled physique. His uniform fits him perfectly. I can't help but smile.

He steps closer, pressing his hard body against mine. "Like my uniform?"

"Yes, very much. I love the man inside it, too."

He caresses my neck and holds my lower back. "The way you look at me and the way you touch me … Angel, I've died and gone to heaven."

"That's what your look and touch does to me. I'm hot, instantly."

"Hold that thought until Friday."

"What? Why?"

Bryce grins from my reaction. "Tonight is hockey, then after the game, the guys want to hang out at The Bull. Thursday night—I've been forgetting to tell you because I've had too much on my mind lately—is dinner and a medal ceremony for the fire department. I want you to wear that dress I like."

"Oh, I'm invited?"

"Always, Angel. You're invited everywhere I go."

"Don't forget we've got the gala Saturday night," I say.

"Right. Fire department Christmas party next Friday."

"What should I wear to that? Is it formal?"

"Yes, big event. Tuxedos and gowns, dancing after dinner."

"Oh, okay. Jeez, you weren't kidding when you said it was a busy week. On my way home, I'll grab something to eat for the ride to the arena."

"Sounds good. Better get moving, we'll be late." Bryce smacks my butt then takes me by the hand, pulling me to the front door. He gives me a scorching kiss, revving up my libido.

I don't have time to recover before he pulls me out the front door.

We stop abruptly. Lindsay is standing there. She's crying.

Oh, crap. Did she hear about Bryce proposing to me? I spin my ring to the inside of my finger and cover it with my right hand, trying to conceal it.

Wait. Why should I care if she sees it?

Because Bryce doesn't need her hysterical when he's trying to get to work on time.

Bracing myself for a fight, I stand stock still, waiting for her to lunge at me at any moment. Bryce must be thinking the same thing because he moves between the two of us, protecting me. But she just keeps crying, wiping her tears, and trying to say something unintelligible.

"Lindsay, I can't understand what you're saying," Bryce says, clearly irritated.

Abruptly, she stops crying.

That's pretty impressive. I frown. *What game is she playing?*

"He broke up with me," Lindsay spits out.

Jeez, that's a surprise.

"I don't have time for this. You'll have to cry on someone else's shoulder, I have to get to work." Bryce guides me to my Journey in the garage, leaving Lindsay standing at the front door, shocked.

"See you tonight, Angel." Bryce kisses me and then climbs into the driver's seat of his truck. He pulls out of the garage first and I follow, maneuvering around Lindsay's car.

I look in my rearview mirror.

She has her arms crossed and she looks miserable.

Bryce is finally learning how she manipulates people.

I'm proud that he's not taking her crap anymore.

Leena sinks into the passenger seat when I pick her up at Austin's. "Hey girlfriend, how was your romantic evening with Bryce?"

"Amazing!" My mind does a recap of all the impressive moments yesterday. "He says he's not romantic, but he blows me away with unexpected surprises. And you knew the whole time."

She chuckles. "And I almost gave it away."

"Hey, how would you like to help me with the arrangements for the wedding?"

"Really?" Leena squeals. "Oh my God! This will be the event of the year." She claps her hands together.

"Bryce wants to get married on a beach or in a church and then have a big reception. He's thinking maybe three-hundred-and-fifty people. Oh, and he wants this to be arranged in six months."

"What? You've got to be kidding."

"I know. They have a huge family. Did I ever mention that Garrett has ten siblings and Deana has eight?"

"Get out! I have to get working on this right away."

"Oh, I forgot to tell you. We had an unexpected visitor this morning."

"Who?"

"Lindsay."

Leena's eyes widen. "No! What happened? Catfight?" She looks me over. "You look pretty good for having a catfight."

I giggle. "No catfight."

"Damn! Kay, what happened?"

"She was crying, wiping her tears. Bryce told her he couldn't understand what she was saying and she stopped crying," I say, snapping my fingers.

"Really? Just like that?"

"I know. She's up to something."

"So what'd she say? Did she find out about your engagement?"

"I don't think so. She blurted out, 'He broke up with me.'"

"Did she really think the new guy would put up with her crap?"

"Bryce said, 'I don't have time for this, you'll have to cry on someone else's shoulder.'"

"Really?" She nods. "Well, good for him!"

We pull up to the studio and start our trek up two flights of stairs. "I know, eh, I'm glad he's not taking her crap anymore. He was actually kind of rude to her."

"Do you think he would've acted differently if you weren't standing right there?"

"I don't know. I'm hoping he's done with her."

When we enter the studio, a ten-foot Christmas tree decorated with fancy ornaments and thousands of lights catches my eye, along with a fireplace and mantle and furniture to make it look like a cozy living room. Leena and I sit on the plush sectional. "Shyanne this looks great. And this couch is comfortable."

"It turned out good. We borrowed the furniture, so be careful people and let's get to work."

Leena and I head over to the high-backed chairs, where the makeup artist goes to work applying Avionté cosmetics. Then they have us wear shimmery party dresses for the Christmas scene. After lunch, we have a few more wardrobe and makeup changes and some close-ups.

The day flies by, we're so busy.

Wednesday night at the arena, Leena and I settle into our usual spot in the grandstand behind both teams, people-watching, gabbing, and waiting for the guys to come out on the ice. A three-year-old girl with long blonde ringlets is jumping from one step to the other. Leena and I smile at each other. She's so cute. Her big blue eyes and little voice are infectiously adorable.

"That's what your little girl will look like."

"Think so?"

"Oh yeah, you and Bryce will have gorgeous kids."

"Thanks, you and Austin will too."

Leena nudges me. "Here comes your friend."

16

J LOOK OVER TO see Blake staring at me as she passes by to sit in her usual spot thirty feet away.

"What was that look for?" Leena asks.

"I know, that was a weird smirk. Makes me wonder what she's done now."

"Maybe that was a congratulating smirk for your engagement."

"Yeah, right."

"You know, the way she looks at you has me thinking she's plotting something. She's got an evil look in her eye."

"I know. I don't like her. She's one of those women who thrives on creating chaos."

Bryce skates onto the ice and starts taking practise shots at the net. I instantly dismiss the look Blake gave me. When he's done, he skates toward the bench, looks up, gives me his gorgeous dimpled smile, and nods his head. Damn, he's irresistible. That sexy, cool persona he displays in front of everyone else has me clenching my thighs together, remembering how he made love to me last night. He flips a switch when he's out in the public eye. He's admirable, responsible, the kind of man every man wants to be. But when he's with me, I see his playful, vulnerable side, and I wouldn't want him any other way.

"Did you hear me? Hello? Earth to Keera. You in there?" Leena taps her finger on my temple. "Christ you've got that fuck-me look on your face. Did I interrupt your sex- filled dream?"

"Yes, you did. What?" I ask a little irritated.

"You are too funny. Although, I have to admit, watching Austin play hockey gets me hot, too. Anyway, I was saying she keeps throwing darts your way. I don't think she likes you too much."

"Ignore her. I am." I nudge Leena. "Look, Austin and Bryce are facing off."

The ref drops the puck and Bryce and Austin shove at each other, digging frantically to gain control of it. Austin wins the faceoff and skates toward the firefighter's end of the ice. Bryce skates after him and the moment he checks Austin, he passes the puck to one of the other cops. Dante slides in next to the cop with the puck and they fight for it, inching closer to the net. The Cops score their first goal in the first two minutes. Austin grins ridiculously as Bryce shakes his head, smiling. The firefighters try hard to get a goal, first period, second period and then they finally succeed in the third period. Jax pops that one in, top right corner of the net. Cops 1, Firefighters 1.

Both teams gather around their benches for pep talks. Dante stands, turns toward us, and waves. I wave back and Bryce playfully thumps him in the back of the head to pay attention.

When Bryce's line skates back out on the ice, so does Austin's. Dante faces off with the cop that scored.

Dante steals the puck from him and passes to Bryce. Bryce and Jax head down the ice, passing constantly. Dante joins them and, between the three of them, the cops can't touch the puck. Bryce shoots the puck between the goalie's pads and scores.

Firefighters 2, Cops 1, with three minutes left on the clock. The intensity of the game shoots through the roof and I find both Leena and I are becoming louder, more aggressive, shouting from the edge of our seats.

The other line of firefighters skate onto the ice and keep the cops from scoring.

Bryce's line enters the ice with only one minute left on the clock. The arena is erupting. Adrenaline is rushing through my veins. It's so exciting!

Jax steals the puck away from one of the cops during the faceoff and passes to Bryce. Bryce and Dante head down the ice, passing back and forth. Jax joins them, checking one of the cops. When he regains his stride, Dante passes him the puck. They inch closer to the net with ten seconds left on the clock. Jax fakes a shot to Dante, quickly changing his mind, and passes it to Bryce. Bryce shoots and scores, top left corner of the net. Jax and Dante jump on Bryce's back trying to tackle him to the ice, congratulating him, but Bryce holds them both up and skates to the bench. My cheeks hurt from smiling. I look over at Austin. He can't hide his grin either.

Firefighters 3, Cops 1.

We file out of the bleachers and into the warm lobby, where we lean against the wall, waiting for the guys.

Leena tugs my arm. "Come on, got to hit the little girls' room. Maybe Blake will follow us and we'll get the dirt on what she's been up to."

"You love drama, don't you?"

"Hell, yeah."

There's a lineup in the washroom, so we have to wait for a stall. Once inside, to my surprise, Leena doesn't say a word. I assume she's listening for Blake and Trish to enter.

When we leave the washroom, Blake is standing against a railing, talking to Trish. She scans my body, inspecting me.

Glad I wore my favourite jeans.

I nonchalantly look her way. *Crap! She looks good.*

Feeling uncomfortable, I turn my back to her.

Leena stares over my shoulder. "Forget the darts. She's throwing knives at your back now. Damn girl! She doesn't like you."

"The way she's staring is making me feel uncomfortable."

"I can tell."

The guys burst through the double doors with their equipment over their shoulders and sticks in hand. They are freshly showered and looking hotter than ever with their wet hair, and they smell fantastic.

Bryce drops his equipment next to me and wraps his arm around my waist. His eyes gleam as he looks in mine. "Feel that?"

I smile. "Yes, I feel it." I pull him down to whisper in his ear. "I want you so bad right now." Electricity crackles all around us.

Bryce smiles and then kisses me.

"Good game," I say. "Two goals."

Bryce's hand lowers, skimming across my butt. "Thanks, Angel."

Dante slides in next to us. "Hi, Keera."

"Hi, Dante."

"Are we heading to The Bull?" he asks.

"Yeah, in a couple of minutes." Bryce glances around, searching. "Mom and Dad here?"

"No. I was looking for them," I say, glancing around.

"Let's get out of here." Bryce tosses his equipment over his shoulder and leads the way out of the arena. "We'll see them tomorrow night."

At The Bull, after Bryce, Austin, Jax, and Dante greet all the regulars by slapping them on the back, we head over to the table we normally occupy.

The waitress comes over and then disappears with our drink orders. She's back in a flash, distributing drinks as the guys finish recapping the game filled with lots of laughter. It doesn't take long for the place to fill up after a game. All the cops, firefighters, wives, and girlfriends occupy the tables at the back of the bar. When we finish our first drink, a good song comes on and Bryce and I follow Leena and Austin to the packed dance floor.

After a couple of songs, we sit down, waiting for the waitress to come over. Bryce squeezes my knee. "Be back in a few. I'll get us a drink." I watch Bryce's sexy ass saunter to the bar, where he waits patiently to place his order.

Out of the corner of my eye, I see Dante looking at something under the table.

Looking more closely, I see it's a picture of Blake. Naked. "Where'd you get that?"

He looks up from the picture to see me staring at it. "Bryce gave it to me. It was stuffed in his locker." His eyes widen. "Oh shit! By the look on your face maybe I shouldn't have told you that, eh?"

My face feels warm as I look over to the bar where Bryce is standing.

What was he thinking when he found it?

"When did Bryce find that?"

"Maybe I should keep my mouth shut. Bryce will kill me."

I narrow my eyes, hoping Dante sees my look as saying, *Don't fuck with me right now.* "When?" I demand.

"Okay, okay. It was today."

That bitch! She was grinning at me because of the picture. She must have heard around the station that Bryce proposed to me and she's trying any tactic to get his attention.

I glance Bryce's way again and see Blake tunnelling through people to get to him. She touches his shoulder. When he turns to look at her, he moves over and pays. He grabs our drinks and leaves her standing there. That was a little rude on Bryce's part, but if she's hounding him constantly, she deserves the cold shoulder.

Bryce distributes drinks around the table and then sits beside me, squeezing my thigh. I stare at him, waiting for an explanation. He looks sideways at me. "What?"

"I saw that."

"Angel, I didn't say a word to her."

"I know. Do you have anything tell me?" I talk next to his ear because the music is loud.

"Like what?"

I glare at him.

Dante turns red, sliding off his barstool to stand. He touches Bryce's back. "Sorry man. She saw me looking at the picture."

"Fuck's sake! I was going to tell you tonight when we got home. Sorry you had to find out this way."

"So what exactly happened? How'd you get the picture?" I need to see if Dante's story and Bryce's are the same.

"I opened my locker and it fell to the floor. Dante picked it up and said, 'Holy fuck, this is Blake.' I automatically looked at it, but I didn't know she was naked until I saw it. I told Dante to keep it because I could care less. She's conniving, manipulating … I try to keep my distance from her."

"At the arena, she walked by me grinning and I knew she was up to something."

Leena gives us a concerned look from the other side of the table.

I'll have to tell her in the washroom where it's quiet.

"Ignore Blake. She's not ruining our evening." Bryce runs his hand down my back, reassuring me. "Come with me. I want to dance." Bryce takes my hand and I slip my butt off the high-backed barstool. A slow song comes on and we're lost in the music, slowly swaying to the beat, holding each other tight.

Bryce looks into my eyes, concerned about how I'm dealing with the naked picture. "I'm sorry. Should've known Dante wouldn't keep it to himself. I wanted to tell you once we got home. It's too hard to carry on a conversation in here."

"I know. It's loud."

"Do you want to get out of here? We can go home."

"It's early. Don't you want to hang out with your friends?"

"I want to be with you."

I pull him down for a soft kiss. "I love you. You know that?"

"Yes, I see it in your eyes. I love you, Angel."

The song ends and Leena nudges me. "Time to hit the ladies' room."

"I'll be waiting for the next dance," Bryce says as he slowly lets go of my hand. Bryce and Austin head back to the table.

Leena takes my arm and leans into me. "What's going on? I'm in the dark here."

Once we get inside the washroom, the loud music is muffled and we can talk now. There's a small lineup. Leena and I rest against the wall.

I tell her what's going on, talking low. "Blake slipped a naked picture of herself into Bryce's locker."

Her eyes widen. "Get out! That's why she was grinning at you. That evil bitch! Does she think that'll help her get Bryce?"

I motion for her to tone it down.

"Sorry," she whispers. "So, what did he do when he found it?"

"It fell to the floor and Dante scooped it up before Bryce had a chance to look at it. Dante said this is Blake, so Bryce automatically looked. Bryce told Dante to keep it. I caught Dante looking at it underneath the table."

"I was wondering what he was doing over there. And then I saw the look on your face and I knew something was up."

"He started spilling his guts and then he said, 'Oh shit, by the look on your face maybe I shouldn't have said anything.'"

"Dante," Leena says, shaking her head. "He's clueless."

"I asked him when Bryce found the picture and he clammed up right away. He said, 'Bryce will kill me.' I gave him a look and he spilled it. Blake stuffed it in his locker today."

"So Tuesday, Bryce proposes and Wednesday she slips a naked picture of herself into his locker? She's not giving up, is she?"

The stalls become available and we slip inside.

On the way out of the washroom, the short and stocky guy from last week stands in my way and I stop abruptly.

"What the hell?" Leena says, irritated, as she bumps into me from behind. "Why is it you always stop, coming out of the washroom?"

I move sideways so she can see.

"You're here again," he says. "I was hoping you'd be here. Can you save me a dance?"

I open my mouth to speak and Leena says. "Have you seen her fiancé? Wishful thinking on your part. He'd kill you. Out of the way!" She shoves his shoulder.

I turn to look at her as we're squeezing through people. "Leena, that was rude!"

"He's the jackass from last week. You need to shut assholes like that down."

I chuckle and climb on the barstool. Bryce and Jax are talking and laughing at something. Bryce squeezes my knee, a sign that he's happy I'm back. With his other hand, he slides a cold beer in front of me. "Here, Angel."

I run my hand down the inside of his thigh. "Thanks."

During the course of the evening, the volume of the music lowers for ten minutes, allowing people to talk. This is one of those times. We talk and laugh, enjoying everyone's company.

When the music starts to play again, the short, stalky guy stands next to me and touches my arm. "Can I have this dance, Keera?"

I look over at Leena and she's glaring at him.

"Sorry, I'm dancing with my fiancé. Ready, Babe?" I look at Bryce, who's giving the guy an icy stare. I take his hand and pull him to the dance floor.

"That's the little bastard who was hounding you last week."

"Yeah."

"He'd better disappear."

I rub his back while we dance to calm him.

After two dances, Dante squeezes Bryce's shoulder. "Come on, Jax is riding the bull!"

Bryce looks at me for confirmation. I smile and he tugs me, but I grab Leena and motion for her and Austin to follow us.

We stand at the bullpen waiting for Jax's turn. He climbs on, wraps the rope around his hand, punches his fist closed, and lifts his other arm in the air. The bull operator starts out slow. When he sees Jax holding on, he moves the joystick side to side, then up and down, trying to knock him off.

A couple of times, I think Jax will go soaring but he holds on, lasting the entire eight seconds.

We all cheer, patting him on the back. When I turn to look at Leena, I see the short and stalky guy speaking with Blake.

Dante slaps Bryce on the back. "Your turn, big guy."

"Some other time," Bryce says.

Short, stalky guy tugs at my arm again as Blake looks on. "Can I have that dance now, Keera?"

Bryce protectively slides in front of me and glares down at him. "You bother my fiancé again and we're going outside."

Dante, Jax, and Austin gather around. Austin blurts out, "We got a problem here?"

Three of short and stalky's friends crowd around with their chests heaving.

Oh crap! This isn't good.

Short and stalky throws his hands up. "No problem." He walks over to the bar and his friends follow.

Austin says, "I knew he'd see it my way."

A moment later, the guy walks over to Blake, laughing and shaking his head. She laughs with him, and that's when I read her lips. "You tried."

I look over at Leena, who's clearly seen what I did. I talk against her ear. "What is she up to?"

"Looks like she's trying to keep you busy so she can sink her claws into Bryce."

"Not happening."

I get close to Bryce and rub against him. "I thought there would be a fight."

"He'd better back off and leave you alone."

"Come on, let's get another drink and then we'll dance."

The rest of the night goes smoothly, hanging out and dancing, having a good time with everyone. By the time we leave, I have a glow on. Bryce protectively grips my waist, guiding me to the truck. After saying our goodbyes to everyone in the parking lot, Bryce helps me into the truck.

I giggle when I clumsily lift my leg and fall back into his embrace.

He chuckles, picks me up in his arms and tosses me on the seat like I weigh absolutely nothing. When he gets in the truck, he glances sideways at me, twice. "What?"

Running my hand across the bulge in his pants, I smile seductively, lick my bottom lip, and bite on it.

"Aw, shit! We're supposed to wait until Friday."

"But I don't want to wait, I want this." I cup his balls and grab the outline of his cock through his jeans.

"Let me pull out of the parking lot." He pulls the seat back and I fumble to get his pants undone. He lifts his butt off the seat and I help shimmy them down to his knees. Wrapping my fingers around his shaft, I can feel his cock grow in my hand. Lying across the seat kicking my feet in the air, I lick my lips and take him deep in my mouth.

"Aw fuck, Angel." He groans. "Your mouth feels so good."

My pussy clenches instinctively with the sound of his husky voice. I go to work lifting and lowering at a very fast pace, while I stroke simultaneously.

"Oh yeah, like that."

I reach down to fondle his balls and they tighten within seconds. "You're going to make me come." I keep up the same relentless rhythm. Bryce rubs my back. "Angel, you've got to stop!"

I keep going.

He taps my butt. "Angel, I want to come inside you."

I run my finger on the soft spot below and then grab his balls giving them a slight squeeze one last time. I lift and wipe with the back of my hand. "Let's hurry, I can't wait to fuck you."

He chuckles as he steps on the gas a little harder. "I'm driving as fast as I can."

Inside the house, Bryce kicks the front door closed and attacks my clothing. Piece by piece it's strewn about in the foyer, up the stairs, and down the hall. We try to keep our lips fused in a hot, steamy kiss. We pull apart, panting, when I lift Bryce's shirt over his head. Then I push him against the wall and work on his pants, pulling them down. He steps out of them.

Pinning me against the other wall, a glass picture falls, hitting the floor without breaking. We look at each other and laugh before our lips meet in another hot kiss.

When we make it to the bed, Bryce places his hand on my chest and pushes me down onto the mattress. He climbs up my body, slowly, stealthily, ready to pounce. He hovers, pinning my hands on either side of my head. "I should make you wait until Friday, like we agreed," he says with a wicked grin.

"I never agreed to that! And you wouldn't dare!" I try to pull my hands free to tackle him but he's too strong and I've learned if Bryce decides he wants to hold me in a certain position, he will until he sees fit to let me go.

"Wouldn't I?" He gives me his mischievous grin.

I get one hand free and grasp his cock, stroking up and down fast. He moans and his body jerks from my touch. "We wouldn't want to waste this."

He closes his eyes, absorbing the sensations. "I might let you have a little fun." He kneels up, releasing my other hand. I rise from the bed, throwing my body against his, trying to tackle him, but I can't move him an inch. He smirks at me and then gives in, falling to the bed.

With me now on top, I straddle his hips, placing his cock between my pussy lips. I twine our fingers together, trapping him against the mattress, my hair surrounding our faces.

"Now what are you going to do to me?" he asks in a deep gruff voice.

I seal my lips to his, kissing him softly at first, then deepening the kiss. I make my way down his body, kissing lightly, travelling south. "I'm going to finish what I started in the truck."

He opens his legs and I settle between them. When I look up, he has his hands behind his head in a sexy pose I love.

I lie on my belly kicking my legs back and forth in the air, staring at his large, shaved balls. I grin and lick upwards. They tighten immediately and I'm rewarded with his body quivering. I do it again. One side, then the other, and up the middle again.

"Fuck, Angel, that feels so good."

I straddle his calf, grinding into him. Taking hold of his shaft, I lower my mouth onto his cock. He groans and grips my head, guiding my mouth up and down.

I work him into a frenzy within two minutes. Then without warning, he snatches it away from me. He spins and pushes me down onto the mattress. "My turn." He opens my legs roughly and then dives for it, pleasuring me with his finger and magical tongue. My fingers find their way through the silky strands of his hair, gripping tightly, holding his mouth to my clit as he flicks it wildly. My breathing slows and sweat starts to form at my temple. His finger pounds the hell out of me, not stopping. When he sees I'm close, he hits that concealed button inside, taking me higher and higher, sending me over the edge, quivering.

"Babe, it's so good." The strength of my orgasm has me lifting my butt off the bed. I grip the sheets. When I lower, my legs shake uncontrollably. He doesn't stop until he sees I've gone limp. Giving my clit one last flick that makes my pelvis spasm, he kisses his way up my belly to my nipples, covering them with his warm mouth. He holds himself up with one arm, muscles bulging, and positions his cock at my entrance, slapping the head back and forth, saturating it with my juices, and then slamming balls deep in one fierce drive.

I gasp. "That's what I want."

"And I'm the man to give it to you."

Bryce gives it to me hard, maintaining the same relentless pace where sweat starts to cover his skin from the intense workout. "Angel."

I know he's close. I reach between us and circle my clit. He grabs hold of my ankles, spreading my legs as wide as they can go in the air. His muscles are bulging everywhere. My eyes inspect and admire everything about him. His abs tighten as he slams into me repeatedly. His cock disappears inside me. He gives me everything he has every time he makes love to me.

"You're so sexy and beautiful. Christ, Angel, you turn me on!"

"I'm with you. Let go."

He doesn't. He holds out until he sees me shaking. Two more fierce drives and he comes hard, emptying himself inside me. I watch the beautiful features on his face strain. His eyes close and then open again. Every muscle in his body tightens and releases and then tightens again.

Breathless, he collapses, his full weight falling on me and his cock jerking inside. Grasping his ass cheeks, I pull him into me. When he catches his breath, he says, "You want more?"

"Always."

"I'll have to give you a rain check on that." He yawns, rolls over, and nuzzles in my neck.

"You're exhausted," I say.

He doesn't answer me and I think he's pretending he's fallen asleep. I wait. He's not moving.

I lift a fraction to wake him but there's no response. If he's had a busy day at work, followed by a hockey game where he's given a hundred-and-ten percent, I find it drains him and he needs to sleep. He never denies me though.

Did he fall asleep?

He mumbles, "I love you."

I caress his cheek. "I love you, Babe. Sleep."

I set the alarm and then cuddle into Bryce's side.

17

THURSDAY AFTER WORK I have to pick up Bryce's tux for the gala Saturday, then I have to rush to get ready for the medal ceremony at six.

A quick touch up to my hair and makeup, then I change into the dress Bryce likes.

On the drive to the medal ceremony, Bryce apologizes over and over for falling asleep last night. I tell him he's allowed to be exhausted. I snuggle into his side and say, "Besides, it may happen to me one day." He squeezes me and kisses my hair.

When we arrive at the banquet hall, it becomes clear this event is a big deal. We check in with highly decorated men and women in full dress uniforms at a table to our left. They cross off our names, finding the table we're assigned to and escort us to it.

Bryce's parents come in shortly after we sit.

To my relief, they are assigned to our table.

Bryce stands and pulls out his mom's chair.

"Thank you," Deana says with love in her eyes as she caresses her son's hand and kisses his cheek.

She sits and touches my arm. "You look beautiful, Keera."

"Thank you. So do you. I love your dress."

She hugs me. "Congratulations on your engagement. I'm so happy for you two." She takes my hand in hers and looks at the ring Bryce gave me. "It's beautiful."

"Thank you. Bryce had it made like the one we saw in Aruba. I love it. I can't stop looking at it."

A loud noise at the room's entrance diverts our attention.

Garrett makes his way closer to the table, shaking a few hands and then sits when he hears the bagpipes playing.

We watch a procession of firefighters and chiefs in full dress uniforms file into the room and fan out at the stage.

A highly decorated chief stands at the podium to introduce himself and address the crowd. "After dinner, we will start the medal ceremony." He takes his hat off, bows his head, and says grace.

During dinner, Bryce leans over to speak to his dad a few times, but the conversation that stands out is when Bryce asks, "How's that transfer coming along?"

"In the works," Garrett replies.

"Good. It's getting worse!" Bryce says with a stern look.

I wonder what they're talking about, but soon forget when the waiter asks me if I want tea or coffee.

Once the tables are clean, the medal ceremony starts.

With every medal awarded, the Deputy Chief describes the situation. If they have pictures or video, they play it on the big screen behind the stage. Some of the survivors of accidents or fires get up on stage with the firefighters to thank them when they're presented with the medal.

"Bryce Hamilton," the Chief calls out. He squeezes my knee as he rises from his chair, then he makes his way to the stage. Everyone is watching him. My eyes lock on him too, unable to look away from his powerful, confident stride. Once on stage, he turns toward the audience and I can't help but smile from his stunning good looks and the way his full dress uniform fits him to perfection.

I'm proud he is mine.

A man and woman follow Bryce up when they are called. They show pictures of the accident and it strikes me then: this is the accident at Highway 11 near the off-ramp when Bryce saved the mom and two kids. He handed the children out the back window to Austin and had just released the mom's trapped foot and got them out safely when the vehicle went up in flames.

They play the video and I tense seeing how close Bryce was to losing his life.

Oh, God! I could have lost him that day.

When the video ends, I glance over to Deana and see she has tears in her eyes. The woman hugs Bryce and thanks him for saving her babies. Her chest heaves for her next breath as her emotions get the best of her. The woman's husband shakes Bryce's hand and thanks him for saving his family. Bryce receives his medal of bravery from the Chief and gets a standing ovation for his selfless act of courage. I grab the napkin off the table and dab at the corners of my eyes, then continue clapping.

Why didn't Bryce tell me he was receiving a medal? Did he want to surprise me?

Well, he did that. I'm blown away.

As Bryce makes his way to our table, several people stop him to shake his hand.

Clearly, we are not the only ones who are proud of him. He's made a lasting impression on everyone.

Bryce sits down grasping my knee, and looks into my eyes. He glances at Deana and then looks back at me. He squeezes my knee tighter and I welcome his reassurance after seeing the video. When he shows me the medal, I run my fingers over it and then hand it to Deana and Garrett.

The ceremony finishes after a few more names are called out and then we get up to dance.

Deana and Garrett join us. Deana hugs Bryce and tells him how proud she is. Garrett shakes Bryce's hand, congratulating him. When I look in Garrett's eyes, they're glossy.

A lump forms in my throat once again. They're as proud as I am.

Bryce amazes me every day.

Did Lindsay not see the admirable and respectable side of him? Or maybe she did, but it was too overwhelming. She did whatever she could to keep him to herself. She was afraid of losing him, so she tried to control him. In the end, that was why she lost him.

Bryce sees the look on my face and tugs me into his side. I pull him down to talk against his ear. "I'm so proud of you. You amaze me every day."

"Thank you, Angel."

We dance like we've been professional partners for years and when I look at Deana and Garrett, they're smiling at us. I give them my biggest smile, loving how they dance to perfection. Their gracefulness is a lesson Bryce and I need to perfect. I look around, noticing how many people are watching them as they glide effortlessly around the dance floor. My smile is also a silent thank you to Deana for teaching Bryce how to dance.

The evening is memorable and when we make it back to Bryce's house, I step closer, helping him undo the buttons on his uniform shirt. "Why didn't you tell me you were receiving a medal?"

"Wasn't one-hundred-percent sure. Had a feeling because they invited us. Then once I heard my parents got an invite, I was a little more positive I was receiving one."

"Babe, watching that video … I was getting emotional. I was so scared for you. Austin was scared, too. It was written on his face. But once you got her out of the car, I was so proud of you. I love you." I hug him tightly. "Please don't die on me," I whisper.

Bryce separates us to look into my eyes. "Angel, I'm not going anywhere." He picks me up in his arms and kisses me. His lips are soft and skilled, and he shows the perfect amount of aggression. I'm only vaguely aware that we're moving until we've reached the bedroom.

Bryce sets me down beside the bed and holds my face in his

hands. "I don't want you worrying." He stares directly into my eyes. "Listen to me good. We will be together forever." His lips meet mine in a heated kiss. When we pull away, he reaches behind to unzip my dress. "Now let's see this fall to the floor."

As I'm making breakfast Friday morning, Bryce sneaks in from behind and kisses my cheek. "I told myself I needed to grow a set of balls to come out here and tell you. I've been trying all week. I'm sorry."

I spin in his arms. "What's wrong?"

He holds me tighter and I know something is desperately wrong. "Grant told me that lunatic stalker only got fifteen months because he had no priors. His lawyer seems to think it's too much time and is appealing the decision. The time he's served reduces his sentence. He could be out in a year."

"Oh, God!" I shake my head. "Will this ever be over? Will I worry for the rest of my life? I guess writing my victim impact statement didn't do a damn thing."

"Grant said the prosecuting attorney read it at his trial and the judge was moved by it but because he had no priors, his lawyer fought to get his time reduced."

"I was enjoying life with no worries."

"I know, I'm sorry. Grant said he'd let us know the moment he gets out of jail. He said they'll have a police officer following him and if he comes anywhere near you, they'll throw him back in jail."

"They'll follow him for a couple of weeks." I put my head down, sad and disgusted.

Bryce lifts my chin, forcing me to look up. "I'm sorry Angel, I've been meaning to tell you but I wanted you to sleep at night."

"No. I need to know."

"The moment he gets out of jail, you're staying here with me in Barrie. When I get a couple of days off, we'll go to the cabin."

"Babe, I can't abandon my house because of that lunatic."

"You're right. You'll have me with you. Always. There will be no staying at Leena's. Whenever we're in Huntsville, I'll be right beside you. He's never getting the opportunity to abduct you again."

Monday, Bryce worried about Colton showing up at my new job. Tuesday, he worried about the proposal and whether everything would go smoothly. Wednesday, he found the picture in his locker and he had to deal with me when I found out. Thursday was the medal ceremony. There wasn't a good time to tell me, we've been so busy. What a huge burden to be carrying around all week. Bryce is always trying to protect me.

"Babe, I don't want you worrying. You need to tell me as soon as you get new information. I'm a big girl. I can handle it."

"I can see that."

My first week with Avionté Cosmetics has gone well and I enjoy working every day with Leena. We accomplish a great deal.

Bryce calls me on his lunch break to tell me he'll be busy after work at his dad's helping Jax fix his truck, so on our way home from the studio, Leena and I stray to the naughty shop superstore.

When we walk in, my eyes widen at the huge selection of lingerie and intimate apparel at the front of the store. Along the wall close by is a variety of quality costumes with accessories to finish off the ensembles. Leena grabs a nurse's costume off the rack and holds it up against me. "Keera, you've got to try this on."

"Yeah?"

"Oh, yeah. It has your name written all over it." She pulls me to the dressing room. "Here, this one's available." She pushes me in with the costume. Moments later, she's throwing stockings over the stall door. "Slip those babies on with these fuck-me heels." She slides the shoes under the door.

I slide the lace-top stockings on and shimmy into the tight

mini-dress in record time, knowing she'll be asking what's taking so long.

"Christ, you making a career out of it? Hurry! I want to see." She claps her hands together. "Get your ass out here!"

"I am. Wait a minute. Oh crap!"

"What?"

"I can't come out there. My ass is showing."

"Open the door. Let me see."

I open the door reluctantly.

"Oh my God, Keera! This will blow Bryce's mind—and his load."

"Think so?"

She pulls me out of the dressing room. "Girls, what do you think?" She looks at the two girls behind the counter in the middle of the store and they're smiling from ear to ear.

"He'll love it!" one says.

"Wow! You look great!" the other one says.

I'm feeling self-conscious about my ass hanging out, so I try to yank it down.

"Quit doing that. You've got a great ass." Leena spins me around. "Doesn't she have a great ass?" She smacks it and the girls laugh. "You are not leaving this store without it!"

"Okay, okay." I go in to change and when I come out Leena is in the dressing room. "What are you trying on?"

"Cops costume."

"Hurry up! I want to see it." I try to irritate her like she did to me.

"Hold on to your horses, I'll be out in a sec."

Leena comes out wearing thigh-high black boots, showing some major cleavage, and looking amazing.

"Wow! That is sexy. Spin." I motion for her to turn around. "Your ass is showing, too." I smack it and I hear the girls behind the counter laugh. "You have to get that. Austin will love it."

"We are having fun tonight. I'll handcuff him to the bed."

"We have quite an assortment against the far wall," one of the girls points out.

After Leena changes, we check out the selection of handcuffs and then make our way toward the vibrators. "Holy crap! Look at this one. You'd have to be loosey-goosey to fit that thing inside you. It's huge!" Leena says, loud enough that everyone in the store can hear her.

I turn to see the girls behind the counter giggling once again.

Leena picks up another vibrator with a cord attached to it. "This is the Hitachi!" She spins it around to get a closer look. "Jesus, look at this thing. It's the Binford 2000. That'll make ya squirt."

I laugh. "Leena, you are something else."

"What?"

"Everyone can hear you," I whisper, embarrassed.

"So maybe they shouldn't be listening if I'm offending them." She saunters closer to the girls behind the counter and whispers, "Will this make ya squirt?"

She's loud enough that I can hear her. I look over to see the girls smiling but they do answer her seriously.

"They've been known to do that."

"That's our top-selling vibrator."

"I'm getting this, too," Leena says. "My first pay cheque is already spent."

I take the same vibrator to the counter as Leena looks at an assortment of leather whips.

"Keera, come here. I want to try this on you."

"Hell, no! Try it on Austin." I turn to see her smacking her own butt. "Are you done, or are you buying everything in the store?"

"I'm done." She slides the four-foot whip on the counter. "I'll take this, too."

"I do have to say, I've enjoyed having you two come in the store. Most people are uptight," one of the girls says as she rings us up. "You're hilarious."

"Yeah." I smile. "What an experience this has been."

"You love me and you know it," Leena says proudly.

When we walk outside to cross the parking lot, I notice Lindsay sitting in her car watching us.

"Lindsay alert! Three o'clock," I warn Leena.

"Blue car?"

"Yeah."

"Does she follow you everywhere?"

"Not that I've noticed. The mall, when we were jogging that day, a couple days ago, and now."

"She's not hiding. She obviously wants you to see her."

"Maybe she's getting up the nerve to hit me with her car."

"If she wants to talk to you, why wouldn't she come in the store?"

"Lindsay's not into that S&M shit."

Leena chuckles. "Girl doesn't know what she's missing."

We get into my Journey and, as I leave the parking lot, I watch her follow us onto the road in my rearview mirror.

A few blocks away, we stop to get a couple pizzas and she stops too, observing us when we walk in and out of the store.

"She's kind of freaky, you know that?"

"What does she want?" I ask as we get in the car. "I'm tempted to tap on her window and ask."

"Think she found out about the proposal?" Leena's eyebrows shoot up.

"I don't know, could be."

"I was expecting her to come into the pizza joint and cause a scene."

"Boy, do we think alike." I pull onto the road again and Lindsay follows closely behind to Austin's house.

Leena gets out of my Journey and looks directly at Lindsay as she sits in her car on the road. "She is definitely different. Let me know if you have any problems with her."

"Okay. See you Monday." I wave.

Leena gathers her bags from the backseat, grabs a pizza, and heads for the door but waits to see if Lindsay will follow me.

She does.

I drive two roads over and pull into Bryce's garage.

Bryce is home so I dash into the house and hide the bag from the naughty store in the front closet.

I want to surprise him. I've been waiting for everything to calm down from our busy week and Friday is my night to show Bryce how much I appreciate all he's done for me. His amazing proposal will be etched in my mind forever.

He hears me come in. "Angel?" he says as he strides to the top of the steps.

"Hi," I say as I close the closet door. A tingle runs through my body and I can't hide it. "How was your day?"

"Better now," he says.

I crinkle my nose. "Maybe you spoke too soon."

"Why?"

"Lindsay's been following me." I tip my head toward the door. "I think she pulled into the driveway." I hand Bryce the pizza and give him a kiss.

He places it in the kitchen and then walks to the front window. "Damn it!"

"Maybe she'll leave."

The doorbell rings.

"Don't answer that. I'll deal with her," Bryce says as he walks past me. He opens the door and steps out, leaving the door open a crack.

"What now, Lindsay?" His voice is angry.

I stand behind the door, eavesdropping.

She sighs heavily.

There is silence for a few seconds. *Is she crying again?*

"What does she have that I don't?" Lindsay asks in a soft, shaky voice. "Why her, Bryce?"

I hear Bryce huff out a deep breath—a clear sign, he's trying to be patient. "Do you want the truth? Will you listen to the truth?"

"Yes, I need the truth."

"Keera doesn't play head games with me. Our relationship is easy. We get along great. Never fight. Someday you'll realize that people will not put up with your shit. You can't manipulate people and think they'll stick around. You've got to change."

This is my chance to get the bag into the bedroom. I grab it from the closet and as I'm about to turn, I hear, "I can change. Please don't marry her."

18

HE FOUND OUT about the proposal. I dart up the stairs and hide the bag in the bedroom closet. I rush back, stepping gently so she won't hear me, and I eavesdrop again.

"You need to move on with your life."

"I can't. I tried. I love you."

"Try again. You'll find the right guy. I've got to go."

I sit on the stairs and listen intently.

"Bryce, please."

"Bye, Lindsay." Bryce comes back in and locks the door behind him. I wait for him to speak, gauging what kind of mood he's in. He holds out his hand for me to take. "Come on, let's go eat, I'm starving." I don't say a word while I warm up the pizza under the broiler. Bryce takes his pager and phone off his hip, charging them on the counter. "I wanted to have a nice quiet evening getting lost in you."

"We can still do that." I get closer to Bryce and rub against him. He's quiet. Thinking.

I wait for him to say something.

"She found out about our engagement."

"I heard. I was listening." I walk to the stove, turn on the light, and then turn to look at him again. His face looks grim. "And this is exactly what she wants. She's playing you. It's another one of her games."

"I know. But the look on her face ... I hope she doesn't do something stupid."

"Not your problem anymore. Do you see how she's manipulating you? She's fucking with your head again. It's the guilt trip," I say calmly.

"I know." He's silent throughout dinner.

I wait momentarily and then tell him my thoughts. "I don't mean to be a heartless bitch, but I see how she's playing you. She knows how to get to you. Screw with your mind. The other day, when she caught us outside, she stopped crying instantly when you told her you couldn't understand a word she was saying. Who can do that? I know I can't. She's a damn good actress. It's all in her game." I make a face and raise one eyebrow.

No response. Crap!

I wait until he's done eating and then I ask softly, "Do you regret proposing to me?"

He brings me to the couch. "Come here. Lay with me."

I look deep in his eyes, trying to determine his mood and what his response will be.

"Never, Angel. How could you think that?"

"Your mood has drastically changed from when I stepped in the door."

He lets out a deep breath of air, hesitating for a second. "It was the look she gave me. That look has been stuck in my head forever from when she hurt herself."

"I'm sorry you had to deal with that. Did she cut herself bad? Was it deep?"

"No. Enough to make her bleed but at the time I thought it was bad."

"Has she done anything to harm herself since then?"

"No."

Jeez, that's a surprise. She would do absolutely anything to keep him. And it worked. He stayed with her for a couple more months.

His lips brush my cheek and he holds me in a tight embrace as his mind wanders. We're both silent and I worry.

What if he gives in to her again because he doesn't want to break her heart? What if he breaks my heart?

"Come with me. Let's fix this." Bryce stands and pulls me into his arms.

"Fix what?" We shuffle over to the stereo and Bryce pops in Brantley Gilbert's, "Fall Into Me."

"My mood."

We dance, lost in the moment, lost in each other. But something tells me he's still thinking about the look Lindsay gave him.

I try a distraction when the music comes to an end. "Will you do something for me? I'll return the favour."

"For you? Anything."

I run to the bedroom closet and hurry back with his tux in my hand. He makes a face, rolling his eyes. "You got me," he says, clearly annoyed.

"Please, we have to make sure it fits. If it doesn't, we have to get alterations in the morning."

"Fine." He starts stripping right there in the living room.

My eyes are having a hard time turning away but I know I have to so I can pull this off. "I'll be right back." I sprint to the bedroom and quickly dress in the nurses' costume while he's busy in the living room. Once I get the lace stockings, nurse's cap, and high heels on, I look in the mirror. "Ready for this Bryce?" I ask my reflection softly.

Walking down the hall, I see him adjusting his tie in the mirror. He sees me out of the corner of his eye and stops what he's doing. Turning slowly, he gawks. His eyebrows arch as his eyes travel the length of my body.

A mysterious smile forms on his beautiful mouth and I wonder what he's thinking.

The way he looks at me diminishes my thoughts of Lindsay and makes me feel like I'm his whole world. I'm cherished by this Greek god standing before me in a dashing tuxedo.

He clears his throat but doesn't speak. His eyes devour my body.

I think he's at a loss for words.

I couldn't have asked for a better reaction.

"I heard you weren't feeling well," I say seductively, closing the space between us. My eyes scan up and down his body, loving how his black tuxedo fits him perfectly.

I don't think I've ever seen a man look hotter. I can't take my eyes off him. "Heard you need a nurse to make you feel better." I purr.

"You're trying to kill me. Angel, are you hot!"

"Thank you." I inch closer and run my hands behind the silk lapels of his tuxedo jacket. "But I'm supposed to make you feel better. Not kill you."

"I'm feeling much better," he says in a slow, husky voice as his hands roam freely over the curve of my butt. Around and around he caresses my sensitive skin behind the garters.

"I feel that," I say seductively.

He pulls me hard into his steely erection. "Feel that?"

"Mmm, yes. I want it!"

"Anything for you," he says in that sexy drawl.

"Look at you." I hold him at arm's length as my eyes inspect his muscular body beneath this debonair tuxedo. "Damn, Babe! I've never seen a man look so hot! You are definitely getting laid in this."

"A sure thing, eh?" Bryce sticks his finger down my cleavage, slowly caressing one breast and then the other. My breath hitches and I hold it in, watching as he sets the mood and my skin on fire. "So soft." His eyes move from my cleavage to my lips and his hand weaves through my hair. His other hand holds my lower back, pulling me hard into him once again.

Oh my, he's rock hard.

He likes my costume.

His luscious lips hold steady, half an inch from mine, hesitating, driving me mad. He's the one killing me, of anticipation. A tingle shot through me the moment I saw him in his tux and now all I want is for him to take away this edgy, restless feeling. His hand moves from my neck to my cheek and he runs his thumb over my bottom lip. "So beautiful."

"Kiss me."

His lips curve wickedly, then lower to mine in a slow, sensual kiss, sending that tingle south once again.

Taking him by the hand, I lead him down the hall to the bedroom. When I glance back, his head is tilted sideways and he's focusing on my ass. "Nice view," he says in a deep resonate voice.

"You, mister, are being a naughty boy. I may have to punish you."

His infectious grin makes me smile.

Once in the bedroom, I spin him around and start slowly, peeling off his tux.

He watches my every move.

After hanging the tux back in the closet, I turn to see him straightening from a bent position.

He was checking out my butt!

"On your back, bad boy." I point to the bed. "Time for your massage."

Bryce doesn't say a word. He gets into position and I climb on stealthily as he does to me. I straddle his hips and go to work massaging every aching muscle.

His eyes widen when he sees my skirt riding up. "Jesus, Angel." He shakes his head and smiles. "You're every guy's wet dream."

"Thank you."

His hands skim my thighs and I grab them, stopping them from moving up further.

"Uh-uh." I shake my head. "No touching your nurse."

He smirks.

"Arms up," I instruct, and he does it. I run my hands over his, massaging all the way to his armpits. I continue to his massive chest, down his washboard abs, to his hips, making sure to miss his vital organ. I massage his large thighs, working out the tight muscles in his calves and then I rub his feet. He flinches when I get to his instep and he pulls away.

"Roll over." I motion.

I straddle his butt and start at the top, digging my thumbs into the hard muscles in his back, gripping his shoulders, squeezing and kneading. I dig my fingers into his neck muscles with circular motions. He moans.

"You like this don't you?"

"You're good at this, Angel."

"Nurse Johnson to you."

I get a side view of his cheeks bunching up as he smiles. Making circular motions with the palms of my hands, I splay my fingers massaging his large, powerful back for a few minutes. I can tell he's enjoying it immensely from his deep, throaty moans.

Moving to his lower back, I poke my thumbs into the tight muscles and then I rub his perfect tight ass.

Before I finish, his big arm pushes me down and he tackles me, climbing on top. I giggle.

"My turn," he says, pinning me to the mattress.

I wasn't able to give him his sponge bath. He takes over, controlling me, taking his time, caressing and massaging every inch of my body. A night I'll never forget. I don't think he will either.

The camera flashes blind us as we step out of the limo upon arrival at the Alaina Gala. Bryce protectively wraps me in a hug as he holds my waist.

One photographer gets too close and personal, so Bryce holds his arm out, shielding me, making sure the photographer keeps his distance while we walk the red carpet to the ballroom entrance.

All this attention has my head spinning, wondering what the big deal is. We're not anyone of significance. Why are they acting like this? I turn to see if anyone famous is behind us.

No. It's just us. I look up at Bryce and he glances at me, grinning, almost like he can read my mind.

Once inside, a beautiful brunette in a stunning royal-blue dress ushers us over to the coat check and then to the cascading waterfall fountain where a photographer takes mine and Bryce's picture.

From there, she walks us over to the two massive dynasty floor vases, which stand on each side of the curved grand marble staircase.

I halt and stand stock still, looking around.

This massive royal ballroom is decorated in pink and could hold at least three-thousand people. The five floor-to-ceiling rounded-top windows are spaced on the opposite wall to look out onto beautiful Lake Ontario. I can see the night skyline of lights. It's beautiful.

Over the PA system, I hear, "Miss Keera Johnson and Mr. Bryce Hamilton."

Down below are twenty-five steps or more and all the guests converge and mingle amongst themselves in the main auditorium.

I tense.

"Don't worry Angel, I won't let you fall."

How does he know what I'm thinking?

Lifting the bottom of my dress a fraction, I grab his hand that's holding my waist and we gracefully descend the stairs. All eyes seem to be upon us.

Holy crap! I'm so nervous.

When I hear a grumble from Bryce's throat and I feel him tense, I look to see why.

Following his line of sight to the people down below, I see Colton making his way through the crowd.

He's stopped by several people who want to speak with him but Colton's eyes stay glued to us as we walk down the stairs.

When Bryce hoisted me up in his truck to come here, me in my beautiful evening gown, I thought he was a little paranoid because we were driving to the limo company. His plan was to divert Colton from finding out where he lives. Bryce doesn't want an unexpected visit from him one day.

Obviously, he wasn't being paranoid.

Colton is here. He wasn't lying when he said he'd be back in three weeks.

We finish our descent and I'm relieved when I make it to the bottom of the marble staircase without tripping.

Chaz is at the front of the reception line with his staff, smiling and greeting everyone who enters.

"Hi, Chaz, nice to see you again. This is my fiancé, Bryce."

"Good to see you. You look beautiful." He hugs me. "Fiancé?" He holds me at arm's length for a moment while he recovers. "Nice to meet you … Bryce?"

Bryce shakes his hand firmly. "Nice to meet you."

"Well, you two enjoy yourselves this evening," Chaz says, looking a bit confused.

We move down the line shaking hands with Brent, the photographers, and the assistants who helped with the Alaina photo shoot. Then, out of the corner of my eye, I spot Josie wearing a dress that matches her beautiful auburn hair. I make my way down to her.

"Look at you," she says, smiling, as she holds my hands and looks me over. "You're beautiful. Who did your makeup and hair?"

"I did," I say proudly. "I had a good teacher." I give her a hug. "I love this colour on you." I say, touching her curls. I turn and run my hand down Bryce's back. "Josie, this is my fiancé, Bryce."

"Fiancé?" Josie touches Bryce's arm. "Congratulations."

Bryce surprises Josie by giving her a hug. "Thank you," he says, blinding her with his perfect white-teeth smile. "Keera told me how she really enjoyed working with you at the photo shoot."

Josie is noticeably flustered now from Bryce's irresistible charm.

I stand back and watch, proud he's mine.

She takes my hand. "I want to hear all about the proposal after," she gushes.

I'm sensing Chaz and Josie are surprised by our engagement. I think they were hoping to hook me up with Colton.

Josie touches Bryce's arm again. "It was nice meeting you. I'll see you two later."

Bryce and I make our way through the rest of the reception line and then head through the crowd, toward the bar.

"That wasn't fair, what you did to Josie," I say.

"What? What did I do?"

"You know damn well what you did. You were charming the pants off her. Or should I say dress?"

Bryce smirks at me.

A waiter, holding a tray of colourful crystal champagne glasses, stops before us. "Champagne?" he asks, handing me one before I have a chance to answer.

"Thank you," I say, taking the flute from him. When he turns away from us, I shrug my shoulders at Bryce.

"Don't drink it if you don't want it. We'll bring it to the bar."

"I'll try it." I take a sip. "This is good. Try this." I lift the flute to Bryce's lips.

Bryce shakes his head. "No thanks."

I glance around the room, noticing how many waiters and waitresses are dressed in short black tuxedoes with tails. They mingle, distributing appetizers and champagne to all the guests.

A larger-than-life picture of me in the red dress catches my eye. It's from the photo shoot. It hangs high above our heads, on the wall behind Bryce. "Babe, look at that picture!"

Bryce turns, taking a look, and then motions his head the other way. "There's a couple more of you along each wall."

I scan the room in a circular motion. "Holy crap, I was so nervous coming down the stairs, I didn't notice." I stop dead at the picture of me in my bikini. "Damn it! Why did they have to hang that picture up there?"

A husky voice invades our conversation.

"Because you're so beautiful." Colton steps out from behind someone, targeting my lips for a kiss. But I quickly turn and give him my cheek.

19

OW! RIGHT IN front of Bryce. What is Colton thinking?
"Hello there, beautiful. How have you been?"
Colton nods in Bryce's direction. "Bryce."

A growl emerges from deep within Bryce's throat. "Colton," Bryce says, sounding irritated.

"Good. How have you been?" I say, trying to break the icy stares and tension between the two of them.

"I'm good. Our new CD is topping the charts. 'You Belong in My Arms' hit number one," Colton says, throwing it in Bryce's face that he wrote a song for me.

"Congratulations," I say not wanting to be rude, but I can see Colton trying to get on Bryce's nerves already.

Bryce wraps his arm around my waist. "Maybe we can have this conversation later. We were making our way to the bar." Bryce leads me away. "I need a drink." He says next to my ear.

"I'll come with you," Colton says from behind.

At the bar, a spot becomes available and we squeeze in, leaning against it, waiting for a bartender to take our order.

I hear a familiar voice from behind and feel a hand on my hip, so I turn to see who it is. "Reese, how are you?"

Reese's eyes float up and down the length of my body. "Wow! That's all I've got to say is, wow!"

I smile, remembering he said that exact phrase the day I wore my slinky, pink bikini in Aruba.

The bartender slides our drinks in front of us. I finish the champagne and pour my Bud Light Lime into the crystal flute. Can't walk around looking like I'm drinking beer while dressed up like this. My mom wouldn't be impressed.

Reese and Colton slide in, ordering their drinks just before they close the bar for dinner. I don't think Bryce noticed when Colton rubs against me as he squeezes by.

I ignore it because I'm paying attention to Chaz over the intercom ushering everyone into the dining room.

Down the hall, at one of the arched doorways, several decorative boards on easels illustrate where each guest has been assigned to sit.

We find our table and get comfortable on the crisp, white-linen, high-backed chairs. Pink silk ribbons with large bows hold the covers in place.

Looking around this massive dining room, my eyes dart from one spot to another taking in the beautiful pink decorations, noticing how much time and energy must have gone into preparing for this event. It is absolutely amazing.

The centrepiece is a two-foot, etched-glass hurricane vase filled with bubbling water. A blue, pink and purple light at the base illuminates the cylinder and a candle floats on top. It's mesmerizing. Everyone who sits at our table comments at how stunning it is.

The champagne and beer are running through my veins now, helping me relax somewhat, but I'm still in a quiet mood.

My mind wanders and I replay the look Bryce gave me when I came out of his bedroom with this dress on.

He'd seen the pictures of me wearing it, but in real life, it must be better because he couldn't take his eyes off me. A half smile formed on his beautiful face and his eyes travelled my body, zeroing in on my cleavage. He inched his way closer and then tugged me into his semi-erect cock. His finger caressed my breasts and he followed the outline of the opening, which shows exposed skin half- way down my belly. I shivered and smiled at him, feeling his cock grow between the two of us. He said, "Angel, you're beautiful! Gorgeous! I can't take my eyes off you."

Seeing Bryce in his tux—muscles bulging beneath the fabric, groomed, his hair styled to perfection and his body smelling of his cologne—made my mouth water. No man could look hotter. I wanted him bad at that moment.

Glancing sideways at him, I come back from my internal thoughts and shiver.

He grasps my thigh and gives me a knowing smile.

Looking around, I people watch, paying attention to the different hairstyles, the beautiful evening gowns, and how refined the men look in their tuxedos.

I look down, making sure I don't have a wardrobe malfunction. I smooth out my dress for no apparent reason, feeling nervous and self-conscious.

Then I go to my happy place, a place in my mind where I think of Bryce and me at the cabin, snowmobiling, or on the ATV in the wilderness. There, I don't have to worry about what people think. It's just me and him, enjoying each other's company.

Bryce notices I'm quiet. "Are you okay, Angel?"

"I'm okay. I feel out of my element here. It's a ritzy event. How are you doing?"

"I thought I was used to this kind of thing with the fire department. They host some pretty impressive parties, but none of this scale and nature."

"Yeah, I'm blown away. Chaz said it would be something to see."

Just then, a beautiful woman walks past our table and looks at

Bryce as he's speaking to me. "Yes, they did spend a lot of money on this event," Bryce says, paying no attention to the way she's looking at him.

I notice her. I notice what she's wearing, as does everyone in the vicinity. Her deep, V-neck, off-white, lace gown with a slit to her thigh is a sexy dress I would love to find. It has beads and large cut-outs on both her sides showing mostly skin. When I turn to look at Bryce, his eyes are on me. When I look back at her again, I pay attention to the way her hair is styled and the jewellery she's wearing.

Bryce doesn't turn her way. His eyes stay glued to me.

I wouldn't blame him if he did look at her. She's stunning.

A voice from behind, has Bryce and I turning around. "Hi Miss Johnson, I'm a representative for Transformations, a new cosmetics company. We'd love for you to consider us when you pick your next photo shoot. Here's my card. I won't bother you anymore."

"Thank you," I say, taking his card.

Just then, someone pulls out the two chairs to my left that were vacant.

I look over to see Colton and Reese settling in.

Oh crap!

Bryce lets out a heavy sigh. "Un-fucking-believable!" he mumbles.

"Hi," I say, covering up his outburst from the people sitting at our table. I turn to look at Bryce on my right. He doesn't look impressed. I turn back to Colton. He's grinning mischievously.

I'm learning that Colton thrives on pissing Bryce off.

Looking over at the next table, I see the rest of the band waving. I smile and wave back.

If I remember correctly, there was a Mr. and Mrs. Something-or-other assigned to sit next to me. I frown at Colton.

Did he bargain with the couple to trade seats?

Colton's leg touches mine and I move over instantly.

He moves his chair closer and plasters his leg against mine.

What do I say to him? I don't want to be rude and bring attention to it. Bryce wouldn't be happy. I feel how tense he is already with Colton next to me.

When the waiter and waitress start serving dinner, I use the opportunity to move closer to Bryce, away from Colton.

"Salad, Angel?"

"Yes. Please." I smile and run my hand down his thigh, feeling every hard muscle beneath his pants.

Bryce dishes salad onto my plate and then his, a habitual and considerate gesture that shows how thoughtful he is of me. The rest of the meal—pasta, roast beef, chicken, roasted potatoes, and vegetables—comes out in a steady stream.

I stare down at the silverware, not knowing which one to pick, and furtively look around the table at what everyone else is choosing. Colton runs his right hand down my thigh while, with his other hand, he shows me which fork he selects.

Bryce's leg is touching mine on the right and Colton's leg is against me on the left.

How awkward is this?

Occasionally, I move my leg away from Colton, but he finds his way back to touching me.

After dinner, I hear another voice behind me and Bryce, and we both turn to see who it is.

"Keera?" The man clears his throat. "Excuse me. Miss Johnson, I'm the vice president of Blue Caribbean swimwear. Here's my card. We would love for you to come work with us. I've sent you an e-mail with the details. Your pictures will be in all the top magazines. Please, consider us."

"Thank you," I say smiling, watching as he disappears. "Jeez, that's the second offer."

Colton pipes up. "Of course, who wouldn't want you?" He grins sideways at me. "They'd be fools not to scoop you up."

I grin at his comment.

"Need to hit the ladies' room?" Bryce asks. "I'll come with you."

"Sure."

Bryce stands and holds his hand out for me. As we make our way through the tables of this very large room, two more people stop to hand me their business cards, which I stow away in my purse.

When we make it down the hall to the washrooms, Bryce expresses his thoughts. "I think Colton's trying to piss me off. What do you think?"

"Yeah, I was thinking that earlier."

"What is he doing here anyway?" Bryce runs his hands through his hair as he paces the floor. "Stupid question. Forget it. I know why he's here."

"Babe, ignore him. I'm here with you. My fiancé. Who I love very much."

Bryce gives me a molten-hot kiss, curling my toes. When we separate, I'm breathless. "I'll be right here waiting," he says, in that deep, resonate voice.

"Be out in a few," I say, a bit disoriented.

The washroom is vacant so I look in the mirror, smiling, fixing my makeup.

How does Bryce do that? I'm like a teenage girl with a huge crush.

When I exit the washroom, Bryce is speaking with an older gentleman with salt-and-pepper hair. I lean against the wall across from them, waiting for Bryce to finish his conversation.

Bryce's apologetic eyes tell me he's trying to be quick.

People come and go, walking the hall to use the washroom. When I look up, Colton is standing before me. "I had to come here tonight, even though you sent that video. I need to see for myself if you still have that sparkle in your eye for me."

"Video? Colton, first, I don't know what you're talking about. And second, there is no sparkle. I love Bryce."

"You didn't send it? The video of your engagement?"

A vision of Shyanne handing Bryce the memory stick flashes

through my mind. I look around Colton and Bryce's eyes are locked on mine while he answers the gentleman.

"No. I didn't send it."

But I know who did.

That was Tuesday night after Bryce proposed to me. I woke and reached for Bryce beside me in bed, but he wasn't there. I searched for him down the hall and he was at the breakfast bar closing my laptop. He said he couldn't sleep. He wrapped his arms around me and urged me back to bed with him, where I fell asleep in his arms.

Bryce sees my wheels turning and he knows I know what he was up to that night: he was intent on sending the video to Colton.

"I had a feeling." Colton holds my hand to his heart. "It killed me seeing that." Lifting my hand, he looks at my ring. "If you were mine, you'd be wearing at least three or four karats."

I pull my hand away. "This is what I wanted. Something that big would be too much for my finger."

"I could give you the world—and I would, if you were mine."

Bryce stands beside us and clears his throat. "Ready, Angel?"

"Yes."

Bryce leads me away with a gentle touch on my hip.

Back at our table, the servers are clearing plates and distributing dessert. Bryce and I stand out of the way until they're finished and then Bryce motions for me to switch seats.

Bryce waits until the guests at our table are engrossed in conversation. "That fucker is still hitting on you."

"Babe, don't worry about him. I see no one but you. You've got me wrapped around your finger."

"You're right. He knows you're mine."

I have to ask even though I know the answer. I need to hear it from Bryce's mouth to see if he'll tell me the truth. "You sent Colton the video of our engagement?"

"Yes, so he'll back off and quit sending you e-mails. But obviously that didn't work."

"He'll eventually give up."

"Bar's open," Reese says standing behind our chairs.

"Thanks." Bryce gives Reese a nod and a smile.

I can tell Bryce likes Reese because he's not a major obstruction, unlike his older brother.

"Drink, Angel?"

"Sure."

Bryce stands to get drinks for us, but when he sees Colton in the vicinity, he holds his hand out for me to come with him.

I slide my hand in his and when we walk past the guys in the band, they stand, greeting us, and then follow us to the bar.

The line-up to get a drink is quite long and it takes a while to move to the front. We talk and joke, and they playfully slap one another on the back. Reese and Colton join us, animatedly talking about a few crazy incidents during their tour. I've missed these guys. We had a good time in Aruba.

Bryce looks like he's having a good time too. He seems to be more relaxed now that Colton isn't right beside me.

When Colton is finished speaking, he stands across from me and his eyes stay glued to the opening in my dress. It's distracting and it makes me feel, very uncomfortable. As the bartender distributes our drinks, we hear Chaz speaking into the microphone, testing it from the other room. He asks for his guests to return to the main auditorium.

We file out into the hallway with Bryce holding my waist and the guys in the band following behind.

Once inside, we notice they've opened large curtains to reveal a stage with stairs on each side.

Behind the stage on the large screen are pictures of Chaz's wife, Alaina. The video shows how Alaina started the modelling agency years ago from a small, two-room studio, to now, in the Alaina building. And how the company has grown to the massive empire it is today in every major city. The memorial picture states she died seven years ago.

My mind flashes back, remembering the huge picture of Alaina on the wall behind Chaz's desk. Josie had told me Chaz loved her dearly and he still grieves for her.

"This Alaina Gala marks ten-years since my beautiful wife started this amazing event. It was close to her heart and I think we've done a great job keeping it alive. We always try to raise money for her favourite charity, the Breast Cancer Society, and every year we try to surpass the amount we donated from the year before. We do this by having our top ten models come on stage to be auctioned off to the highest bidder in exchange for a dance with a beautiful woman. So, how about it ladies, would you like to help raise money for Alaina's charity?"

Jeez, nothing like being put on the spot. I tense and I feel Bryce tense, too.

I look at him, tilting my head to one side and shrugging my shoulders. He kisses my forehead. "It's okay. It's only one dance."

I smile at how understanding he is and grip his hand, letting him know how much I love and appreciate him.

Turning, I make my way through the crowd of people and up the stairs to the stage where the models are assembling. I search for Bryce in the crowd and see he's slowly inching his way closer to the stage. His eyes lock on mine.

I can barely take my eyes off him, but I do for a moment noticing how most of the women he's squeezing by can't take their eyes off of him, either.

Forget it, girls! He's mine!

Chaz introduces the first model to his right. She has short blonde hair and she's wearing a stunning, deep purple evening gown. She's beautiful. The spotlight pans over to her pictures on the wall. "How about it, gentleman? Who would like to dance with our lovely, Serenity?"

The auctioneer stands to our left, behind the podium talking fast into his microphone.

"Sold!" The auctioneer points. "Eleven-hundred dollars, to the man in the black tuxedo." The crowd applauds and laughs.

The model on Chaz's left is up next. She has a dark tan and long, black hair, and she's wearing a long, cream-coloured, off-the-shoulder gown.

She looks a little like Fiona, if I'm not mistaken. I watch as the bid goes from a man with blonde hair to Reese, who won't give up. They bid back and forth. Reese is having a good time irritating the poor man. In the end, Reese wins and the man shakes his hand, smiling.

"Sold!" The auctioneer smiles and points. "Twelve-hundred dollars, to the man in the black tuxedo."

The audience laughs again.

Chaz auctions off five more models, making me nervous every time he skips over me, and they leave, gracefully departing the stage.

I'm dying up here. I don't like this attention. I want to get off this stage!

A woman named Brandy is called next. She's wearing a teal Vera Wang dress, which fits her like a glove. She's stunningly beautiful, with brown wavy hair that falls to the middle of her back. We've been bonding a bit, standing up here whispering to each other about how nerve-wracking this is. This is her second year at this event, so at least she knew what was coming.

A good-looking man with brown hair bids back and forth with Drake, one of the guys in the band. I find myself hoping the man wins because of the way he looks at her.

He must be her husband.

"Sold!" The auctioneer points to Drake with his microphone. "Nineteen-hundred dollars to the screaming lunatic." Drake is hooting and hollering, jumping in the air, pumping his fist. The audience breaks out with laughter.

Brandy leaves the stage and I'm left with one more model.

They call her name next.

Crap! My eyes meet Bryce's again. He can tell how nervous I am. He cocks his head slightly and furrows his brows in a show of sympathy for me.

The last model is auctioned off, leaving the stage, and I'm left with Chaz and the auctioneer.

Chaz pulls me to his side. "You're looking a little nervous. Are you okay there, Keera?"

"Yeah. No. I'm fine." I blush and the audience laughs.

Oh, God! Let's get this over with!

"Okay, let the bidding begin for our beautiful Miss Keera Johnson." The spotlight moves from us to the pictures on the wall of me.

"Do I hear one-hundred dollars?"

Bryce lifts his hand and the auctioneer points at him, accepting his bid.

"Do I hear two-hundred dollars?"

"Five."

Everyone turns toward the voice and I see Colton's hand descending.

Oh, no!

"Do I hear six?"

"Six!" Bryce says.

The auctioneer says, "Seven-hundred dollars?"

"Twelve hundred!" Colton blurts out, and the whispering amongst the audience begins.

How awkward is this?

"Thirteen!" Bryce counters.

"Two grand!" Colton shouts.

With pleading eyes, I beg Bryce to stop. People begin to back away until there's an open circle with Bryce on one side and Colton on the other, staring each other down.

"Three!" Bryce says, his voice, loud and irritated.

"Four grand!" Colton says, slowly.

Bryce turns away from Colton and looks at me on the stage.

I shake my head no and plead with my eyes again.

He can't afford to hand out that kind of money. He has a house and a truck to pay for.

"Do I hear forty-one hundred?"

There's a pause of silence.

"Going once … going twice."

"Five grand," Chaz says, smirking at me.

What the heck is he doing? I thought this was over.

"Six grand!" Colton counters.

"Seven!" Chaz says, smiling mischievously at Colton.

What is he up to?

Oh, I get it. He's driving the price up for his wife's charity, knowing Colton won't stop until he gets what he wants.

"Ten. Grand!" Colton pauses between each word.

20

*T*HE AUDIENCE ERUPTS.

Oh, God, please let this be over.

"I'll let you off this time," Chaz says into the microphone, grinning at Colton.

"Sold!" The auctioneer points to Colton.

Colton holds his stare on me as if to say, *You are mine.*

Turning, I head down the stairs and over to Bryce.

He wraps me in a hug. "Sorry, Angel."

"Babe, you can't afford to compete with Colton. It's one dance."

He mutters something I can't understand.

"It'll be okay." I give him a warm, lush kiss.

"If I could have everyone's attention," Chaz says into the microphone, "Against the far wall is our silent auction with some wonderful gifts to be handed out to the highest bidders at midnight. I'd like to thank everyone for participating in our Tenth Annual Alaina Gala Auction. You've helped raise a lot of money for Alaina's favourite charity. Thank you all. We'll start with the auction dance if everyone can move to the side of the dance floor."

Bryce and I walk hand in hand to the wall waiting for everyone to disperse.

Looking across the room, I see Colton requesting a song from the DJ and then he struts contentedly through the crowd toward us to claim his dance.

All eyes are on us when Bryce wraps me in a hug, kissing me longer than what he normally does when people are watching.

When we separate, Colton is watching and waiting.

Is Bryce letting everyone know I'm his so Colton will behave himself on the dance floor? Is this another tactic in their pissing contest?

Whatever it is, I don't like how I feel. I'm a pawn in a chess game, tossed back and forth.

Although, I feel bad for Bryce. I try to put myself in his position. How would I feel losing to Lindsay, Fiona, or Blake? It would kill me. Rip me to pieces.

I place my hand on his cheek, pulling him down and then rest my forehead against his. "I'll be right back." I hesitate, waiting for a reaction from Bryce.

He's silent. His eyes tell me everything.

I turn and Colton takes my hand, leading me to the dance floor. We bump against Reese and his model, and Drake with Brandy.

The music starts to play and I tense the moment I hear the lyrics.

Oh, God! Bryce will lose his mind.

The song is, "You Belong in My Arms."

Colton takes me by surprise, swinging me around in one smooth move, wrapping me in his arms.

"I think you should behave yourself since everyone is watching," I say.

"Hell, no! I've got you in my arms and I'll enjoy every second of it. I've missed you." He hugs me tighter.

I pull away to speak to him, trying to distract him from this awkward moment. "Colton, you paid way too much for a dance."

"Money doesn't mean a thing to me, but you do."

Damn it! Walked right into that one.

"I knew Bryce was the one who sent that video and not you. I knew you couldn't break my heart like that."

"He sent it so you'd give up and move on."

"No. I don't give up easily. You're not married yet. And even if you were, people have affairs all the time."

"Colton, I'm not like that. When I marry Bryce, it'll be until the day we die."

"There are a lot of different circumstances that break up marriages and I'll wait for that day."

I sigh heavily. "Colton, I love Bryce. You need to find—"

Colton holds his finger over my lips shutting me up. "Does Bryce know we slept together?"

"No. We. Did. Not!" I say it slowly. "And you know it!"

"I don't know … I've got pictures on my phone that suggest otherwise."

I frown at him, disgusted. "Colton don't be like this! It doesn't suit you."

"You're right. I'm sorry." He wraps his arms around me. "Let me hold you for the rest of this dance. Please." We're silent as we dance slowly, swaying to the beat. He pulls back slightly and his eyes float to my cleavage where they hold steady, examining me. "Christ, that body of yours. You're so beautiful. I was counting the days, waiting to see you." Colton pulls me in by my waist. I tense, feeling his cock grow. He holds me tighter, sticking his nose in the crook of my neck and breathing in deeply. "You smell good." His lips and tongue run down my neck. I pull away.

"Colton!"

"Please. One night! Give me one night with you! You're all I think about! You know I could treat you better than him."

I look over at Bryce and he's pacing, running his hands through his hair.

"You know it will never happen. I love Bryce."

"That I don't believe. We were close in that hotel room. If you'd given me five more minutes, I would've had you back in that bed, making love to you. Your body was telling me yes. Too bad your mind told me no."

"I will always tell you no."

"But one of these times, your mind might deceive you. I could get you so hot, you wouldn't think straight. And you will give in to me. You'll be mine."

My mind does a replay of when Bryce seduced me the first day we were together. I tried to resist, but I failed.

Would my walls crumble in the heat of the moment with Colton?

No. Bryce has that special characteristic no one else has and I could not resist. Love. He is the one I will love forever.

I shake my head. "This is getting me nowhere."

"I know what I felt in that room. You felt it too."

I roll my eyes, shake my head, and purse my lips together tightly.

"Don't get mad at me. Please, let me hold you. Let me dance with you."

We dance in silence again, swaying to the beat.

There is one thing I need to know, it's been bothering me for a while. "I heard you set up the photo shoot with Chaz."

"I told you, when I want something bad enough, I will do absolutely anything to get it."

"You did? You set up the photo shoot?" I scowl at him.

"Don't be mad at me. I knew you'd be a great model."

I start to walk away, but he pulls me back. "I had to see you again." He holds me tight and won't let go. Half a minute later, he talks against my ear. "I can tell you're not dancing like you normally do. You're holding back for some reason. I want a personal dance like the one you gave Bryce in the hot tub."

I push him back at the chest but he holds me steady at my waist. "You were watching us!"

Colton smiles. "Damn, the way you move, I could watch you forever."

Heat crawls up my neck and face. I'm furious. I glance over his shoulder, see how many eyes are on us, and try to keep it together. *Calm down Keera, don't let him get to you.* It feels like my head wants to spin around three times and pop off.

That loud noise behind the fence in Aruba, it was Colton. Watching us.

And he has the nerve to tell me?

Does he have some kind of fetish about watching people have sex?

I knew it! Or I had a feeling he was watching us that night. *What is it with this guy?*

The song ends and I'm relieved.

I follow Brandy's lead by curtsying and tipping my head.

"Thank you for the dance, beautiful."

I turn to walk away but he grabs my hand and tugs me back, flattening me against his chest. "You can't leave me like this. Please don't be mad at me. I need you to know how much I love you and I would do absolutely anything to get you."

"You're welcome," I say, hoping he'll let go this time without creating a scene.

He loosens his grip and I turn to walk away. I march back to Bryce, take his hand, and lead him to the dance floor. People are still watching. I try to calm both him and me by rubbing his back and dancing like we normally do.

"What did he say?" Bryce asks.

The third degree. Here we go. "Can I tell you later? I don't want you to be any angrier than you are now. He's trying to get a reaction from both of us. Don't let him get to you."

Bryce breathes deeply. "You're right. He's not ruining our evening. He got his dance and that's all he'll get!"

By the time the song is done, Bryce has calmed down and we make our way to the bar.

Chaz is there with some of his staff and I finally get a chance to talk to Josie while Bryce lines up for our drinks.

I tell her how Bryce surprised me with his amazing proposal, how he planned everything from the ring he had made, to borrowing the firetruck and climbing the ladder to the balcony. And then I give details about the amazing restaurant he chose for dinner.

We both look over to Bryce at the bar.

"You are one lucky woman. And he's a fireman? Does he have any good-looking friends?"

I chuckle.

"Look at him," Josie says. "He can't take his eyes off you."

"I can't take my eyes off him."

"I see that." Josie smiles. "Neither can all the other women in this place. He sure does draw attention."

"I know, eh? And he's all mine."

"Look at you two." She looks from me to Bryce. "Now that is love. I was rooting for Colton but now that I've seen the way Bryce looks at you, I can see it's true love."

"Will you to come to the wedding?" I ask.

"Yes. I wouldn't miss it for the world." Josie points her chin toward Bryce. "Better go get him. Someone's moving in on your territory."

"I'll see you later." I touch her arm gently.

Moving slowly toward Bryce, I watch how he handles being hit on.

He smiles politely, saying only a few words to the woman and then turns his attention back to the bartender. When he turns and sees me, he's one-hundred-percent focused on me. I hope that look never fades.

When I make it over to Bryce, the woman who's been hitting on him stops talking. She can see the way he's looking at me.

"Ready, Angel?" Bryce nods her way, trying to be polite, and then guides me through the ballroom.

I stop abruptly after we've moved out of earshot. "Was she hitting on you?"

"Why?"

"Because I'm curious what she said."

"I'll tell you, when you tell me what Colton said."

"Fine," I say, frustrated, and continue to the washroom. I lean against the wall, holding Bryce's beer.

The moment Bryce disappears inside, Colton walks down the hall toward me. "Shit!" I whisper.

I watch as he approaches me.

Is he following us?

"See? You've still got that look in your eye for me."

"Colton." I shake my head. "I was wondering how you know where we are? Are you following us?"

"I need to talk to you."

"About what?"

"You and me."

"Colton, there is no you and me."

"Yes, there is. I'm not giving up. I'm sending you an e-mail."

"Please don't."

"Why? Because Bryce doesn't like it? You should be able to have friends. He shouldn't be controlling your life."

I remember that night in Niagara Falls when Colton tried to put a wedge between me and Bryce. How he said he worried about my safety because Bryce has a temper. Colton is still trying any tactic to break us up.

"I wouldn't like it if Bryce was e-mailing other women."

Just then, Bryce emerges from the washroom and takes my drink and his. "Colton," he says, icily.

"Bryce," Colton says, returning the ice.

"Oh, I don't have to go," I say quickly.

I can't leave them alone. They'll kill each other. I take my drink back from Bryce and lead him away from Colton.

"He's really pissing me off, hovering, waiting for the moment I leave you alone."

"Let's go dance," I say, coaxing him to stay in a good mood.

On the dance floor, we bump into Reese and his model, and Brandy with her husband.

Bryce's baritone voice rumbles against my neck as he sings, "The Lady in Red" to me, and it's the sweetest sound, sending delicious chills throughout my body. His mood starts to thaw as we dance. He's holding me tight and moving his hips like that night he did the strip-tease for me. The man can move.

I glance around the room noticing how many women are paying attention to the way he's moving and then I see Colton walk over to Reese. They talk and then Colton takes over dancing with Reese's model but he stays on the other side of the dance floor. Reese leaves to talk to the DJ.

A few moments later, Reese is standing beside us. "Hey, big guy. Can I have the next dance with Keera?" Bryce is silent, hesitating for a moment. "Please, I requested the perfect song." Bryce doesn't look happy, but he gives in only because he likes Reese. Bryce releases me and steps back. "I promise I'll give her back after this song."

Bryce takes a hold of Reese's shoulder, squeezing playfully. "You don't have a choice. One song. That's all you get." Bryce struts over to the wall, leaning in a relaxed position, but he watches closely.

Reese swings me around and dips me backward. I can't help but giggle. He's adorable. "But seriously, I need to tell you something." Reese instantly straightens, changing his form of dancing to professional. "We tell Colton all the time you're with Bryce and to forget about you, but do you think we can get that through his thick skull? We've tried to set him up with some hot models. He went out for one date and that's it. He can't stop thinking about you. I really do think he loves you."

"How? He doesn't know me."

"We've asked him the same question, many times."

"Reese, I'm going to marry Bryce."

"I know. Colton showed me the video. God, was he screwed up after he got that e-mail. He disappeared again after our concert in New York. Nobody could find him. We later found out he hopped on a plane to Toronto and then took a helicopter to your house. You weren't home."

"How did he find out where I live? I've never told him."

"When Colton wants something, there's no stopping him."

I'm learning that, real fast.

Colton and the model move in close, dancing beside us.

Reese shoves Colton playfully. "Hey, look, dumb ass, I didn't have to pay ten grand to dance with her." Colton gives Reese an irritated look, playfully shoving him back, and then his eyes move to me.

Bryce cuts in the moment the music ends. "I'll take over, thank you." He leads me away. When Bryce spins me around, I see Reese dancing with his model again and Colton is speaking with Chaz. His eyes stay glued to us, dancing.

After our dance, we saunter over to the silent auction, filling out Bryce's name and number for some of the gifts, hoping he wins the hockey tickets—Detroit Red Wings versus Toronto Maple Leafs.

It's after midnight now and we still have a long drive home from Toronto to Barrie. We both agree to head out.

Josie notices we're making our way to the marble stair-case, ready to leave, and she rushes over to give me a hug and say goodbye.

Chaz appears, trying to convince us to stay, but gives up when we tell him it's a long drive home.

The band members wave goodbye from a distance and we wave back.

Once we make it to the top of the stairs and down the hall, I stop abruptly in front of the washroom. "Babe, I've got to go. I won't make it back to Barrie."

"I'll wait for you here."

Five minutes later when I come out, Bryce is leaning against the wall in that sexy pose I love. He wraps me in a hug and nuzzles in my neck. "This was a good night."

"Yes, it was."

"Except for the shark trying to piss me off."

"You did a great job handling him. I'm proud of you." I run my hands down his hard chest and smile. "I can't wait to get this tux off you," I say, "because I know what's underneath."

Bryce leads me down the hall with that simple touch to my lower back. "Come with me. The faster we get home, the faster I get this dress off you." He grins with that gorgeous, corner of the mouth smile.

In the grand foyer, the guys in the band and some of the Alaina employees gather around the coat check waiting for the attendant to find their coats. She's overwhelmed and flustered from the flood of people. I feel bad for her and want to help. Josie and Chaz join us and are speaking with the photographers.

When the attendant finds our coats, I dig into Bryce's pocket and give her a hefty tip. She smiles. When I turn, Colton is right there in my personal space.

He pulls me into him by my waist, holds the back of my head, and seals his lips to mine, kissing me.

Holy shit!

Bryce shoves Colton back hard and I quickly move out of the way.

Colton shoves at Bryce, knocking a table over.

The brawl begins and swear words fly through the air as their hard bodies collide against one another.

Women scream in the background.

When they separate for a second, Bryce makes a fist, cocking his hand back. Colton does the same, ready to throw the first punch.

I step back farther to get out of the way.

Chaz and the band members spring into action separating and restraining them.

I look from Bryce to Colton.

Both their chests heave for air as rage consumes them. They look like they want to rip each other's heads off.

What the hell just happened?

I glare at Colton. *What are you thinking?* I shake my head at him. Disgusted.

He grins back at me.

All night he's been trying to piss Bryce off. Is this because of the proposal video? Whatever it is, Colton has pushed Bryce to his limit.

Bryce and Colton surge forward to fight again and women scream once more.

21

*A*LL THE GENTLEMEN close by jump in to restrain them again.

"Enough already, Colton!" Chaz shouts, holding him by his chest. "Keera, take Bryce home!" He says, looking my way.

Bryce turns to see the look on my face. He fixes his tuxedo jacket, regaining his composure.

To save us from further embarrassment, I grab Bryce's hand and lead him out of the building toward the limo waiting for us at the curb.

Big fluffy snowflakes are falling slowly, covering the red carpet with at least three inches. The temperature has dropped considerably. But at this moment, I don't care that I'm freezing without my coat on. I'm intent on moving past these photographers.

Our driver opens the door for us. Before I slip in, I use the limo door to shove back hard against a photographer who is leaning in with his large lens taking pictures through the opening.

I climb in first and Bryce follows.

"That fucking asshole!" Bryce punches the seat. "All night!

All-fucking-night he's been pushing my buttons!" He runs his fingers through his hair.

The limo driver starts to pull away from the gala, saving us from several blinding flashes as the photographers take pictures through the smoked-glass window.

I'm silent as I wait for Bryce to vent and calm down. My mind wanders to the ride here in the limo—how the sexual tension between the two of us crackled, leaving me with an edgy feeling. Neither one of us had made a move, most likely because we were dressed up and we didn't want to ruin his tux or my dress, but I had pictured how I wanted to seduce him later and what his reaction would be.

I look behind me, studying the smoked glass divider, making sure the driver can't see us.

Sitting across from Bryce, I pull my zipper down, slowly.

His eyes widen but he remains silent, watching my every move.

Then, his eyes squint and his right dimple appears when he sees me shimmy out of my dress.

Thank God I lost five pounds when I thought Bryce broke up with me, otherwise I'd never get this dress off.

Bryce smiles appreciatively when he sees I have nothing on underneath. "I had a feeling," he says. He's no longer in a bad mood. He's grinning and it's the sexiest grin I've ever seen. He takes my breath away.

I toss my dress on the other seat and prowl toward him on all fours, resting between his muscular thighs.

He tosses his tuxedo jacket and it lands next to my dress as he gets ready, positioning himself on the edge of the seat—a position that's sexier than all hell.

My fingers wrap around his hard cock and I massage him through his pants. "I want this."

"You can have it. Anything for you."

I go to work undressing him, kissing him fiercely as my fumbling fingers try to undo the buttons on his shirt, fast. Breathless and panting when we pull apart, Bryce rips open his shirt and the buttons scatter, falling to the limo floor.

I lean back on my heels. "Damn, that was hot!"

His shirt flies past me and he tugs his pants down, kicking them off with his shoes. His movements are fast and deliberate. He wants me. He wants me bad.

He pulls me in for another molten kiss.

He's gloriously naked now, positioning himself in that sexy pose with his hands locked behind his head. His jawline tightens as he stares back at me, a clear sign he's fighting the urge to lunge at me.

I'm kneeling before him. Admiring. "My God. Look at you!" His arm muscles bulge everywhere. My eyes float to his perfect chest and then down to his washboard abs. His thighs are huge and they're spread, waiting for me. My eyes follow straight to his beautiful cock. I lick my lips and climb aboard, holding his shoulders for support as I straddle him.

Grabbing his hard cock, I place it where I want it, grinding deliciously up and down, stroking myself against him. Then I focus on his muscles, which are bulging because of the pose he's in. He knows I can't resist running my hands down his arms. Taking his face in my hands, I kiss him slowly. Sensually. When we separate, I'm panting, my chest heaving for my next breath. Shifting onto one knee, I take hold of his heavy cock, rising enough to place his length beneath me, saturating the head with my juices. I sink down slowly.

"Christ! You feel good." He moans.

"Mmm, I've been waiting for this all night."

The limousine stops in traffic and teenagers in the car beside us hang out the window trying to see inside. I don't care who sees us. I want Bryce. I've wanted to seduce him in a limo from the first ride we took in Aruba, but Austin and Leena were with us at the time.

The tinted windows help to conceal what's really going on

inside and it makes me feel wild and reckless. Cars stream by us at a steady pace as I set a slow rhythm, lifting and lowering. I take his face in my hands, kissing him slowly, letting him know I'm not mad for what happened with Colton. But regret is etched on his face. "Sorry, Angel. I didn't mean to ruin your evening."

"Babe, you didn't ruin it. Any night with you is a great evening." I lift and lower. "Colton was trying anything to piss you off."

"Yeah." Bryce is in deep thought.

"Let's forget about what happened." I reposition myself, placing my feet on the seat, changing the angle as I descend. "Let's focus on this."

Bryce grasps my butt cheeks, guiding me up and down on his hard-as-stone cock. "Angel, that pussy of yours. Jesus, you fuck me so good."

"Your cock is so hard right now. Babe, ahh … it's so good."

"That's what you do to me. You drive me wild."

I find a steady rhythm, lifting and lowering.

"Did I not tell you we'd fuck like wild animals? That our love would be so strong you'd never be able to extinguish the flames?"

I hold his beautiful face in my hands and kiss him slowly, our tongues entwining. When we separate, I run my thumb over his bottom lip. "That was the first time you seduced me. I tried to resist. But you got me so hot and you've been doing it to me since then."

"Promise me whenever there's chaos in our lives, we always end up making love."

"I promise."

I wrap him in the biggest hug and kiss him. The kiss is hot and intense, almost to the point that I feel my lips swelling. My skin is misted from the workout and Bryce notices. He reaches over and turns the heat off. He's always in tune with my needs.

Lifting and lowering at a steady pace, I can see the signs he's losing control by his facial expressions and groans. A moment later, he tackles me to the seat and now he's on top. "No. We're taking this slow. We've got more than an hour's drive back to Barrie and I'm taking advantage of it."

He yanks me down with rough hands, positioning my body where he wants it on the seat as he settles between my thighs. "Let me see if my sweet pussy is wet." Bryce inserts his finger, holding his stare, watching my reaction as he explores inside me. "Christ, Angel, you're soaked."

"I've been like this from the moment I saw you in your tux. You're hot and you're all mine."

"And you are all mine!" He shakes his head, inspecting me. "Look at you. You're so sexy."

His magical hands caress every part of my body, gliding slowly, setting my skin on fire. His fingers flutter the soft skin between my thighs, and I find myself straining toward his hand so he'll keep touching me.

Bryce is showing me his dire need to make things right between us, even though I told him not to worry.

"I need to taste you." His wicked tongue torments and teases me to the brink of orgasm over and over again all the way home to Barrie.

When Bryce and I hear the beeping sound from the keypad buttons of the front door lock, we look down the stairs, wondering who is trying to enter his house this early in the morning.

Leena stumbles through the doorway, but quickly recovers making her way up the stairs to the kitchen to join us. "Oh, good. You're home."

"I told you we'd be home today."

Leena assesses Bryce with his uniform on. "Going to work?"

Before Bryce has a chance to answer, I do. "They called him in due to the snow we got last night."

Bryce collects his phone and pager, strapping them to his belt, then gives me a kiss. "Bye, Angel. You two have fun. Bye, Leena."

Bryce knows Leena will be digging for drama about what happened last night at the gala. I can hear it in his tone.

Leena waits until Bryce closes the door. "What the hell happened last night?" she asks, her face lighting up with excitement. "The pictures are all over the internet. Who got the first punch in? Colton or Bryce? Did you notice I was checking out Bryce's face? He looks pretty good so Bryce must've connected with Colton's. Did Bryce beat him bad? Are you going to answer me?"

"Not until you shut up! Jeez, I can't get a word in. They were about to throw a punch but Chaz and the guys in the band pulled them apart."

"So what happened?"

"Why? What pictures did you see?"

"Where's your laptop?"

"Dining room table."

Leena grabs it off the table and rushes back. "I could not wait to get here this morning!" She sits at the breakfast bar and I hand her a tea. "Explain this one," Leena says pointing to the screen.

"Let me start from the beginning. From the moment we got to the gala, Colton was right there making comments trying to piss Bryce off. He followed us everywhere. To the bar. To the washroom. Twice."

"I can't believe he showed up there."

"The moment I heard Bryce grumble when we were coming down the marble staircase, I had a feeling it was because of Colton. So the evening starts with Colton slipping out from behind someone and he targets my lips for a kiss. But I quickly turned and he got my cheek."

"I've never met a man with bigger balls."

"Yeah, I know. We were making small talk and then Colton tells us how his new album is topping the charts and his song, 'You Belong in My Arms,' hit number one. Bryce says, 'Maybe we can talk about this later, we we're making our way to the bar,' and he steers me away but then Colton follows us."

"Colton had you in his sights and he wasn't letting you go. Also, kind of conniving how he threw that dig in about him writing a song for you, don't you think?"

"I noticed right from the beginning how Colton was being a mischievous bugger. Like at dinner, when I look on the board for our assigned seating, Colton was at another table away from us. But somehow he coaxed a couple from our table to switch spots with him. Bryce wasn't impressed when Colton pulled out the chair next to me."

Leena laughs. "I wish I could've been sitting across the table from you guys. Bryce would've grumbled and his facial expression would've been priceless."

"You're getting to know him well. So during dinner, Colton kept touching me. I'd move away, but he'd find my leg again. The moment I finished dinner, Bryce asked me if I needed to go to the washroom."

"Bryce couldn't wait to get you away from Colton."

"When I came out of the washroom the first time, Bryce was speaking to an older gentleman, so I waited until he was finished. But of course, here comes Colton to talk to me. He asked me if I e-mailed the video of our engagement. Right then, I knew it was Bryce. I saw Shyanne hand him the memory stick the day he proposed to me. I questioned Bryce on it when he took me out for dinner that night. His answer was he wants to add it to our wedding video when we get one."

Leena scoffs. "No. Bryce knew all along what he wanted that video for. To rub it in Colton's face. To get him back for all the problems he's caused. Wow! I didn't know Bryce could be so devious."

"In Bryce's defence, he does whatever it takes to keep us together. He once told me that from the moment he saw me, he knew I was the one. He did everything in his power to get me, and now all he thinks about is keeping me. He's the type of guy who, when he wants something, he fights for it. So anyway, Colton said he had to see for himself whether I sent the video. But when he asked me, I was clueless. You should have seen the looks Colton and Bryce were exchanging."

"Oh, I bet."

"So then we head to the bar and into the ballroom where Chaz is up on stage raising money for Alaina's favourite charity. And the way they do that is by auctioning his top models off to the highest bidders. The winner receives a dance." I roll my eyes.

"Get out!"

"It was quite embarrassing, especially when the bidding war was between Colton and Bryce."

Leena rubs her hands together and squirms on her chair. "This is getting exciting!"

"The bidding begins with Bryce for a hundred dollars. Then I see Colton lowering his hand after bidding five hundred. Colton was then bidding by the thousands. I think Colton was trying to embarrass Bryce, knowing he couldn't compete."

"I can see Colton doing that. And he was probably enjoying every second of it."

"He was. Everyone could see the smirk on his face. So then the crowd opens up and they stare each other down. You should've heard the whispering going on in the crowd. They were enjoying the spectacle of dirty looks passed back and forth."

"I would've enjoyed it too."

"Once the bid got to three thousand, I was begging with my eyes for Bryce to stop. And he did, but then Chaz took over, raising the price for Alaina's charity, knowing Colton wouldn't back down until he got what he wanted. Colton bid ten-thousand dollars for a dance with me."

"Ten grand?"

"Yeah. So Colton got his dance but he wasn't behaving. He requested his song, 'You Belong in My Arms.'"

Leena chuckles. "Oh, another stab in Bryce's heart."

"I know. So once he gets me in his arms he says, 'I knew Bryce was the one who sent that video.' I say, 'He sent it so you'd give up and move on.' He says, 'No, I don't give up that easy. You're not married yet and even if you were, people have affairs all the time.' I said, 'I'm not like that. When I marry Bryce it will be until the day I die.' He comes back with, 'There are a lot of different circumstances that break up marriages and I'll wait for that day.'"

"Jesus, Keera, he's really thought this through."

"So then I told him again he needs to find someone new and he cut me off by saying, 'Does Bryce know we slept together?'"

"Get out!" Leena says, her eyes wide open. "He said that?"

"I know, I couldn't believe it either. I said, 'No, we did not and you know it.' He said, 'I don't know, I've got pictures on my phone that suggests otherwise.'"

"See, I told you he took more pictures of you! That's why he took your clothes off."

"I hope he's bullshitting about that. There better not be any more pictures of me. Anyway, I gave him the look."

"I know that look. The-don't-fuck-with-me look."

"I said, 'Colton, don't be like this, it doesn't suit you.'"

"What did he say?"

"He said, 'You're right, just let me hold you for the rest of the song.' So there we were, quiet, dancing slowly and then I felt his cock growing. He stuck his nose in my neck and said, 'You smell good,' and then he ran his lips down my neck. I pulled away. He said, 'Please. One night. Give me one night with you. You're all I think about.'"

"Keera, he has it bad for you."

"At that point, I looked over at Bryce and he was pacing, running his fingers through his hair."

"A clear sign that he's ready to lose his shit." Leena laughs.

"I don't know how he kept it together, but he did."

"He didn't want to cause a scene and embarrass you."

"I think you're right. Anyway, I said it would never happen because I love Bryce."

"That's good. You're telling him straight out."

"Yeah, but he's not listening. He thinks if he would've had five more minutes in that hotel room, he would've been making love to me. I said, 'Colton, I'm not like that.' He said, that one of these times my mind might deceive me, that he could get me so hot, I wouldn't be able to think straight and I'd give in to him, I'd be his."

"Holy fuck! He just doesn't stop."

"I know. It's like talking to a wall. So then he says, 'You're not dancing like you normally do. You're holding back for some reason.' He said, 'I want a personal dance like the one you gave Bryce in Aruba.'"

"What does he mean by that?"

"I forgot to tell you this? I was dancing for Bryce in the hot tub and we heard a loud noise beyond the fence. Turns out Colton was watching us have sex again. And then he has the nerve to tell me. I was furious and I couldn't do a damn thing because everyone was watching."

"He gets off on that, eh?"

"I think he has some kind of fetish. Anyway, I was relieved when the song ended. When I went over to Bryce, everyone was watching so I pulled him on the dance floor to calm him down. It took a while. He was mad."

"I would've loved to have been there watching the action go down."

"So later, when I'm standing outside the washroom waiting for Bryce, Colton walks down the hall toward me. He says, 'See, you still have that look in your eye for me.'"

Leena chuckles. "Conceited bastard, isn't he?"

"I said, 'How do you know where we are? Are you follow-ing us?' He side-steps the question and says, 'I need to talk to you.' I said, 'About what?' He says, 'About you and me.' I said, 'There is no you and me.' He said, 'Yes there is. I'm not giving up.' He wants to e-mail me something. I said, 'Please don't.' He said,

'Why? Bryce doesn't like it? He shouldn't be controlling your life.' I said, 'I wouldn't like it if Bryce were e-mailing other women.' That's when Bryce comes out of the washroom and takes both drinks from my hands. I take mine back and say, 'Oh, I don't have to go.' I couldn't leave them alone. They would have killed each other, going by the looks they were exchanging."

"To be a fly on the wall."

"So then, Bryce and I go dance and Reese cuts in. He tells me they set Colton up with a beautiful model. He went out on one date. He said Colton can't stop thinking about me. He said he thinks Colton loves me. I said, 'Reese, I'm going to marry Bryce.' He said, 'I know. Colton showed me the video.' He said Colton was screwed up after getting that e-mail. He disappeared after their concert in New York. No one could find him. He hopped on a plane to Toronto, then he took a chopper to my house. I wasn't home at the time."

"Wow! He really does have it bad for you. He's obsessed."

"I asked Reese how Colton found out where I lived. You didn't tell him. Did you?"

"Nope. Wasn't me. Don't think Austin would've said anything either."

"He found out. Maybe from Chaz. Anyway, that picture you're pointing at is after Colton kissed me with Bryce standing right there."

"What! He's got huge balls."

"I'd say so. We were at the coat check and I dug into Bryce's pocket for a tip. When I turned, Colton pulled me into him by my waist and held the back of my head. He kissed me right there with everyone watching. Bryce shoved his shoulder and once I backed up it was a free-for-all. Colton shoved back, a table crashed to the floor, and then they were in an all-out brawl. You should have heard them. It was like two buffalo colliding, crashing into one another. Women were screaming in the background."

"Damn it! I missed it all."

"Leena, it was terrible! All I could do was stand back and watch. If I'd gotten between them, I would've been crushed."

"Good thing you didn't."

"So anyway, this picture here." I point to the screen. "Is them getting ready to throw the first punch."

"Nobody connected?"

"No. All the men who were near the coat check at the time jumped in to separate them."

"That must've been so exciting! I wish I'd been there. So what about this picture?"

"They went at each other, pushing and shoving again."

"And this fight is because Colton's pissed that Bryce sent the video of your engagement? Or is Colton provoking Bryce so you'll see Bryce has a temper? Colton doesn't want you to marry Bryce."

"I never thought of that. He was trying any tactic to piss Bryce off."

"And he succeeded."

"Yes. Colton was a different person. He was pissing me off too."

"So what happened next?"

"After Bryce saw the expression on my face, he knew it was time to go. These pictures here are us leaving. See how mad Bryce is?"

"Yeah, I see that. He looks like he wants to rip someone's head off."

Leena plays a video.

I chuckle. "The paparazzi were right in our face. By the time we got to the limo, I'd had enough. This guy," I point, "had his camera right in the door. I used the door to shove him back. I was pissed."

"You go, girl! Don't take that shit from those leeches. What did Bryce say once you got in the limo?"

"He said, 'That fucking asshole! All night! All fucking night he's been pushing my buttons!' He finally calmed down when he saw me taking my dress off."

"You did not!" Leena says. "You did?"

"Yup! Made love all the way home. Something I've wanted to do since our first limo ride."

"That's on my bucket list, too. So, it was an eventful evening?"

"Definitely." I hold out my hand to show Leena. "Look at the cards I got from different companies wanting me to endorse their products."

"That's fantastic! Maybe I could be your assistant again?"

"Yeah, sure."

"Anything else happen?"

"No, that's pretty much it."

"All righty, then," she says, and drains her teacup. "What do you want to do today?"

"I was thinking I'd get my Christmas shopping done and look for a knockout dress for the fire department Christmas party."

"Great, let's go."

22

*B*RYCE WILL WORK most days around the clock this week to make up for needing last week on the day shift. He had to call in a few favours from his fellow firefighters to switch shifts with him to arrange the proposal and go to the medal ceremony and the gala.

It is my last week working for Avionté Cosmetics. It keeps me busy during the day while Bryce is working. Monday night, I work out and research the companies whose name are on the business cards I got from the gala.

Leena surprises me when she comes through the door at seven-thirty.

"What are you doing here?" I ask.

"Austin had to go to the station for some reason. I thought I'd come and see what you're up to."

"Doing research on some companies for my next job. Want a tea?"

"Would love one." Leena sits down at the breakfast bar behind my laptop and starts clicking away.

"By your tone, I'm guessing something is going on with you and Austin?"

"Last week was great! This week, I don't know what the hell his problem is. Maybe he needs space because he's used to living alone. I don't know. I haven't got a clue."

"We can hang out. You can stay over if you want. Bryce has to sleep at the station all week."

"Yeah, maybe. Aww, Keera, did you see these e-mails and pics from Colton?"

I hand Leena her tea. "No." I come around to look at my laptop. "Oh, shit!"

"I told you he had more pictures of you!" Leena opens the first and the next, and they progressively get worse as she opens them. "Did you read this?" Leena points.

"Life on the road is hard. I catch myself daydreaming, looking at these pictures and it helps me make it through the day. I dream of you waiting for me to get off stage and you jump in my arms congratulating me with a hug and a kiss. Then I can't wait to get you back to the bus to make love to you. Life on the road would make sense with you by my side and in my arms. Keera, my angel eyes, I need you! Call me, E-mail, please, I need to speak with you. I need to apologize. I love you. Colton."

"Is he out of his mind?" I ask.

"How will you explain these to Bryce?"

I start to pace back and forth, gathering my hair in a ponytail looking at the screen on my laptop. "I don't know! He'll most likely break up with me for conveniently forgetting some of the details of that night."

"You're going to show Bryce these pictures?"

"I have to. I thought I could spare Bryce the heartache but I need to get this out in the open. I should have told him the truth from the beginning. But I had no idea Colton could play dirty like this. He knows Bryce will see the pictures and Colton is hoping to break us up. Look at this one." I point to the one with Colton lying next to me in the hotel bed. He's naked, his body is plastered against mine and he's wearing a mischievous grin. The sheet rests, barely covering my nipples, making us both look like we're naked. But you can clearly see I'm sleeping. "Bryce will lose it! What am I going to do?"

Leena stands and holds my shoulders to stop me from pacing. "Calm down. Relax. Bryce loves you. Explain everything to him. He will understand. Bryce knows how manipulating Colton can be."

"Right. Bryce saw it at the gala and knows Colton will try to piss him off again." I look at the computer screen, my eyes glancing over the pictures, and I cringe, remembering how mad Bryce was at the fire station when he told me to leave. He'll lose his mind over this. "I don't know, Leena."

"Don't show him then. Delete them. Get a new e-mail address. There. Problem solved."

"I like my e-mail address. Besides, all the companies I've been in contact with have that e-mail."

"Send them a new one." Leena starts clicking away as I make her another tea.

"What do you think of this Gmail account?"

"One minute." I squeeze honey into Leena's tea and then open the fridge and pour some milk in the cup. "I don't want another e-mail."

I hand it to her. "Too late!" she says.

"What do you mean?"

"It's all taken care of. New e-mail and the pictures are deleted."

"Leena! I was still thinking that through."

"They're gone! Now you don't have to worry about telling Bryce. They were never sent."

"Jesus, Leena!"

"What? Don't sweat it. It will all work out."

"You didn't give me enough time to think."

"Too late. You're too slow. Don't worry. You'll probably never see Colton again."

"That's what I thought the last time and the time before that."

Bryce calls me twice Monday night. The first time is to make sure I made it home safely from work and the second to talk dirty while he's in bed thinking about me at the station.

Tuesday night, while I'm making a salad for dinner, I hear the beeping sound of the keypad on the front door.

I walk to the foyer entrance. "Angel?" Bryce says closing the door behind him.

"What are you doing here?"

"We were in the vicinity for a car fire. I had the guys swing by the house. Quick! Come here and give me a kiss."

Bryce is wearing his full firefighting gear looking hotter than hell with black soot on his right cheek. I run down the stairs and launch myself into his arms from the third step. He catches me and wraps my legs around his waist. "I've missed you!" he says, as our lips meet in a frantic kiss. "I couldn't stand another minute without you."

"I'm happy you stopped by."

"Tomorrow night I'll get to see you after the game. We're not going to the bar. I told the guys we won't be there. They didn't like it too much, but too bad. I've got a date with an Angel."

I kiss him hard, thinking my lips will bruise, and then I slide down his body until my feet reach the floor. "You'd better go."

Bryce opens the door and gives me another burning kiss. We hear the firefighters in the truck yelling out, "Give her one for me." I turn beet red as Bryce tries to rub the soot off my face.

"Look," he says, "I got you dirty."

"It was worth it. I got to see you."

"Bye, Angel. I love you."

"See you tomorrow. I love you, Babe."

Bryce runs to the truck and gets in. I wave to the firefighters and they wave back.

Ever since Bryce told me about that lunatic stalker only getting fifteen months in jail, my mind is side-tracked thinking about it. Will I live in constant fear every day now that I know what he's capable of? Will I have to make Barrie my permanent home, only visiting my house occasionally?

With all this playing in my mind, I wake a few times with nightmares. In the morning, I'm moving slowly from my restless night's sleep.

When I pick Leena up, I'm ten minutes late. "I was about to call," Leena says. "Thought you weren't coming."

"Didn't get much sleep last night."

"Nightmare?"

"Yeah. Bryce told me that lunatic only got fifteen months. He could be out sooner than we expected."

"I get vague pictures in my head of what he looks like and it gives me the creeps. Can't imagine what you're going through. You probably see his evil eyes and feel him touching you." Leena sees the frown on my face. "Sorry, you know my filter's broken."

"That's okay. I know my freedom is coming to an end. Wish he would've got more time."

Our day at work flies by we're so busy and I look forward to the hockey game and seeing Bryce afterwards.

Bryce is running late for the game because they were cleaning up after a house fire. I tell him to save time I'll meet him at the arena.

When I'm walking across the grandstand to sit in our usual spot, I notice Leena talking with Sidney and Angie above. I slow my pace to watch the expressions on their faces. Sidney doesn't look impressed. Her face turns angry and then she expresses her thoughts to Leena. I watch as they squabble back and forth and then Leena raises her hand in a motion for Sidney to stop talking.

Furious, Leena turns and heads down the grandstands.

"What was that all about?" I ask.

"I told Sidney not to waste her time thinking her and Austin will get back together, but she's not listening."

"What did she say?"

"She said, 'Who the hell are you to tell me what to do?'"

"I can't believe you went over there."

"I was sitting here with nothing to do and I kept thinking about it so I thought I'd take care of the problem."

I chuckle. "You've got more balls than I do."

"Speaking of another problem." Leena nudges my arm and I follow her line of sight.

Here come Blake and Trish walking across the grandstand, three seats below. Blake stares directly in my eyes and we watch as they pass by us.

"Ooh girlfriend, she doesn't like you. That was quite the evil look, don't you think?"

"Yes, it was. What has she done now?"

"We're not making too many friends here tonight, are we?"

I nudge Leena. "Look, here come the guys for warm up."

My diversion works for a couple seconds and then Leena looks off to her right again at Sydney.

After the face-off, both teams come out skating hard, trying to get the first goal. But as time ticks away and they have a couple of close calls, we find ourselves on the edge of our seats with no one scoring.

In the second period, Austin checks Bryce into the boards, hard, and Bryce's natural instinct is to fight back. They both drop their gloves and lunge at each other. After a few punches, they wrestle. Bryce kicks Austin's feet out from underneath him and they fall to the ice. The refs jump in, separating them.

They both get sent to the penalty box with two minutes

for fighting. Once inside, Bryce stands, looking down at Austin through the glass as he sits on the bench. Bryce yells at him. "What the fuck is your problem!" Bryce shakes his head at him and goes to sit.

While the guys are serving their penalty, the cops score.

Austin rises, grinning down at Bryce, and then stands at the door waiting for the seconds to count down to when his penalty is over.

They both dart out the doors, skating hard to catch up to the play.

The moment the puck comes toward Bryce, a very large cop covers him, slowing him down. I can tell how frustrated Bryce is, but he plugs away, trying to shake him.

At the beginning of the third period, Jax scores. Cops 1, Firefighters 1. Leena and I, are on the edge of our seats cheering them on. Both teams work their butts off trying to score, but when the buzzer sounds, the game ends with a tie. The schedule is tight at this arena and the next two teams are ready and waiting for their upcoming game.

As our teams step off the ice, we leave the cold grandstands to the warm lobby beyond the double doors.

The warmth from the fireplace and the aromas from the concession stand are a welcome feeling—one I've become accustomed to, enjoying weekly.

With the way the cops were hovering over Bryce the entire game, it has me wondering if Austin gave them a pep talk in the dressing room to prevent Bryce from scoring.

When the guys burst through the doors with their equipment over their shoulders, Bryce is smiling and laughing, looking mouth-wateringly delicious with his hair wet. His jeans fit to perfection and his t-shirt is skin tight, showing every well-defined muscle. I can't help but smile. It's been four days since I've made love to him. I can't take much more. I need him.

His eyes make contact with mine and that's where they stay

while he closes the gap between us. Before he reaches me, his eyes scan the length of my body.

"Hi, Angel."

"Hey."

He hovers, looking down my top at my cleavage. "You look hot, Angel!"

"Thanks, so do you."

Dante and Jax move in beside us. "You two are coming to The Bull, eh?"

"No. Not tonight." Bryce says looking into my eyes and then back to my cleavage.

"You're kidding, right?"

"I told you we weren't going." Bryce takes a quick glance toward Dante and then back at me.

"I thought you were bullshitting me."

"Nope. Ready to go, Angel?"

"Ready when you are." I smile at Dante and Jax. "Bye guys." I grab Leena's arm before we leave. "See you tomorrow."

As we're passing by, Austin and his cop buddies shove through the double doors. Bryce meets Austin's eyes for a second and then they look away.

The moment we get in the truck, Bryce expresses his thoughts. "I don't know what's up Austin's ass, but he's pissing me off."

"I could tell you weren't impressed with him."

"He knows I'm not."

"Leena was in a feisty mood tonight, too."

"Come here." Bryce slips his hand behind me, sliding my butt across the seat. "I've missed you."

"It's been a long week. I've missed you too."

We're barely inside the front door of Bryce's house when he attacks my clothing, throwing them wherever they land in the foyer and up the stairs. He picks me up and carries me to the couch, dropping me right there and stripping out of his clothes in seconds. He lowers his hard, naked body to mine and our lips fuse in a heated kiss. This is what I've wanted all week: his strong, beautiful body next to mine.

Friday night when Bryce comes into the bedroom, I'm squeezing into my new electric-blue, off-the-shoulder gown. He leans against the door frame, inspecting me. He looks me up and down, his eyes stopping at the slit at the top of my thigh. "Oh, by the way, thanks for sewing the buttons back on," he says, doing up his shirt.

"No problem."

"Angel, you look beautiful."

"Thanks, Babe." My eyes scan the length of his body. "You in this tux does me in every time. You are hot." Bryce closes the gap staring down my cleavage. "What?" I ask.

His finger runs between my breasts. "I want you to stay right beside me tonight."

"Okay," I say, wondering what's up.

"Dante and Jax will be all over you in this dress."

"Babe, you shouldn't worry. They know I only see you."

"Yeah." Bryce is deep in thought and I wonder what's going on in his mind. "Come with me, beautiful, we better hurry or we'll be late for the party." He holds my coat and I slip my arms inside.

The banquet hall is decorated with deep burgundy accents throughout, from the tablecloths to the burgundy chair coverings. Deep burgundy napkins are folded in the shape of a fan and the centrepieces at each table have deep burgundy fibre-optic flowers in a tall crystal vase. The peacock ice sculptures catch my eye the moment we walk in.

Bryce watches my reaction.

"This is beautiful. The fire department sure knows how to throw a party."

"The organizers out-do themselves from the year before."

My eyes float across the room, noticing how many people are here: there must be more than two-hundred.

Bryce sees Dante and Jax at the bar. He takes my hand and leads me over.

Dante steps forward, moving in for a hug, but Bryce stops him with a hand to his chest. "Back off! She's mine!" He gives Dante a dazzling grin. It makes me smile to see how great they get along.

"What? I just want a hug."

"Hands off, fucker!"

"Hi, Keera. What a greedy bastard, eh?"

I smile. "Hi, Dante. Hi, Jax."

Jax runs his hand down my back. "You look beautiful."

"Thank you, Jax."

Bryce tugs me close and we line up to get a drink. We're joined by Bryce's mom and dad and another couple. Once the introductions are finished, I hear Chief Anderson say, "That problem you were having, is it solved?"

Bryce pats him on the back. "Yes, thank you."

I wonder what they're talking about, but completely forget when Deana asks me where I found my dress. We talk for a few minutes before Deana and Garrett lead the way over to the table were assigned to.

Jax and Dante are at the table beside us.

As everyone sits, I realize Deana and Garrett are good friends with all of them. They laugh and talk about events that happened years ago. The men work with Garrett at Station One, in Investigations. I assume they are all highly decorated.

When everyone is seated, the waiters distribute our meal of salad, filet mignon covered with mushrooms in a wine sauce, baked potato, cheese ravioli in Bolognese sauce, sesame garlic asparagus and, for dessert, a delicious tiramisu.

Once dinner is over, the music begins to play and some people get up to dance. I lean into Bryce. "I'll be back in a minute." I run my hand over his thigh and he grins down at me.

"Back left corner," he says, motioning his head.

As I rise from my seat, I see Bryce eyeing the slit at my thigh. I smile and rub his back, appreciating the look he gives me. He slides my chair in and I make my way to the other side of the room.

Later, when I'm washing my hands, I notice someone staring at me out of the corner of my eye. Turning, I see Blake's eyes following the length of my body. She spins quickly, her hair whipping through the air, and disappears out the washroom door.

I'm glad I wore this dress. She looks good in her form-fitted red gown. Her hair is curled and floats in waves down her sexy, open-backed dress.

I look in the full-length mirror, self-consciously adjusting my dress. I add some lipstick and then head for the door.

When I sit down at our table, there are only two wives talking. Everyone else has left to mingle or they're up at the bar where Bryce is.

I observe how stunning Blake looks and how she's hovering, trying to get Bryce's attention. But he's speaking with a man and a woman.

Dante pulls out the chair next to me distracting my thoughts of why he and Blake didn't hook up. "You look gorgeous tonight," he says.

"Thanks, Dante. You look great in your tux." I hesitate, wondering if I should ask. "I'm curious, the last couple of times I saw you with Blake, you were all over her. What happened?"

"She's not my type."

"Oh, really?" In other words, he got his piece of ass and then moved on to his next target. That's why Dante doesn't have a steady girlfriend. He's a player.

"But you are," he says, rubbing my knee.

I lift his hand off. "You know what Bryce would say if he were here?"

"Yeah, I know. He'd say, 'Hands off, fucker!'"

I laugh. My eyes dart back to Blake and the way she's acting. She's anxious and circling. She doesn't speak to Bryce because he's in deep conversation with Chief Anderson.

Dante follows my line of sight and scoffs. "She must still be pissed at Bryce."

"Why?"

"Bryce must've told you Blake slapped him across the face."

My eyes meet Bryce's. His meet mine.

I pretend I know to get more information from Dante. "Yeah, he told me."

"She can't get over the fact she couldn't make it at our station and she's blaming Bryce for having her transferred."

"Why is she blaming Bryce?"

Bryce looks periodically at Chief Anderson but, for most of their conversation, he has his eyes on me.

"I heard Blake telling Trish that Bryce couldn't get over the shower incident or the picture in his locker," Dante says.

Thinking back, I remember every conversation I've heard between Bryce and Garrett, and then tonight, with Chief Anderson. I also remember Bryce saying he'd take care of the situation.

"Do you think Bryce had anything to do with her being transferred?" I ask Dante.

"Wouldn't blame him if he did. She doesn't belong with us at our station. It's been chaotic since she was hired. That one is wicked. Didn't see it right away, but I see it now."

A couple of men join in the conversation with Bryce, slapping each other on the back and laughing. I observe how they honour and respect Bryce, lining up, vying for his attention and it makes me proud that he's mine.

Bryce finds a way to excuse himself from the conversation and comes back with a drink for me. "Sorry, Angel, Chief Anderson was talking to me."

"No problem."

"I was trying to hurry back because I saw dickhead sitting beside you." Bryce playfully squeezes Dante's shoulder.

"That's okay, go back and talk to Anderson. Keera and I were getting cozy."

"Jackass! What did I tell you about hitting on my fiancé?"

"I don't know. I can't remember."

Bryce gives Dante a disgusted look and then holds his hand out to me. "Dance, Angel?"

"Sure." Once on the dance floor, Bryce holds me tight and talks against my ear over the music. "Sorry Angel, for some reason they all want to talk to me tonight. They found out about our engagement and I think they want an invite to the wedding."

"Really? How many people in this room would you invite?"

"At least a hundred."

My eyes widen.

"A lot of them I've been working with over the years and quite a few are good friends with my parents. You'll get to know them eventually. I didn't want to overload you with introductions."

An older couple dance beside us. "Bryce, good to see you again. And who is this lovely lady next to you?"

"Chief, Mrs. O'Donnell. This is my fiancé, Keera."

"Fiancé?" Mrs. O'Donnell sounds surprised as she touches my arm. "Nice to meet you, dear." She looks back at Bryce. "Bryce is getting married and off the market."

"I'll be expecting an invitation to the wedding." Chief O'Donnell chuckles, patting Bryce on the back.

Bryce gives them a blinding smile. "We'll get one in the mail, soon." They smile back and dance away.

"I see what you mean. You're a popular guy tonight."

"The news is spreading fast."

"I don't mean to change the subject but why didn't you tell me about Blake's transfer and how she's blaming you?"

"Dante." Bryce glances in his direction.

"Don't be mad. I pumped him for information after we saw the way Blake was circling you, looking like she wants to talk to you. Dante said Blake must still be pissed at you. What's going on?"

I search his eyes, but he's silent.

"Did you fuck her, too?" I ask softly.

23

*B*RYCE QUICKLY PULLS me past some people dancing and beyond the double doors to the hallway. He spins me around and looks both ways to make sure we're alone. "No, Angel. I did not! Do not compare me to Dante! I'm not like him!" He runs his hands through his hair. "I've been keeping my distance from her since day one and yes, I did get her transferred. We don't need that kind of chaos at our station. She's manipulating everyone. She doesn't belong there. I didn't tell you because I didn't know if my connections could pull this one off. But they did. And yes, I'm glad she's gone."

I'm listening, but my gaze is off in the distance. "Angel, look at me." He lifts my chin, forcing me to look at him. "I would never—hear me out—never cheat on you!" He hugs me and then bends to look at me. "I don't want you worrying. I can see how this is affecting you. I'm not proud of what I did but the problem is solved. Do I regret it? No. I would do it again. I told her to stop, that it could cost her job, but she didn't listen." I relax, melting into his arms as I realize again that everything he does is to keep us together. "Now, can we put this behind us and move on?"

"Yes."

"Are you okay?"

"Yes."

Bryce pulls me close, kissing my lips, rubbing my back, reassuring me as we head back into the banquet hall.

On the dance floor, I reach up, pulling him down to talk above the music. "Did Blake talk to you yet?"

"No. Why?"

"Because she looks like she wants to talk to you."

"Not happening."

"I thought I'd give you the heads up."

"Thanks. Now let's enjoy the evening."

Garrett and Deana dance next to us, smiling.

I hope they didn't see the drama unfolding. I needed to know what was going on. There are times Bryce tells me exactly what's bothering him and then there are times when he holds it all in, thinking he can spare me the worry and solve the problem on his own without telling me. In the end, I always find out, usually thanks to Dante.

Blake stays close, waiting for the opportunity to speak to Bryce, but he is either on the dance floor with me or he's speaking with a firefighter, captain, or chief.

While Bryce is speaking with them, I head for the washroom. When I come out of the stall, Blake is leaning against the counter with her arms crossed.

Oh Jesus, here we go!

I wash my hands and Blake clears her throat. "Obviously, you heard what your boyfriend did?"

I glance over, not saying a word, and continue rinsing my hands.

She hesitates for a moment. "This is not over! I'm issuing a complaint with human resources, the association, or anyone who will listen to me."

I wipe my hands. As I'm walking past her, I say, "Enjoy the

rest of your evening." Before the door closes behind me, I hear a loud bang.

She must have hit something. I think she's pissed off because she didn't get more information or the reaction she wanted from me.

It is well after midnight now and most of the guests have gone home. Deana and Garrett, Dante and Jax, and a few other firefighters join us at the main entrance.

Dante wraps Mike in a headlock and knocks on his skull. "Garrett, you'll never believe what our rookie here did this week?"

Garrett smiles back at Dante. "What?"

Dante pulls out his phone, showing Garrett and Deana a video. Bryce and I watch over Dante's shoulder.

The video shows Mike holding the hose, but the pressure is too much to handle. He loses control and the hose slips from his hands, flopping around erratically until Mike dives on it. By the time the video ends, we're all laughing, congratulating him on saving the day by getting it back under control.

Dante lets Mike out of the headlock and holds his phone to Mike's face. "This is what not to do. Next time, let us shut the water off."

"What? I had the situation under control."

We all laugh.

Garrett shakes their hands and then he and Deana leave with big smiles on their faces.

We say our goodbyes and leave shortly after.

Before we make it to the truck, we hear the sound of high heels closing in on us from behind and turn to see who it is. "Bryce!" Blake stands with her fists clenched and her body tense. "You're not getting away with this! I'm lodging a complaint with the association and human resources."

Bryce is straight-faced. "Do what you've got to do." Bryce

opens the door of the truck and we watch Blake furiously stomp toward the banquet hall.

I climb in as Bryce walks around to get in the driver's side. He grasps my thigh and searches my eyes.

"She told me the same thing when she cornered me in the washroom."

"Sorry, you had to deal with that, Angel."

"That's okay. Think she'll be a problem?"

"Not worrying about it. Chief Anderson will shut her down."

"Oh."

"Besides all the Blake drama, did you have a good time?"

"Yes, it was a great evening. I always have a good time with you."

Once we get inside Bryce's house, I drop my purse on the breakfast bar and turn to see Bryce watching me closely. "What?"

"Did you really think I'd risk losing you for a quick fuck with Blake?"

"When you're quiet and keep things from me, that's the first thing that enters my mind."

Bryce takes a step closer. He runs his hands down my back, reaching my butt, grabbing a handful and flattening his body against mine. "I'll try from now on to involve you, let you know the details. I don't want you thinking I've cheated on you." His serious look shows his honesty.

"I'm sorry. But I needed to know what was going on. Sometimes you're too silent."

"What this means is, I need to work on my communication skills. Come. Let me show you how much I love you." Bryce takes my hand, leading me to the bedroom. He spins me like one of our dance moves and then dips me backwards, holding me in his big, strong arms. His lips meet mine and we kiss. When he pulls me back up, I'm light headed.

His fingers find the hidden zipper down the side of my dress. It surprises that he knows where to look. But then I should know his mind is always thinking of how to extricate me from my clothing. He takes my hand and helps me step out of my dress. It falls to the floor, pooling at my feet. I stand before him with only my thong and high heels on. "So sexy."

"Let me undress you."

"I'm all yours," he says in a deep resonate voice, raising his hands in the air. I slide his tuxedo jacket off and throw it on the chair. I quickly undo the buttons on his shirt before he rips it open and I have to sew them back on.

He smiles down at me, knowing I can't help but touch his washboard abs. My hands caress his pec muscles and then move to his shoulders, pulling his shirt off, slowly. I toss it on the chair and work on taking his pants down. My thumb follows the dusting of hair to his happy trail. I glance up at him and he's giving me that mischievous grin.

I get on my knees and finish taking his pants down.

My new job, working for Blue Caribbean Swimwear, starts Monday and it will bring in a whopping one-hundred grand for a week of my time. I also negotiated with them to come to Barrie. They rented the same studio where Bryce proposed to me during my last job, with Avionté Cosmetics. I love the architecture of the old red-brick building with black awnings. It holds a special place in my heart.

In the morning, as we're saying goodbye in the garage, Bryce kisses me long and hard. "If you find anything unusual, call me. I'm only ten blocks away."

"Babe, why do you worry? Everything will be fine."

"Humour me."

"Fine."

I sink into my Journey and roll down the window. Bryce kisses me again. "Love you, Angel. See you tonight."

"I love you, Babe."

Bryce feels more at ease when Leena is working with me every day, but this time she can't get a leave from the bakery so I'm going alone.

When I pull up to the red-brick building, a few guys are carrying in some props. I grab some expensive camera equipment from one of the guys and carry it upstairs. I notice there is an older gentleman directing everyone around and he's a little moody. I stay quiet and out of the way, letting the man vent.

The moment I come through the door, a nice brunette greets me by name. "Keera, I'm glad you came to work for us. My name is Miranda and the grumpy old guy over there is your photographer."

"I'm only grumpy because I have to carry all this shit up the stairs."

That would be my fault, but I don't say a word.

He shakes my hand. "My name is Hudson. Good to meet you. While you're getting changed, we'll finish setting everything up."

Right to business.

Miranda leads me to a room they've sectioned off as a dressing room and salon. "Don't mind him. He'll loosen up and relax once we start."

The day is filled with bikini changes, poses, touch-ups to my makeup and positioning different backdrops. Hudson keeps us busy. As soon as he's done with one shot, he's directing the next. We stop for a quick lunch and just as quickly return to work. The day flies by.

On my way home Monday night, I have a visitor, tailgating me. It's Lindsay.

When I pull in the driveway at Bryce's, I hit the button for the garage door and back in next to Bryce's truck.

I'm expecting Lindsay to be standing outside the garage door when I open it, but she's not. The garage is obstructing my view, so I walk over a few feet to see if she's driven past the house.

She hasn't.

She's sitting at the end of the driveway in her car.

I wave and then go inside the house.

When I enter, Bryce comes to the top of the steps. "Babe."

"Angel," he says at exactly the same time and we both smile.

That familiar tingle travels through my body and I shiver. "Should I lock the door?" I ask. "You have a visitor out there."

"Who?"

"Lindsay."

Bryce frowns. "Great!" He goes to look out the front window. "She's gone."

"That's good." I toss my purse on the counter and, minimizing the space between us, I give him a kiss. "She must've followed me this morning and I didn't see her. She was waiting next to my Journey when I came out tonight. Couldn't miss her."

"Any confrontation?"

"No. She watched me walk past her car and then she followed me here."

"Any other visitors today?"

"No. Just Lindsay."

"I started dinner, since you were running behind."

I lift the lid, inspecting what's in the pot and discover spaghetti sauce boiling.

"Hudson keeps us working right until the end. He's a grumpy old bugger."

"Good thing you've only got one week with them."

I throw the noodles into the boiling water and make a salad. "Miranda is nice and everyone else who works for them."

"That's good. What do you think about working out at the fire station after dinner?"

I crinkle my nose. "I really should since I'm prancing around in a bikini."

"It's settled then."

Tuesday morning after I get ready for work and I'm leaning against the counter having my tea, my mind wanders, replaying the way Bryce made love to me last night. He told me he was hoping the station would get another fire call like the last time, but we weren't that fortunate.

Bryce said he couldn't stop thinking about it and by the time we got home he was so hot for me, he stripped my clothes off right there in the foyer. We stumbled up the stairs and he flattened me against every wall leading to the bedroom, then he picked me up and threw me on the bed.

Just then, Bryce walks down the hall, slipping his jacket on. "After the game tomorrow night, do you want to go to The Bull or do you want to come home?" Bryce sees the expression on my face. "What are you thinking about?" He grins mischievously.

"You. And this body." I step closer, running my hands down his chest. "Boy, did you rock my world last night."

"So did you. I'll be thinking about it all day. All week."

Something catches my eye down the stairs. I chuckle seeing our clothes thrown everywhere. "Found some down the hall this morning too." I start down the stairs, picking them up and throwing them in the laundry basket in the bathroom. Bryce has my coat ready for me to slip on. "We'd better hurry. We'll be late."

"To answer your question. I like The Bull. That's our date night."

"All right. It's settled then."

When Bryce opens the garage door, our eyes land on the words written across my windshield. I turn to Bryce. "Lindsay." We say at the same time. The words slut, whore, and homewrecker are written in permanent marker across every window on my Journey. My eyes scan the paint to see if there is other damage.

Bryce holds me. "Angel, don't let this bother you. She's pissed that we're engaged."

"I see that."

Bryce grabs the brake cleaner and rag off the shelf. "This should take care of it." He starts scrubbing it off.

Placing my purse on the hood, I grab a shop towel and we clean it together.

When we finish, Bryce holds me tight. "Are you sure you're okay? Next time I see Lindsay, I'll tell her not to come here again."

"I'm okay. I'm trying to put myself in her position. I'd be heartbroken knowing you're engaged. It would be quite the blow."

"Still, she doesn't need to come here."

"Think she'll listen?"

"Probably not. Give me a kiss, Angel, I'll see you tonight. I love you."

"I love you too, Babe." I give Bryce a kiss and then slide into the driver's seat. I pull out of the driveway first and Bryce follows. I make it to work with one minute to spare.

At Wednesday's game, they try to slow down the top scoring players on the firefighter's team and it works. The Cops tie the game and Austin is grinning from ear to ear because his team is improving—they're banding together. Austin and Bryce seem to be getting along better than at last week's game, when they were sent to the penalty box for fighting.

After the game, when we enter The Bull, the short and stalky guy is at the bar with his friends and all the regulars. Bryce strides past them, slapping Junior on the back. Junior's a big guy who habitually wears denim overalls and a cowboy hat. He occupies that same bar stool, weekly.

Junior turns to me and blushes. "Hi, Keera."

"Hi, Junior. How are you tonight?"

"I'm good." He turns away, his face beet red.

I smile and rub his back. I'm getting to know all of Bryce's friends and this one is a big teddy bear. He's so sweet.

Feeling uncomfortable with short and stalky guy's eyes on me from behind, we head over to our usual spot at the back of the bar. Leena and Austin follow. Bryce tugs me into his side. "That's unfair what you did to Junior."

"What?" I smile. "All I did was ask him how he is tonight."

"He probably blew his load talking to you," Bryce says. "Did you see his face?"

"He is too cute when he blushes like that."

We settle onto the bar stools and Bryce lifts his arm for the waitress. She comes over and takes our order.

Bryce leans to speak to me. "You don't think I notice how men react around you, but I do. They love what they see."

Just then, there's a scuffle at the bar. Leena turns her bar stool to get a better look and then climbs back on as the rest of us observe the commotion.

Junior has picked up Short-and-Stalky and is holding him by the shirt at his throat.

Dante and a couple bouncers are calmly talking, reaching up and trying to convince Junior to put Short-and-Stalky down.

Junior, the seven-foot giant, looks down at Dante and speaks again. They talk back and forth for a minute, with Short-and-Stalky still suspended high in the air, kicking and yelling. Junior puts him down and shoves him back. Junior bends to the floor, pointing at Short-and-Stalky, speaking his mind, and then he sits down on his bar stool. He looks furious.

Dante pats Junior on the back and walks over to us, laughing.

"Keera, Junior was defending your honour." Dante chuckles. "That little prick over there was talking shit about you. First, he showed Junior your picture on his phone. Then he was describing in full detail the things he could do to you. Junior lost it! Said, 'You don't disrespect women like that!' He wanted to kill the little bastard. I convinced him not to."

Bryce tenses and closes his fist. I rub his hand, helping him relax.

"That was nice of you, Dante." I smile.

Leena pipes up. "Next time, let him kill the little prick."

The waitress comes back with our drinks and collects the cash.

The sound of the music lowers for ten minutes so people can talk but it's quite loud now that the bar is crowded. Most of the firefighters and cops have gathered around our table to do a recap of the game and laughter fills the room.

I look over at Leena, observing her smile and her eyes roaming. She's having a great time with all these hot guys standing next to us, wearing tight t-shirts and jeans.

When the music comes back on, Bryce squeezes out, extending his hand to me. "Dance, Angel?"

"Sure."

As we dance, I glance around the room looking for Blake. This is the first time since she was hired at the fire department that she's not here. She wasn't at the game either.

When the song ends, we head back to the table. I poke Leena in the side to get her attention. "Time to hit the john."

"You're making me leave? Now?" Leena's eyes widen.

I giggle. "Yes. I've got something to tell you."

Leena lets out a heavy sigh and slides off her bar stool. "Fine. Let's go."

She leads the way and I follow.

When Short-and-Stalky sees us coming, he leaves the bar and purposely stands in our path. Leena shoves him out of the way and keeps walking, without missing a step. When I look back, he's snickering.

The lineup is long so we stand against the wall, waiting. "So, what's up?" Leena asks.

"When I came out of work Monday, Lindsay was parked next to my Journey."

"No. What happened?"

"She watched me walk past her car and then she followed me home. I expected her to be standing outside the garage when I came out, but she wasn't. She was waiting at the end of the driveway. She left and there was no incident. Never thought any-thing of it until Tuesday morning when Bryce and I went into the garage."

"What did she do?"

"I shouldn't have waved at her. I think I set her off. She wrote slut, whore, and homewrecker on the windows of my Journey with a sharpie. Bryce helped me get it off. I was almost late for work."

"She's pissed that you two are engaged."

Two stalls become available and we slip in.

When we come out of the washroom, I see Short-and-Stalky at the end of the hall, waiting. Leena sees him, too. She pushes me to her left and shoves him out of the way with her right arm, stomping past him and tugging me along.

He follows. "Keera? Keera, can you sign my poster? It'll take two seconds." He holds the pen up. "My name is Kane."

Junior immediately catches sight of Kane and starts plowing through the crowd toward us. As soon as he's within arm's reach, he picks Kane up by the scruff of his neck. "What did I tell you?" I stop and pull Leena back to watch. "You stay away from Keera. You better not harass her again. I'll squish you like a bug. You got that? I can't hear you! Say it! Louder!"

"Okay, okay!" Kane shouts and Junior drops him to the floor.

I grab Junior's hand, pulling him down for a hug. "Thank you for looking out for me."

He hugs me back. "No problem, Keera." He turns red and returns to his bar stool.

When we make it half-way across the bar, Bryce is walking toward us.

I'm learning, Bryce is always watching, keeping a close eye on me from a distance when I venture to the washroom.

"What happened?" He asks.

Before I have a chance to talk, Leena starts rambling, letting Bryce know the details.

Bryce looks over at Junior, tipping his head and then steers us to the bull pen. "Dante's riding the bull." He wraps his arm around my waist and pulls me tight against him. "That jackass better stay away."

"I think Junior fixed the problem."

We watch Dante climb aboard, punching his fist closed around the rope and lifting his other arm high in the air. The operator starts out slow and when Dante is still hanging on after four seconds, he tries every tactic to jostle him from the saddle. When Dante conquers it, he pulls his hand free and lays back on the saddle. His chest heaves for air and then both his arms shoot out. We all cheer for Dante. It was a wild ride and he's happy he lasted eight seconds.

Jax is next. He enters the bull pen, pulling Dante off the saddle, letting him fall to the padded mat below. Everyone cheers again. Jax has the same routine but this week the bull operator almost throws him. It's a miracle he stays on. When Jax jumps down, he congratulates the bull operator. They do a funky hand shake and smile at each other. I've come to the conclusion Jax doesn't get thrown too often and he's quite proud of the fact.

Bryce slides his hand around my waist and guides us to the bar, finding an opening next to Junior.

Bryce playfully slaps him on the shoulder. "How's it going tonight, Junior?"

"It's going good as long as that midget stays away from Keera." Junior glances at me, his face turning red, and then he looks over at Kane.

Bryce slides a beer in front of him. "Thanks for looking out for Keera."

"No problem. Anytime."

We head back to our table with drinks for Leena and Austin. Bryce slides a beer in front of Austin and I watch as they exchange a silent, brotherly truce. It makes me smile as they nudge each other.

The rest of the evening is filled with laughter and dancing. It's a good night.

Hudson, my photographer for the swimwear shoot, gets moody a few times near the end of the week when things don't go as planned, but he quickly remedies that by walking onto the balcony for a cigarette to calm his nerves.

Friday morning, Bryce wants me to stay home because I'm not feeling well when I wake up, but I go anyway knowing it's my last day and I'll be home in eight hours.

After a few bikini changes during the day, Hudson wants to get some shots of me wearing an expensive Swarovski bikini under a palm tree.

The backdrop is an electric-blue ocean with a boat in the distance pulling a para-sailor with a rainbow parachute.

Maranda has me sit on the padded lounge chair leaning to my right to show more cleavage while Sarah pats my nose and forehead with mineral powder. They love how the navy and forest-green bikini hugs my body. They attach dangling Swarovski jewels at my hips and position hot lights around me.

As I follow Hudson's instructions of leaning forward and tightening my abdominal muscles, suddenly, my temperature rises and I feel warm. I start sweating at my temples and my stomach churns.

A clear sign, this will not be a good situation.

Shooting up off my lounge chair, I head to the washroom in a hurry. "Sorry Hudson, I'll be back."

24

*A*S I RUN to the toilet, I hear Hudson say, "Make sure the bikini doesn't leave that room! It's worth a lot of money!"

I make it there just in time, throwing up my breakfast.

Wiping my mouth, I lean back on my heels, wondering why I feel this way.

I drag myself to the sink and dab a cold paper towel on my face. I fix my makeup, rinse my mouth, collect myself, and head back to the studio to get the shot before Hudson's mood sways again.

Lunch comes and I pick at my sandwich, still not feeling one-hundred percent.

I can't wait for this day to end.

A few more bathing suits and backdrop changes have me hoping everything goes smoothly. I want to wrap this up and go home early.

When Hudson calls out, "That's it, we got some great shots," we shake hands and thank each other. I gather my purse and then give them my address in Huntsville. They can send my portfolio there. I then help them carry down some equipment to the truck.

Bryce is waiting for me when I enter his house. "Angel?" He stands at the top of the stairs with the oven mitts in his hand. "How are you feeling?"

"I'm okay. How was your day?" I try to disguise how I really feel.

He tosses the oven mitts onto the counter and comes down the stairs to hug me. "Mom sent her famous chicken dinner for you. She hopes you're feeling better."

"That's nice of her. Maybe once I eat something."

"Come with me, beautiful. Let me take care of you."

He takes my purse off my shoulder and we walk upstairs to the kitchen. "Sit. Or would you rather lie down?"

"I'll sit and watch you."

Bryce takes two casserole dishes out of the oven and arranges food onto the plates. He collects our silverware and comes to sit beside me on the bar stool.

I smile at him. "Mmm, smells delicious. I'll have to thank your mom next time I see her."

"She's worried about you and so am I."

"I'll be fine."

After dinner, Bryce takes my hand and leads me to the couch where he wants me to lie down. He places a cold cloth on my head and kisses me. "Take a nap while I do the dishes."

Since I'm not feeling well, we stay in Barrie and Bryce takes good care of me, fussing all night, making sure I return to normal. I tell him it's not necessary, because I'm feeling better after eating but he insists on waiting on me.

For the next five days, Bryce works around the clock, banking his hours so he can have a couple of days off during the holidays. I'm still not feeling great, but Christmas dinner is at my house this year and I'm looking forward to it. Gramps says he'll come to

Huntsville with Mary and they'll stay overnight, leaving Boxing Day.

I'm shocked, because previous years since Gram died, I've always had to travel to North Bay for the holidays.

He hasn't been the same since her death. He's never set foot inside my house again. I think it was too painful for him, knowing this was where she died.

When we talk on the phone, I ask him if it's okay to invite a few more guests and I'm shocked yet again by his answer. He says, "The more the merrier." He's changing since he's met Mary.

Days before the guests arrive, I ask them not to say anything about the case or the ordeal I went through because Gramps doesn't know. It would kill him.

I make sure all the preparations are done well in advance. I hope if this Christmas is memorable, maybe Gramps will want to come back every year.

Christmas morning comes and Bryce rolls over, kissing me. "Merry Christmas, beautiful. Our first together and many more to come."

"Yes, a lifetime of them together. Merry Christmas, Babe." I give him a searing kiss that sends a direct hotline to my groin and a tingling sensation throughout my whole body. It's affecting him, too. I roll over quickly, straddling his hips, capturing his hands against the mattress. Grabbing hold of his cock, I stroke it up and down. His body responds from my touch. I lean down, pressing my lips to his, kissing him slowly, passionately.

His hands move up my thighs and reach around, grabbing my butt cheeks as he helps glide me along his stiff shaft.

I lean down and give him a quick kiss. "Rain check. I've got to get the ham in the crock-pot and the turkey in the oven."

"You can't leave me like this." His voice is deep.

I chuckle and climb out of bed. "Tonight."

"Un-uh. Your grandfather will be down the hall."

"That's okay, we'll be quiet."

Bryce shakes his head and grins—a look of disbelief and amusement at the same time.

"Besides, I need to get something in my stomach."

"Still not feeling good, Angel?"

"I'm not bad. I just don't feel one-hundred percent."

Bryce crinkles his forehead in a worried frown.

After cleaning up our breakfast, Gramps and Mary arrive early, which leads me to believe he didn't sleep well. It's about forty-five minutes before the rest of the guests arrive at one o'clock.

"Good to see you." I give them both a hug and a kiss. Bryce takes their overnight bags and places them in the spare room and I watch Gramps closely, but only when he isn't looking. He's inspecting the house, looking at everything, from the kitchen to the living room. I look at Mary and she rolls her eyes.

"Looks good, Giggles. I like the change."

"It's a little more modern now."

He stands at the doorway of the adjoining two rooms, staring at the picture of my parents above the fireplace mantel. "That's a good picture. I've always loved that one." He walks farther into the living room.

Mary steps close, whispering in my ear. "He's been worked up for a week now. I hope he relaxes soon."

"I know what will work." I sprint to the fridge and pull out a couple beers. "What would you like to drink Mary? I have pretty much everything."

"What kind of wine do you have?"

"Chardonnay or red. Which would you prefer?"

"Chardonnay, please."

Bryce joins us in the kitchen. "I'll get that, Angel." He grabs the bottle from the fridge, pops the cork and pours the wine, handing Mary a crystal wine glass.

"Thank you, this is delicious."

I walk into the living room and see Gramps holding the snow

globe. He's staring at the picture inside. I stand beside him, waiting for him to speak.

He turns to look at me. "How'd you get that in there?"

I hand him his beer and take the snow globe from him, turning it upside down, showing him how the picture frame slides out. "See, you can put any picture inside the frame and pop the frame back in the globe."

"I remember the day we had that picture taken."

"I do, too. I was fourteen at the time."

Mary and Bryce join us in the living room. Mary walks over to the bench Gramps made for Bryce and I and runs her hand over the leaves and vines on the backrest. "James, you do fine work. It's beautiful."

Gramps looks at Mary and smiles.

"Would you like a tour of the house?"

"Yes, please," Mary says to me.

We wander down the hall to the laundry room with Gramps and Bryce following. "I like the cabinets and how it helps hide everything," she says. "And the island to fold laundry. It's very organized."

"I had an idea and it all came together. Gramps made my cabinets." I touch them and smile proudly at him. "I gave him the measurements and when I hung them, they fit perfectly." I rub Gramps' back as I pass by him to leave the room.

We walk next door to the spare room, but Gramps stays in the doorway, not entering. He peers in, staring at the bed.

Once he sees it's a different bed from where Gram passed and I have changed the room totally, he speaks. "I like what you've done. It looks good."

He steps inside and looks around.

When I glance back from the doorway, he's standing next to the bed in deep thought.

I hook my arm in Mary's and guide her to my room. Bryce follows. "I think Gramps needs some time alone," I say, softly.

"I think so, too," Mary whispers. "He's been anxious and upset about visiting. We discussed it and I told him it's a normal reaction to feel the way he does. I told him it's hard for anyone to revisit the place where their loved one has passed. I went through the same thing when Ray died. I think he'll be fine."

"This is my closet."

"This is huge!" Mary says, her eyes wide.

"Part of this was my old bedroom. The other half I used to increase the size of my bathroom." I open the door. "It was too small. It's a perfect size now."

"It looks great. Your house is beautiful."

"Thank you, Mary."

We stroll into the kitchen and when I glance in the living room, I notice Gramps is still in the spare room. I try to keep Mary occupied to give Gramps time alone.

"Would you like more wine, Mary?"

"Please, it's delicious. Are you going to have something?"

"Maybe in a little bit."

"I'll get that, Angel." Bryce pours Mary's wine and I take out appetizers.

Mary points. "What's this one?"

"That's a veggie pizza."

"Looks healthy."

"Yes. Most of it is healthy. Try it, Mary."

"I think I will." She takes a bite. "Oh, I like this."

Just then, Leena and Austin come through the back door.

"There they are."

"Smells good in here," Leena says, placing a pecan pie on the counter.

I rush over to Austin, giving him a hug to whisper in his ear. "Remember what we talked about?"

"I know, Blondie."

I turn and give Leena a hug.

"Mary, this is my good friend, Leena, and this is Austin,

Bryce's brother." Mary looks from Bryce to Austin and back again but she doesn't comment. She keeps it to herself.

Gramps joins us and I introduce Austin to him.

Not five minutes later, Katie and her new boyfriend, Jacob, arrive, and Ma and Constable Grant come through the door at the same time.

Once the hugs and introductions are done, Bryce helps me with the drinks.

"Constable Grant, what would you like?"

"Please call me Dave, unless we're at another crime scene. I'll take a beer."

My eyes widen at Leena because she told me she warned Constable Grant not to mention anything about the case.

Her eyes widen back at me and she shrugs her shoulders.

I look at Gramps and he's speaking with Austin. I don't think he heard the comment.

"Would anyone like to come into the living room where it's more comfortable?" I rummage through the fridge, finding a few more appetizers and when I turn back, I see that everyone's standing, moving toward the living room. When they're not looking, I tug Leena back by her arm. I whisper next to her ear. "I thought you warned him?"

"I did. He must've had a brain fart. Hopefully, he'll realize what he said and zip his mouth for the rest of the evening."

"If you get a chance, refresh his memory. But quietly!"

"Okay. Do you want me to bring these?"

"Yes. Thank you."

Leena places the appetizers on the coffee table and then sits on one of the love seats next to Austin.

I motion to Bryce. "I'll sit on your lap."

We settle in the living room talking and I watch how Gramps and Mary ease into the conversation until they feel comfortable. There's a knock at the back door and Bryce gets up to answer it. I join him and see Deana, Garrett, and Ciara have arrived. I take the bags from Deana, give them a hug, and Bryce gets them a drink. We join everyone in the living room and introduce them.

After giving a tour of the house again to everyone who hasn't seen it, I sit down, content that all the preparations we've made have come together and I see everyone is happy.

The turkey is in the oven, the fire is burning, and the smell of a Christmas candle is an aroma that will be set in my mind as a special moment in my life.

I glance over to see Jacob whispering in Katie's ear.

It's been three months since we last saw her. She's grown her auburn hair to just past her shoulders and added strawberry highlights. It looks good on her. She's wearing tight jeans and a t-shirt, both accented with crystal bling. I pay attention to how Jacob treats her. They look like they get along well. She looks happy as she smiles back, whispering in his ear.

Later, all the women help me in the kitchen while the guys watch the hockey game in the living room.

The expressions on Deana's and Mary's faces are priceless when Leena bluntly asks Katie how good Jacob is in bed.

Katie blushes and looks over at Deana and Mary.

"Oh, come on Katie. Spill it! Mary doesn't mind, do you Mary? Deana's used to me by now."

Mary chuckles. "No. I don't mind. I like our girl talk."

"See Katie. Mary's enjoying this."

I say nothing. I just smile and return to thickening the gravy.

Leena always wants the details. "Well, I'm waiting!"

"Yes, okay. He's good in bed."

"Just good? Or, blow-your-mind, send-you-into-orbit good?"

"Yes, blow your mind, okay."

I glance over at Katie and she's rolling her eyes at me. It's a sign, she needs me to save her from Leena's overbearing personality.

I walk from the kitchen archway to the living room and motion for the girls to look.

When we peek in, Gramps is on the reclining love seat with

his feet up. He's enjoying himself, hanging out with the guys. He's relaxed now compared to when he first came through the door. They're laughing at a few comments passed back and forth amongst the men in the room as they watch the hockey game.

Leena's attention shifts from irritating Katie to the conversation unfolding about the hockey game. When Leena expresses her thoughts regarding two of the hockey players, Katie gives me a silent thank you with her eyes.

Bryce looks over at me and I wink. He stands and walks toward me, affectionately holding my waist. "Do you need some help, Angel?"

He sets up two six-foot tables and, with the help from the ladies, we distribute the food, decorating as if our Christmas meal will be featured in *house and home* magazine.

We call the guys into the kitchen and form a line on each side, dishing our food onto Mom and Dad's fancy china. Once everyone sits around the kitchen table, Mary asks, "Would it be okay if I said a prayer?"

"Yes, please."

"I would like to thank the Lord above for allowing us to enjoy this delicious meal and for all the special people in my life, new and old."

I watch everyone's eyes shine with excitement as they dig into the food.

I find, since my parents passed, I've become very sentimental. I try to absorb every special moment in my life, knowing all too well how quickly it can be taken away.

The turkey is tender and juicy and the glazed ham with pineapple is succulent. The homemade stuffing with cranberries fills the house with the smell of a traditional Christmas meal. I eat too much and I'm a little worried with all the modelling jobs I have lined up that I'll gain weight. But aside from the food tasting so good, the aromas evoke rich memories of holidays when my parents were alive.

Mom and Gram would be in the kitchen preparing dinner, teaching me to cook by the time I was nine or ten.

They would give me a job and, while I was accomplishing the task, I'd watch Dad come in the kitchen and rub against Mom, coaxing her to give him a bite. Gram would say no, you'll spoil your dinner, but Mom would always give in. Gram would smile, knowing she was wasting her breath. But she'd love the display of affection they showed every time. I did too, smiling so hard my cheeks would hurt.

Once the dinner dishes are cleaned, we file into the living room, where Bryce and I hand out gifts from under the tree. The room overflows with smiles and laughter.

Everyone was too full for dessert after dinner, but now that it's two hours later, we make coffee and tea and arrange the pies, pastries, and cheesecake on the table.

The day and evening fly by, but I tuck the memories away, along with the pictures I've taken of the best Christmas I've had since my parents have passed.

The next morning, I get up early, trying not to wake Bryce as I shimmy out of bed. After throwing some clothes on, I quietly open the door and head to the kitchen where I start making coffee and breakfast.

Gramps is first to come down the hall. "Good morning, Giggles."

"Good morning, Gramps. How'd you sleep?"

"Slept well."

"Great! So did you have a good time yesterday? Will you come to visit next Christmas?"

"Definitely. Had a great time. It was nice meeting everyone in your life."

Mary joins us in the kitchen. "I really enjoyed myself, too. Your friend Leena is a wildcat. I love her spunky personality."

"Yes, Leena, you've got to love her. She always speaks her

mind." I shake my head. "She has no filter. We've been friends with Katie since JK. It was great seeing Katie. I've missed her."

Gramps pours a coffee and starts the kettle for Mary's tea.

Bryce saunters into the kitchen in his black jogging pants and a tight white t-shirt, looking hot with his hair tousled. My eyes scan every delectable muscle under his shirt, then slip lower to get a glimpse of the outline of his beautiful cock. I shiver and my muscles clench.

We were both too tired to have sex last night. Bryce sees the look in my eyes and gives me a smile. He knows he's in for a wild ride the moment Gramps and Mary leave.

Shortly after Christmas, Leena and I search for the perfect hall and church in Barrie for the wedding. The church Bryce referred us to was where his mom and dad were married. The moment we pull up to it, Leena's eyes float to the clock and the large bell in the steeple tower. "I love it already. Look at the architecture. I hope it's as nice inside."

"Let's find out."

There are three sets of large carved-wood double doors at the entrance. Leena pushes the wheelchair accessible button on the stone wall and the middle doors open. Once inside, our eyes float to the beautifully painted eighty-foot ceiling. "Holy shit! Look at this place!" Leena says, her voice travelling and echoing. I give her a nudge.

"Right! No swearing. Aww, crap! I'm going to hell."

"This is amazing!"

"I'm already picturing how we'll decorate in my head."

We walk down the main aisle with at least fifty carved wooden pews on both sides. Halfway down, we spin to look at the sun shining through the stained-glass windows, which act like prisms refracting small rainbows across the interior of the church.

"I can't get over this place. It's gorgeous!"

"Thank you." We turn to see the priest walking toward us.

"Your church is beautiful. I'm Keera Johnson and this is my friend Leena Ericson." We take turns shaking the priests' hand.

"Nice to meet you. I'm Father Connery. What can I help you with today?"

"We would love to book this church for Bryce and Keera's wedding."

"Bryce? Bryce Hamilton?"

"Yes. Bryce and Keera are tying the knot and we'd love to have their wedding in this church."

Father Connery smiles. "I know the Hamilton family very well. See them almost every Sunday. I married Deana and Garrett many years ago right at that alter. Let's go see what dates we have available."

Bryce has two days off and needs to get away from his busy life in Barrie. We've had several snowstorms and Bryce has been going non-stop trying to help out at the station. He wants some quality downtime with me. He plans to stay at my house for a day and then head to the cabin for a ride on the snowmobiles.

When we enter the back door, there's a puddle of water on the floor. It's a good thing we came to my house first. The slow leak saturated everything in the cupboard and eventually ran out. I rush to clean it up so Bryce can fix the pipe.

Bryce never hesitates to do anything for me, from fixing my car to repairing the garage door to throwing in a load of laundry. And now he's under my sink fixing my leaky faucet. I couldn't ask for a better man. His torso is in full view and all I want to do at this moment is climb aboard, but as I think it through, I change my mind, worrying he might hit his head on the pipes.

"Damn it!" He struggles to get his muscular body out from under the sink. "I have to go to the hardware store. Angel, you can't use the water. I've got it shut off."

"Okay, I'll wait to do laundry and make dinner."

He climbs out and collects what he needs. "This won't take long. Ten, fifteen minutes."

I give him a kiss.

He throws on his coat and boots and I watch him walk out the back door.

While I wait for him to return, I put our chicken back in the fridge to cook later and then collect laundry from around the house.

As I'm rounding the dividing wall from the kitchen to the living room, I hear the back door close.

"What'd you forget?" I say, stopping mid-step, holding the wall, looking in the direction of the back door.

I'm frozen—with excruciating fright!

The sadistic eyes of that lunatic stalker stare back at me. He's standing not twenty feet away from me, inside my house.

25

H, GOD!

Time suspends in the air, forever it seems, as we stare at each other. My mind spins uncontrollably. When did he get out of prison? Why didn't Grant warn us? Where's Bryce?

My hands start to shake, and I drop the dishcloths as panic and fear engulf me. *Bryce left the house only moments ago. Did that lunatic ambush him on his way out? Bryce! I need to find Bryce!*

I glance from his evil eyes to the knives in the chopping block on the counter. His eyes follow mine and then he turns back, holding his cold stare on me once again.

He knows I'm ready to make my move. I have to before he does.

In my mind, I see myself slamming the bedroom door and locking it. But I need to detour him away from the bedroom, which is to the right of the kitchen. I want to buy some time and make it around the other way to my bedroom, where the rifle is stored beneath the bed.

I turn quickly behind the wall that divides the living room and hall and run toward my bedroom.

I'm a little more than halfway there when my feet slide out from under me. My body slams hard to the floor as he drags me by one foot back toward the kitchen. "You can't run from me!" He yells, his voice harsh and demonic.

With my hands, I'm clawing, grasping for anything to hold on to. I grab the floor moulding that separates the two rooms and my nails shatter as he yanks me roughly.

Flipping onto my back, I kick him square in the face, hard, with my other foot.

Oh shit!

He shakes it off and grabs me roughly, climbing up my body, digging his fingers into me. Red surges upward from his neck to his face, and his eyes bulge.

Oh, God! He's so angry.

I'm fighting him, trying to keep my hands free, when his fist lands hard across my cheek.

The overpowering stench of gasoline wakes me. As I reorient myself, I remember he punched me in the face and must have knocked me out. Trying to look around, my head frantically whips from side to side searching for that psychopath. I feel the room spinning.

The pain in my head and jaw are intense.

I try to touch my face, but realize my hands are bound with cable ties. I try to get up but my ankles are shackled together. I flip on my side, stretching to look in the living room and see where the noise and odour are coming from.

That lunatic is pouring gas everywhere, saturating my couch.

No! He plans to set my parents' house on fire!

My eyes scan the huge picture of my parents hanging above the fireplace mantle. I can't take my eyes off them.

Oh God! I'm going to die like this! I'm going to burn to death!

I can hear my parents' voices in my ears: *Don't give up baby. Fight! Fight to stay alive!*

Looking above and seeing he's preoccupied with dousing the furniture, I roll my body the length of the kitchen floor to the counter and use the cupboard handles to pull myself up.

Just as my hands land on a knife, he startles me by squeezing my hand so hard, I drop it.

He stands behind me, grabbing my throat, choking me as he talks against my ear. "What do you think you're doing?"

Instantly, a feeling of complete disgust flows through my whole body remembering how he abducted and drugged me. I start to shake as fear overwhelms me.

"Un-uh. You're not getting away from me this time! We'll be together forever like I told you before." He yanks me backwards, shoving me hard onto the floor, and I hit my head on the ceramic tile.

I wake to that psychopath straddling my hips, slapping me across the face. "Wake up, beautiful. Wake up!" He pulls duct tape from a roll. "I need you awake for this."

"Please don't do this! All my families' memories are…" He shuts me up by slapping tape over my mouth. A harsh groan escapes from my throat as my head thrashes from side to side.

He holds my hands above my head and leans to talk against my ear. "I had plenty of time sitting in that jail cell thinking about you and our relationship. And I've come to the conclusion that you'll never truly love me unless that prick is out of our lives for good. I thought long and hard how I want to do this." The rawness of his voice scares me and I realize I'm shaking uncontrollably.

Oh God! Where's Bryce? What has he done to Bryce?

"I've got nothing to lose," he says. "They took my house. They took my truck. The only thing left—is you. You belong to me! Who does he think he is?" he shouts. "He thought he could come into our lives and steal you away from me? You've always been mine!" He leans down and kisses my cheek. "I bought a truck and worked out so you'd notice me. I was trying to get your attention. But nothing worked! So, my solution—is that we die together! If I can't have you in this life no one will. But we'll be together forever in the next life."

He reaches to his side and picks up a knife.

No! Please don't do this!

He slices my shirt wide open.

A groan surfaces from somewhere deep within me.

"Shh, baby. It'll be okay." He leans down to hug me, placing his head on my breasts. "We will live in paradise, forever. I'm not going back to that hell hole," he says, lifting his body, looking directly in my eyes. "Do you have any idea what I went through in prison? I had to play the game." he says in a low, chilling voice. "I had to survive. Those fucking perverts!" He shakes his head, showing disgust on his face. "I won over one guard at a time and they protected me. I was a model prisoner. My mother helped by bringing meals to the guards. They looked forward to them. They loved her. She told them how I was falsely accused and the only thing I've ever done wrong was falling in love with you. She can't understand why I still love you." He runs his hand over my cheek and leans down kissing me. "But I do. I will love you forever, and beyond."

He fondles my breasts. "I've missed these. I've missed you!" Leaning sideways, he searches for something as he rambles on. "They let me out, day parole with supervised visits to see my mom. They trusted me. I waited for the perfect time. I didn't want to kill him. He was my friend."

He killed someone?

Reaching into his pocket, he takes out a box of wooden matches. I try to protest by shaking my head and screaming, but only a muffled sound releases. "Shh, everything will be fine," he says, taking a match out of the box. "Don't worry, you'll be just as beautiful in our next life." My eyes widen and I try to yell as he strikes the match on the box.

No! Please, no!

It doesn't light.

He lets out a growl before striking it again, and again. Frustrated and furious, he flips the box over and strikes it on the other side.

It lights.

"I'm not going back to prison!"

He throws the match and I hear the gas ignite. It sounds like an explosion. I feel the heat on my hands and hair from the flames engulfing my living room. I twist my body to look that way and see the flames rolling across the ceiling. The fire climbs the wood mantle, reaching the large picture of my parents.

No!

Suddenly, pain surges through my neck. He's biting me! A scream escapes from my throat. I twist and pull my hands free from his and push his head away.

He gains control of my arms again, forcing them to the floor. He's grinning, mesmerized by the flames, not even realizing what he's done to me. The sadistic look on his face is terrifying, I shake uncontrollably.

I try to get up but he holds me down by lying on top of me. My bound hands are now sandwiched between us. I can't move.

He grabs my breast again, fondling as he grinds into me. "See what this does to me. My cock is so hard! I've been waiting for this moment!"

He talks against my ear. "It won't be too long, baby. Before you know it, you won't feel a thing."

I try to roll my body to get him off me but his weight holds me down. *Get off me!* I struggle and attempt to scream, but then tears start to flow as I realize I can't do anything. *I'm going to die like this!*

I start to pray. *Please dear God, Mom and Dad, if you're listening, I need you again. I'm going to die. Please help me!*

He grinds into me at a fast, steady pace as he looks off, mesmerized by the fire.

Out of nowhere, I feel the weight of his body lifted off me as some invisible force tosses him against the wall and he lands on the floor, as limp as a ragdoll.

Bryce!

That lunatic stalker gets up and charges toward Bryce in a rage.

Bryce picks him up by the throat and slams him to the floor. But that psychopath doesn't stop. His arms and legs thrash around in a frenzy. He moves at lightning speed to get out of Bryce's grasp, lunging towards the counter and reaching for a knife from the chopping block. No sooner does he have it in his hand, then Bryce smacks it away.

They wrestle again. Bryce pins him to the floor, grabbing his shirt collar and punches him in the face, knocking him out.

A tidal wave of relief washes over me until I realize we're not out of danger yet.

The flames are now covering the ceiling and walls in the kitchen and it's hard to see and breathe from the thick billowing smoke.

Bryce picks me up and kicks the back door open, carrying me to safety outside.

Running from the house, he places me on the snow thirty feet away from the deck and pulls the tape from my mouth, slowly. Both of us cough, trying to clear our lungs. "I'll be right back, Angel." He runs up the stairs and into my house. The interior is engulfed in flames.

"Bryce!" I shout. "No!"

The windows shatter from the intense heat and flames shoot out.

Their voices are faint, as if they're whispering. But that's when I really pay attention to what they're saying.

Bryce! Where's Bryce?

"Look at her. Look what that psychopath did to her." I feel someone grab my hand. "Twice, that relentless bastard has put her in the hospital. Excuse my language but I'm pissed," Leena says.

"Understandable. We've sent Keera for a CT scan to see how severe her head injuries are. We're thinking she has a concussion from blunt force trauma. The results should be here any moment. She has multiple cuts and bruises to her neck, head, face, and lower extremities. As you can see, she's been through quite a bit. She's traumatized."

"When will she come back to us?" I hear the concern in Bryce's voice.

Bryce! He's alive! I can feel tears welling up in my eyes.

"Could be an hour. Could be a few days, but right now we have to take her to ultrasound to make sure the baby is fine."

"Baby!" they all shout.

"The blood tests we took earlier show positive."

Silence fills the room for a moment.

"I see by your reaction this pregnancy is a surprise."

I'm pregnant? Me? There's a baby in there?

That would explain why I've felt queasy and need to eat something first thing in the morning.

"How far along do you think she is?" Bryce asks.

How can I be pregnant? I've been taking my pill all along, not missing a day.

"We'll find out right now. You can come along if you'd like."

"Can we all come?" Leena asks.

"Yes."

I hear and feel everything, but I can't wake up. They move me from the bed to the gurney and as they wheel me down the hall, Bryce takes my hand, not letting go until the gurney slows and then stops at our destination.

They expose my belly. I jump when they squirt the cold gel on me.

"Angel?" Bryce takes my hand in his.

"Did you see that?" Leena asks.

Bryce splays our fingers and holds them tight with his other hand. "Angel. Can you hear me?"

There is pain and concern in his voice.

The technician runs the wand over my belly, skimming lightly and then pushing harder in certain spots. I hear clicking of the mouse and a dinging sound as she takes images.

"Is that the baby's heartbeat?" Leena asks.

Bryce is silent, rubbing my hand gently.

"Yes."

"It's most likely too early to find out if it's a boy or girl? Correct?" Trust Leena to dig for more information.

"Yes, it's too early. According to this, Keera is six weeks pregnant."

"Does everything look okay?" Leena asks.

"I'm not allowed to say. I give the report to the physician. They will inform you. The only thing I can do is print some images for you."

I hear the printer spitting out paper and then Bryce's hand leaves mine for a moment.

When the technician is finished, she wipes the gel off my belly and they wheel me down the hall. Bryce holds my hand, not letting go until I feel them lifting me onto the bed.

Once I hear the door close, Bryce finally speaks. "I'm going to be a dad."

"You okay there?" Austin asks. "You look like you're in shock."

"I am. But I'm happy." Bryce hesitates. "My mind is all over the map. I'm worried about Keera."

Bryce's phone wails with the sound of firetrucks. "Hello. No, she's still unconscious. Still waiting for the results of the CT scan."

There's silence in the room for a bit and then I hear Bryce say, "What? This can't be happening." The door opens and his voice fades.

Moments later, the door opens again and I hear Bryce and the doctor speaking. "I hear congratulations are in order."

"Thank you," Bryce says, rubbing my hand.

"Results from the CT scan show no cerebral edema—brain swelling. But I'm diagnosing mild traumatic brain injury—concussion. Everything looks good. When she wakes, she may be dizzy, confused, have headaches, be sensitive to light or noise, and in extreme cases, she may have memory loss. Keep talking to her and let the nurses know if something doesn't seem right. I'll check on her in the morning. Do you have any questions?"

"Is Keera in pain and can they give her something for it, knowing she's pregnant?"

"We won't give her anything right now. If she starts to wince or moan, let the nurses know and they will give her acetaminophen. Fine to take while pregnant."

Bryce's hand leaves mine. "Thank you."

The door opens again and I assume the doctor has left.

"I can't believe it! You're having a baby! I'm going to be a godmother. I take it by the look, Keera didn't mention that to you, eh? We discussed this years ago. Bryce are you okay? You seem to be preoccupied with something. Did you want a baby right now?"

"Yes! I couldn't be happier."

"Oh, because the look on your face—"

"Leena, you stay here with Keera. I'm taking Austin to the house to see if we can salvage anything."

"Oh, okay."

"Call me the moment Keera wakes up or even moves."

"Okay, bye."

The door closes and the room is still.

I feel the bed dip beside me and a body next to mine.

"I am the godmother of this little bambino, right?" Leena's hand rubs my belly as she lays her head on my shoulder.

"I'm sorry this happened. I wish we would've known that psychopath escaped. We could've kept you safe in Barrie."

Leena is quiet again for a few moments.

"You have to wake up. Bryce and your baby need you ... I need you."

I feel moisture on my shoulder. Leena lifts her head, sniffles and lays her head back down.

I think she's crying. Leena never cries.

"Leena!" Bryce raises his voice. "You were supposed to be watching to see if Keera moves."

Leena jumps up. "Sorry. I must've fallen asleep."

"Did Keera move?"

"Umm, don't think so."

"You don't know."

"I would've felt her move," she says with an attitude. "You found her pictures?"

"Found the snow globe, too," Bryce says. "It was broken but the picture inside is fine."

"Which is odd," Austin says. "I'm still freaking out about that."

"Metal objects mostly. But it's something," Bryce concludes.

"It looks like all her pictures are here," Leena says. "She'll be so happy."

"Grant let us look for the metal box, but we ran out of time. We had to get the hell out of there. The investigation team was close."

"And they don't want you anywhere around there," Austin says.

"They're wasting taxpayers' money," Bryce says, clearly irritated.

"What's going on?" Leena asks.

"That phone call I got earlier ... it was Grant giving me the heads up: they're investigating me."

"For what?" Leena asks. I can hear the disbelief in her voice.

"They think I had something to do with that lunatic not getting out of Keera's house."

"I wouldn't blame you if you did do something. Look what he did to her."

"I didn't! I couldn't get back in the house. We were lucky to get out."

"Why do they think you had something to do with it?"

"His mother showed up and overheard there was remains of a body inside. She lost it, screaming, 'He killed my son!' She was hysterical, pushing her way through the police barricade spouting off to any cop who would listen to her. They had to make a report."

"Don't sweat it. What's Grant saying?"

"He has to stay out of this or he's compromising his job. But he did tell me to get to Keera's house to grab anything salvageable and then he gave us the heads-up the investigation team was on their way and to get out."

"I couldn't believe it when we drove by. Only parts of the brick from the fireplace remain. The rest is rubble. The investigators won't find anything."

Oh, God! My house is gone!

"Keera will be devastated when she wakes up," Leena says. "But at least you found her pictures."

Every memory I have of my family in my parents' house plays like a movie in my head.

Their voices fade.

Someone kisses my lips softly. "Angel, please wake up. Come back to me. I love you!" Bryce rubs my stomach.

"Angel, we're having a baby! You don't know how happy I am. I need you to wake up. I need to know you're okay."

He rubs my belly again.

"I wonder if it's a boy or a girl. I hope she looks like you. Wait—maybe not. Once she gets to high school, I'd have to keep the shotgun at the front door to scare away the horny little bastards sniffing around."

I giggle inside.

After a couple minutes of silence Bryce says, "Angel, I need you. Our baby needs you!"

I hear the door open.

"How are you doing this morning?" a woman's voice asks. "That bed is a little small for the two of you."

Bryce moves to get up. I hear the chair dragging across the floor. "Uncomfortable, too. We're good. She hasn't moved yet."

"I'll take her vitals."

She wraps the blood pressure gauge around my arm and starts to pump. I feel the pressure and tightness as it fills with air and then relief when she lets the air out slowly. I hear the sound of Velcro ripping. "Blood pressure is a little low. Also potassium and iron are low. You look like you need a coffee. The cafeteria is on the first floor."

"I'll have my brother bring one. Do you think she's in any pain?"

"Doesn't seem like it. I'll come back after my rounds. Keep talking to her."

"Thank you."

The door opens and I assume the nurse has left.

Bryce takes my hand. "We need a lifetime of memories with our children, your Gramps and Mary, my mom and dad, with Austin and Leena, my pain-in-the-ass sister and Katie."

26

*T*IME PASSES. I'M not sure how long I've been in this hospital.

I move.

"Angel!" Bryce squeezes my hand.

I open my eyes.

"You're awake! I love you. Speak to me. Let me know you're okay."

"Babe." I touch his arm to see if he's real, that I'm not dreaming.

When I focus, I see him smiling. He holds me tight. I can feel his big body shake. He takes a deep breath, nuzzling in my neck. "Did you hear me, Angel? I love you."

"I love you, Babe."

He squeezes me again and I feel wetness on my neck from his tears.

My tears start to fall.

"Angel, you gave me one hell of a scare."

"Babe, I thought I lost you. I thought you died. I saw you go in the house and then the windows shattered."

"Shh, it's okay. I'm here. What you saw was me entering the back door. When it flashed, or I should say exploded, I dropped to the floor and covered my head with my jacket. Blew me away from the house and I landed ten feet away from you. Think it knocked me out for a few seconds. Then I went to see if you were okay. You were out but you were breathing. I called fire and ambulance and got you to the hospital. I've been waiting for you to wake up. I've been going out of my mind without you."

"Where is he? Is he in jail?" I ask in a panic.

"Angel, he'll never hurt you again. He died in the fire."

"Are you sure?"

"Yes. I'm sure. Grant said they identified him by his dental records."

"It's hard to believe."

"I tried to get back in the house to save his ass. I wanted him to go to jail for the rest of his life, but I didn't make it in time. We were lucky to get out."

"Does that mean my house is gone? My parents' house..."

"Angel, we found this." Bryce hands me the metal box.

I open it and glance at my family pictures, making sure they made it through the fire. I close it and hold it tight to my chest. "Thank you."

"Angel, we can build you a new house. Better than it was before."

"It's gone?"

"I'm sorry. Yes, it's gone."

"If he died there, I can't live there."

"I understand."

"This is over? I don't have to worry about him abducting me? Attacking me?"

"It's over. He will never hurt you again."

"You saved me. I was so scared thinking he ambushed you on your way out."

"No. He was out of sight, waiting for the perfect time. We

should have gone to the store together. I should never have left you. I had just entered the store when Grant called me. When he told me that lunatic had escaped, my heart dropped. I ran to my truck and beat the hell out of it to get to you. I was stupid letting my guard down."

"We both did. We were enjoying our freedom."

I touch Bryce's face and run my thumb over his singed eyebrow. "Look at you. Your eyelashes and hair are singed and you've got a cut—"

"I'm okay. It's happened before. It'll grow back."

Bryce reads an incoming text. "Angel, everyone is on their way to see you right now. I've got a couple things to tell you before they get here. Everyone means your Gramps too."

My eyes widen. "Gramps knows?"

"Grant texted me before you woke up. He said your Gramps showed up at the scene and told Grant he needed to start talking right away. Grant had to tell him everything."

"Oh, God! Now he knows, he'll be mad at me for not telling him."

"Angel, I'll talk to him, tell him how you didn't want to worry him. He'll understand—eventually."

"You don't know my Gramps very well. He'll be pissed for a while."

"The moment he sees you, his heart will be breaking."

"Why?"

Bryce walks to the sink and grabs a hand mirror. He helps me sit up a bit.

"Oh."

"What?" he asks, alarm in his voice. "What's wrong?"

"My head ... hurts. And moving makes the room ... spin."

"Okay, you take it easy. The doctor said you'd have symptoms like this." He fluffs pillows behind my back, and I wait for the room to stop spinning. "How's that, Angel?"

"That's a bit better." He hands me the mirror and I hold it up. "Look at me!"

"You're still beautiful."

I touch the bruise on my cheek. The cut above my forehead is deep enough that it needed—stitches. *Damn it! I hope it doesn't leave a scar.* When I move my neck a certain way it hurts. As I look at my neck in the mirror, I see teeth marks and a bruise starting to form. I look at my shattered nails and the memories start coming back to haunt me. I replay everything from beginning to end.

Tears start to fall. "He bit me. And he dragged me down the hall."

"Angel, get that shit out of your head right now. He will never hurt you again. I'm here." Bryce leans, kissing me gently, trying to hug me tenderly, without hurting me.

"He said he killed someone. Can you find out if that's true?"

"I'm asking Grant right now."

Even with Bryce here reassuring me, it's hard to believe this is finally over. "You know, I've been trying to be strong throughout all of this but—" I can't stop my tears from flowing.

"Angel, you're the strongest woman I know. We'll get some counselling. We'll get through this. Together."

"He had me pinned to the floor and I couldn't move. I was praying, I knew I was going to die. You saved me. Again. I love you so much!"

"I love you, Angel." Bryce wipes my tears and kisses my lips softly. "Please don't cry. This is over. We never have to worry again." He climbs on the bed carefully, trying not to jostle me too much. "Is that okay?"

"Yes," I say. "It feels good to have you beside me."

He slips one arm behind my back, gingerly, and rolls onto his side. Then he wraps his other arm around me. "You are safe right here in my arms."

I lean my head against his chest, wincing slightly at the pain in my neck, and we stay like that in silence. When I lie completely still, the pain stops and I can just enjoy the feeling of his big, muscular body next to mine.

With everything that's happened in my life since I've met Bryce, there is no doubt in my mind: my parents sent him to take care of me—to save me.

I look up at him. "What?" he asks.

"You're my guardian angel. You were sent to save me and you did."

He squeezes me gently and kisses my temple.

An incoming text disturbs our special moment. "Angel, they're on their way up. Before they get here, I've got to tell you one more thing. You're pregnant. We're having a baby!"

"I'm pregnant! I remember bits and pieces of conversations before I came to…"

"You could hear us?"

"Yeah. It was weird. I could hear you, but I couldn't respond, or open my eyes, or move anything. I remember a little about the ultrasound … I'm pregnant. We're having a baby! Are you happy?"

"Happy?" Bryce says. "Are you kidding me? I can't wait! Nine months is too long." He pauses, looking into my eyes. "What about you? Are you happy?"

"Yes." I smile, but then wince from the pain as I move slightly. "Ouch! That hurts, but yes, I'm happy."

Bryce hugs me gently and gives me a soft tender kiss. He pulls back. His gorgeous smile is infectious.

I smile, holding my bruised cheek. "I don't know how when I've been taking my pill every day."

"Remember when you told me we have to be careful. You were taking antibiotics for a bad cold. That was about six weeks ago."

"I'm six weeks?"

"Yes."

Just then, the door opens. Bryce rolls carefully off the bed and stands next to me, holding my hand. Leena and Austin, Gramps and Mary, Ma and Grant, Deana, Garrett, and Ciara come walking through the door.

I'm surrounded by everyone I love.

"There she is. She's awake."

"You gave us one hell of a scare."

"Look what that psychopath did to her." Ciara says.

Deana gives her a nudge. "How are you feeling?" Deana asks in a concerned voice, touching my leg.

"I feel like I've been run over by a truck."

Gramps squeezes in to hug me and when he pulls back, I see his eyes are glossy. "Look what he's done to you. He's lucky he's dead! That's all I've got to say."

"I'm with Gramps." Deana nudges Ciara again. "What? He has every right to be pissed off," Ciara says.

Mary rubs Gramps' back and he lets her squeeze by to give me a hug. "I've been praying for you, dear. Everything will be fine."

Bryce moves to the other side of the room and is speaking with Grant. I wonder what they're discussing.

Everyone takes turns leaning in to hug me as gently as possible.

"Keera, this is an ongoing investigation," Grant says. "But as it stands right now, all signs point to him killing his chaperone. We've spoken with a few guards at the jail. He manipulated everyone. He had this planned. We also found he had punctured the gas lines. It was a slow leak and once it built up enough gas, the house exploded. You and Bryce got out just in time. I've already spoken with victims' services and they're coming to speak with you and Bryce."

I don't want to speak with anyone. I'm fine. I can deal with this on my own.

"I can tell by the look on your face you think you can handle this situation but please, listen to them. They've dealt with this kind of thing before. They can help you. Promise me you will listen to them."

I'm bombarded with comments from everyone in this room and I don't really have a choice.

I realize by their comments, they're looking out for my well-being and want me back to normal.

"Fine. I'll listen to them."

They love me. And I'm lucky to have every one of them in my life.

Leena bends to talk against my ear. "Tell them your surprise."

My eyes widen and I purse my lips. "I just found out myself before you walked in. Can I let it sink in a little bit?"

"I'm excited. And we need some good news."

I look around and everyone is staring, wondering what Leena is talking about.

"Umm, Gramps, you know how I told you Bryce and I are engaged? Well, we have the church and hall booked for the wedding at the end of June. We might have to postpone it until the end of the year, or move it up to say, April."

Bryce says, "April."

"Why?" Gramps asks. "I don't understand."

"Umm, I'm pregnant."

The room explodes with chatter and then Bryce and I get hugs and handshakes congratulating us. Gramps is smiling, so I guess he's not too upset.

"Our first grandchild. I'm so excited," Deana says.

"I'm going to be an aunt," Ciara says, "I can't wait to see what this little munchkin looks like."

Garrett stands back with a big smile on his face and he tugs Deana into his side. They gaze into each other's eyes and then turn to Bryce squeezing in next to me. They look overjoyed.

Later, when it quiets down and everyone's feet are sore from standing, they say they will visit tomorrow and head out.

"Mary and I will get a room and we'll be back early to speak to you about what's been going on."

Oh, great! Now I've got all night to think about what I'll say.

"How'd you find out Gramps?"

"Mary saw it on TV. The reporter said it happened in Huntsville. Mary said she saw the before-and-after pictures of the explosion and she was convinced it was your house. I tried to call. There was no answer. We got in the truck and drove here as fast as we could. But that's enough for now. I'll let you rest. We'll see you in the morning." Gramps and Mary give me a kiss on the cheek. "Congratulations, Giggles."

"Thanks, Gramps."

They leave and it's just Bryce and me.

"He'll leave me to stew all night," I say. "He used to pull this crap when I was a bad kid. Gave me the silent treatment to make me think about what I'd done wrong."

"I know what that's like." Bryce snickers.

"I should never have kept it from him."

"I don't know. I think you made the right decision. Your Gramps probably would've beaten that lunatic to death. Did you see the look on his face when he first saw you?"

"Yes. I think you're right. He was a soldier. He wouldn't hesitate to put a beating on him and then bury him somewhere. I've heard stories of what he lived through. He's a badass."

"It's hard to tell, but I think he's happy we're having a baby."

"Yeah, he's ecstatic."

I start to yawn. "I'm really tired."

Bryce carefully climbs back on the bed with me and I lie my head on his shoulder. "Get some rest, beautiful." He bends to kiss my lips. "I love you, Angel."

"I love you, Babe."

"Good morning!"

Bryce jumps up at the sound of Gramps' deep voice and stands at attention next to the bed. "Good morning."

"Boy, when you said you were coming early, you meant early," I say. "What time is it?"

"Seven."

"Here, Mary, you sit here." Bryce slides the chair closer and Mary sits.

"Start from the beginning," Gramps says, getting down to business. He pulls the other chair next to Mary and sits.

I look at Bryce and he looks at me. "It all started the day Keera and I met. I noticed how that jackass was looking at her in the grocery store. Thought it was weird. I followed him out of the parking lot from a distance. Turns out, he was following Keera to her house. I sat three doors down and watched him. At first, he was gawking through her windows. I snuck up on him and scared the shit out of him. He took off after that, so I drove Austin back to the cabin. I thought about how crazy he was acting so I went back to Keera's to see if he came back. He was there again. I could tell he wasn't normal. I knew I had to protect Keera. Keera stayed with us at the cabin for a week and when we went back to her place to shut the water off, the first note was on the door. We took it to the cops. That's where we met Grant. There were a few more notes and some encounters with him. He started setting fires to get our attention. Cops set up surveillance at Keera's and they couldn't catch him either. First, he burnt the Fishers' wheelchair ramp. Then Keera's neighbours' garages on both sides. Two separate incidents. And then a couple houses around town. Keera would come to my house in Barrie or we'd go to the cabin when we didn't want to deal with him. Other times, I'd try to draw him out of hiding to catch him. Keera was upset with me, once, and decided she wanted to stay with Leena for a few days. I wasn't able to change her mind even though I told her I had a bad feeling about it." Bryce turns to me, his jaw set in a scolding manner. "That lunatic broke into Leena's house, drugged Keera, and kidnapped her."

The angry look on Gramps' face intensifies as Bryce speaks.

"I drove like a madman to get to her, hoping the police had some leads."

"You didn't think something like this was important enough to tell me!" Gramps raises his voice.

"Gramps, it was my decision not to tell you. Anyway, they found me and he went to prison. I was fine. I didn't want to worry you. We went to Aruba to get away from it all and had no worries. He was in prison ... until now. Bryce went to the hardware store to get a part for my sink. We both let our guard down. We didn't know he had escaped."

"We found out he's been watching Keera for two years now."

Gramps is silent as he thinks.

Bryce and I look at each other and wonder if we should say anything else.

"I've been living too far away from you. Mary and I have been talking and we're selling our houses and moving to Huntsville as soon as possible. This never would've happened if I lived here."

"Gramps, even the police couldn't catch him."

"What's the address of your cabin? Mary and I would like to buy property on the outskirts of town."

"I'm heading to the cabin today to get Keera some clothes if you'd like to see the area. I can lead the way." Bryce offers. "It's hard to find."

"Giggles, you don't mind if I steal Bryce for an hour?"

"No, I don't mind. You have to see the cabin. You'll love it."

Gramps hugs me. "You'll be safe from now on. I'll make sure of it."

"We'll come later and bring you something good to eat," Mary says.

Bryce gives me a kiss. "Be back in a bit, Angel. You stay in that bed!"

"Okay, bye, love you."

They leave and the first thing I do is call the nurse to get rid of the wires and take the catheter out of me.

When she's done, she says she'll be back shortly to help me to the shower.

The moment she leaves, I shuffle out of bed and slowly make my way to the washroom holding on to anything to keep from falling. I'm still dizzy.

I make it to the sink and notice Leena has brought me the essentials for taking a shower.

The warm water is a welcome feeling except for the initial sting to my open wounds. Taking inventory, I examine the lacerations and wonder how many cuts will be permanent scars. I twist my neck to get a better look in the mirror of the bite marks. The memories of violent abuse start the tears flowing. I shake them off and climb in the shower, then I adjust the spray of water so it doesn't hurt as much.

When the nurse comes back in, I'm lying in bed combing my hair, gently.

She shakes her head and smiles. "Had a feeling you'd get in there on your own."

"That took all my energy, I'm exhausted now. I never knew taking a shower could be so tiring."

Just then, Leena walks through the door holding a bag. "Brought you some of my clothes. Hopefully, you'll get out of here today."

"Thanks. You're the best. You're always here for me. Give me a hug."

"Where's Bryce?"

"He's showing Gramps and Mary where the cabin is. After we told him the whole story, he said he and Mary are selling their houses and moving to the outskirts of Huntsville. He said he's lived too far away and this never would've happened if he lived here."

"You know how your Gramps doesn't say much, but when he does, it's meaningful. He had us all at attention downstairs, laying into us. He was pissed that we kept this from him. Christ, it was like when we were little kids. Remember how I'd always convince you to do something bad with me and then we'd both get in trouble from Gramps. He still scares the shit out of me."

I giggle. "It sounds like he'll be living close to us."

"Is that a good thing or bad?"

"I think it will be good. I'll probably still have to go see him. Where's Austin?"

"He got called to Barrie for a case."

"You don't sound too happy about that."

"I don't know what's going on with him lately. He's preoccupied with something ... or someone."

"Do you think so?"

"He's acting strange and he's distant. I'm getting tired of it."

"Well then, give it back to him."

"That's the plan."

The door opens and a doctor strolls in. "Hi, Keera, I'm Doctor Kendall. Great to see you're awake and alert."

"Nice to meet you," I say, shaking his hand. "When can I go home?"

He laughs. "Let's check you out first. Then we'll see what we can do. Come to sit on the edge of the bed."

Dr. Kendall steps toward me and pulls out a light. "I want you to stare at the door. Eyes forward." He shines the light in my eyes and then takes out a pencil and has me follow it. Next, he checks my reflexes. "And you feel well enough to go home?"

"Definitely. I promise I'll go straight home and take it easy."

He holds his hands up and wants me to push against them. He then checks my breathing and chart. "Other than your potassium, iron, and blood pressure being low, everything else seems to be good. I want you taking prenatal vitamins as soon as possible. And I want your family doctor following up with you. They will send you to an OB/GYN. Straight home and get some rest. I don't want you out dancing all night." He smiles at me. "I'll get the paperwork going. Could be a couple of hours."

"Thank you."

The doctor leaves.

I look for my phone on the table and in the drawer, realizing it was in the house when it exploded. "Damn it! I'll need a phone right away. Can I use yours to call Bryce?"

"Sure."

"How long have I been here?"

"This is your second day in the hospital."

"Two days too long."

"I can buy you a new phone and clothes. We are the same size and I've got great taste." Leena chuckles. "Besides, I've got nothing better to do since Austin is so-called busy."

"You'd do that for me?"

"Oh, yeah."

"Can you buy me a laptop too?"

"Same as before?"

"Yes. You're the best friend anyone could ask for."

"I know," Leena says.

I call Bryce. "Hi, what are you doing? Oh, okay. The doctor says I can leave today. In a couple of hours. Okay, I'll see you then. Bye, love you."

I hand Leena her phone.

"Don't you guys ever **not** get along?"

"We've had our moments. But most of the time, we get along great. I love spending time with him and he tries to get every moment with me."

"So maybe Austin and I should give this up."

"You guys got along great at first."

"Something is going on. I have two days off. I think I'll take a shopping trip to Barrie."

"Bryce wants to go to the cabin."

"Great! This works out then. Can I sleep at Bryce's?"

"Sure. Are you going to spy on Austin?"

"Me? No. Do you have any binoculars?"

"Bryce has a pair downstairs on the shelf near his hunting equipment."

"Perfect! Don't tell Bryce."

"My lips are sealed."

"I'll keep all the receipts and you can pay me when you get a bank card."

"I never thought of that. Licence, health card, passport … Hand me that box, please." I open it and sift through to the bottom. "Passport. It's here!"

"Everything else, you can most likely fill them out online."

"What a pain this will be."

"Wait until after you're married for your licence unless you're not changing your last name. Have Bryce drive you."

"My Journey!"

"Your Journey was in the garage?"

"Yes."

"Not sure how that made out. You'll have to ask Bryce. From what I saw, your garage collapsed. You have insurance, correct?"

"Yes. But will they pay? I don't think a stalker blowing shit up is in the insurance contract."

"They better! That was out of your control—and as if you haven't been through enough. We'll sue their asses!"

"Leena, you should have been a lawyer. You always make a great argument."

"Well, I'm off to investigate why Austin is being a total jackass. I'll see you in two days."

"Love you. Be careful!"

She rubs my belly. "Take care of yourself. You'll get through this. It'll make you stronger. And take care of this little bambino. Bye."

Sifting through Leena's clothes, I find four outfits as well as a down-filled winter coat and leather mukluk boots with fur around the top. It will work until we head back to Barrie, where half my clothes are in Bryce's closet.

When Bryce walks in, he's surprised to see me dressed. "You look beautiful, Angel. But I thought I told you not to get out of that bed. I knew you wouldn't listen."

Bryce is freshly showered. My eyes float up and down his body appreciating how his t-shirt clings to every muscle and then my eyes stop at the bulge in his pants. I lick my lips. "I listen sometimes."

"Who are you kidding?" Bryce gives me his cute corner-of-the-mouth smile.

"How did it go with Gramps? Is he still mad?"

"When I left here, it felt like I was going on a covert operation with him. Have to admit knowing he's a former badass soldier, the thought crossed my mind you'd find me MIA in the forest." Bryce chuckles. "No. I showed him and Mary the cabin and Mary was saying, 'This is what I want.' Then we took a tour of the garage, and Gramps was saying, 'This would make a great wood shop.' I showed him the large door at the back and told him he could get the wood in the forest and carry it in with a John Deere Gator. His eyes lit up, I think. Hard to tell. But he did start asking questions about our builder. I told him I still have the plans. Then we went to see a huge lot. Three acres, half a mile down the road from the cabin with a stream running through it. Mary fell in love with it. Gramps says he'll call about it. Umm, they're coming to the cabin instead of the hospital. They said they'd bring dinner."

"Okay."

"Are you sure? I can call them."

"It'll be great to have them over. Keep my mind off things."

"Did victim's services show up?"

"Yes. They asked me some details about what happened but I got emotional, so they stopped. Told them maybe in a few days I'll be ready to talk. They gave me these." I show Bryce the pamphlets. "They want me to call them."

"You are smooth."

"What?"

"You did not want to speak with them."

"You're getting to know me well."

"I know exactly what you're like. I watch you. I've seen how you try to cover your fear. You'll try to bury your thoughts, denying everything that's happened and when you wake from a nightmare, you'll bury it even further."

I raise my eyebrow and purse my lips together.

He chuckles. "Surprised?"

"Yes."

"I know everything about you. Every detail."

The doctor put a rush on my discharge paperwork and I'm cleared to leave earlier than what I thought I would be. It only took an hour-and-a-half.

As we're driving down the road to the cabin, I notice six inches of fresh snow, which brings the total to three-and-a-half feet. The pine tree branches are weighted down with the thick heavy snow. Most of the small lakes and ponds have frozen over except for the streams with rushing water.

Bryce turns off the road, pulling up to a gate. Getting out of the truck, he undoes the chain and opens both sides, exposing a long laneway. The snow is packed down from Gramps' and Bryce's trucks earlier in the day. Bryce hops in the truck, grabs my knee, and drives a quarter-mile in. He comes around my side of the truck, picks me up, and starts trekking through the snow. It's deep, and I wonder how he's not falling with me in his arms.

"Babe, I can walk."

"No. You're staying right here in my arms. I love holding you."

"You won't be able to do this when I'm nine months pregnant."

"Yes, I will."

"What if I gain eighty pounds?"

"You'll be beautiful and I'll still be able to pick you up."

Bryce stays in the footprints that he, Mary and Gramps made earlier.

Once we get to the stream he says, "Can you picture it? The log cabin will go here and the wood shop will go there." Bryce points with his chin.

"I can see why they fell in love with it. This is what Gramps needs instead of being in North Bay."

"I can picture what it will look like when it's finished. The driveway will be here and Mary said she wants a bridge, right there, over the stream leading to the massive garden she wants. They'll have land as far as the eye can see in the forest. We've already made a trail, so you can visit any time you like. That's how I knew about this place. I hope they can get it."

I think Bryce is more excited than Gramps and Mary. I smile at him.

"What?" he asks, smiling back.

"Nothing. You're just gorgeous. You know that?"

"Are you cold, Angel? Let's get you to the cabin where it's warm."

Once we get to the cabin, Bryce comes around the truck to pick me up, but I'm already out. "Babe, I'm okay, I can walk."

"You're supposed to take it easy."

"I will."

Bryce wraps his arm around my waist and leads me to the cabin and then to the couch. "You're still dizzy from the concussion. I want you staying right here."

I don't argue because I know he's right.

He covers me with a blanket and hands me the remote, then adds more wood to the fire. "Tea or hot chocolate?"

"Tea please."

I flip through the channels for five minutes, not really finding anything I want to watch.

Then I see an explosion and flip back to that channel. The news reporter says, "We have new video from a house explosion in Huntsville, which killed a man. No identification yet. We've also learned there is an investigation against this man, firefighter Bryce Hamilton." They show a file photo of Bryce at a car fire.

"Babe, Bryce! Come here! You've got to see this!" I raise my voice in panic.

Bryce stands between the kitchen and living room staring at the TV and then turns to me. "I didn't get to tell you. I'm being investigated."

"What? This can't be happening. Why?"

"They think I had something to do with that lunatic not getting out of your house."

"That's ridiculous. You tried to get back in to save him."

"I told them in my statement what happened."

I turn back to the TV. "Oh, my God! Look at it. There's nothing left. How can they find anything? It's gone!"

Bryce takes the remote and changes the channel. "I didn't want you to see that. And please, don't worry about the investigation. We're working to clear my name." Bryce sits on the edge of the couch and hugs me. "Are you okay?"

"Yes, but I'm worried about you and your job."

"Don't worry about me. I've got my dad and Austin on it."

"Everything is gone," I whisper.

Just then, there is a knock at the back door.

27

*J*TENSE AND BRYCE notices. "Are you sure you're okay?"

"I'm good." I move to get up and Bryce holds my shoulder.

"You stay here."

He walks over to answer the door and I peer over the couch, waiting anxiously.

I look down and see my hands shaking.

How do they know he died in the fire? Maybe he got out of my house. What if he followed us from the hospital?

I'm on the verge of yelling out Bryce's name when Mary and Gramps come through the door. *What is wrong with me?*

I exhale deeply, realizing I was holding my breath the whole time. I smile, but deep down inside my stomach is in knots.

I need proof he's dead or this fear will never go away.

"Hello, how are you feeling?" Mary asks.

"I'm good," I say, choking out the words.

"You stay there dear and I'll fix you a plate."

"Thank you, Mary."

Bryce looks at me, his forehead furrowed. He can see something is wrong, but keeps it to himself.

Gramps comes to give me a kiss. "How is my Giggles doing?" He asks and then goes to sit on the other side of the sectional.

"I'm doing good. Did you find out about that property?"

"It is for sale and we're negotiating back and forth. Look, I got a cell phone."

"Are you trying to give me a heart attack?" I ask, disguising the fear I was showing only moments ago.

Mary and Bryce join us in the living room and Mary sits next to Gramps with their dinner—fried chicken, mashed potatoes, gravy, and salad.

Bryce places both our plates on the coffee table and gives my knee a reassuring squeeze.

"Looks good," I say. "I'm starving!" I look down and see my hands aren't shaking as much.

Bryce has three possible plans for Gramps' new log cabin laid out in front of us on the coffee table. Gramps starts to sift through them without touching his food.

"This is the plan I originally wanted but Austin talked me out of it. Said it wasn't in our budget. It would have been another sixty grand and since we wanted the best of everything in the interior, we had to compromise."

I finally feel the tension leave my body and Bryce notices, running his hand down my thigh.

"I absolutely love the wrap-around porch," Mary says.

"So do I," Bryce agrees. "That's why this front porch is larger than the plans. We had to change a few things, but it worked out in the end. You don't have to follow the plans exactly. If you hire our builder, he will work with you. He wants his customers happy."

"The interior will be a work in progress," Gramps says. "I'll want to do the trim myself."

"I knew you would," I say, smiling at how excited Gramps, Mary, and Bryce are about this project.

Just then, Gramps' phone rings. He fumbles to get it out of his pocket. "Hello? Hello? I don't know how to use this damn thing."

We all smile.

"Gramps you have to tap the green button."

"Hello? Yes, this is him. I see. Well … I'll talk it over with Mary and see if we can go that high. I'll call you back. Yup. All right, bye."

Gramps looks at Mary, and sighs. "He came down ten grand."

"That's okay James, I have the money in my savings account. If you want it, buy it."

"No. I'm letting him stew for a day or two. He told me he hasn't had any bites on the lot since he put it up for sale. I want him to come down another twenty grand."

"Gramps, let me pitch in. I earned a lot of money from my last job. I want to help."

"No. It's the principal of it. He doesn't need to charge that much."

Gramps starts to eat as he eyes the plans. "If we don't get this lot, we'll buy somewhere else. But I do like this log cabin. What do you think?"

"That's my favourite too," Mary says. "I love the layout with the large front porch and big kitchen."

Gramps tugs Mary next to him, hugging her.

This is the first time he's shown affection to Mary with us in the room. It's adorable.

"Besides, that extra twenty grand will help pay for the John Deere Gator." Gramps smiles at Bryce.

I think Gramps is enjoying Bryce's company, and with this project, they will bond further.

Gramps and Mary stay for a couple more hours and I feel lazy with Bryce and Mary waiting on me. Every time Gramps wants to see parts of Bryce's cabin to get ideas for building his own, I'm told to stay on the couch. I stay as long as I can and then nature calls.

It's nice having Gramps and Mary over, they're keeping my mind busy.

I tell them they can stay overnight in Austin's room but Gramps has paid for the hotel.

They'll be back in the morning he says. He wants to inspect the garage again.

Next morning, Gramps and Mary come in early with Tim Horton's coffee and tea. "Good morning. We brought you something."

"Good morning."

"We knew you couldn't make it to the store," Mary says, walking to the couch, handing me a bag from the drug store. "Your grandfather wants you taking these vitamins right away," she says, lowering her voice to a whisper.

"Thank you. I will."

Standing, I walk to the kitchen and give Gramps and Mary hugs. Gramps frowns. "Shouldn't you be taking it easy?"

"I'm good now, not as light-headed and dizzy as before."

"I want you taking it easy."

"I will."

After eating breakfast, we dress warmly and head to the garage with Bryce protectively watching over me.

As we're showing Gramps around, he gets a phone call and fumbles for his phone again. "Damn thing! Hello? Yeah. Which lot is this again? Oh, okay. Yes. Mary and I discussed it and that's the highest we can go. We're looking at other lots more in our price range. Yeah, sure. Bye."

"What did they say?" I ask.

"He said he'd speak with his wife."

Moments later, his phone rings again. He lets it ring three times and then answers it. "Hello? Yes. All right. What's the address? We'll come to sign the paperwork and bring a down payment. See you in an hour."

Mary holds Gramps' arms and looks in his eyes. "What did he say?"

"He took it. We got three acres for a hundred grand. That's a good deal, eh?"

Mary hugs Gramps. "I'm so excited!"

"I'm happy for you two," I say.

"Whenever we're down from Barrie and you need help, give me a call," Bryce says.

After Gramps and Mary leave, Bryce and I snuggle on the couch, talking. "Babe, you don't have to stay here with me. Go for a ride on the snowmobile."

"No. I'm staying right here. What spooked you yesterday when I went to answer the door?"

"You saw that, eh?"

"Yes. Will you tell me what's going on in that pretty little head of yours?"

"How do you know for sure he's dead? I need proof, or I'll never be at peace."

"I'll see if Grant can get a copy of his dental records and we'll compare them ourselves."

"Thank you. Shouldn't you be going back to work tomorrow?"

"I was going to call and tell them I need another day."

"But then you'll have to make it up some other time. I'm okay to travel back to Barrie."

"Are you sure?"

"Yes. I'm sure. Weren't you supposed to work for George?"

"Yes, but he'll understand. Shit happens in life that we can't control."

"What about the investigation against you? Did the fire department find out about it yet?"

"Yes. My dad and Austin are trying to clear my name."

"You're not temporarily suspended?"

"No. The Chief said he will not suspend me unless someone higher up demands it."

I get off the couch and grab his hand. "We've got to get you back to work! They'll see there is no way you could've done what they're accusing you of."

"Okay, okay," Bryce chuckles. "I guess we're going back to Barrie."

"I would die if you lost your job because of that lunatic."

"Angel, everything will be fine. Let me text Grant and see if we can pick up a copy of the dental records on our way through. I don't want you worrying over this."

I rush to collect our things and we are out the door, making a quick stop at police headquarters. Then we head south on Highway 11.

I text Leena with Bryce's phone:

This is Keera. We're coming back to Barrie.

Leena texts back:

Damn it! I need one more day. Can I stay at Bryce's tonight?

Sure. Bryce has to go to work.

Perfect! See you later.

We make it back to Barrie with an hour to spare so Bryce can cover for George on the afternoon shift. Before he leaves, Bryce gives me strict instructions to take it easy and relax. I also get a simmering kiss and he holds me tight, not wanting to leave me.

Once Bryce is gone, I call Leena on Bryce's home phone asking where she is and where she's hiding my new phone and laptop.

"I'm sitting in my car waiting for Austin and his new female partner to come out of police headquarters."

"Oh, no!"

"Everything is in the front closet. This is why he's been acting like a jackass. He wants her."

"I hope you're wrong." Something in her voice tells me she's upset.

"I'll see you later. Bye."

Finding them, I start the painstaking task of setting up my new phone and laptop.

Hours later, when it's dark, Leena comes through the door and stomps up the stairs.

I can tell by the look on her face the news is not good. I lean in to give her a hug and she backs up, holding her hands in the air.

"No! No hugs. I'm not crying over this asshole! We're done! He's got a lot of nerve treating me like shit because he's sniffing around her. Fucking dog! I'm pissed!" Leena turns and walks into the living room, then spins quickly and chuckles. "Funny thing is, she has a big, gorgeous husband and two beautiful little babies. Too bad, Austin. She doesn't want you! And now, neither do I!"

"You're always there for me, helping me through the tough times, and when I want to support you, you push me away."

"I'm pissed right now and if you hug me, I'll cry. I don't cry!" Leena turns and starts pacing again.

"What exactly did you see?"

"I sat across from the cop shop with the binoculars and watched them go to the cruiser. I can tell by his body language how he's trying to impress her. He did that with me when we started dating. He's rubbing against her, smiling, opening her door, and trying to charm his way into her heart. She smiled back a couple of times but mostly she's all business, proving she can do the job. I was wondering why she doesn't look interested, so I followed her."

"You did?"

"Fucking right I did. Her massive gorgeous husband met her at the daycare and they picked up their two adorable kids together. That's when I saw the wedding rings. They look like you and Bryce, all lovie dovie. I zoomed in to the bulge in his pants

324 | Book 3

and holy shit that thing looks like a python. No wonder she's happy with what she has."

"Leena, you crack me up."

"Anyway, I've decided I'm not calling Austin. I want to see how long it takes him to call me. And when he does, I'll tell him you're obviously preoccupied with someone, so it's time for us to move on."

"You go, girl! Give it to him! And if it's meant to be then you'll get back together. If not, make him suffer."

"I plan on it."

"Did you set up your phone and laptop? And did you see the clothes?"

"Yes. Clothes, I haven't dug them out yet."

Leena runs to the front closet and back and spreads the clothes out on the couch. "This burgundy and grey baseball shirt and these ripped bootcut jeans will go great together. And this army green shirt tucked into the front of these jeans will look fabulous. Oh, and look at this sweater and these boots. I couldn't resist."

"Wow! I love them all." I pick up a boot and unzip the side. "When did you have time to shop when you were spying?"

"Investigating."

"Right."

"When I knew their shift was done, I went to the mall. I was starving by that time."

"Thank you. I owe you."

"Oh, while I was bored in my car, I was surfing the net, using my data, and I found out Colton has a new girlfriend."

"Good. I'm glad. Now he won't bother us. He could tell at the gala I wasn't impressed with his games."

"Where's your laptop?"

I point to the dining room table.

"You've got to see this." Leena clicks away and brings up a picture. It shows Colton and his new girlfriend dressed up at an awards show.

"Look at her. She could be your twin," Leena says.

"She does look a lot like me."

"Ya think? But you're cuter and you've got a better body."

"I don't know."

"Oh, yeah."

"Thanks, you're too sweet."

"Maybe I'll call Reese when Austin and I break up."

"Really? You'd do that?"

Leena chuckles. "Maybe I'll ask him if he's free to be my date for your wedding."

I laugh. "That would be devious."

Leena's eyes light up as she clears my new clothes off the couch. She then goes to hang them up in Bryce's closet and is back in a few moments.

We lie on the couch relaxing, feet touching.

"So how have you been?" Leena asks.

"Good."

"Come on, Keera. Spill it! I can tell something is wrong. Are you getting headaches?"

"I've had one since I woke up."

"For two days you've had a headache?"

"Yes."

"Did you tell Bryce?"

"No. It'll go away. I'm not taking anything, except vitamins."

"Stubborn! If it's not gone by tomorrow, talk to your family doctor."

"I will."

"Don't bullshit me."

"I'm not. I'll tell her."

"Good."

"I should've known I was pregnant. There were quite a few signs and there were times I felt sick but once I ate something it would go away." I chuckle. "Except for the last day working for Blue Caribbean Swimwear. They stuck me under the hot lights and I could feel it brewing. I ran to the washroom and what little breakfast I had, came up. I couldn't wait for that day to end."

"You're six weeks pregnant and I got to see your first ultrasound before you did."

"We should be able to see more in the next one. I've been trying to pinpoint when we conceived. Six weeks ago we were at Gramps' house. It was the first time they met and Bryce wanted to give Gramps the best first impression. Bryce didn't want to have sex but I got him so hot, he couldn't resist. But then, he was still anal about being quiet, so it was a slow, sensual fuck. It was amazing."

"So, it was a naughty, could-get-caught-at-any-moment, kind of fuck?"

"Yes, it was." I get up and walk to the kitchen cupboard, taking out my cheque book to pay Leena. "After my shower the next morning, I overheard Bryce asking Gramps for his blessing to marry me. I'll always remember it. I believe we conceived that night at Gramps' house."

Leena takes the cheque from me. "Ah, this is too much."

"Take it. You came to Barrie and you shopped for me."

"I came to investigate. And had fun shopping."

"Thank you again. You're the best."

The next morning, Leena heads to Huntsville early, before the snowstorm hits. She has to work for the next three days but afterwards, we make plans to look for bridesmaid's dresses.

Around noon, Bryce calls me on his home phone. "What are you doing?"

"I'm lying in bed, filling out information for my new health card."

"How's my Angel today?"

"I'm taking it easy. How's your day going?"

"It's good. Are you sure you're okay? And how are you filling out information if you have no computer?"

"Still not one-hundred percent. Leena went shopping for me. Bought me a new computer, phone, and clothes. She stayed overnight."

"I'm worried about you. But that's great Leena came to visit. Still the same number?"

"Yup. Same number. Oh, I called the church and hall and the only date available for both was April twenty-fifth. Hope I'm not showing too much."

"You'll be the most beautiful bride ever."

"Thanks, Babe."

"Did you hear how much snow we're supposed to get?"

"Eight to ten inches."

"Now they're saying ten to twelve. It'll be crazy around here," Bryce says in his deep voice. "They asked me for overtime. I told them I'd see how you're feeling."

"Work it if you want. I'm just lying around anyway. This way you can bank your hours for the summer when it's beautiful out. Maybe we could go camping or take the ATVs for a trip."

"Sounds like a great plan. Okay. I'll text later. I wanted to call last night but we got back to the station late after a house fire and I didn't want to wake you."

"That's okay. Be careful in all that snow. Bye, I love you."

"I will. I love you, Angel."

The next morning, I wake to cramps in my lower abdomen. It's strange, and it worries me. When I go to the toilet, I notice blood on the toilet paper.

What the heck is going on?

I throw on a pad and make my way to the kitchen, filling the kettle to make my tea. I look out the front window and it looks like a blizzard. My first thought is, *Bryce is outside in this bad weather.* I get closer to the front window and, by holding my hand near it, I can feel how the temperature has dropped with the strong winds.

I want to call Bryce to see if he's okay but I change my mind and text him:

How are you? I hope you're not out in this crap.

The text shows delivered and he texts back:

We stopped at Timmies to get something warm. It's been busy, but now it'll be crazy with rush hour traffic. There will be accidents everywhere.

Stay safe! I'll be thinking of you all day! I love you! Be careful!

I will! I love you too, Angel … Dante says him, too. Lol!

I smile at my phone, loving how great they get along and knowing they have each other's backs.

The cramps are more severe now, reaching my lower back, so I take my tea with me and cuddle the pillow and heating pad in bed.

Within an hour, I'm up, changing the pad.

I text Leena, scared out of my mind:

Are you at work?

No. I couldn't get out of my driveway. Besides that, Manny called and said not to come in. The bakery is closed for the day due to the storm. What's up?

I woke up to cramps and I had to put a pad on.

Now, don't get too excited there. A lot of women spot while they're pregnant.

This is more than spotting. This is my second pad.

Oh. So what are you thinking? Miscarriage?

I hope not!

Does Bryce know?

He's working outside in the storm. I don't want to bother him.

Keep monitoring it. Pay attention to all your symptoms. Keep me updated.

I will. Has Austin called?

No. And I am getting more pissed off as the days go by.

Sorry. I didn't mean to bring it up.

That's okay. Text or call me. And don't stress yourself out.

Okay.

For most of the day, I keep my mind busy with my phone and laptop—that is when I'm not dealing with the excruciating pain of the cramps and changing my pad. I get tired of lying in bed and walk to the front window to check out the storm. I think to myself, if I wasn't in pain, I'd get outside and push the snow off the driveway. But the thought disappears when the pain becomes so intense, I'm doubling over. I make my way back to bed, slowly.

Tears start to flow when I look at the ultrasound picture Bryce saved and I think of how I could lose this precious little baby inside me.

Two hours later, Bryce calls me. "Hi, Angel."

"Hi."

"Are you okay?"

Wincing, I let go a soft moan of pain.

"Angel, what's wrong?"

"I've been spotting and cramping all day."

28

"WE'RE ON OUR way!"

"Babe, I don't want everyone to know."

"Too late! We're coming down our road to get you."

"I'm not dressed."

"You better get dressed because they're most likely coming in the house."

"Bye!" I rush as fast as I can to the bathroom and fix myself up and then get changed. I'm sitting on the side of the bed when Bryce comes in the room wearing his bunker gear.

"Come on, let's get you to the hospital."

"I've seen enough of the hospital. I don't think it's urgent, the cramps might go away."

"It is urgent! I saw you buckling over with pain. Come on, let's go. Besides, this is a different hospital."

Bryce slides my coat on and picks me up in his arms.

Dante covers me with a blanket. "She is a stubborn one."

I turn and frown at Dante and then I feel Jax sliding my slippers on my feet. "You, little missy, are giving us a scare lately," Jax says.

"Sorry, I don't mean to."

"Dante, grab Keera's purse. Dresser."

"Got it."

Once we get to the foyer, Dante tucks me in the blanket. "It's damn cold out there."

"You guys get ahead of me and I'll hand her up to you," Bryce says.

The snow is blowing wickedly, blinding us as Bryce walks through the deep snow. The howling gust of wind shoves Bryce sideways and I feel the cold beneath the blanket. It's hard to breathe as my nose hair feels like it's freezing from the extreme cold.

Jax and Dante motion to pull me up into the firetruck. "Babe, I can get in myself."

"She's a stubborn one," Dante says as he tries to help. Then he runs around to get in the front seat and Bryce climbs in next to me. The wind whips up again and snowflakes engulf the doorway, scattering throughout the cab of the firetruck.

Bryce uses force to close the door. "That wind is unbelievable," he says, pulling me close. We watch out the front window as the firetruck plows through the streets.

"Hi, Keera."

"Hi, George."

"Are you okay?" Bryce asks, squeezing my knee.

"I am now." I smile at him and he wraps his arm around my shoulder, holding me tighter.

Once we get to Main Street where there aren't as many houses and the road opens up, the wind strength is incredible. George fights the wheel as the wind hits the side of the truck. He struggles to stay in the middle of the road.

The snow drifts are scattered here and there and the truck slows when it hits larger accumulations forming across the roadway.

Minutes later, George pulls up beside an ambulance stuck in a large drift and Dante rolls down the window to speak with the driver. "Need some help?"

"Yes. We need to get this VSA to the hospital. He's stable at the moment."

"Be back in a minute, Angel."

I watch as the guys spring into action, rushing to get out of the truck.

George and I stay in the firetruck. He pulls in front of the ambulance and I watch through the side mirrors trying to get a glimpse of—well, anything. It is mostly white but when the wind dies down for a second or two, I see the reflective stripes on their turnout gear from the ambulance headlights. I hear a knock on the driver's door and then George rolls down the window.

"All hooked up. Nice and slow." I see Jax in the mirror directing George. "Little more, little more," Jax yells above the howling wind. "Good. She's tight. Okay. Give 'er all she's got."

With the window rolled down, it is now cold in the cab of the truck and I shiver, grasping my stomach from the pain and I wrap the blanket around my body.

George steps on the gas and the firetruck jerks a bit and moves forward.

"Keep going ... more, more. Good. Back her up a bit," Jax shouts.

I see the ambulance pull up beside us and George waves. They turn their lights and sirens on, and I watch as the ambulance disappears down the road into the whiteout.

Bryce, Jax, and Dante hop in the cab of the truck and we follow the ambulance to the hospital.

"That was exciting!" I say.

Dante and George look back and smile. "That was nothing," Dante says. "We should have you with us at some of our other calls."

I picture Bryce and his best friends fighting a fire and how they would do absolutely anything to protect one another. They're like brothers. They have a strong bond and I see that now.

They've accepted me into their firefighting family and I'm happy to be a part of it.

When we pull up to the hospital, the ambulance attendants are transporting their patient inside.

George hesitates outside the carport overhang.

"Pull up beside them on the left," Bryce directs George. "It's fourteen-ten. We're twelve-eight. Lots of room." George follows Bryce's directions.

Dante jumps from the passenger seat with the truck still rolling. "I'll get the gurney."

Bryce tugs me into his side. "Are you in pain, Angel? Tell me the truth."

"Yes."

"Let's get you inside."

Bryce jumps down from the firetruck and I slide into his arms. He struts over to the gurney, placing me gently down on it, and covers me with the blanket. They wheel me from the cold blowing wind to the warm waiting room inside.

I notice emergency is totally vacant from the bad weather outside as they push me down the hall and over to admitting.

Dante hands Bryce my purse and he finds my temporary health card number. The nurse asks a few questions and types the information into the computer.

Jax and Dante chat with Bryce while we wait for a room and I stifle the waves of pain that hit me now and then.

A flock of nurses nearby are talking amongst themselves and looking our way. I watch as Dante catches a glimpse of them and excuses himself from the conversation.

Jax and Bryce watch him go.

Bryce looks from Dante to me, rolling his eyes and shaking his head with a look of disbelief—Bryce's typical response to Dante's womanizing ways.

I can still remember at the fire department Christmas party when Bryce said, "Don't compare me to Dante. I'm not like him."

Bryce loves Dante like family but he doesn't always agree with the way he acts.

When the nurse is done admitting me, another nurse wheels me into a room and Jax and Dante follow.

Bryce places two warm blankets on top of me. "How's that, Angel?"

"Feels great!"

"Got the hot one's number," Dante says, holding up his phone.

"You did not!" Jax says, doubting him.

"Look!" Dante holds his phone to Jax's face. "Mikaela."

"How do you do that? Seriously." Jax shakes his head.

Just then, all their pagers go off with a loud beeping sound, alerting them to the next fire call. "We better get back to work."

"Thank you for your help. You guys are the best."

"No problem," Jax says, surprising me with a kiss on my cheek.

"We've always got your back," Dante says, squeezing my hand. Dante looks at Bryce. "We'll cover you."

Bryce pats Dante and Jax on the back. "Thanks, eh."

As they're heading out the door I hear, "I got a kiss from her."

"On the cheek, asshole. Not considered a kiss." Dante corrects him.

They shove each other and Jax smiles back at me. I return a smile and wave.

After they leave, Bryce turns to me, stepping out of his turnout gear. "I want you to tell the doctor every symptom you're having. Don't leave anything out. I know what you're like." Bryce scolds me with his eyes.

My eyes float down the length of his body, appreciating how good he looks in his tight t-shirt and jeans.

"You always do that," he says.

"What?"

"Look at me like that when I'm giving you shit and then I can't think straight afterwards."

A bad cramp hits. I grasp my abdomen, wincing in pain.

"Angel, are you okay?"

"Yeah. Just another bad one."

Bryce takes my hand in his, holding it with his other hand. "I wish I could take your pain away."

"I'll be okay."

Two nurses come in and out of my room taking my vitals, making small talk as they fill out my chart. I find them staring at Bryce and me as we talk. It's distracting.

Ten minutes later, another nurse comes in, introducing herself as the head nurse. She asks about the cuts and bruises on my face.

"These are from an incident that happened last week. Today, I'm here because I'm pregnant, spotting, and have bad cramps."

She checks my blood pressure, marks it on my chart, and disappears.

Half an hour later, the two nurses who were in earlier say they're taking me to ultrasound.

"Is it okay if my fiancé comes?"

They look at each other, hesitating for a few seconds.

The short one finally says, "Yes."

Their hesitation is strange because Bryce told me at the hospital in Huntsville, we had a room full.

The nurses push the gurney down the hall to the elevators and then to ultrasound. Bryce sits next to me and holds my hand.

This will be the first time I'll see our baby. I'm so excited!

The technician exposes my belly, squirting the gel, rubbing hard in certain spots, clicking away at her mouse and on the computer screen.

I only see dark and light shades and wonder what she's measuring.

"Is it still too early to find out the sex of our baby?"

"Yes. Usually between eighteen to twenty weeks." The technician says.

"Do you see anything unusual?"

"You should get the results from your physician within a couple of hours, or less."

"So that means you can't tell me anything."

"I give the report to the physician and they inform you."

"Just thought I'd pry, hoping to get some information."

"Almost every patient tries." She smiles.

When she's done, she wipes the gel off, covers me up, and rolls me out to the hall, where the nurses are waiting to transport me to my room.

As we're travelling in the elevator, I think about how short the ultrasound was and the fact that she didn't give us a picture of our baby. It worries me.

I look into Bryce's eyes and see the same look of concern.

My eyes start to water but I hold the tears in and think of something else.

Once the nurses leave, I turn to Bryce. "Was the other ultrasound longer? And why didn't she give us any pictures?"

"Yes, the other technician was a little more thorough than this one."

"I'm worried."

"We have to wait for the doctor. No stressing yourself out." Bryce hugs me and then sits in the chair and holds my hand.

The two nurses return after about five minutes and look at Bryce. "Can we ask you to go down to the waiting room for five minutes while we check Keera out?"

"Sure." Bryce squeezes my hand. "I'll be back in five minutes. Do you want anything from the cafeteria?"

"Maybe an orange juice. Thanks, Babe."

"Sorry," one of the nurses says. "You can't have anything until the doctor sees you and says it's okay."

The moment Bryce leaves, the nurses turn to me. "We have great programs to help victims," the short one says.

"The programs will help you think differently and you'll meet other women who have gone through the same situation," the other one says.

"You'll learn this is not the way life is supposed to be."

"If you give us the word, we will have security detain him and you can fill out a restraining order to keep him away from you."

"You'll never have to see him again or fear him from this moment on. If you need somewhere to live there are places we can contact and you can stay there until you find a more permanent place to live. Do you have any family members who can help you?"

They stare at me while I process what they're saying.

I point to the door and then my face. "You think Bryce did this to me?" I shake my head. "No! Bryce saved me. A stalker did this to me."

"Overcoming denial is the first step."

"Wait a second. Bryce did not do this to me! Bryce would never hurt me. Ever!"

They still have looks of disbelief.

"Look." I grab my phone out of my purse and do a quick search. "Right here. Look. This is what I went through last week. The stalker who has been following me around for over two years escaped from prison and beat the hell out of me. Then he torched my house. Bryce saved me just before my house exploded."

They take my phone and watch the video.

"I know it sounds unbelievable but it really did happen."

"We're so sorry," the short nurse says, touching my leg. "Sorry you went through that."

"We apologize. We get a lot of abuse victims and they refuse to see they have a problem."

"I'm glad the staff is aware and try to help the victims of abuse. And if I ever need your help, I'll come to see you." I smile at them.

"We'll let our head nurse know we were wrong about this one."

"Thank you."

They leave and I shake my head. *Unbelievable! That's why they were looking at me strangely.*

A few minutes pass and then I hear a knock at the door. "Come in."

"All clear?" Bryce asks, popping his head in.

"Yeah. They left."

"Did they check you out?"

"No. They wanted to have a discussion."

"The results of the ultrasound?"

"No. They started rambling about victims and meeting other women in the same situation. Then they said in the program I'll learn this is not the way life is supposed to be. They said they would call security to detain you and I'd never have to see you again. They'd call to find me a place to stay and they asked if I have family to help."

Bryce makes a face of misunderstanding. He frowns and crinkles his nose. "What?"

"They thought you beat the hell out of me. When I finally realized what they were insinuating, I told them you would never do this to me. You would never hurt me. Ever! You saved me from that lunatic."

"What did they say?"

"They still didn't believe me. I had to show them the video. Then they apologized."

"Unbelievable."

"Said they see this kind of thing all the time. I told them it's great the staff is aware of the problem and help their patients."

"I was wondering why the head nurse was giving me dirty looks. Should've known when she asked about your cuts and bruises."

"I forgot about them with the pain in my stomach."

"How are you feeling now?"

"The pain comes and goes."

An hour later, Bryce is still shaking his head. He can't believe the nurses would assume he had beaten me.

Just then, an older gentleman opens the door and introduces himself. "Hello, I'm Dr. Branson."

"Bryce and Keera." Bryce shakes the doctor's hand firmly.

"I've been looking over your test results and your ultrasound and I don't know how to tell you except to be blunt. I'm sorry.

You've had a miscarriage. But everything looks good and you should have no problem in the future having a baby."

Bryce turns to look at me, squeezing my hand, and then turns back to the doctor. "Can you tell me what happened?"

"To be frank, we have no way of knowing," the doctor says. "This is very common. At least twenty-five percent of pregnancies end in miscarriage. It can be caused by stress, thyroid, hormones, chromosomal abnormality, and insufficient development of the embryo."

The doctor sees my tears falling. "But you don't need to hear all of this right now. I'll give you some time and I'll be back later to answer your questions."

Bryce says, "Thank you." He doesn't wait for the doctor to leave. He leans, hugging me tight. "Angel, I'm sorry. We'll have another baby. The moment the doctor says we can."

"He did this! He took our baby from us! I was eating healthy, taking vitamins. I didn't even take a Tylenol for the headaches."

Bryce sits on the edge of the bed wiping my tears. "Angel, you heard what the doctor said. Many factors can lead to miscar—"

I cut him off. "You heard the doctor. Stress!"

"I refuse to give that bastard the satisfaction," he says, his voice firm and clear. "He is out of our lives. Gone. Forever!"

I put my head down and think about what Bryce is saying.

He pauses, letting his powerful words sink in.

He's right. From this point on, I refuse to think about that psychopath. He is gone. Forever!

"My mom had miscarriages. Maybe our baby wasn't developing properly."

Bryce lifts my chin. "My aunts had miscarriages and then later had healthy babies. No one knows why. It just happens. We will get through this and we will have healthy babies."

I try to process what Bryce is saying and then my mind drifts off to our precious baby we'll never get to meet.

"Angel, look at me." Bryce holds his hand on my cheek. "Life can be devastating at times, sending us in a tailspin, but I'm telling you, if we can make it through these tough times, we can handle anything life throws our way. I promise you, life will get better."

"How do you do that? You always know what to say and you're always here for me."

"I love you, Angel."

"You are the best thing that's ever happened to me. I love you, Babe."

Bryce climbs on the bed, holding me tight, and wipes away my tears. "I hate seeing you hurt like this."

We lie in silence for I don't know how long, alone in our own thoughts.

"Angel, are you okay?"

"I'm okay. I was thinking about our baby again. I wonder if it was a boy or a girl."

"All I know is, you will be a great mom."

"Thanks, Babe. I needed that."

The doctor comes back in to answer our questions and then he signs the release forms.

Once he leaves, Bryce calls Dante to swing by the hospital with the firetruck. It's our only way of getting home in this snow storm.

The ride home is worse than the drive to the hospital. The brunt of the storm is hitting us full force, five hours later. Cars and trucks are stuck everywhere in the three-foot snow drifts.

Jax, Dante, and George are quiet on the way home. I'm assuming Bryce told them about my miscarriage and they don't want to upset me by asking questions. I can tell they know from the sympathy in their eyes. And Dante is never this quiet.

As we pass by abandoned vehicles stuck in snow drifts, the guys check to make sure the occupants have made it out safely. As we're turning onto Johnson Street, a car with its flashers on catches Dante's eyes. "Hold up there, George. I want to get a close look at this one."

Dante jumps from the firetruck and treks through the deep snow.

He brushes the snow off the window and knocks, then turns and whistles for help.

Bryce and Jax jump out.

They are back in a flash with two small children and their mother. Bryce hoists them up and I pull them into the back seat with me and tuck them in under my blanket.

Their mom sits on the other side of them. "It's so cold. I was scared when we got stuck. There was no one on the roads for at least two hours. I didn't even see a snow plow. I got the sleeping bag and an old t-shirt out of the trunk and used it as a flag, hoping someone would see it. Our gas ran out about an hour ago and we were freezing so we cuddled in the sleeping bag. I'm so happy you came down this road and found us. My name is Julie and this is Jameson and Kade."

"Dante. Nice to meet you." Dante reaches back and shakes Julie's hand. "I'm glad we came down this road, too," he says.

There's a look on Dante's face I've never seen before.

"Mom. We're in a firetruck," says the oldest boy, Jameson.

Julie slides the youngest one, Kade, on her lap as she answers her older boy. "I know, honey."

"You don't have to be afraid anymore," Jameson says as he gently touches his mom's cheek.

"I know. The firemen will take good care of us." Turning to us, she says, "Riding in a firetruck has been a dream of his for a couple of years now."

"You'll have to bring him to the station one day and we'll show him the other firetrucks," Dante says. "Give him a tour."

"I will. He'll love it. Thank you so much."

"I'm Bryce, my fiancé Keera, Jax, and George." Bryce points to everyone. "And you've already met Dante."

"Nice to meet you," we say together.

Julie smiles. "It was getting a little scary out there."

"No problem," Dante says. "We're here to help."

We hit another snow drift and it flies in the air, covering the windshield.

Julie holds onto her children, protecting them.

I look over and smile. They're an adorable family.

My mind wanders to our baby we lost. *Will we be able to have children? Will I have multiple miscarriages like my mom?* I'm so deep in thought, I don't realize George has pulled up in front of Bryce's house. He won't pull into the driveway, fearing they'll get stuck in a large drift.

"Thanks, guys."

"You take care, Keera."

"I will. It was nice meeting you. Bye everyone."

"Bye." They wave and Bryce climbs down from the truck. He waits with open arms as I lower myself down.

Dante exits the front seat and holds our door, bracing it from the harsh winds. Jax switches to the front seat and Dante climbs in the back, next to Julie and her boys.

We give them one last wave and Bryce treks through the deep snow with me in his arms. Once we're inside and I'm in our nice, warm bed, he stays with me, fussing and pampering me, until I fall asleep.

Later, I wake from a dead sleep, crying, as I remember the details of the dream that woke me.

Our baby boy had black hair with Bryce's beautiful eyes and perfect nose. I was holding him in his blanket and he smiled at me. The love I feel for him breaks my heart.

When I reach for Bryce, he's not there.

I wipe my tears and throw back the sheets, sliding out of the bed, covering myself with my housecoat.

Wandering around the house, I search every room looking for him.

In the distance, I hear the sound of an engine and I head over to the front window to look outside. Bryce has cleaned five of his neighbours' driveways of snow. I stand at the window and watch him, proud he's mine.

He sees me and signals that he'll be one more minute. When he comes through the door, he says, "What are you doing up? You're supposed to be sleeping. Come on, let's get you to bed."

"Only if you're coming with me," I say, snuggling into his side. "I had a feeling all that snow was driving you crazy."

"This way, the neighbours can get out of their driveways in the morning."

We climb back in bed and he holds me until I fall asleep again.

Bryce's pager goes off five times during the night. I can tell he's curious about what's going on, but he stays with me.

When I wake, he has a tray with breakfast and tea off to the side. "Good morning, beautiful." He props up my pillows and positions the tray in front of me.

"Good morning Mr. Tall, Dark, and Gorgeous. It looks delicious." I hold his face in my hands. "I love you."

"I heard your stomach growling."

"You didn't get much sleep last night."

"Too much thinking," he says as he sits on the bed facing me. "I noticed your eyes were a little red when I came in the house last night. Were you crying?"

"Woke out of a dead sleep remembering the dream I had. I was holding our baby boy and he looked like you. He smiled at me..."

Bryce wipes my tears. "I think I had the same dream. It seemed real. Our boy had black hair and you were holding him in a blanket."

"That is strange we had the same dream. He was a boy. Our first baby was a boy!"

Bryce leans forward and hugs me long and hard.

"Angel, we'll get through this. We'll have more babies. I promise."

29

A MONTH LATER, OUR lives return to something approaching normal. Bryce is either working at the station or studying for his captains' course. If gets the captain's position, he wants to transfer to headquarters, where his dad works. It's always been a dream for him.

I'm just as busy with my job, wedding preparations, and booking our honeymoon to Greece. At night, I try to keep my mind busy researching my next job. Sometimes Leena comes to Barrie and we shop, preparing for the big day.

In no time at all, it seems, our wedding day is only six weeks away.

Bryce will be away at Ontario Fire College in Gravenhurst for his captains' course for the next three days. We arrange that I'll drop him off and travel to Huntsville for a surprise visit with Leena and Ma.

At the Gravenhurst exit, I think of Ken and Sue and wonder how Sue is doing after her husband's death. I cuddle next to Bryce and I think he instinctively knows what I'm thinking. He tugs me closer and kisses my temple.

Through the winding roads of the beautiful Muskoka region, we see a moose sloshing in the marsh and a large beaver dam in one of the many small lakes along the way. We pull up to a brick wall sign saying Ontario Fire College and Bryce follows the road around to the residence building.

I know the importance of this course for Bryce and the promotion to captain once he passes his exams. He's wanted this job for years and he's been studying hard for weeks, but it breaks my heart being separated from him for three days and nights—although I should be used to it by now with him working so much. But at least when I'm in Barrie, there's always hope he'll stop by the house to give me a hug and kiss.

He holds me tight, hugging me hard. When he releases me, he holds my face in his hands. "I know this course is bad timing and I'm sorry about that."

"That's okay. Leena and Ma will be surprised."

"If you don't feel comfortable at their place, go to the cabin."

This is the first time I've visited Huntsville since the horrific ordeal with that lunatic stalker. "I'll be okay. I have to face my fears."

"Call me after six or text me if you need me."

"Thanks, Babe. I'm wishing you luck. I know you'll pass your exams. You got this. I'll miss you."

"I'll miss you more than you know. I love you, Angel."

"I love you, Babe."

"Be careful," Bryce says. "Text me when you get there."

"I will."

Bryce gives me a passionate kiss and holds me tight. I can tell he's having a hard time letting me go, and so am I. As I pull away, I feel overwhelmed with sadness. "I'll miss you more than you know."

When we finally part, I climb into the driver's seat and he kisses me again. "Be safe!"

He grabs his duffle bag from the back seat and I watch him

walk to the building with that powerful stride. "Damn you're hot! Too sexy, baby," I whisper.

I travel through the streets of Gravenhurst until I come to Highway 11, then follow it north to Huntsville. Luckily, the weather cooperates for the trip. The first thing I do when I pull up to Leena's house is text Bryce to let him know I made it safely.

Then I stare at Leena's house for a few minutes, remembering the details of that tragic evening. I shake off the disgusting feeling creeping over me. "You can do this. Get him out of your mind. He's gone. Forever!" I whisper to myself as I head to the front porch.

The door is locked so I fish out the new key Leena had made for me. When I come around the wall to the kitchen, Ma is standing there with big eyes and a knife in her hand. "Oh, Jesus! You scared the hell out of me."

"Sorry, Ma. I thought I'd surprise you."

"I'm glad you're here. It's just whenever Dave is working and I hear noises ... I get a little scared."

I give Ma a hug. "I'm sorry this happened in your house. This ordeal obviously left an impact on you, too."

"How are you doing?" she asks, changing the subject as she holds me at arm's length and looks me over. "I'm sorry. As if you haven't been through enough."

"It's tough. I think about our baby all the time. We had a boy."

"I was wondering who you were talking to," Leena says as she emerges from her room.

I give her a hug. "I thought I'd surprise you."

"Where's Bryce?"

"Ontario Fire College."

"This is great! How long can you stay?"

"Tonight, for sure. Gramps was talking about staying at the cabin for two days to check on his contractors. I'll have to let him in." It's an excuse in case I'm not comfortable sleeping here more than one night. Which is true—Gramps did mention it.

"Perfect. Here, give me your stuff." Leena walks to my old room and tosses my bag on the chair.

I peer in, glaring at the bed.

Visions of that lunatic hovering over me leave me frozen and I think of how I could've prevented it, from the first encounter.

Suddenly Leena steps in front of me, pushing me out and closing the door. "I'm such an idiot. I didn't even think. You sleep with me in my room. I have a new king bed. Lots of room." She tugs me by the arm and throws my bag on her chair. "Looks good, eh? I redecorated. I needed a change after Austin."

Shaking the terrible thoughts from my mind, I walk over to touch the wood on Leena's four-poster mahogany bed. "Wow! This is gorgeous! It looks great. I swear you should've been an interior designer." I say as my eyes scan around the room.

"Got everything cheap, too. Except the bed."

"I hope you and Austin will get back together. It can't be over. I see the love in both your eyes."

"I thought so, too. Whatever! I don't want to talk about him. Come on, let's go have a drink with Ma."

As we enter the kitchen, we see that Ma has made us her famous Caesar cocktail with a pickled asparagus and bean, olive and celery, and a stick loaded with a chicken wing, mozzarella stick, onion ring and a pickle spear. It's a meal in itself. "Thanks, Ma. Looks delicious."

We talk and eat and drink and Leena finally opens up about her feelings for Austin. After a few more drinks, we talk about the wedding and I vent, trying to hold back the tears as I talk about the loss of our baby.

Ma switches to piña coladas later and when a good song comes on, we dance and laugh. I've missed this: Our girl time.

When it's time for bed, I dismiss my thoughts of that lunatic and climb in next to Leena. Knowing she's right next to me gives me comfort and I fall asleep quickly.

At seven a.m., Gramps calls, saying he's leaving North Bay and should be at the cabin in an hour-and-a-half.

Leena and Ma come with me and we do a fast dusting and change the sheets in Austin's room.

We don't want Gramps in Bryce's room wondering what's in the locked cabinet.

Gramps and Mary say they'll only be sleeping at the cabin. The rest of the time they'll be shopping for flooring, light fixtures, and countertops.

Gramps has been hard at work making cabinets. The interior of their cabin is almost finished. The brick layers for the stone around the fireplace will be there this morning.

Bryce wants me to show Gramps how to close the cabin so he and Mary can use it anytime they want while he's doing the woodworking.

Later, we follow Gramps down the road to see their cabin.

The exterior is approximately twenty-five-hundred square feet, all on one floor.

Gramps has made several pathways through the snow and we follow him to the front of the cabin.

"I can't believe how much is done. This looks amazing."

"Thanks, Giggles."

Two large windows on each side of the grand entrance catch my eyes first. The bluish-grey metal roof and three dormers, including one large one over the grand entrance, add to this cabin's amazing exterior. But what really catches my eye is the wrap-around deck and carved wood double doors at the grand entrance.

We climb three steps and wait for Gramps to open the door. He fishes out his key. "I think I'll get one of those keypads you got."

"Gramps, these doors are incredible," Leena says.

I touch the medium-stain carved tree with leaves. "I've never seen a door as stunning as this."

"We've been working on this for a while. Mary helped me."

"It's a work of art," Ma says. "Just amazing!"

Gramps and Mary give us a tour of the interior, describing what it will look like once it's finished.

They've got shopping to do, so we girls head back to Leena's until later tonight.

Gramps has taken us up on our offer to provide a few helping hands around his cabin.

Ma and Leena enjoy cleaning and Gramps and Mary agree with a few of Leena's decorating suggestions. It's a fantastic weekend with lots of laughs. Mary loves Leena's uninhibited personality.

Friday night, I hear the buttons on Bryce's front door keypad beeping and the first thought that runs through my mind is Bryce in the vicinity, stopping by to see me.

Leena shoves through the door and runs up the stairs holding a dress and a bag.

"What are you doing here?" I touch her hair. "Wow! Looks great! Love the highlights."

"Blondes have more fun!" She smiles and shrugs her shoulders. "I thought I would bring some happiness to our boring lives."

I frown. "What do you mean?"

"Come on, we've hit a rut. It's like you and Bryce are an old married couple already."

"I like my life."

"We need to change it up here. I've realized since I'm still not over Austin and you're depressed from the shit you've been through and the miscarriage, we're going out and having fun." Leena holds her finger to my lips. "Trust me on this. Bryce is working tonight, right?"

"Yes."

"Good. Promise me you won't ask any questions and you'll come along for an exciting ride."

"Okay. I like surprises and excitement."

"I know you do. Come with me." Leena grabs my hand and pulls me down the hall to Bryce's closet. "Find your favourite short, sexy dress," she says, opening the doors. "So, do you like the blonde?"

"Yes. It looks fantastic. I think you should've done it years ago." I pull out a sequined dress. "This one will work."

"Nice choice."

While I search for matching shoes, Leena slips on her dress. "And no, I didn't change it because she's a blonde. I've been thinking about it for a while now. Even before I met Austin." Leena looks in the mirror, making the final adjustments. "We are looking hot tonight. And we're curling our hair," Leena says, heading for the bathroom.

I slip my dress on and join her.

"Damn girl, I'm borrowing that one day," Leena says, looking over my champagne-coloured spaghetti-strap dress. "Love how the sequins cover in patches, but then, you get a peek of skin showing. That is sexy!"

"Thanks. So is yours. We'll swap sometime."

Leena's dress is a red chiffon mini with a deep V-neckline.

I fluff the layers of chiffon. "Better hope it's not windy tonight."

"Eh, so they'll get a shot of my ass."

"It is very sexy. Love this dress on you." I chuckle. "And your ass."

"Thanks. Wish I had your butt. That is a J-Lo ass," she says, smacking it. "Oh, we'll need to take your new Grand Cherokee. Can't be slumming with my car in a place like that." Leena rubs her fingers together. "Very ritzy."

"Now you've got me curious. But I won't ask. Just going for the ride."

Leena claps her hands together excitedly. "This reminds me of when we were little kids, always getting into trouble."

"Oh, Jesus! Should I be scared?"

"No. We'll have a great time."

The GPS takes us through the streets of Barrie and as we travel, the houses in the residential area get larger and larger.

Leena looks over at me with a smirk on her face. She's wondering what's going through my mind.

At first, I thought we were going to a bar, dancing. Now, I'm thinking some kind of rich house party.

The lots are noticeably bigger now and the mansions are set back, far from the road. The GPS tells us to turn right onto a long, two-lane driveway. The entrance is guarded by a spectacular fifteen-foot stone and wrought-iron gate.

The metal work design is impressive.

Two, three-foot black antique lanterns attached to the stone pillars light the surrounding area.

The gates open as we approach and I drive through.

Trees line both sides of this long, curved driveway. "This must look amazing in the summer with all the leaves on the trees," I say.

"Yeah, it would be like you're driving through a tunnel. I'd hate to plow this driveway. It never ends."

"They probably have maintenance staff."

"No doubt. Look at this place!" Leena says. "It's amazing! And Fort Knox. How many gates do we have to go through?"

We pull up to a guard shack, which looks like a small replica of the large brick mansion beyond the eight-foot decorative wrought-iron gate.

A massive, muscular man in a tuxedo emerges from one of the rooms inside and approaches the window. He hits a button, the window slides open, and he leans out. "Good evening, ladies. How can I help you?"

"Leena Ericson," she says, leaning over to look at him.

He taps at his computer and smiles at us. "You ladies have a wonderful evening." He hands me an envelope and I pass it to Leena.

He hits another button and we watch the wrought-iron gate slide sideways out of our way. We wave to him and as I pull away. Leena and I yell, "The Rock! Dwayne Johnson!" We both laugh.

I roll up my window and check my driver's mirror. The guard is hanging out the window, waving at us. "Leena, I think he heard us," I say snickering.

"Damn, he was hot! If I don't find any action in here, maybe I'll come to see The Rock. Bet he's hung like a horse."

"You would not let me sit in my truck waiting for you to fuck him."

"Fucking right, I would." Leena points. "Pull in next to the Escalade. Look at this place, my God it's beautiful. And look at the vehicles. It's all SUVs right now but wait until summer when the Ferraris, Lambos, and Bugattis are out. We're coming back."

Beyond the fence is a large, circular, stamped-concrete drive-way with parking along the outer edge. In the middle is a large fountain and a ten-foot marble sculpture of a naked couple, noticeably in love.

I look around as we get out of my Cherokee, walking to the back to join Leena. "What is this place—forget it. Just going for the ride."

As we pass by two men standing next to their vehicles, they stop talking and stare at us. I look over at Leena as she winks at them.

"Oh, no. You're in one of those moods."

"Well, I think it's time for me to move on, since Austin doesn't want me. I'll find someone else."

"Really? You seem like you love him."

"How would you feel if one day Bryce stopped calling you? It's been a frickin' month."

My brain wanders for a second thinking about my relation-ship with Bryce and how, lately, we're busy, working a lot to pay for the wedding. Or is it an excuse? We haven't had sex since the miscarriage. Is this our coping mechanism?

"It's been a month?" I ask. "Do you want me to talk to him? Snoop around."

"No. If he doesn't want me, then I don't want him. End of story."

The grand entrance has four white-marble pillars, two on each side holding up the large balcony above. The matching rounded-top doors, below and above are magnificently eye-catching, as is the large crystal chandelier lighting the way.

We walk up five stone steps to the large entryway but before we make it to the etched-glass double doors, they open and two couples stroll out. Each of the women are carrying a bag in one hand and a cattail leather whip in the other.

What is this place?

We glance at them and keep walking silently.

Leena slows to a crawl and cocks her head slightly, suggesting I follow her line of sight.

The man she's staring at, behind us, looks like one of the cops from the arena who plays hockey with Austin and Bryce.

He nods his head and smiles at her. She does the same and then we turn and continue.

The moment we walk through the double doors to the grand foyer our eyes glance everywhere, trying to take in the beauty.

The first thing that catches my eye is the magnificent staircase of fifteen steps to a landing above, where it branches off to the right and left taking people to the next floor. The height of the ceiling must be forty-feet high.

Three massive crystal chandeliers refract prisms of light on the shiny marble floor. To the right of us is a gold metal elevator with doors carved like peacocks, their fanned-out tail feathers covering the bottom portion. The workmanship is outstanding. "Holy crapper! Look at these doors."

"Better close your mouth," Leena says. "Wouldn't want you to drool on this floor."

"I've never seen anything like it in my whole life."

"Okay, from this point on we have to act as if we belong here."

I walk over to touch the doors. "These are amazing! I can't get over this."

Leena smacks my hand.

"Ouch." I frown at her.

"Don't get your fingerprints all over it."

"I had to touch it."

"Is that what you say to Bryce?"

"Aren't you funny."

Leena taps my hand several times to get my attention. "Here comes somebody. Try to be good."

"I should be saying that to you," I whisper.

"Good evening, ladies." He extends his hand and we shake. "I'm Dawson. I'll be your host for this evening. Is this your first visit to The Mansion?"

"Nice to meet you. Leena and Keera. Yes, this is our first visit. This is amazing."

Dawson is a tall, good-looking man in his late thirties to early forties. He has salt-and-pepper hair and he's wearing a sharp, black tuxedo.

"May I take your coats?" He hands us a ticket for the coat check.

"Thank you," we say in unison.

"I can give you a tour or you can visit the viewing area above on the right, privately. Your choice. You can't get lost: it loops around to the reserved rooms on the left."

"I think we can handle this on our own," Leena says.

"Bar to the right, coffee shop on the left, if you'd like something before you go upstairs."

"Thank you, Dawson."

He tips his head and bows slightly. I watch as he walks over to the coat check.

Leena grabs my arm. "Bar first. It'll help take the edge off."

The interior design throughout this massive room is Victorian, with over-stuffed, burgundy loveseats and chairs placed in groups with highly polished cherry wood tables. The bar itself is thirty-feet long with carved cherry-wood covered in multiple coats of lacquer. Gramps would be impressed by the intricate carvings and blinding shine. A round gold rail surrounds the bar and gold metal artwork encompass this entire room.

Leena orders our drinks from the bartender while I'm still mesmerized by the décor.

She nudges me to get my attention. I look at her and her eyes roll to one side. Following her glance, I turn to look around the room. We seem to be the centre of attention.

I turn back around and the bartender hands me my drink. Leena cocks her head, motioning to a quiet spot in the corner.

Once seated, her eyes scan the room. "Have you noticed all the hot men here?"

"I'm too busy checking out the décor."

"I see that. I'm more interested in a different kind of décor. Check it out. It's a meat market in here."

I look around the room, sipping my drink. "Good thing we dressed up for this, eh?"

"You wonder what these people do for a living. Doctors, Lawyers, CEOs ... They sure as hell don't work in a bakery."

"That's what it was like when we went to the gala. I was out of my element there. It felt strange."

"Check out the guy at the bar who's turned around and staring at us. Bet he's a model. Look at that face. God, he's gorgeous!"

"Here comes his beautiful wife, or girlfriend."

He turns and speaks with her and then they both stare at us.

"Aww, I get it. They're swingers. He's scouting out the new recruits."

"Really? Could you do that?"

"No. When I love someone, I hope it's for the rest of our lives. But at this point, I'd do whatever it takes if it meant Austin was back in my life."

"I knew it! I knew you still loved him!"

"Come on, suck it back. They look like they're ready to come over here. Better go."

I do, plopping my glass on the table and following Leena as she leads us on the long trek up the stairs.

Once we get out of everyone's earshot, I whisper to Leena. "How much did you pay for this evening?"

"You don't want to know."

"Yes, I do."

"A grand … each."

"Are you kidding me?"

"Shh, lower your voice."

"I'm paying you back."

"I knew you would."

By the time we make it to the top of the stairs, our legs are on fire. It's a good workout.

Down this very wide hall approximately twenty-five people are scattered about, staring into glass viewing areas on the left. I look down to the end and approximate the length of the hall at well over a hundred feet. It is very modern, with dark cappuccino walls and gold-embossed ceilings. There are pillars every fifteen feet with large, eye-catching, spiral crystal wall sconces to light the way. The granite floor is the same colour as the walls and the ceiling lights refract off it, showing the magnificent shine. I'm entranced by the modern, majestic architecture of this hallway. Leena tugs at my arm, pulling me from my thoughts.

We slowly pass by the first room and my eyes almost pop out of my head.

I turn to look at Leena and she's trying to hold in her laugh by covering her mouth. "That expression was priceless. So, what do you think?" she asks.

"I had no clue. I thought maybe dinner and a party afterwards. Wasn't expecting this."

"Surprise!"

30

*B*EHIND THE GLASS is a naked man. He's fit and muscular. He's just finished tying a woman to the bed and he stands back, admiring his handiwork. Then he turns and walks slowly to the wall, where an impressive assortment of tools-of-the-trade hang in a wood cabinet.

I catch a glimpse of his profile. Beneath his thin, trimmed beard is a strong, sculptured face. He has brown hair and is very good-looking.

He grabs a blindfold and walks back to the bed with a slow animalistic stride.

This is not his first walk in the park.

He's shaved and his cock is hard, standing at attention.

Leena grabs my hand and pulls me to the next window. "That could take a while. I want to see some action."

"But … I … I was getting into that," I say, pointing.

In this window, two men are pleasuring one woman. The burgundy padded table they're on is at the perfect height. They have her legs spread wide and one is about to enter inside her. Her back arches with pleasure. The other man grabs her hands roughly and holds them over her head. He leans, taking her nipple in his mouth while caressing her skin with his other hand. She is over-stimulated, and so am I.

"Isn't this hot?" Leena asks.

"Now I see why Colton gets off on watching people have sex."

Farther down the hall, across from the glass viewing area, there's a scuffle. A man has a woman against the wall. He's holding her hands above her head and kissing her ferociously. Their lips separate and he rips open her blouse, exposing her bra. He shoves her against the wall again, grinding into her, grasping her breast. I think they're going to fuck right here with everyone watching.

Most of the people on this floor have stopped viewing what's going on behind the glass to watch this couple.

Twenty seconds later, the couple realizes they're being watched. The man pulls her around the wall to a more secluded spot.

We all resume watching what's going on behind the glass.

A minute later, Leena pulls me to the next window.

In this room, a naked man is handcuffed to a large wooden cross and two women are dressed in leather dominatrix costumes. One is touching him gently, running a feathered wand over his chest. She captures his nipple between her teeth and pulls. When she's done, the other woman takes over, whipping him with her leather cattails, then soothing the sting by licking the area she hit.

Leena grabs one of the headsets and places it on my ears. Then she grabs another headset for herself. As we turn to each other, her eyebrows shoot up and she smiles.

Watching what's going on in the room is a turn-on but when you can hear the moans of pleasure and groans of pain, it's like you're right there in the moment. It is very erotic.

We listen and watch for a few minutes.

Out of the corner of my eye, I see Leena shifting restlessly from foot to foot as she sways back and forth. This is noticeably affecting her. She pulls me to the next room.

This room has six people in it.

A blonde with a rockin' body wearing thigh-high black leather boots and a dominatrix outfit is beating the hell out of a giant man cuffed to a cross. She looks good in her black leather bunny ear mask. The man is wearing a black thong and leather mask with a ball in his mouth.

Leena shoves headphones on both our ears and we listen as she whips him over and over again. Every time he grunts with pain, she hits him harder.

Another man, who is cuffed to a chair, says, "Enough, Sarah!"

Her head spins and she frowns, her forehead furrowed and eyes narrowed as she slinks toward him. She steps on his balls with her high-heeled boots and he lets out a sound of excruciating pain.

"What?" she says, digging deeper. "What is my name?"

"Madame ... Madame Arianna!"

"Don't ever forget it!" She twists the pad of her foot into his balls as if she's snuffing out a cigarette on the ground.

He grunts with pain. "Christ!"

The tall blonde drops to her knees, pushing the other woman out of the way, and takes the man's cock deep in her mouth.

She gives him a good workover, changing his pain to pleasure.

He starts to moan and thrusts his hips toward her mouth.

She pulls away. "Did I hurt you?" She strokes his cock as she looks over at the man on the cross. "Did I hurt your boyfriend?" she asks, her voice dripping with fake concern.

She finishes what she started, taking his cock in her mouth, simultaneously stroking, working him over, giving him a mind-numbing blowjob.

Leena is clearly turned on as she moves from left to right. She turns to look at me and her eyebrows shoot up. She pulls her headphones off and motions for me to do the same. "I love her! She's a badass! Isn't this hot?"

Her line of sight leaves mine and she looks beyond me, down the hall. "Speaking of hot ... what is he doing here?" Leena's happy voice turns to anger.

I turn to see Bryce marching down the hall toward us. Austin stops to look in each room and then tries to catch up to Bryce.

"How did they know we were here?" I ask.

"His cop buddy when we first came in, I'll bet," Leena says. "What I want to know is why Austin is here?"

Bryce is unmistakably on a mission to get to me fast, dodging people when they move in his path.

He's wearing his black formal pants and silky white dress shirt. His powerful stride and the way he moves sends a tingling sensation through my whole body. I've missed this feeling. I haven't felt this way in a while.

I can see his muscle mass clearly beneath the fabric. He looks really good.

Several people, men and women turn and follow him with their eyes.

As he strides closer, I can see his facial expression and feel the power in his physical presence.

He looks mad.

Why is he angry? He wants me to hold onto my innocence? He doesn't want me to see other men naked? Or he doesn't want me to compare our sex life with the people behind the glass? But I already have and Bryce is a sex god. These women would love to have him in the same room, even if only for a moment.

He stands before me, holding my arms and breathing heavily. "What are you doing here?" His voice is deep and angry.

"I should ask you the same question. Why aren't you at work?"

He frowns and his facial expression hardens—a clear sign I shouldn't mess with him. He's in a mood.

"Leena wanted to surprise me. I thought we were going for dinner and dancing."

"I don't want you here!"

The blood instantly rises to my face and neck, and my body temperature skyrockets. "Now you're telling me where I can go and where I can't!" I start to walk away and he holds me.

"Come here! Calm down! Look at me!" His grip tightens on my shoulders. "Angel, a place like this, we need to be together." He pulls me to the other side of the hall, away from people and the viewing area.

He glances into the room across the hall. "Call me selfish and overbearing, I don't care, but I want to be with you when you experience happiness and pleasure."

"You haven't touched me since we lost our baby."

He glances again.

"Don't say that." His voice softens. "I've touched and kissed you and we consoled each other. Maybe I could've handled this better if I wasn't working as much. I thought if I kept my mind busy, I'd get through it. It's been tough. I'm always thinking about him."

Bryce avoids showing his feelings most of the time. But when he does, I had better be listening.

"I'm sorry," I say, as the tension in my body gradually eases. "I had no idea this was affecting you as much as me."

"I should've taken time off. We should have taken a vacation together and talked it through. I'm sorry, Angel. I should've been there for you."

"You are always here for me. Through all the tough times." I give him a slow, soft kiss. "I don't think we'll ever get over this. We'll always be thinking about him. That's what parents do."

"We may get through this in time. It always takes time, Angel."

Bryce holds me tight, not caring who sees our intimate moment.

Seconds later, a scuffle to our left draws our attention, and we see Austin has Leena pinned to the wall and is kissing her, ferociously.

We smile at each other, hoping they'll get back together.

I glance at them again and then look back at Bryce.

Bryce's kinky side has him curious. He's once again watching the activity in the room.

Pulling him to the glass, I slide the headphones on his ears. Then I stand out of the way and watch the expressions on his face.

He's enjoying the show.

Just before I place the headphones on my ears, I hear arguing. Leena and Austin are now in a heated discussion. Her body language tells me she's angry.

Bryce pulls me in front of him and wraps his arms around my shoulders. He bends his knees, rubbing his cock against my butt. He pulls the headphones off, resting them on his shoulders. "Do you like this, Angel?"

I turn to look at him. "Yes. I think you do, too."

"Only with you by my side," he says, turning me to face him, holding my waist. "I would never come here without you!"

"I've never heard of this place. Have you?"

"Yes. That's why I had to be here with you. Dante and Jax come here. They've been exhibitionist."

A confused expression crosses my face.

"They've participated with masks to be discreet." Bryce clarifies. "We're public servants. We can't be seen doing this kind of thing."

"In the same room?" I ask.

"Yes."

"I'm looking at them differently now."

"Look around. There are a lot of prominent people here. Judges, councillors, surgeons, pro-athletes. Come from Toronto, I've heard."

"Have you been here before?" I ask, wondering if he'll dodge the question.

Bryce looks me straight in the eye. "No. I haven't been here. That's why I brought Austin."

"Austin's been here?"

"Yes."

"In one of the rooms?"

"He won't give me a straight answer on that, but I'm assuming."

I look over at Austin and Leena and they're still in a heated discussion.

Bryce turns me again and we watch as the tall blonde stands before the man on the cross. She places clamps on each nipple and then walks over to the table deciding which torture device she wants next. She stands before him again, licking her palm, taking hold of his cock, stroking him until he's good and hard. She places a double cock ring around his cock and balls and then stands back, taking a picture.

"This is erotic. Is this making you hot, Angel?" Bryce's big hand cups my breast and he searches for and finds my nipple erect. "Mmm, I love this," he says, nuzzling my ear.

Rubbing against him, I feel his cock grow between us and he grinds harder, holding my hip.

"You look so fucking hot tonight."

"So do you, Babe." I spin in his arms, facing him, and take hold of his cock. I glance both ways to see if anyone is watching. "I think you're enjoying this." I run my hand along his length and he lets out a throaty moan.

His eyes move to my cleavage and my nipples protruding beneath the fabric of my dress. "Angel, you are so sexy, I can't take my eyes off you."

"The moment I saw you walking down the hall, my body was tingling. You do it to me every time. I've missed you."

"I've missed you." He holds me tight and I feel myself melting in his arms.

Leena and Austin catch my eye again. He has her against the wall in a desperate and frantic kiss. Bryce spins, looking in the same direction.

Leena pulls Austin over to us and hands me a key card. "This is your room. Better use it. Paid a lot of money for that. Whatever toys you use, you bought them. Take them home with you. And don't worry, they sanitize each room from top to bottom. Very thorough. They assured me because I know what you're like."

Austin pulls Leena down the hall and around the corner, anxiously.

Bryce and I smile. "You knew if he saw her, they'd get back together," I say.

"Yeah. You know, sometimes he needs a swift kick in the ass." He spins me so I'll watch the activity in the room instead of questioning him about Austin.

We make our way down the hall, watching and listening to what's going on in the rest of the rooms.

The last room has ten people in it. My eyes dart around the room remembering Colton's pilot, Craig, having an orgy with all the naked bodies on the floor.

Bryce places the headphones on my ears and his, distracting my thoughts.

We watch for a few minutes as he splays his hand across my stomach, tugging me back against his hard cock.

He pulls my hair to the side and runs his lips along my neck. That tingling sensation flows through my whole body and I melt from his touch.

He lifts one side of the headphone off my ear. "I can't take much more. I need you! I need to be inside you." He takes our headphones off, returning them to their place, and then takes my hand, pulling me to the end of the hall.

Looking down this hallway, I see there are rooms on the left with numbers on each door. Half way down the hall, Bryce slides the key card in, opens the door, and pulls me in the room. The door hasn't closed yet before Bryce starts pushing me against the wall and kissing me fiercely.

I've missed this feeling. It's been too long since he's touched me and made love to me.

He undoes his belt and button, sliding his zipper down at lightning speed. His big hands grasp my butt, lifting me, and I wrap my legs around his waist.

He shoves me aggressively against the wall and my dress rides up, revealing my pussy. He leans back, tilting his head, searching for a better look. "I knew it! Bad girl!" He smacks my ass. "I think a punishment is in order."

His stance and voice changes before my eyes to the domineering Bryce.

"Why? What did I do?"

"You know exactly what you did," he says, narrowing his eyes as he grinds his cock into me. Our lips meet in a searing, desperate kiss and I run my fingers through the hair at the back of his neck.

When we pull away, we're both panting from the intensity.

"You came here without me!"

I open my mouth to explain and he shuts me up with another scorching kiss.

"And you came here with no panties."

"I can't wear them with this dress, you'll see—"

He shuts me up again, kissing me hard. I'm vaguely aware that we're moving until Bryce sits me down on a leather table.

Before I know it, I'm pulled off and face down with my upper body lying across it.

I move to stand up, but he has one big hand on my back, holding me down. "Don't move!"

He lifts my dress to my waist and gently caresses my butt cheek, first the right and then the left. He kneels and kisses each cheek several times, sending chills through my body. "The things I could do to this sweet ass."

I turn to see what he's doing.

"Eyes forward," he says in a deep, commanding voice.

For some reason, I listen to him this time.

He kisses a few more times and then nothing. I wait for his touch.

Out of nowhere, I feel a silk mask slide over my eyes.

"Don't take it off!" he says sternly.

He leaves and I hear movement a few feet away, behind me, where the new toys are stored in a tall wood cabinet.

What's he up to?

After a long minute, he's back and I feel the heat of his body next to mine as he rubs against me. He lightly skims his cock along my butt and I know he's taken his clothes off. "This sweet little ass is mine!"

"I didn't know we were—"

"Quiet!" He smacks my left butt cheek.

His legs spread mine and he probes inside me.

My head drops down on my hands and I moan, enjoying every sensation.

He smacks my right cheek and squirts an oil. Then he messages me gently, around and around on both cheeks.

A quick smack to both cheeks, again.

When he sees me tense for the next hit, he stops and inserts his finger inside me. "Do you have any idea how you send me over the edge, crazy for you?"

"Babe, you don't have to worry—"

"Quiet!" I feel a quick sting and I know he's used the three-foot cattail on me. A couple more cracks to my butt. It's not his hand. It feels like a flogger. He switches between the cattails and the flogger so the pain isn't as intense. He wants me to feel the different sensations.

I know he doesn't want to hurt me. This is something his dominant side needs and enjoys. He always knows how much I can take and how much I can't.

He leans over my back, wrapping his hand around my throat. We're skin on skin. "You thrive on driving me crazy." I feel his abs tighten as he speaks.

"Babe, I didn't—"

Bryce's hand moves from my throat to my mouth. "Quiet! Yes, you do. You want me to chase after you like a crazed lunatic."

He won't let me speak to set him straight. I roll my eyes knowing he can't see me.

"I think you've been punished enough." He rubs my tender

cheeks, soothing the pain. Then I feel gentle kisses and I know he's on his knees, kissing my butt.

He lifts my upper body off the table and cradles me in his arms. He kisses my lips tenderly and I know it's his way of showing his gratification.

Little does he know the slight sting makes me hot.

Bryce gets off on this, showing his dominant side. I like it too, when his aggression takes over and he loses control.

I feel us move to the other side of the room. He places me on the bed and pulls my dress off. Bryce splays his hand on my chest, pushing me down, and lies beside me. He runs his hand around the plump globes of my breasts, feeling the weight of them. "How I feel for you, it scares the shit out of me. Sometimes I don't know how to control my emotions. It suffocates me. I can't breathe."

I open my mouth to say something and he covers it.

"Don't say anything. I need you to know how much you mean to me." I feel Bryce get off the bed and hear him moving things around.

He loves me. He really loves me.

After a few moments, he's back, tying my ankles. Then there's no movement and I wonder where he's gone. After a minute, he startles me by dropping something between my legs. It rubs my thigh.

He chuckles. "Did I scare you?"

"Yes."

"Good. I want to add a little fear into the mix of emotions you're feeling."

I'm ready to explode and he's hardly touched me.

He ties my wrists and I know I'm in for long, erotic, torturous foreplay.

Bryce starts with a feather, running it from head to toe.

Then, something else. It's cold and he's rolling it like a ball, from my chest to my thighs. Whatever it is, it has my nipples standing erect. Hard as a rock.

Bryce runs his finger across each one, slowly. "Jesus, Angel, I don't think I've ever seen these this hard. They're beautiful!"

His warm mouth covers my nipple and his tongue flicks it rapidly.

He switches to the next, giving my other nipple his undivided attention.

I'm on fire and he knows it.

He walks away and I let out a heavy sigh.

"Babe!"

"Patience there, Angel, patience."

I hear the mini fridge open and a cork popped.

Silence fills the room. *What is he doing?*

I feel something against my lips. "Sip, Angel?"

"Mmm, that's good."

The cold liquid dribbles down my chin and neck.

"It's champagne." Bryce licks it. "Mmm, delicious. And you smell amazing."

"Thanks, Babe."

Unexpectedly, I feel the cold bottle run across my nipples. Then he pours a little bit over each one, quickly lapping the champagne.

Next, it feels like a cold oil. Bryce massages my body, loosening the tight muscles at my neck and shoulders. "Mmm, your hands are amazing."

"Do you like this?"

"Yes. I love this."

He continues down my body, touching every inch.

Then he's gone and I hear the fridge open again.

I jump when he places something cold and heavy on my clit, running it back and forth over my wide-open lips.

"That feels like your tongue, but cold. Babe, I need you. I need you inside me."

His big, muscular body climbs on the bed and he nestles between my legs. His tongue and finger go to work doing magical things to my body.

After making love, we lie there for a while, cuddling, talking about the loss of our baby boy. We reconnect and our love for each other feels stronger than ever—a bond no one can break.

Three hours later, we emerge from the room, toys in hand and smiles on our faces, totally satisfied.

31

ONDAY AFTERNOON, A week before the wedding, I'm shocked to see Lindsay standing outside, ready to ring the doorbell. "Shit!"

"I didn't mean to scare you. I'm sorry. I've been standing here arguing with myself as to whether I should bother you again. Please, hear me out. I haven't been myself for a few years now. The doctors had me on different medications and some turned me into a raging lunatic. Unfortunately, you got to see me at my worst. I never meant to say the things I said." She takes my arm and shakes it. "Please, relax. I won't hurt you. I'm taking the right medication now."

Flashbacks of Lindsay with my hair in her hand and her punching the brick wall invade my mind.

"Can we go inside to talk?"

I hesitate, saying nothing.

"Please, it's cold out here."

I turn my body, keeping one eye on her as I open the door.

Bryce's and Leena's voices ring loud and clear in my head. *Quit being naïve.*

I hesitate in the foyer as she closes the door behind her.

"Can we go upstairs and have a tea? That is, if you have time?"

"I was running to the store to grab something."

"I promise, I won't keep you long."

Damn it. There is no getting out of this.

I start to walk up the stairs sideways, keeping her hands in sight, ready to strike if she makes the wrong move. "Tea, coffee, or hot chocolate?"

"Tea is fine."

"Any specific kind? I have English breakfast, orange pekoe, green tea, or oolong tea."

Lindsay gets to the top of the stairs and scans the rooms. "Still looks the same."

Well yeah, you were in here five months ago stealing Bryce's phone. "We haven't had a lot of time to change anything with our busy schedules. Besides, Bryce likes it this way."

"Oolong would be great. I'm on a health kick right now."

"That's good."

"I have to fit into my wedding dress in six months."

"That's great! Congratulations. Same guy?"

"Yes. We worked it out. Landon is great. I really love him. And he's there for me when life gets crazy. He doesn't work long hours and I need that. I need a husband who will be there for me." Her eyes widen. "Sorry. Me and my big mouth again."

I hand Lindsay her tea and she takes a couple sips.

She's nervous. I can tell. Her hands shake and she glances into my eyes periodically, quickly turning away to look elsewhere.

"No. That's okay. I've accepted Bryce's job and he accepts mine. It works for us."

"What do you do?"

"Clothes and cosmetics model."

"Figures." She rolls her eyes. "Had a feeling with that body."

"I have to exercise and watch what I eat."

"Well, I'm glad it doesn't come naturally."

"Wish it did. So how'd you meet Landon?"

"At the office. We worked together. But now he's moved up in the company. I hardly see him he's so busy. But he always makes time for us at lunch. He's making a lot more money now and we're in the process of buying our first house. Life is great."

"That's fantastic."

"Umm, now that I'm feeling better, I had to come here and apologize. I'm sorry for the problems I caused. I hope you don't hate me."

"I'm glad you're better Lindsay. And no, I don't hate you."

Lindsay finishes her tea. "Well, I won't keep you. I have an appointment to see a house. I'm hoping this is the last one. By the pictures, I think it will be. I'll bring Landon on the weekend to see it. He says he doesn't care where he lives as long as it's with me. Isn't he sweet?"

We walk to the front door.

"I think you've found the right man. I'm happy for you."

Lindsay gives me an awkward hug. "Thank you. And I'm sorry again for my outbursts. Also, congratulations on your engagement," she says as she turns and leaves.

Leena texts me:

What are you doing?

Just got back from the store. But guess what I was doing before that?

I don't know. What?

Having tea with Lindsay.

Are you kidding me!!!

Leena calls. "Start from the beginning."

"I was coming out the door and she was about to ring the bell. She scared the crap out of me. I think I'm still skitzy or skittish, whatever you call it from that stalker."

"I would be, too, with what you went through. Did you ever find out what his name was?"

"I don't want to know. He's out of my mind. Gone. Forever."

"Did you call for counselling yet?"

"No. I'll deal with it on my own."

"You're so stubborn!"

"Yeah, so anyway, Lindsay said she was arguing with herself whether or not to bother me. She said she hasn't been herself for a few years now. The doctors had her on a few different medications that turned her into a raging lunatic. She said unfortunately, I saw her at her worst. At that point, I was picturing her with my hair in her hands from the mall incident and then when she punched the brick wall."

"Don't forget the sharpie on your windshield."

"Yes, there were quite a few encounters with her. But she said the doctors have her on the right medication now."

"I don't know. Don't trust her."

"She smiled at me and shook my arm. She said, 'you need to relax, I won't hurt you.'"

"And you believed her?"

"She seemed like a different person. She was nice. Then she wanted to come inside to talk because it was cold. I hesitated in the foyer. She then asked if we could go upstairs and have a tea."

"Ding, ding, ding. Here's your sign."

"I know. I could hear you and Bryce in my head, telling me to quit being so naïve."

"Did you have visions of her stabbing you in the back?"

I laugh. "I walked sideways, keeping an eye on her hands while I was asking what kind of tea she likes."

"I would've never let it get that far. I would've said, 'Don't have time for this' and slammed the door in her face."

"No, you wouldn't. Not if you saw her struggling with her feelings."

"You're too nice, Keera."

"You know, I tried to put myself in her position, having to deal with uncertain mood swings on a daily basis. It would be tough.

And at the time, in her eyes she thought I stole her boyfriend, even though they'd split up two months earlier. No one knows until you've walked a few miles in their shoes. Mental illness is a growing concern. It can happen to us one day. I've been researching and they say causes can be horrific trauma in a person's life. I've had that. I'm telling you, it could happen to me with what I've been through. I'm learning more every day. I didn't understand it before, but I do now."

"You're finally admitting it. If you start acting strange, I'll drag you to counselling myself."

"I know you will."

"So how did the rest of the tea party go?"

"Lindsay said she's on a health kick so she can fit into her wedding dress."

"Really? Do you believe her?"

"Yes, she said Landon and her worked it out. She said he doesn't work a lot and she needs that. She needs a husband who will be there for her. Then she apologized for her big mouth. I said, 'that's okay, I've accepted Bryce's career and he's accepted mine.'"

"See, I think she's trying to persuade you to cancel your wedding."

"I don't think so. By the end of our conversation, I truly believe she loves Landon."

"Until they break up again."

"She seems happy. You know, I saw a different side of her today, and I can see why Bryce still had feelings for her and didn't want her to hurt herself. Bryce saw the good side of her, which no one else saw. You can't shut off your feelings for a person. It takes time."

"Yeah, I know what that's like."

"See? You understand then."

"I'm trying."

"Bryce has a good heart, too. I understand what he was going through."

"How long did she stay?"

"Not long. Ten minutes. She had an appointment. Lindsay and Landon are buying their first house. She gave me an awkward hug and congratulated me on our engagement. I think she's finally moved on and I'm happy for her."

My eyes open and the first thing I see is Bryce's mega-watt smile as he hovers over me. "Good morning, beautiful."

"Good morning, Mr. Tall, Dark, and Gorgeous."

"I've been waiting for you to wake up."

"How long were you waiting?"

"About twenty minutes." Bryce kneels up, holding a bag with tissue paper. "Open it."

"What's this?" I prop my pillow up and lean against the head-board. "Babe ... I ... I didn't think we were buying each other gifts."

"Leena hinted and I'll have to thank her because now I can't wait for you to open it."

"I feel bad because I didn't get you anything."

"Angel, all I need is you. Seven more hours and you'll be my wife."

"Aww, come here." Leaning down, he kisses me—slow. "I love you."

"I love you, Angel. I would like you to wear this today but if you have something else..." Bryce's voice trails off as I open the first box. "That isn't crystal. It's the real thing."

"Babe, it's beautiful. I love it!" I touch the solitaire diamond necklace pendant. "I would love to wear this today."

"Open this one." Bryce hands me the second box.

I pull out the matching halo-drop diamond earrings. "Wow! You've got great taste in jewellery. These are gorgeous."

"Last one."

I open it to find a white-gold tennis bracelet, diamonds all the way around. "Babe! This is too much. It's gorgeous!"

Bryce stands beside the bed, holding the necklace. "Turn. Let me see this on you." I twist my body, holding my hair to the side. His fingers gently touch my neck as he clasps the necklace. He takes my hand and wraps the bracelet around, clasping it to my wrist.

I hold out my hand, admiring it. "Babe, you spoil me."

"Come with me. We've got to get moving."

"Wait." I grab the earrings and sprint to the bathroom, where I quickly insert them.

Bryce leans on the door frame watching me.

"I love them. They're gorgeous, like you." I smile. "Thank you, Babe."

Bryce grabs my housecoat off the back of the door and covers my body. "Here. We're limited for time, otherwise, I'd have you bent over that bed. Come with me. Breakfast is made."

"You made me breakfast on our wedding day? Thank you."

Bryce leads the way to the kitchen, where he motions for me to sit at the breakfast bar. He hands me a plate.

"You're welcome."

"Oh, Jesus! Look at the time! I slept in."

Bryce chuckles. "That's what I've been telling you."

We eat quickly and Bryce checks the weather. "Shows it will be sunny and seventeen today."

"Really? We hardly ever get a spring day this warm." I look up to the ceiling and whisper, "Thank you."

Bryce smiles at me, knowing I'm talking to my parents again.

After I've stowed the plates in the dishwasher, he takes my hand. "Let's take a shower. I have to be at Austin's in twenty minutes."

"All right. I'm moving."

Leena opens Bryce's bedroom door and pokes her head in. "Need some help?"

Five seconds earlier, I squeezed into my dress and covered my breasts. "I'm glad you're here. It would be great if you can zip me up and help with these buttons down my back."

"Sorry, running a little late. Jesus! Look at you! You're gorgeous!"

"Thank you. You look amazing, too. Damn girl, look at the cleavage on you." I stick my finger between her breasts like she normally does to me. "I love what you've done with your hair."

"Martina. She worked her magic. Told her I have a hot date."

"With who?"

"You'll see. It's a surprise."

A quick knock at the door and then Ma opens it and peeks in. "Can I—oh, my lord." Ma steps inside with Katie and Ciara following behind. Ma holds her fingers over her mouth and tears well up in her eyes. "You are stunning. I've never seen a bride look as beautiful as you are today."

Katie gives me a hug. "You look amazing."

"Wait until Bryce sees you. He'll lose his mind," Ciara says.

This is one of those moments I think about my mom and dad and wish they were here.

I start to get teary-eyed.

Leena says, "Oh no! No one is crying today. This is a happy day." We all break out in laughter.

Ma touches the jewels and sequins around my waist. "This dress. I love the off-the-shoulder, corset style. It's perfect! I can't get over how gorgeous you are."

"Thanks, Ma. You look amazing too. You all look so beautiful."

"Oh God! Look at the time," Leena says. "We have to get moving. Limo's here."

My bridesmaids fuss with the long train on my dress as we wait in a secluded room for the guests to arrive at the church.

Gramps hooks his arm in mine and pats my hand. "Are you ready for this? You seem a little tense."

"I always get nervous when the attention is focused on me. Never liked it as a kid and still hate it as an adult. Have I told you how handsome you look in your tuxedo?"

He chuckles. "Yes, you have. Several times. Maybe we should've had a few beers. That would've calmed the nerves."

"The girls gave me one on the way here in the limo."

Leena sticks her head out the door and motions for us to set up in the main entrance. My bridesmaids fix my train and rush to get into position.

"Why is it I have an awful urge to dance down the aisle?" Leena says, smiling.

"You better not!" Ma scolds her.

Just then, the double doors open and I hear the noise from everyone shuffling in their seats to look at the back of the church.

My bridesmaids are lined up in front of us and as each one leaves to head down the aisle, I feel a little more nervous.

Gramps pats my hand. "Our turn." He starts to walk, guiding me down the aisle.

I see some familiar faces smiling at us but mostly, people I don't know from the fire department, Investigations, or the hospital where Deana works.

Then, when I turn to my left, I catch a glimpse of Reese. I smile but I'm frantically searching for Colton because, wherever Reese is, Colton is usually with him.

I want this to be our special day with no distractions or drama.

Josie steps out into the aisle and whispers, "Wow!" I smile at her in passing as she takes as many pictures as she can.

When we're almost to the front of the church, I see Mary, Deana and Garrett, and a great surprise: Pops made the trip from Aruba.

Bryce steps from the right of the pews to the middle of the aisle and I can't take my eyes off him. He is dignified and debonair in his tuxedo. He's perfect.

The look in his eyes and his smile, are making me smile.

His eyes flow down from mine, the entire length of my dress, the inspection so intense, I shiver.

As I approach, he steps closer. My eyes inspect his gorgeous body. No one could look better.

I'm about to marry this Greek god. My best friend, my lover.

32

GRAMPS PULLS HIS arm free, distracting my thoughts.

Bryce shakes Gramps' hand firmly. "I promise, I will take care of her for the rest of her life."

Gramps gives me a kiss and I give him a big hug. When he pulls away, I see his eyes are glossy. "Save me a dance."

"I will." This is the first time Gramps has shown any emotion. I try to hold back the tears.

Gramps walks over to sit with Mary.

Bryce slides his hand to the small of my back and guides me to the altar.

As we wait for the priest, Bryce leans in. "You look so beautiful! I'm the luckiest man alive!"

"Do you know what you do to me? Babe, you're perfect. I want you right now!"

The priest clears his throat and starts to speak.

Now that Bryce is standing next to me, I finally relax. He doesn't seem nervous at all.

Right on cue, as we rehearsed last night, Leena and Austin place chairs behind us and we sit.

My mind wanders while the priest is speaking. Leena and Austin, our maid of honour and best man, are trying to be civil, only speaking when necessary at the rehearsal, dinner, and now. Leena told me their night at The Mansion was perfect. She said they had three hours of the best, most erotic sex to date, yet Austin hasn't called her since. So now, she's called Reese to be her date. Leena is tired of Austin's games.

None of us can figure out what Austin's problem is.

My parents enter my mind again and I hope they're with us to celebrate this special day.

I look at Bryce periodically and wonder what he's thinking.

He smiles and squeezes my knee.

The rest of the ceremony is a blur, except for our vows. I'm nervous but I say them perfectly.

Bryce's vows are filled with all the romantic verses he's said to me since we've met and it's a heartfelt statement I will remember forever.

Forty-five minutes later, the priest finally says, "May I present Mr. and Mrs. Hamilton. You may kiss your bride."

Bryce's kiss is so passionate, it makes my knees weak and I melt in his arms.

I faintly hear clapping in the distance.

When I come back to reality, I see smiling faces and a few tears.

Everyone heads to the back of the church to congratulate us. Kisses and hugs from all of them.

The photographer takes some pictures inside and out and then Leena takes my hand, pulling us to the limo. "We're limited for time," she says, gathering my train and stuffing it in the limo door. "Bryce will explain."

We wave goodbye to everyone and the limo pulls away from the church.

"Now that we're alone, come here, my beautiful wife." Bryce wraps his arm around my waist and pulls me close. "I love how that sounds: my wife."

"My husband. I like it. Just don't call me your old lady, or an old bag. That gets on my nerves when men say that about their wives."

"Demanding, already." Bryce gives me an adorable smile.

"No. It's one thing that's always bothered me."

"All right. No, old bag."

I tickle him and he holds my hands, chuckling and grinning ridiculously. "I can't get over how beautiful you are." His eyes leave mine and travel to my cleavage. "I can't take my eyes off you. Come a little closer."

I feel for his cock and find it hard. "Mmm, it would be a shame to waste this." My lips lock on his and I kiss him.

"I've been hard since I first saw you. And while the priest was talking, all I could think about was ten different ways I could make love to you. But we can't start this now."

The limo pulls into the parking lot of the Barrie fire department headquarters. "Leena wanted to surprise you. She wants a photo shoot with the firetrucks."

"Oh. Do we have time for this?"

Bryce chuckles, noticing the disappointment in my voice. "Leena has us on a tight schedule."

The bus with our wedding party pulls in beside us and Leena is the first one standing at the limo door grabbing my train.

"We have half-an-hour to get these pics. The photographer is set up already."

"Leena, you are the best maid of honour a girl could ask for."

"You wanted a wedding planner, you've got one. Let me know if I'm being too pushy."

"No. No. You're doing great!"

We capture approximately fifty pictures inside and then Dante suggests pulling the ladder truck outside to get more. We're only ten minutes late for the photo shoot at Kempenfelt Bay.

Forty-five minutes later, the limo pulls up to the reception hall. Before we go into Salon A, where our guests have arrived, my bridesmaids gather my train and hook it to my butt, making it look like a bow.

The DJ starts to play "Fall Into Me" by Brantley Gilbert. "May I present, Mr. and Mrs. Hamilton," he says into the microphone.

Bryce guides me with his hand on the small of my back and we walk into the room.

Everyone starts to clap and all I can think to do is smile and wave.

When we get to the middle of the dance floor, Bryce spins and dips me and when he pulls me back up, he kisses me, a sensual kiss that leaves me melting.

Did he plan this? I never even thought of it, I'm so nervous. He holds me close and we dance to our favourite song. "Aren't you nervous?" I ask.

"I am but I could see you needed my help. It could've been a disaster but you followed my lead and it went smoothly."

"Thanks, Babe. I'm not as nervous now."

"I'm glad." He smiles at me and it's the most gorgeous smile.

"You're great at hiding your nervousness."

"I've been in some sticky situations. You learn to roll with it."

"See, you're always there for me."

"For the rest of your life."

"This has been a great day. You were right. I was nervous for nothing."

"I knew it was the 'marriage is a big step' idea. And I knew you'd be fine once we got to this point. Me, holding my wife in my arms, dancing to our favourite song."

I hold his face in my hands, pulling him down for a kiss.

"Angel, I can't express how happy I am right now."

I smile. "I am too. I love you."

"I love you, Angel."

When our dance is finished, Leena ushers us to the head table.

As our servers bring out the salad, Leena starts her speech at the podium.

She has everyone in stitches when she tells a few stories about when we were younger. I can't help but laugh, too. At the end of her speech, she says she tested me a few times, asking, "Are you sure Bryce is the one?" She said she knew she was wasting her breath. There was no mistaking the love in our eyes.

Leena comes to hug Bryce and me. "Great speech," I say. "You did a fantastic job."

"I wasn't nervous at all." She chuckles.

When Austin gets up for his speech, I'm a little scared of what might come out of his mouth. But he does a great job telling stories of their childhood—stories I've never heard before that have everyone smiling and laughing, hanging on every word. He finishes with, "I knew you would marry Keera the first week you were together," and then he comes over to hug us both.

As we're eating our wedding meal of penne with meat sauce, roasted potatoes, fried chicken, tender roast beef with mushrooms and gravy and green bean casserole, I finally get a chance to look around.

Gramps, Mary, Deana, Garrett, Dave and all of Bryce's grandparents are at the nearest table.

Reese is sitting with Pops and Josie with her date. I don't see Brooke. Pops didn't bring her?

Reese has everyone at their table entertained. They're all laughing as he animatedly moves his hands while speaking.

Dante and Jax leave the head table to speak with two beautiful women. Did they bring dates? The one on the right looks like Julie. I wonder how her boys are.

My eyes scan the room and I see many of the firefighters and wives from the hockey games and the Christmas party.

After dinner, the servers bring out the most amazing dessert, which I swear I won't eat until everyone starts raving about it. Turns out, it's Leena's recipe and her bakery made them. It's a warm cheesecake wrapped in filo pastry with raspberries and chocolate drizzled on top. The best dessert I've ever had. Well worth the calories.

It's our turn. Bryce and I get up to the podium and thank everyone for coming. We thank Leena for all her hard work, our bridesmaids and groomsmen for standing in our wedding, and everyone who came from out of town for our special day.

The DJ starts to play and the first few couples get up to dance. Everyone at the head table scatters.

This is our time to thank everyone personally. First, Bryce introduces me to his grandparents. Garrett looks like his dad and his mom is a little petite woman with beautiful features and short grey hair. Deana's mom is the spitting image of her daughter. They're like twins, though her mom is obviously older. Deana's dad is tall and thin with grey hair. He stands and gives me a hug and shakes Bryce's hand.

We go from table to table, meeting uncles and aunts, cousins, friends, and family, and it's all a blur.

I look over and see Austin staring like he's in a daze. I follow his line of sight and notice Leena and Reese sitting close to each other, laughing, having a great time.

Deana and Garrett come over. "Now that we have you all to ourselves, I want you to know how proud and happy you make us."

"Thank you." I give them a hug.

Gramps walks over, touching my arm. "How about that dance you promised me."

"Sure."

The DJ plays a slow song and we dance. I look over and Bryce is dancing with his mom. The love she has in her eyes for him makes me smile.

While we dance, Gramps expresses his happiness because he sees me more often than before with him living closer. And then we talk about the improvements they've made with their cabin.

Halfway through the dance, I look over to the bar and Austin is leaning against it, staring at Leena and Reese again.

When the song ends I give Gramps a hug and he holds me longer than he normally does. It makes my eyes tear up. He didn't mention our miscarriage but I think he wanted to tell me how sorry he is. With his tough exterior, he often stifles his emotions. Gramps leaves the dance floor and I look over at Bryce still dancing with his mom.

Reese slides in, standing before me. "May I have this dance, beautiful?"

"You sure can. Glad you could come. It's good seeing you. How have you been?"

"I'm good. I'm happy for you and Bryce. You make a great couple."

"Thank you, Reese. How's the touring going?"

"Good. Colton doesn't take off anymore. He's focused again and working on some new music."

"That's good."

"I can't tell you what Colton wants me to relay. I'll tell him I told you. And ... he'll eventually give up. Christ, you're married now."

"Isn't he with a beautiful model?"

"Yeah. She's not like you. You're always happy."

Bryce stands beside us and slaps Reese on the back. "Hey." Reese backs up and shakes Bryce's hand. "Congratulations, bud. I'm happy for you two."

"Thanks," Bryce says. "Glad you could come."

"Love weddings. Makes me feel normal."

"Still touring?"

"Yeah, Wisconsin tomorrow night. Leena asked me to come and it worked out."

Chief Anderson and his wife dance next to us. "Congratulations are in order for you two."

"Thank you," we both say.

I touch Reese's arm. "We'll talk later. Thanks for the dance."

"How's life treating you, Bryce?" Chief Anderson asks.

"Good, now. Thanks, Chief. I really appreciate you pulling some strings in the investigation."

"No problem. Anyone could see they were bogus allegations."

"No shop talk," Mrs. Anderson says. "Anyways, congratulations to both of you."

When our dance is finished, Bryce is pulled away from me. In the opposite direction, I see Josie sitting with her date and I go over to speak with them. "You are stunningly beautiful." She gives me a hug. "I'm so happy for you."

"Thanks for coming. I'm glad you're here."

"Wouldn't miss it. Dinner was great and dessert was amazing! Oh, and I got some great pictures. Wait until Chaz sees these."

Someone else comes over and I'm tugged to the dance floor.

I wave to Josie. "Talk in a bit."

Leena and Austin have an awkward moment when the entire wedding party gets up to dance. Leena hesitates on the sidelines for ten seconds until Austin pulls her into his arms. She doesn't speak to him. They're silent for three minutes until she walks away.

Austin goes back to leaning on the bar.

Time has flown by. Before we know it, the night is nearly over, and it's now past midnight. Leena gives me a hug. "Your wedding planner is now leaving the building. You're on your own."

"Thank you for everything. This wedding would've never turned out so beautifully without you. The decorations and dessert were amazing. Love you."

"Thanks, Leena," Bryce says.

"I'll call in two weeks to see how your honeymoon in Greece went. Have fun."

We watch Reese join Leena and then they leave together.

I turn to look at the bar and see the look on Austin's face. He looks angry and disappointed.

Leena didn't see that she was breaking his heart. Or she didn't care.

By one-thirty, there are only twenty guests left.

Deana whispers in Bryce's ear as she looks over at Austin at the bar. Then they hug us and leave.

Bryce and I haul what's left behind to the limo and come back for Austin. We hook our arms around Austin's waist and he hugs us both. "I love you guys. Oh, congratulations, by the way!" He mumbles something I can't understand.

Before we get him to the limo he says, "I can't believe she left with him." He mumbles something else and passes out on the seat.

I look at Bryce and smile.

"Not too often you get to see Austin drunk," Bryce says, smiling.

"I know. That's why I'm enjoying every moment."

Five years later…

Mr. and Mrs. Fisher are doing well. After the fire, two of their children moved to Huntsville to be closer and we see them now and then when Bryce and I visit.

Occasionally, I see Colton on TV with his girlfriend and Leena tells me after all these years he still hasn't popped the question or had any children with her. She's beautiful. What's wrong with him?

Bryce and I helped Gramps with his cabin whenever we had time off. They finished all the woodwork a year after they started and it's amazing to see. It is definitely unique—a work of art they are proud of—and Gramps and Mary love living close by. They come over with the Gator or we ride over on the ATVs or snowmobiles.

Bryce and I have date night once a week and, to keep our sex life exciting, we venture to The Mansion a least once every three months for a night of ecstasy.

Bryce pulls his truck into the garage at the cabin and we habitually open the doors to help Savannah and Maverick jump down from the truck. They run over to Austin's and Bryce's ATVs, each climbing on their own, pretending they're driving. Maverick is now two and looks exactly like Bryce with his black hair and perfect features. When we compared their baby pictures, we can barely tell the difference. The resemblance is uncanny. Maverick sits atop "his" ATV sticking his tongue out, his cheeks bulging as he makes the sound of the motor running.

Savannah is three-and-a-half and people say my baby girl is my twin. She has perfect little features with long blonde hair, and when I wrap it around my finger, it curls, making ringlets. Savannah looks over at Bryce. "Daddy, can we go for a ride? Can we go see Gramps and Gram?" she asks in her adorable little voice.

Bryce can't hide the love in his eyes and the smile on his face as he looks at our children.

I smile as he looks over at me.

I followed my heart. I had no doubt in my mind, Bryce and I could have the kind of relationship my parents had. Like Bryce's parents have.

Our life isn't perfect. And it was crazy at first. We have setbacks—chaotic moments. But we work through them. Bryce is not perfect. He has flaws like I do. I accept his and he accepts mine. We respect, care, and love each other.

They say the first few years of a relationship are the hardest because you're getting to know every little thing about one another. You go through insecurities and jealous rage, and once you know your partner and best friend loves you unconditionally, it all falls into place and you build a loving home, striving for the big picture in the end—having children and grandchildren and growing old together.

Bryce knew what he wanted. So did I.

A lifetime of love and happiness.

The End

If you like the Unforgivable series, please help spread the word.

Authors need reviews, if you could please,
take the time to write a review

on, Goodread's, Amazon, Indigo/Chapter's, Kobo, Google,

iBooks, and Barnes and Noble.

It would make my day!

Thank you so much!

Thank you for buying the Unforgivable series.
I appreciate it more than words can say.
I would love to hear if you like it. Please find me on
Facebook, Twitter, Pinterest, and Instagram or
check out my website @ www.shayleesoleil.com
for more information and upcoming news.
Lots of love from Shay Lee Soleil.

www.ingramcontent.com/pod-product-compliance
Lightning Source LLC
Chambersburg PA
CBHW030649120726
47905CB00001B/134